THE BRASS HORSE

THE BRASS
HORSE
J. C. PIMENTEL

HIGH MEADOW PUBLISHING
Siskiyou County, California

WRITTEN DURING THE 1970S
BY J. C. PIMENTEL
COPYRIGHT © 2014 BY B. J. GRUBB AND JACK LAVAL PIMENTEL
EDITING/COVER & INTERIOR DESIGN BY MIKE SLIZEWSKI
FRONT COVER PHOTOGRAPH BY PIA TORELLI PHOTOGRAPHY
WWW.PIATORELLI.COM USED BY PERMISSION
BACK COVER POPPY ARTWORK BY B. J. GRUBB
ALL RIGHTS RESERVED.
ISBN 978-0-9848231-1-6

PRINTED IN THE UNITED STATES OF AMERICA

FOR BETTY RUTH, B. J., JACK,
AND FOR JOHN MAXWELL'S LIFE;
AND DEDICATED TO THE IDEA OF LIVING
EVERY MOMENT TO ITS UTMOST.

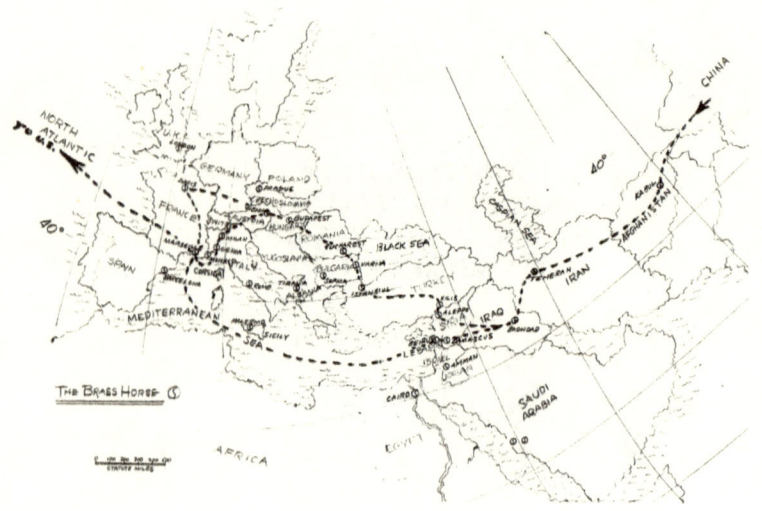

Smuggling route map from J. C. Pimentel's original manuscript

THE BRASS HORSE: *Principal Characters*

Julius Harte (American): US Ambassador to Lebanon.

Bogart Schuyler III (American): Career Foreign Service officer; First Secretary under Ambassador Julius Harte.

Jefferson Ryder (American): Aviation marketing executive for commercial airliner sales abroad.

John Maxton (American): Aeronautical engineer; close friend and business colleague of Jefferson Ryder.

James Crawford (American): Central Intelligence Agency official, Washington, D.C.

Mohammed Rafat (*rah-FAHT*) (Iranian): Aged, wealthy, and powerful underworld figure. Involved in illicit smuggling.

Hassan Rafat (Iranian): Eldest son and chief aide of Mohammed Rafat.

Asad Tabet (*TAH-bett*) (Palestinian): Second-in-command of Al Fatah, the Palestinian terrorist guerrilla movement.

Luigi Carini (American): A Mafia Don, overlord of illicit narcotics importation through the US Eastern Seaboard.

Dr. Yuan Chang (Chinese): A senior diplomat for the People's Republic of China.

Alfonzo Bonifacio (Corsican): Chief of the Corsican underworld organization processing morphine into heroin, Marseille.

Wahji Ghandhouri (*wah-jee gahn-DOO-ree*) (Palestinian): Wealthy and powerful financial entrepreneur and underworld figure in Lebanon.

Emil Oltu (*OL-tew*) (Turkish): A leading exporter from Turkey of illicit opium.

Claude Thibault (*TEE-boh*) (French): Wealthy French bon vivant and underworld distributor of illicit narcotics in Europe.

Palmer Tuxford Lane (American): Executive Vice President for Marketing; Jefferson Ryder's boss.

Ali Boubahri (*boo-BAH-ree*) (Iranian): Wealthy, legitimate Iranian businessman, acting as local business agent for Jefferson Ryder in Teheran.

Mondo Cat (American): Real name, Raymond Catlow. Young, liberal rebel, alienated from his family, stranded abroad without funds.

General Hakim Rabahby (*rah-BAH-bee*) (Jordanian): Director General of Civil Aviation for Jordan.

Issam Lahoud (*la-HOOD*) (Palestinian): Businessman in Amman, Jordan; covertly importing contraband arms.

CONTENTS

PART 1: A BRIGAND

Hassan Rafat
Teheran, Iran
JANUARY 1966

January's drab cloak lay over the land. Old Mohammed Rafat sat in quiet solitude, staring out at a grayed Iranian landscape from the comfortable warmth of his study. Gusts of cold northwest wind sent shards of sleet slanting into soft clicks against the glass panes of his window and rattled the black bones of bare trees beyond. These small sounds and the measured rhythm from a stately, pendulum-driven clock were all that intruded on the silence of the room.

Time passed as the massive, grizzled old man continued to sit in motionless quiet beside his vast desk, watery eyes fixed in an unblinking stare. Deep in thought, the aged Iranian ruminated with satisfaction on the pyramid of his many winters. Now in his seventieth year, the immense old Persian basked in a rare inner pleasure. He sensed fragments of excitement reviving in his ancient smuggler's soul. Vast wealth and terrible power had been robbers themselves, leaving little to slake an old brigand's thirst for challenge. Now a unique prospect lay ahead.

Finally stirring himself, the old man rubbed a gnarled hand over the mottled dome of his bald head. He grimaced in pain as he tried shifting his gout-swollen leg into a more favorable position. Mountainous corpulence made his every movement difficult. Old Mohammed Rafat guarded his enormous wealth and ruled his underworld empire from the depths of a great upholstered divan adjacent to his desk. Rarely departing from his Teheran mansion or from the divan's comforts, the imperious old man exacted blind obedience from his four sons, deputing to them his own lost mobility.

He lifted a pair of spectacles from the desk and fitted them over his eyes, then reached to the huge world globe beside the divan. A look of shrewd satisfaction appeared on Mohammed Rafat's bulbous features as he traced a knotted finger along an imaginary line arching to the west from Iran and running nearly halfway around the world. The finger followed closely along the fortieth parallel. It paused near the border between Turkey and Syria, paused again at the Mediterranean coast of France, then traveled brusquely over the empty blue span of the North Atlantic and halted against the Eastern Seaboard of the New World.

The old man's silent contemplations were interrupted by a solemn resonance from the great clock's chime. Presaged by a low growl from gears deep within its bowels, the huge timepiece tolled sonorously through the hour of two. Mohammed Rafat withdrew his hand from the globe and removed his eyeglasses. He resumed his contemplation of the wintery scene beyond the window, but his eyes flickered, alert and watchful. Soon he heard the sound he awaited. The door to his study opened and then closed. Mohammed Rafat's eldest son, Hassan, entered the room and stood silently before his father's desk. It was forbidden that he speak until spoken to.

Mohammed Rafat, slowly turning his gaze away from the window, swung to stare through rheumy eyes at the face of his first son. He scanned the narrow features and brooded silently, as he had done numberless times before, over Hassan's strange yet brilliant mind. He inwardly cursed the dreadful flaw that marred this diamond; that disconcerting flaw that had marked the boy and now scarred the thirty-six-year-old man; that terrifying and unpredictable threshold of ungovernable rage that, once passed, erased all vestiges of Hassan's natural mental superiorities. Old Mohammed Rafat continued to silently survey his son.

Hassan, accustomed to the old man's peculiar lapses of inconsiderate silence, occupied himself in a minute inspection of his fingernails. He waited in annoyed boredom for his fat, senile father to decide to speak, irritated that the old tyrant had not asked him to sit down. Hassan knew he had been summoned for something the old man considered important. He had resigned himself to endure the wearisome session, at least until he learned its purpose.

At last the elder Rafat's deep, gravelly voice rumbled ponderously into his formal manner of speech. "Hassan, my son, I will speak with you of the future of the Rafat fortunes. I refer to my acceptance of the alliance with the American Mafia people. The burden of directing the Rafat participation in that alliance will fall largely upon you."

Hassan Rafat, having searched out a fingernail file from his pocket, worked on the tip of one of his fingers. Without looking up he nodded his head and muttered, "Yes, father, I understand. You consider this alliance important." Hassan busily agitated the tiny file.

There was no movement from the immense figure on the divan, no sound, nor any gesture. Yet Hassan Rafat felt a sudden chill of unease. Hastily, he returned the fingernail file to his pocket and glanced up at the revolting pile of flesh that was his father. Coals seemed to burn in the depths of the old man's eyes.

With careful respect in his voice and with full attention now, the younger Rafat tried to retrench. "Is there something you wish me to do, Father?"

The old man enveloped Hassan's attention with his eyes. He did not immediately reply. The deep, slow voice finally sounded, ominous and deliberate. "No! There is something I *command* that you do!"

Hassan's dark, narrow face burned with a sudden flash of anger. Controlling his voice with difficulty, he said, "Yes, Father."

The mountain of flesh continued to dominate Hassan with its eyes. The voice rumbled harshly. "Listen and listen well, Hassan! The ventures we speak of are dangerously new and untried. Handled well, they will produce unprecedented profits. Handled badly, they will destroy the Rafats and the efforts of my lifetime!"

Hassan felt slightly mollified. His father seldom said "we." Hassan stated, "It will be handled well, Father."

The old man's tone became flat and businesslike. "You will meet tomorrow with a man in Baghdad. The man is named Asad Tabet. He is a Palestinian, very high in the command of their terrorist guerrilla movement, which is called Al Fatah, and it is through Tabet's voice that our payment is authorized."

Agitated again, his anger returning, the younger Rafat overcame his sense of intimidation. His lip curled and he said, "And why does the unwashed half-Jew not come here? Why must a Rafat travel in this filthy weather to that pesthole, Baghdad?"

The rheumy eyes blinked patiently, no longer so intense. The shrewd old man said, "First of all, my son, he is a valued client of the Rafats. He is willing to pay outrageously for our services. For such a client, we shall bend to accommodate his small wishes. Secondly, this Palestinian, Asad Tabet, dares not travel freely. His murder is sought by many. You will meet with him in Baghdad."

Hassan complained in petulant annoyance. "Then why tomorrow? If this begging refugee manages his affairs so poorly, let him wait. I have urgent plans for tomorrow."

Heavy lids drooped, half closed, over the watery eyes. The sonorous voice raised, "There is a distinction, I will remind you, Hassan, between what is urgent and what is important. It is seldom these days that I know of your plans. As it happens this time I do. Your 'urgent' plans for tomorrow are to fornicate with the new, foreign, blond, whoring dancer. It is urgent to you, only because you desire to be there ahead of your brother Ishmail! I do not consider that important. What you will do in Baghdad is very important. It is also urgent."

Piqued, Hassan continued to pout rebelliously. He asked, in a faintly insolent tone, "Why do you make so much of this little business, Father? What is so important about a small transaction with those dirty people who have no future?"

Hassan saw the old eyes flame again, and saw his father rub a knotted hand over his bald skull. Old Mohammed Rafat's patience vanished. His booming voice erupted in a bellow. "*You are a Rafat!* You are not a drooling imbecile! Do not behave like one! I told you to listen carefully! I also expect you to *think* while you listen! Your meeting with this Palestinian, as should have been obvious to you from the start, is part of the new arrangement with the Mafia American gangster, Carini! That arrangement *must* be made to succeed! Can you not see that we stand to realize more profit from that arrangement than from *all our other holdings combined?*"

Fearing to further arouse the old man, Hassan Rafat's voice became conciliatory. "I will go to Baghdad tomorrow. I will see to it that the arrangement with the Americans will be a success."

Asad Tabet
Baghdad, Iraq
<u>JANUARY 1966</u>

Alone in the small room, the second-in-command of the Al Fatah guerrillas slouched behind a scarred, timeworn wooden desk and puffed clouds of acrid cigar smoke around his head to dampen the enthusiasm of the relentless flies. The Palestinian, Asad Tabet, seemed oblivious to the choking foulness of the humid air in the dingy, poorly heated, and unventilated room he was using as temporary headquarters during this stay in Baghdad. Under scanty light issuing from a dirty incandescent bulb hanging above his head, Asad Tabet worked with fixed concentration on a pile of papers resting in his lap. The room's silence was only disturbed by the buzzing flies and an occasional creaking complaint from the overtaxed chair under Tabet.

Asad Tabet seemed to have fit himself into the tawdry atmosphere of the room. Heavily bearded, he wore a mottled, mud-spattered suit of army fatigue coveralls. Despite the cold, the coveralls hung open, unbuttoned from the waist up, revealing a matted mass of black hair across Tabet's chest and down his fleshy belly. Steadily sorting through the soiled stack of papers, he sat leaning precariously back in the ancient swivel chair, feet crossed and resting in worn paratroop boots on the uneven desktop. Also resting on the desk, among disorderly, scattered papers, lay a .45 caliber automatic pistol.

The Palestinian leader raised his gaze from the papers, listening. A jumbled sound of footsteps approached. Tabet moved the half-smoked cigar from one side of his mouth to the other, then, clutching a handful of papers in his left hand, picked up the handgun with his right and let it hang out of sight behind the desk. Without otherwise disturbing his half-reclined position he waited, heavy-lidded eyes fixed on the locked door.

The footsteps halted outside. A knuckled signal rapped into the room, followed by the sound of a key in the lock. Asad Tabet continued to sit silently, eyes alert. The paint-peeled surface of the door swung partially inward, admitting an unshaven face, then an arm that swept up in a haphazard military salute. Tabet ignored the salute, remaining motionless in the swivel chair.

The door opened and three men entered the tiny, unpleasant room. The second man to enter was the immaculately and foppishly clad Iranian, Hassan Rafat. The other two were Palestinian guerrilla soldiers dressed in sweat-stained and worn fatigue coveralls identical to Tabet's. The two soldiers wore holstered pistols slung from webbed belts at their waists. They moved, each to a corner of the room, flanking the Iranian visitor and facing Asad Tabet, waiting for his orders.

A cynical smile lurked invisibly beneath the unkempt growth of wiry black beard on Asad Tabet's face as he studied his fashionably turned out guest. The Iranian, Hassan Rafat, in an obvious rage, had recoiled sharply on entering the fetid atmosphere of the room. His slender face, contorted in revulsion, had gone to a greenish pallor. The young Iranian stopped and stood rigidly, barely inside the closed door, working to regain his poise.

Through successive years of exposure to the business affairs of his father, Hassan Rafat had mentally conditioned himself to detest the city of Baghdad. This, despite the long-standing importance of a number of people within the city to certain very lucrative, albeit illegal, Rafat enterprises. On this occasion Hassan's accustomed distaste for Baghdad had flowered into furious outrage after having been met and escorted by the two unbathed Palestinian guerrilla soldiers for the entire distance from Baghdad's airport to this revolting meeting place. In place of an impeccable limousine, he had been transported in a rattling, drafty military jeep. Rather than fawning and banal witticisms for conversation, he had heard nothing but incomprehensible grunts exchanged between the two evil-smelling soldiers. He had found himself delivered not to the shelter of wealth, comfort, and luxury usual to his visits here, but to the most sordid section of the ancient city. Finally, the air in the small office had him on the verge of vomiting.

Hassan Rafat gradually overcame his sickening nausea but not his irritation. As the retching compulsion subsided, his anger and disgust increased. His eyes danced with rage as he glared at the insolently languorous, slovenly figure of Asad Tabet, whose booted feet remained resting on the desk. The young Iranian, in his fury, failed to note the shrewd competence visible in the black eyes that stared emotionlessly back at him.

The Palestinian leader took the cigar stub from between his teeth and gestured lazily with it toward the one remaining unoccupied chair in the room. One of the soldiers lifted the loose-jointed chair and slid it behind Hassan Rafat. Asad Tabet muttered curtly in Arabic. The two soldiers obediently went out the door. When the door had been pulled shut and latched, Tabet swung his feet to the floor and sat up in the swivel chair, keeping his eyes on Rafat's face. He quietly lifted the heavy automatic pistol into view and set it on top of the scattered papers on his desk. "Please sit down, Mr. Rafat. I apologize for the austerity of my headquarters."

Hassan Rafat, his oddly narrow face still ashen from suppressed nausea, continued to stand for a moment as he fought to control the fury that boiled in his brain. Hands quivering, he drew the wobbly chair under himself and sat down. The young Iranian let his contempt show on his face as he stared at the man second only to Yasser Arafat in command of the Al Fatah terrorists. Rafat sneered, "Your headquarters are a pigsty!"

Imperturbably, Asad Tabet agreed. "Yes, Mr. Rafat. We have many demands upon our funds and, sadly, little seems to go toward comfort."

Hassan Rafat's voice advertised his disgust. "If you insist on meeting with me in this stinking closet, then say what you must, and let me get away from here."

The Palestinian gravely nodded his head. "Neither of us cares to waste time with the other, Mr. Rafat. Be kind enough, however, to allow me to inquire into the health of your father. He is a man for whom I have great respect. He is well?"

Suspicious that the inquiry represented a subtle affront, Hassan Rafat abruptly snarled, "My father is elsewhere, Mr. Tabet, and his health is of no concern to the business you and I are here to discuss!"

Asad Tabet sat silently for a moment, scrutinizing the younger man facing him. At length he spoke. "Forgive me, Mr. Rafat, but if I may say so, the health of Mohammed Rafat is of vital consequence to the affairs of a great many people, including myself."

Hassan Rafat, impatient to leave the foul little chamber, relented. "My father's health is satisfactory, apart from his lameness," he stated coldly.

The Palestinian leaned back in his chair, holding a pencil between the palms of his hands. After a moment's silence, he resumed. "Mr. Rafat, I had hoped for a more congenial beginning to our association with one another. You will see in a moment that today's meeting is crucial to the interests of the Rafats as well as to those of my organization. It is because of the critical nature of certain current circumstances that I requested this extraordinary meeting. Otherwise, we would have continued as usual to operate through your local people."

Hassan Rafat, skeptical and still impatient, nevertheless felt a stir of interest. He suddenly realized that the Palestinian had wanted to speak directly to old Mohammed Rafat. Hassan spoke arrogantly. "What you mean is, it is critical in *your* judgment. It remains yet to be seen whether it is critical in mine."

Asad Tabet smiled and shook his head in mock resignation. "You are a difficult man to approach, Mr. Rafat. But then, I always appreciate dealing with a skilled negotiator."

The Palestinian had penetrated Hassan Rafat's armor. The young Iranian reacted to the suggested praise. "The Rafats are all skilled negotiators!"

Asad Tabet leaned forward in his chair and reached toward the papers on his desk. He thumbed briefly through the pile of papers, then withdrew a plain file folder. He placed it, unopened, in front of himself and rested his forearms on the desktop. His manner changed abruptly. "Let's get to the business then. Mr. Rafat, there has emerged, quite suddenly, an external problem which threatens to put an end to our purchases and shipments of weapons through your channels."

Hassan Rafat remembered his father's admonition that this arrangement must be made to succeed. The Palestinian's words were ominous. Rafat said, "The Rafats do not permit their business affairs to be hindered by external intrusion. What is the nature of this alleged problem?"

Asad Tabet opened the plain folder. He placed two typewritten lists side by side in front of himself. "The problem is represented by these lists, Mr. Rafat. These are lists of people who are, to put it bluntly, in the way. They are people who represent alien interests in one way or another, all of whom are determined to interdict our clandestine program of arms shipments." The Palestinian picked up one of the two typewritten pages. "On this rather long list of names you will see that a few of the entries are marked with an asterisk. Those not so marked represent individuals with whom my organization is able to contend. Those are lesser individuals, people who pass along damaging bits of information about us.

They will be removed from interference very soon. The asterisked names"—he picked up the second page and waved it—"are listed here separately. These are the names of people with whom we cannot readily cope." Asad Tabet pushed the second sheet of paper across the desk in front of Hassan Rafat.

Rafat had been staring at the two lists from across the table while Tabet spoke. He could see that the first list was extensive, covering the entire page. The second list, which Tabet thrust in front of him, was quite short. Hassan Rafat picked up the second list and glanced at it. "Obviously, you are giving me the most difficult part of the problem."

Asad Tabet smiled and tilted back in his chair. "It is certainly true that the list you are looking at represents a unique category of opposition. It is a short list, but it is potent, Mr. Rafat. As the saying goes, dynamite comes in small packages. Those people are too much for us. They may be too much for you."

Hassan Rafat sneered at the challenging suggestion. "No matter who they are, those on this list, they are only people. If they are in the way, they will be removed. Such matters are routine. What is so difficult about all this?" He waved the list, then dropped it disdainfully onto the table.

The Palestinian remained silent for a moment, fishing a fresh cigar from his pocket. He lit the cigar and blew a cloud of blue smoke toward the ceiling. He said, cryptically, "It is a question of method and prudence, Mr. Rafat. If you feel you can assist in overcoming these difficulties, I would not presume to doubt your judgment."

Hassan Rafat demanded, "All right, then, what is this 'category' you talk about? What makes these people so exceptional?"

The Palestinian stared into Rafat's eyes. "What makes them exceptional is that those are American and Russian undercover intelligence agents, Mr. Rafat. The best they have. I'm certain you will want to consider the associated implications before you decide on a course of action."

Hassan Rafat returned Tabet's steady gaze, determined to be decisive with the Palestinian. Rafat saw nothing implied of sufficient significance to cause him to hesitate. Furthermore, he was suddenly sure he had in his hands the means by which to score a spectacular coup in the eyes of his father. He picked up the short list and waved it curtly. "I will take this list. These people will be appropriately dealt with."

A flicker of satisfaction darted into Asad Tabet's eyes. "That is excellent, Mr. Rafat. There is only one other thing, then. As you know, an unusually massive shipment of arms is scheduled for movement very soon. It is absolutely vital that the shipment take place, and that its timing remains undisturbed. No delay may be accepted." Tabet waved the long list of names. "The effectivity of every individual on this list must be neutralized before then. They must be held in check for at least as long as it will take to complete that shipment's delivery."

Hassan Rafat, fully confident now, ignored the Palestinian's last statement. He stood, declaring, "I believe you said that was all there is to discuss. I have other pressing matters to attend to. This list you have given me, it is scarcely sufficient information for my purposes. Have you no more on these people than their names?"

Puffing on his cigar, Asad Tabet nodded his head and again scuffed through the disarray of papers on his desk. He came up with a new-looking file folder and held it toward Rafat. "In this folder are extracts of pertinent information on each of the people on your list. This information was selected from dossiers we maintain on them. After you've looked through these extracts, if you feel you need more than is given, please ask us, and we will try to accommodate your requests."

Rafat took the folder. He opened it and glanced superficially at one or two pages. He placed the list Tabet had given him in with the other contents and closed the folder. "I will let you know if these are not satisfactory. Now, I would like to leave."

Asad Tabet heaved himself out of the swivel chair and stepped around Rafat to the door. He opened the door and barked a command in Arabic. Leaving the door ajar, he turned back to Rafat. "One of my men will deliver you to a convenient taxi stand, Mr. Rafat."

The Palestinian extended his hand. Hassan Rafat gave Asad Tabet a desultory handshake and, without another word, turned and departed.

The Palestinian leader stood for a moment in the open doorway, puffing contentedly at the cigar in his mouth and smiling thoughtfully as he watched the dapper figure of the young Iranian disappear down the hall. He closed the office door, then went around the desk to his seat. He worked to open one of the dilapidated wooden desk drawers. He reached into the opened drawer and switched off a tape recorder, then carefully removed the spool of tape from it. After inserting the tape reel into a small box, he dropped the box into his battered briefcase. Still smiling, he said aloud, "There now, you arrogant, masturbating young prig! Maybe someday your own words will help you learn some humility!"

In satisfaction, Asad Tabet turned over in his mind the results of his meeting with Rafat. That reckless young Iranian would never know that the extensive files of data on American and Russian agents were built largely from information procured covertly in Washington, D.C. and supplied to Al Fatah by the American underworld chieftain Luigi Carini. The Palestinian guerrilla leader was certain that Hassan Rafat would heedlessly murder those agents without regard to potential consequences. Carini would be enraged, having so carefully instructed Tabet on the finesse required in the neutralization of these particular intruders. Tabet smiled to himself in sadistic amusement. The American gangster, with all his ferocity, would be powerless to exact any useful retaliation. He would instead be forced to expedite the next planned massive shipment of arms to Al Fatah, which was exactly what Asad Tabet desired. After that, Tabet mused, Al Fatah's weapons needs would no longer be so pressing. Then, all of these scheming, money-hungry foreigners could carry their clamoring elsewhere.

Julius Harte
Beirut, Lebanon
APRIL 1966

Julius Harte, US ambassador to Lebanon, took note of the hour as he put down the telephone and momentarily relaxed. The elegant digital clock on his desk read 10 AM, Tuesday, 12 April 1966. The next hour would be his own.

A man of great ability, Julius Harte was not imposing in appearance. Rather narrow, sloping shoulders over a linear frame gave the ambassador a misleading look of fragility. Harte was wiry and tough, and enjoyed vigorous health. His face was too long to suit the proportions of a slender, medium-height frame. The homeliness lent by a long, slanting jawline and teeth that tended to protrude was more than offset, however, by the undeniable glow of deep intelligence and wisdom showing in his eyes. Homely or not, Harte's face was a kind one. Strength of character and personal force were clearly visible, overlaid by marks of understanding and compassion.

In decades of diplomatic service Harte had learned the value, circumstances permitting, of reserving this hour to himself each morning—a chance to privately contemplate the problems confronting his embassy. With his staff instructed accordingly, and barring the inevitable emergencies, Harte knew that if he chose, he could anticipate an hour free from the customary press of scheduled and unscheduled appointments, conferences, meetings, telephone calls, or callers. In this instance, however, he pressed the signal button that summoned his secretary, Marjorie Mackenzie. "Marge, I'd like to see Boge for a few minutes, now," he told her, "and bring us some coffee when he gets here."

The rotund figure of Bogart Schuyler III, the embassy's first secretary and Harte's second-in-command, entered the ambassador's office a few minutes later. Abundantly aware that Harte normally kept this hour undisturbed, Schuyler paused just inside the door, unsure whether the conversation was to be brief or otherwise.

Harte looked up. "Sit down, Boge. Marge will be bringing us coffee." As Schuyler seated himself in one of a pair of leather-upholstered chairs that faced the ambassador's desk, the secretary entered to deliver a coffee tray, then quietly departed. Schuyler waited until Marge had turned to leave, then furtively watched the movements of her buttocks and splendid nyloned legs as she walked out of the office.

The ambassador stood and turned his slight, wiry frame toward the large window behind his desk, gazing meditatively at the incredible clarity of color presented by the Mediterranean coastline curving away before him. He remained there, saying nothing, and Schuyler busied himself with filling two cups with coffee.

A minute or two passed, then Harte turned from the window. "Thanks for pouring, Boge. Guess I'm not much of a host this morning." The ambassador's lean, long-jawed face looked contemplative and remote. He moved around his desk toward the matching leather chair. He settled himself in the chair and reached for his cup, then said, "Boge, I want to hear your present ideas, and a report of whatever progress you've made since last week on this CIA affair that's coming up. There are some other things I'd like you to do right away on that subject, but we'll get around to those after I hear what you have to say."

Schuyler's pallid and somewhat cherubic face furrowed. He grouped his thoughts carefully, taking time before answering. He was aware that Harte viewed involvement with the particular enterprise concerned, at ambassadorial level, as contrary to his diplomatic instincts.

"Well, sir," he began, "I've sent out priority signals through classified channels, over your name, requesting all available information on the individual the CIA has named." Harte nodded but made no comment.

Schuyler continued, "As of this morning I have Washington's answers, from all the sources they could immediately reach. You were right last week when you said we shouldn't expect State to give us too much. We really didn't get much. Most of it is the usual stuff from the Personal Security Questionnaire forms. Then, there's a credit rating and a police report. Nothing derogatory in any of the data. So far, that's about it." Schuyler then added in a mildly rueful tone, "I'm afraid that in depth, our poop on the man won't come remotely close to the kind of reading CIA will have on him."

The ambassador gestured in mild disparagement. "That's in their field and they're quite expert and thorough. In depth, as you put it." In a new tone, Harte went on, "So. Then our inquiries haven't produced any particular surprises as yet.

We can consider that a plus. Is there anything more on that before we move along?"

Schuyler nodded. "There was one small surprise. We've learned that the man once applied to CIA for employment. He was accepted, but never took the job."

Harte registered interest. "Oh? What sort of job was involved?"

Schuyler answered, "Well, among other things, he's a pilot. CIA wanted him for technical evaluation of foreign aircraft. He was evidently hoping the job might lead to some flight test work, as well as the desk end."

Harte sipped his coffee, then commented, "He seems to have had a healthy motive. In contrast, I mean, to the usual tiresome parade of money-hungry tyros that turn up here as would-be CIA agents. Any idea why he didn't take that job?"

Schuyler shrugged narrow shoulders. "Evidently the Agency took too much time to suit him in confirming their offer. It was reportedly more than a year before they sent him their firm acceptance. My guess would be that they mired themselves in their bog of a security check and lost their man. He got a civilian contract offer in the meanwhile that appealed to him and accepted it, doing experimental flight testing at Edwards Air Force Base in California for one of the big aircraft manufacturers."

"And when was all that?" Harte inquired.

Schuyler was silent for a moment, gazing upward in thought. "Let's see. If I remember correctly, he went to work in that flight test job in April of 1955. That would be exactly eleven years ago this month."

Harte mused aloud, "And during those eleven years since, he's become a rather well-regarded figure in international commercial aviation marketing. Has this all been with the same company?"

The ambassador had risen to his feet as he asked the question, and returned to his accustomed seat behind the desk. The relaxed atmosphere faded slightly.

"Yes it has, sir," Schuyler replied. "From the poop we now have on him, plus our own direct experience with the man, I get the impression that he is steady, maybe even dogged on whatever he sets out to do."

The ambassador closed this part of the conversation with his next words. "Thank you, Boge. That was a good and useful report. I want you to continue to remain on top of this program." He looked squarely at Schuyler. "In fact, it may become necessary that you physically participate in this to an extent that neither you nor I may otherwise care for." Harte finished his sentence and leaned back in his chair.

Schuyler frowned anxiously. "Sir, I'm afraid that you've been talking a little over my head. Do I gather correctly that there is a lot more to this, uh, enterprise than has been apparent? You have referred to a project, or program, that suggests a greater dimension to the effort than I'd been giving it."

"Boge," the ambassador said kindly, "I know you must feel as though you've been purposely left in the dark, but that isn't the case at all. This thing has moved very rapidly, especially over the last few days, and truthfully, I don't know the full implications myself. I'd rather not try to answer your questions until things become more clear. We're out here on the end of the communications limb as always, and it isn't wise to speculate too far afield. I believe we will both have our questions answered later today."

Harte glanced at his watch. "Well, daily doings are upon us. One last thing then. At two thirty this afternoon a man named Crawford, James Crawford, from the CIA, is due to arrive at the airport on a BEA flight from London. Please meet him and get him settled at the Carlton Hotel. And assign a car to him. I don't know whether he'll want a driver or not, so have one stand by." The ambassador smiled and added, "Once he tries sharing the street with our wild Beirut drivers, I imagine he'll yell for help!"

Schuyler, who considered driving among Beirut's traffic an unnerving experience himself, nodded without humor. The ambassador continued, "I'm to meet with Crawford here at four this afternoon. Please remain nearby, because I will want you in on those discussions from the beginning. Keep your late afternoon and evening free, in case the time is needed. Crawford may be here for a couple of days, so please study our planned schedule ahead and acquaint yourself with the open hours and any soft appointments. We may find need to cancel some of them."

Schuyler had risen to his feet. The ambassador came around the desk and walked slowly toward the door with him. Harte's face was solemn and remote. "Listen carefully to this CIA man James Crawford, Boge. His visit puzzles and disturbs me. Whatever the CIA project is, it must be unusually important.

Otherwise, they would have dealt with us through their customary channels. I have no idea where Crawford fits into their picture." Harte then ended the discussion with a question. "By the way, Boge, what is that other name again, the name of this fellow the CIA is interested in?"

Schuyler paused before opening the door to leave. "His name is Jefferson Ryder, sir. He has no middle name."

James Crawford
Beirut, Lebanon
APRIL 1966

Julius Harte, by nature an unobtrusive person, leaned favorably toward people of similar ilk. When James Crawford entered the ambassador's office and introduced himself, Harte immediately liked the CIA man's calm, straightforward manner. The ambassador greeted the visitor, then invited Crawford to relax in one of the leather chairs. Seating himself at his desk, Harte called for coffee. As Marge served the refreshments, Harte studied the CIA man.

Crawford was stockily built, with thinning, reddish hair now tinged with gray. Set above a thick neck, Crawford's round face wore a bland, generally pleasant look, contradicted sharply by an emotionless opaqueness in steel-blue eyes. Harte judged Crawford to be around fifty years of age, about five years younger than himself, and about the same height at five foot ten. Although the subdued, three-button suit made Crawford appear rotund, Harte estimated that the man was in excellent physical tone, and that the filled-out contours of the suit covered a powerful physique.

The ambassador chatted lightly about his neglected tennis game for a few minutes, giving Crawford a chance to feel at ease and to savor a few sips of his coffee. Then Harte swung the conversation toward business. "Mr. Crawford. I believe the ball is in your court. We here at this embassy have occupied only a minor role in the matter at hand thus far. Perhaps you have more to add. Would you care to proceed?"

The CIA man set his coffee cup down and leaned casually forward in his chair, elbows resting comfortably on his knees. "Yes, Mr. Ambassador, there is considerable that I can add for you." He paused, collecting his thoughts. "Starting with a detail, I am here in Beirut right now for two purposes. The principal reason, of course, is to discuss future arrangements with you. I am also here, though, to talk with the man in question, Mr. Jefferson Ryder. He is scheduled to arrive in Beirut tomorrow on one of his usual business trips. He has no idea as yet that we are interested in him."

Harte said, "I see. Then he may be a good subject to begin our discussions with. We'll certainly be interested in what you have to say about Mr. Ryder. Before you begin, however, and if you have no objection, I would like to call in Bogart

Schuyler, my first secretary, for this part of our talk. Boge has a working acquaintance with Ryder. I plan to have Schuyler add this program to his responsibilities along with his present cognizance over embassy security."

With no perceptible hesitation, Crawford nodded. "Certainly, sir. It will be almost imperative that one other person beside yourself in the embassy remains aware of the planned arrangements." Crawford's faint emphasis on the "one other person" was not lost on the ambassador.

"However, before you invite Mr. Schuyler in, Ambassador Harte," Crawford added, "I'd like to spend a few minutes more talking to you alone, concerning this effort as a whole." Crawford paused, then continued. "How you may then wish to include Mr. Schuyler will, of course, be entirely as you please."

Harte looked keenly into Crawford's broad, impassive face. "All right, Mr. Crawford. I must caution you, however, that I do not countenance lack of trust in people whom I have placed in highly responsible positions. If they could not be trusted, they would not be where they are in this embassy."

If the ambassador's admonition disturbed Crawford, it was not apparent. The CIA man calmly continued, "I am certain of that, sir. I believe that you will understand my intent a little better after you've heard what I want to tell you."

After a brief silence, Crawford resumed. "To begin with, Ambassador Harte, we are confronted with a problem of extreme urgency—in fact, an emergency. Possibly the best measure of the gravity of our situation in the Middle East is that the order that has resulted in this meeting came from the Office of the President."

Emphasizing his statement, Crawford stopped speaking for a moment, then went on. "The motivation for Washington's extraordinary level of concern derives from the sudden emergence in recent weeks of an unaccountable and deadly succession of events that directly and seriously threaten the United States' policy position here in the Middle East."

Julius Harte remained silent, watching Crawford's face and reserving judgment on these dramatic-sounding statements.

Unemotionally, the CIA man continued, "The thrust of the Central Intelligence Agency's effort out here is aimed at supporting that policy position. Simply stated, our goal is to assist in the stemming, or better yet halting, of any trend of events that might lead to open war between combined Moslem countries and the Israelis. Further, and at all costs, to prevent such contingencies from leading the United States into any form of armed confrontation with forces of the USSR."

The ambassador nodded without speaking. He noticed Crawford's mouth tighten as the CIA man went on. "As you so fully know, Ambassador Harte, the Middle East has become a tinderbox. Washington relies on, and demands, an uninterrupted flow of up-to-the-minute intelligence data from this region. During the last ninety days, Mr. Ambassador, the United States has been virtually decapitated from its primary information sources *throughout the Middle East*!"

Ambassador Harte leaned forward in his chair, frowning. "Exactly what do you mean, Mr. Crawford?"

The CIA man's level gaze met Harte's. "Over the past three months, our intelligence network has been struck at every level in one way or another. Fringe agents and other routine reporting sources have been suddenly, irrevocably, and cleverly compromised. Covert operators have found themselves summarily exposed. For example, you will be aware of two State Department Foreign Service officers who have recently been kicked out by the country to which they were assigned. In both instances, disgraceful misconduct appeared evident. I'm referring to that mess in Damascus, and then the one in Baghdad, when the Iraqis scalded us with the world watching."

The ambassador, attentively following Crawford's account, asked, "If I understand correctly, you're saying those incidents were conspired into being? That our State Department people were deliberately victimized?"

Crawford nodded. "Beyond any doubt, sir. The situation is much worse than that, however." The CIA man looked directly at the ambassador. "Where such nullifying measures as I have mentioned have failed, or were evidently judged inappropriate, Ambassador Harte, prime agents have simply been eliminated!" Crawford's voice muted down with an implacable undertone. "Three of CIA's leading Middle East agents have been found murdered, sir. Two others have vanished, almost certainly also dead!"

Julius Harte, his composure visibly jarred, exclaimed, "Good heavens, man! How can such actions possibly be accounted for?" The ambassador's voice betrayed a great depth of emotion.

Crawford answered with deadly calm, "That will be determined, sir!" The CIA man paused, then continued, "There is more. As nearly as we can tell, Russia's intelligence system out here has also had many of its sources severed! We know, positively, of at least one of their best agents who has been murdered, and probably two others. Bear in mind, sir, all of this has happened in just under ninety days!"

Harte's face was taut. "Then you don't really know who is behind this!"

Crawford shook his head. "Needless to say, we looked hard at the Russians first. All we could find was that at the same time, they were furiously accusing us! It took a while, eliminating the possibility of a phony performance on both sides. We, and they, have both known from the beginning, though, that the stark extremes employed have been totally unwarranted and utterly uncharacteristic." Crawford shook his head again while he looked at the ambassador. "It was not the Russians."

Harte gestured with a hand. "In its own terrible way, I guess that's a relief. But then, who? And, in God's name, why? If anything, this is even less characteristic of the Chinese! It's completely irrational and out of context!

Crawford's respect for the ambassador's acuity grew. "That is also our conclusion, sir. These blows come from another direction. We have evolved certain theories and suspicions, Ambassador Harte. Frankly speaking, though, they are entirely too vague to be worth mentioning right now. Suffice to say, someone unknown, incredibly enough, has intervened!"

Harte was silent, his face grim. His eyes searched Crawford's face. At length he asked, "Mr. Crawford, you present a forbidding reality. Are there no alternatives than to send untrained and uninformed people into this kind of charnel house? If your best have failed, how do you expect all of our country's Jefferson Ryders to survive?"

Crawford's flat-voiced reply was immediate and flinty. "This wears the face of war, Mr. Ambassador. I'm afraid we are without acceptable alternatives." Bluntly, he added, "The flow of vital information must be reinstated, and immediately."

Harte leaned back in his chair and turned away from the CIA man. Both remained silent for a minute or two. It was Harte who broke the silence. Turning back toward Crawford, he looked earnestly at him. "The terrible truth is, I see you are right. I must tell you too that what you have told me will certainly alter the manner in which I will permit a man like

Bogart Schuyler to become involved. I want you to know that I appreciate your having given me this chance to protect him."

Crawford waved the thought away. "There is no question of gratitude here, sir. This unknown intruder has made a desperate play for time. Patently, he knows this intelligence dislocation cannot be allowed to exist. He knows too that he has invited terrible retribution. This can only mean that he has some similar and vital goal targeted for imminent achievement. To unravel all this with dispatch will require thinkers as well as doers, sir."

Harte saw that Crawford had tacitly offered dignified sanctuary for Schuyler. His respect for this implacable man increased warmly. "I understand, Mr. Crawford. Perhaps now it is timely for Mr. Schuyler to join us." Crawford nodded, and the ambassador turned to the intercom and asked Marge to summon Schuyler.

A silent interval passed, then the first secretary entered. He was introduced to the CIA man, following which Harte said, "Boge, we're going to discuss the possible arrangements to be made concerning Mr. Ryder. I think it will be important that you and Mr. Crawford compare notes on him firsthand, so please sit in with us." Harte waved in the direction of his desk. The three men seated themselves.

The ambassador said to Schuyler, "Mr. Crawford informs me that Ryder is to arrive in Beirut tomorrow, and is unaware that he is to be approached on this. I have explained that you have had closest contact with Ryder here." Harte turned to the CIA man. "I believe that brings us up to date, Mr. Crawford."

"There are one or two things I'd like to hear Mr. Schuyler's comments on," Crawford began. As he spoke, he withdrew an unmarked folder from the briefcase he had carried into the office. He addressed himself to Schuyler. "How would you characterize Ryder, Mr. Schuyler? His personality, I mean. The impression he makes on people. His manner of speech. His conduct, on and off the job. Social habits. What I'm looking for is a sense of the man himself, as you've seen him. I have a wealth of vital statistics concerning Ryder"—James Crawford's hand patted the unmarked folder—"but as you know, there is no way to really put a man on paper. Some of the best-appearing résumés turned out to represent the worst individuals."

There was a pause as Schuyler decided how to begin. "Please let me qualify ahead of time anything I say about Mr. Ryder," Schuyler said, adjusting his glasses. "My personal contacts with him have been mainly official, Mr. Crawford. It was he who first sought us out, here at the embassy, in going about his business affairs. He appears to use every possible avenue of help to promote his business efforts, and to him we represent a potential source of useful information and influence. Otherwise, I doubt if he would come around here much. He isn't one to waste much time on protocol for its own sake." Schuyler's tone made this last comment sound like criticism.

Crawford studied Schuyler. "What can you say about his social conduct, Mr. Schuyler?"

Schuyler flicked imaginary dust from his well-creased trousers. "Socially, Ryder has bought lunch for me a few times, and now and then a dinner. Naturally, I have my own opinion of him from these associations. Then, Beirut being the gossip capital of the Middle East, there is the usual wealth of rumor and speculation about the man. For my tastes, he's a bit on the 'diamond in the rough' side, although all in all, a worthwhile enough individual. Whatever private social interests he may indulge in, he seems to succeed in keeping them well out of sight. Even the Beirut rumor mill evidently hasn't much to go on about him. He's apparently a very interesting man to the opposite sex, though, judging from the amount of time the ladies of the Beirut cocktail circuit seem to spend talking about him. That also appears to be true of the American secretarial help around this embassy," Schuyler added in a mildly waspish voice, "not to mention the embassy wives."

This last comment caused the ambassador to look a little surprised. Schuyler noticed the look and hurriedly changed the subject. "You mentioned 'manner of speech,' Mr. Crawford. That's one peculiar habit of Ryder's I might mention. He is an intelligent and well-educated man, and has a respectable vocabulary when he chooses to use it. You'd never know it, though, listening to his ordinary conversation. He has a habit of talking in a sort of American patois. He ends up sounding and looking and acting like a cowboy in disguise. Oddly enough, that fact might account for his popularity among the Arabs. They have a tendency to judge Americans on a yardstick built on the 'Bonanza' television series. I personally believe Ryder is aware of this, and exploits it deliberately." Again, a note of disapproval had crept into Schuyler's voice.

The CIA man smiled. "Well, how does he behave himself in the saloons?"

Schuyler blinked through his pince-nez glasses. "I presume you mean Ryder's drinking habits. He must handle his liquor very well, Mr. Crawford. I've seen him cope with an Australian bunch that are prominent in one of the airlines out here, and that takes some doing. Those Australian people regularly drink everyone else under the table while they're just warming up. I've never heard of any undisciplined behavior on Ryder's part due to excessive drinking, though." Schuyler stopped speaking, thought a moment, then asked, "Does that help any, Mr. Crawford?"

Crawford had listened intently to Schuyler's remarks. He replied to the question, "Yes, indeed! I wish some of my own people knew how to answer my questions as well. You've given me all I need on that subject for now. There are a few other things I'd like to ask about, if we have time." Crawford looked toward the ambassador.

Harte said, "Time will not be a problem, Mr. Crawford. Both Boge and I have left the late afternoon clear of other business today, to avoid unnecessary interruption to these discussions with you. Please go ahead as you wish."

"I'm grateful for that, Ambassador Harte," Crawford said. "I'll try to keep all this as brief as possible." Turning back to Schuyler, he asked, "Does Ryder always stay at the same place when he comes to Beirut?"

Schuyler's answer was immediate. "Oh, yes. I'm certain he makes a regular practice of staying at the Phoenicia Hotel. It isn't any wonder," Schuyler added, "considering the royal treatment that man receives when he's there! It seems that every last soul on that hotel's payroll knows him by name. They all greet him and fall all over themselves seeing to his needs. I'd thought Ryder probably had attracted all that attention through extravagant tipping. Georges Khalid, the senior assistant manager at the Phoenicia, is a close personal friend of mine. He says Ryder tips sensibly. What it seems to come down to is that the hotel staff people simply like him."

"That's excellent and all to the good," Crawford said. Then he asked, "On Ryder's trips out here, does he always travel alone?"

"No, not always," Schuyler replied. "Occasionally he brings along specialized helpers of one sort or another. There is one man in particular who seems to accompany him fairly frequently."

Crawford asked, "And do you happen to know that man's name?"

"Yes, his name is John Maxton. It is my impression that he has known Ryder for a long time, personally as well as professionally."

Crawford inquired, "What can you tell me about Maxton?"

Schuyler's voice registered distaste. "Very little in a detailed sense. He impresses me as a rough, coarse person. He has a physique like a gorilla, and manners to go with that. Maxton seems to drink to excess. Ryder has had to retrieve the man from local bars on more than one occasion, I'm told."

Crawford pondered for a moment, then queried, "Just one more question, Mr. Schuyler. Do you happen to know if Ryder employs anyone native out here in his business pursuits? An interpreter, or resident representative, or technicians of any sort?"

Schuyler shook his head. "If he does, I don't know of it."

With Schuyler's reply, Crawford leaned back in his chair and rested his hands on the table's edge. "Well, that's all I want to ask right now, gentlemen. Other than laying out a few plans for our effort to meet with Ryder, I'll make no other demands on your time. Of course, I'll be perfectly happy to reciprocate for all the help you've given me by answering, as best I can, any questions you may have." He looked at each of the two men in turn.

Schuyler spoke. "What can you tell us about Ryder, from your collection of information on him'?"

Crawford reached for the unmarked folder. He had evidently expected this question. "I'll try to give you a thumbnail version of the important particulars we have about Mr. Ryder." He opened the folder to its first page and glanced at it briefly.

"Age, forty-six. Six feet tall. Weight, 175. Build, medium. Hair, black, mixed with gray, cropped short. Scars, one on the right side front, below the ribs. Another on the right thigh, and a third—visible—scar on the left cheek, diagonally, starting under the sideburn. Health, excellent. Dental record, not so good. Education, BS in engineering, University of California. Qualified pilot. World War II combat veteran, impeccable military record. Amply decorated. Served a brief period with the OSS during combat service in the ETO. Married in 1946, widowed in 1954. Wife, Margaret, and youngest child, George, killed in an auto accident—passengers in a car driven by a woman friend of Mrs. Ryder. Living daughter, Martha, born 1948, educated in private schools in California. She will enter Stanford University this fall. Ryder's family religion, Protestant. His religious views, indifferent. Politically, an independent voter. An outdoorsman; active in sports."

Crawford was silent for a moment, studying the contents of the folder. He closed the file and looked up. "It appears that Ryder was severely grieved by the sudden loss of his wife and young son twelve years ago. His way of life appears to have changed abruptly with that accident."

Listening to these words, both Harte and Schuyler remembered that Ryder had applied to CIA for employment in 1955, evidently within the year following the death of his wife and son. The ambassador asked, "In what way did his life change, as you see it?"

Crawford replied, "Ever since that auto accident, Ryder has kept himself on the move. He has clearly made a point of severing any ties associated with the life he'd shared with his wife Margaret. He immediately sold the house they'd had, and since has maintained a bachelor apartment in LA. He has succeeded in staying with work that keeps him traveling most of the time. He seems to avoid circumstances that would lead him into regular close contact with any particular group of people. This has been at the expense of various offers he has received for positions in senior management echelons."

Harte listened with interest. Then, as Crawford finished speaking, the ambassador looked down at his watch. He said, "There are still a number of important things we must discuss tonight, but right now I believe we should take a break. I imagine you could use a little rest and some time to yourself, Mr. Crawford, and there are one or two outside matters I must attend to. I propose that we interrupt our meeting and go our separate ways for the next two hours or so. If all this is agreeable to you, I suggest that the three of us resume our talks at eight o'clock this evening, here in my office."

The three men stood and exchanged departure amenities. Schuyler escorted the CIA man out of the embassy, chatting with him about arrangements for their return later in the evening.

Luigi Carini
Tirana, Albania
<u>**APRIL 1966**</u>

Striding along the dim corridor toward a great, age-darkened door at its end, the Mafia chief disgustedly fought an uneasy flutter in his stomach. He fumbled in his pocket for a tranquilizer capsule, blaming his queasiness on an accumulation of little things from earlier in the day.

The morning had started splendidly. The Mafia chief, Luigi Piero Carini, was in the highest spirits, still flushed with the holiday feeling of this unusual trip away from the stale weight of New York. Despite the extraordinary importance of his mission, the en-route, two-day stopover in Sicily had taken the edge from Carini's accustomed tensions. The splendid April weather, boisterous Sicilian welcome, festive reunions with admiring relatives and old friends, the pleasure in revisiting scenes of his youth had, in fact, induced a few moments during which he'd actually dismissed from his mind the real reason for his travels.

The euphoria ended for Carini with his departure from Sicily. All his tensions came back with a rush when he climbed aboard the shark-like executive jet airplane. To begin with, Big Lou Carini, in all his fifty-eight years, had never rid himself of his superstitious fear of flying. To Carini it was bad enough, those huge airliners full of other people who would die alongside you in the crash. Who would know whose bad luck had been at fault? Bad enough. But these bouncing, roaring, fragile-looking little things with almost no wings seemed a suicidal risk.

True to Carini's gloomy expectations, his flight in the little jet from Sicily to Albania amounted to almost an hour of uninterrupted, turbulent discomfort. The pilot's apologies for the rough ride only added to Carini's nervous disgust. As the airplane had at last crossed the Albanian coastline and begun its descent toward the city of Tirana, the already morose Mafia chief found the unfamiliar terrain below depressing. To the Sicilian, the uninviting scenery did not seem to belong near his beloved Mediterranean. He stared down glumly as drab miles of untenanted, lonely looking marshlands dragged by. Then, while mentally commending his Chinese hosts for the flawless ease with which Albanian entry formalities were dispensed with at the airport, he found his accommodations in the Tirana Eagle

Hotel austere and cramped. Worse yet, his bodyguard was situated in quarters identical to his own.

As a final disquieting prod, the prestigious Mafia chief found himself obliged to enter the unfamiliar premises of this meeting place unaccompanied, and that was an unheard of thing for Big Lou Carini. During his Mafia career, Carini had been the target of three known assassination attempts. Now, as chief of the Mafia's narcotics importation for the eastern half of the United States, the number of bodyguards he kept around himself was legion. While the number of his guards varied according to Carini's whereabouts, one thing remained certain. Luigi Piero Carini never went anywhere alone.

A faint smile touched the face of Dr. Yuan Chang of the People's Republic of China as he put down the telephone and leaned back in the unfamiliar chair. For a moment he allowed curiosity to occupy his disciplined mind. The telephone call, from one of his young assistants posted at the downstairs entry, had informed Chang of the American gangster's arrival from nearby Tirana. The American would be entering the room before long.

Dr. Chang, veteran diplomat and currently one of Communist China's senior foreign envoys, would normally have handed down to a man of lesser stature the task that had brought him to Tirana. The concept behind this meeting, Chang's own brainchild, was considered brilliant in Peking, and of crucial significance.

Its implementation, however, could easily have been delegated. Yuan Chang was entranced by the bizarre possibilities implicit in the meeting, though, and had chosen to engage in the novel match of wits it promised in person. Having made that choice, he had personally and industriously supervised every preparatory detail, including selection of this rented Albanian hunting lodge where the meeting was about to unfold.

With the American's appearance imminent, Chang eased his small, bony figure out of the swivel chair and stood behind the desk that he had ordered placed in the room. From behind the desk he faced the hallway door through which the Mafia chief must enter.

Dr. Chang waited, standing, until the large, florid-faced, and silver-haired American had opened the door and seen him there behind the desk. He then moved out to meet the man, extending his hand in a cordial greeting. The Chinese man was gratified to note that Luigi Carini appeared ill at ease. Chang had vehemently insisted on the choice of an Albanian setting for this meeting, rather than to accept the preference for Paris expressed by the Americans, acceded to by some of the people in Peking.

Big Lou Carini's uneasiness drained swiftly away, however, as he scanned his negotiating adversary. He saw a small, wizened old Chinese man wearing a poorly fitting suit and steel-rimmed glasses on a shining, hairless head. Carini asked himself, *how could anybody have trouble with a chop suey headwaiter?* He said, "I'm Lou Carini, Mr. Chang."

Dr. Yuan Chang bowed slightly. "Yes. Mr. Carini. It is my pleasure to meet with you." Chang motioned with a frail yellow hand toward a great, oaken table extending across one end of the room. It stood before a large bay window and overlooked a vast, well-kept garden. The diminutive Chinese man said in a soft voice, "Isn't it fitting, Mr. Carini, that we shall be able to enjoy the sight of growing things as we speak of our business matters, since indeed we shall ourselves endeavor to plant the seeds of something new today?"

Big Lou Carini glanced out the window in feigned interest as he seated himself across the table from the Chinese diplomat. In an attempt at humor Carini replied, "Yeah, that's a pretty sight out there, all right. They should've planted a mess of poppies for us, though!" The American chuckled at his own joke.

Dr. Chang smiled and said, "Deftly put, Mr. Carini. You bring us directly to the point without delay. We will begin our talk. Would you care, perhaps, for some coffee, or other refreshment as we proceed?"

The Mafia chief, reacting to the subtle statement, felt he had seized the initiative. He spread soft, well-manicured hands on the table and said brusquely, "No thanks. Let's get down to business."

"Of course," Chang said. "Then it may be appropriate for me to try to summarize our position at the moment." He leaned back in his chair and fixed keen black eyes on the bulky American. "My country is deeply concerned, Mr. Carini, as are the other great nations, with the current frictions in the Middle East. In consequence, we have stationed many watchers there. Through them we have learned, to our surprise, of the presence of your organization's influence in that part of the world."

Carini smiled fatuously. His hand patted the table. "So we even surprised you, eh?"

Dr. Chang's soft voice smoothly resumed, "Quite true. We had thought your major efforts were largely confined to the geography of North America. With our discovery of your Middle East interest, however, it seemed possible that you might provide us with the solution to a certain pressing problem."

Carini's voice rasped across the end of Dr. Chang's sentence. "So, six months ago you sent a messenger to us, Dr. Chang, about your opium. You know, in our territory we have a pretty good system of 'watchers,' as you call them, too. We spotted a few of your hired hands poking around in our business *before* your messenger ever got there!"

Yuan Chang ignored the hard arrogance in the American's tone. His face remained expressionless. "I'm certain that your organization also investigates the soundness of its trading associates, as we do, Mr. Carini."

Carini guffawed. "You can count on that, Doctor!" Unsmilingly, the Mafia chief continued, "In principal, we're interested in your proposition, Chang, and we can handle the time schedule you laid out. Before we start haggling over details, though, there are a couple of questions."

Dr. Chang inclined his head. "Yes, Mr. Carini. I shall ask some as well. What would you like to know?"

Carini's expression hardened. He tilted his head back and let his eyelids droop. "First of all, why did you come to us? If all you want to do is dump your snow, it's a lot easier for you to push it out in the other direction. East, not west."

Dr. Chang allowed a generous interval to pass before he spoke. "I do not propose to try to deceive you, Mr. Carini. Your question, however, touches on what may prove to be a delicate point. That is, you may feel disinclined to do business with us if we appear to press on your sense of allegiance to your country."

Carini blinked his eyes, then guffawed again. "Well, let me put it this way, Doctor. We're all red-blooded American patriots, you understand, but when it comes to allegiance, my friend, there's only one that counts. It's called hard cash!"

Dr. Chang said, impassively, "Very well, then. You've asked why we come to you. The answer is a simple one, Mr. Carini. The more delicate the operation one wants performed, the more skillful the surgeon one must seek. Your organization is masterful at its business. We elect to associate with the best whenever possible."

Carini set a hard smile on his face. "Okay, so we do all right in our business. You haven't answered the east-west question yet."

The Chinese diplomat removed his eyeglasses and thoughtfully polished them. "Is it not true, Mr. Carini, that in rich times such as these in America, your organization's business tends to flourish in direct proportion to the wider search for pleasure by the American people?"

The Mafia chief frowned, pondering the wording of the question. "I think I see what you're driving at, Doctor, so let's not beat around the bush. Sure, the richer and lazier and sloppier the suckers get, the better we like it. I gather that that suits you too—watching Americans turn themselves into fat, gutless slobs."

The Chinese smiled faintly. "So, it is the lax attitudes that help you, and therefore you take steps to help the attitudes. Is that your meaning Mr. Carini?"

Luigi Carini, warming to a subject dear to his heart, stood and strolled over in front of the window. He chopped at the air with his hands in emphasis. "Of course! It's so simple it's laughable! Help the 'attitudes,' as you call them, then help screw up anything that gets in the way of those attitudes. The fat suckers practically take care of the rest by themselves!"

Big Lou Carini stared out at the garden for a moment, remembering other days. In a reflective voice, he resumed, "The funny thing is, some of the stunts that used to be toughest to pull off are practically happening by themselves these days." He waved his hands in a gesture of wonderment. "Hell's bells, I shudder when I think of the big money we used to have to spend, buying off cops and judges and politicians." Carini looked at his attentive listener. "Naturally, we still do, but it's so easy now! All those types have got their hands out for a tidy share of the easy buck. On top of that, the suckers themselves have all but pulled the wings off the whole damn legal system with no help from anybody! The name of the game for them now is 'Rules Are For Fools'! Honest cops are hamstrung; the courts are mealymouthed; jail sentences have turned into jokes. A crook gets caught, mostly the charge won't stick. If it sticks, he gets loose anyway. So, who should worry? The suckers' heads are out of sight in the sand. Would you believe it, they're convincing themselves there's no such thing as a Mafia? And, by

Jesus, the damned fools are even jackassing J. Edgar Hoover! Why, in over forty years, we couldn't even dump him!" Carini smiled in amazement.

Dr. Chang kept the attentive look on his face. He nodded his head. "We have wondered at the reports deriding Mr. Hoover lately. He has been a worthy adversary of ours as well. I have had much respect for him."

The Mafia chief laughed sardonically. "I'm with you, Doctor! I hate Hoover's guts, but I don't mind saying he's always stayed in our way!" Carini, shaking his head and smiling, returned to his seat at the large table.

The Chinese diplomat waited quietly, to be sure the American had finished his rambling commentary. At length he said, "Mr. Carini, with your own words I think you have helped me answer your 'east-west' question. Perhaps I can sum up our views with a little philosophy. We believe your country is in decay. It has derived its great strength not from its wealth, as so many choose to boast, but from its people. As individuals, they have been exceptionally determined in their self-reliance and durability. Collectively, they have presented themselves to the world with spirited, albeit subconscious, unity. It would now appear, however, wouldn't it, that those values have eroded severely?"

While the thrust of Chang's softly spoken words came through to him, Luigi Carini occupied himself with containing his exasperation over the Chinaman's persistently abstruse colloquy. Threats, veiled or blunt, were old hat to Carini. He dismissed any concern with national well-being and focused his attention on implications affecting the Mafia. He quickly concluded that whatever the Chinese may do now, there was little reason to expect resulting interference with the interests of the Mafia. In fact, the odds were that the probable results would be beneficial.

Chang's quiet voice interrupted Carini's thoughts. "Mr. Carini, now there is a question I would like to ask."

Carini tilted back warily in his chair. "Okay, shoot, Dr. Chang."

Yuan Chang rested his forearms on the table and laced his slender fingers together. "Can you tell me who is responsible for the recent elimination of certain American and Russian intelligence sources in the Middle East?"

Carini's face became expressionless. He stared at the Chinese diplomat. "I wasn't sure until you asked that question. Now, I know."

Chang said, thoughtfully, "Thus you have considered that *we* might have taken the action. Furthermore, you imply that those measures were not directed by yourselves."

Carini thrust his blunt face forward and answered acidly. "That was a fool's move, Chang! We've got enough people chasing us, thank you, without asking for more; especially *those* kind!"

Dr. Chang nodded. "We quite agree. With respect to our proposed agreement, then, what is your estimate of the probable consequences, Mr. Carini?"

The Mafia chief reflected for a moment. "Assuming you and I come to a meeting of the minds today, my feeling is that no great damage has been done; at least not as far as our original schedule is concerned. It will take a while for both of those outfits to glue themselves together again. Meanwhile, we'll be home free. It's the later-on time that'll be tough."

Dr. Chang probed. "And, have you given that problem some thought?"

Carini's fist came down hard on the table. "Enough to know that a certain money-hungry, hotheaded young Pasha is suddenly going to get a whole new education!" More calmly, he went on, "The way I see it, we'll have to shut down while the dust settles and things cool off, after the first big move. Then, we'll have to get a good calibration of what we're up against."

Yuan Chang was satisfied. The answer was the one he thought he should hear, but hadn't expected. The American group was proving to be useful and one to respect. He said, "Then we have nothing more to do, you and I, other than to agree on terms?"

Carini answered crisply, "That's it, Dr. Chang. For this first exercise we're offering you ten million dollars cash for twenty-five tons of processed morphine, delivered by you at the border between Afghanistan and your country. We take it from there. You know the schedule. We can line up the time frame for future shipments later, for the rest of the 'M' and to move more weapons for you to the Palestinians."

Dr. Yuan Chang said, simply, "Our agreement is reached."

Lido di Ostia
Italy
APRIL 1966

Rays from the warm midafternoon sun shattered into dazzling reflections as they caromed against the low sea swell undulating toward the western Italian beach a few miles south of the Lido di Ostia. Across the coarse sand of the quiet shoreline a group of five wealthy and powerful men lounged idly, some standing and watching the sparkling sea, others sprawled in comfortable lawn chairs, engaged in desultory conversation. The group of men occupied the seafront gardens of a majestic villa. A pair of servants in white mess jackets hovered around a portable bar, keeping the idle group supplied with drinks.

Luigi Carini paused inside the villa and, with satisfaction, looked out across the expanse of lawn at the five men he was about to join. He indulged himself for the moment, savoring the announcement he would make to these men as their nominal leader of his success with the Chinese.

Lou Carini had spent more than a year in painstaking search, sorting and handpicking, to assemble this elite international underworld cabal. It had taken almost as long before that to sell this project, his brainchild, to the Syndicate in New York. The burgeoning American craze for narcotics, and Carini's impeccable background of successes for the Mafia, had combined finally to win them over. The investment required was enormous, and admittedly a gamble against more than the usual odds. At stake, however, were potentially astronomic profits. Also at stake, now that the project had been graced with a go-ahead, was Luigi Carini's continued existence.

In concept, Carini's new venture embraced geographical extension eastward, beyond the established clearinghouses in Marseille, of Mafia control over heroin flow to the United States. Building on this fundamental idea, Carini had evolved a complex plan by which ancillary profits were to be derived through side ventures slaved to the basic heroin transfer network. These included movement into and through the Middle East of contraband implements of war. Carini's project had received an unexpected expansion early in its growth.

Buck-passed upward by a leery succession of Carini's lieutenants, a tight-lipped, angry Frenchman had finally penetrated to the Mafia chief's twentieth-floor suite of offices on

Park Avenue. Carini had listened patiently at first, then with astounded attention, as the Frenchman related his message. He was commissioned, the Frenchman declared, by the People's Republic of China, to transmit to the Mafia an invitation to purchase huge quantities of pure morphine. Furthermore, the message went on, as an additional inducement the Chinese would be satisfied, on terms to be negotiated, to entrust the Mafia with the transfer of certain military equipage out of China to Middle East destinations also appropriate to the necessary routings of the narcotics. From that incredible interview, Luigi Carini had evolved an immediate intensification of his already implemented scheme.

Scanning the grouped figures on the lawn beyond the terrace, Carini assigned in his mind an identity to each of them. There, standing and talking with that Frenchman, was Wahji Ghandhouri, the snake-eyed, effeminate Lebanese-Palestinian superpimp. An arrogant son of a bitch who pretends he's doing the Mafia a favor. Shrewd as they come. Treacherous. A wild gambler and a lucky one, so far. His job: to handle the heavy traffic of Mafia goods through Beirut.

Then, the Frenchman talking to Ghandhouri: Claude Thibault. Fawning, sweating Parisian peacock. Heir to a perfume factory. Jet-set playboy. Makes a fortune every year and spends a fortune and a half. Loaded with bad debts. He'd feed his mother piecemeal to the hogs for profit. Now heading up an embryonic but promising expansion of the narcotics underground spreading over Europe.

Then, that one, standing next to the chair the old Turk is sitting in. Alfonzo Bonifacio, the gorilla-shaped Corsican killer. Now, that's a paisano who's easy to understand. Rough as an elephant's bunion. Tough and smart. The only one in that whole bunch who is doing the Mafia a favor! Mastermind of the Mafia-like Corsican heroin manufacturing organization in Marseille. Runs the production hub for underworld conversion of morphine into heroin. A tricky business, managed beautifully. Birds of a feather, those two—Bonifacio the Corsican, and Emil Oltu, the old Turk.

Old Emil Oltu. Turkey must be some country if all the Turks are as sour as that one. Even smells sour, in those bad-fitting pallbearer suits he wears. Every bit as tough as Bonifacio, but no sense of humor. The best at his trade: exporting great tonnages of illegal opium for conversion into morphine—without getting caught.

Then the last one. Hassan Rafat. Pure creep, standing by himself. Oil-rich, snot-nosed Persian misfit, sent here by his brilliant smuggler of an old man. Duded up as usual like a hippie faggot, with that Lord Fauntleroy velvet suit and that pointed beard. Bad look, always, in those twitching eyes. Something wild inside trying to get out. A murdering back-shooter, from the look of him. One to watch extra carefully. Eldest son in a family that runs the biggest smuggling layout in Iran, the organization of that wily old bastard, Mohammed Rafat, too crippled to travel himself these days.

Satisfied with his memory study, Carini stepped into the sunlight and headed toward the waiting group. The five men turned to watch the tall, fleshy, well-groomed Mafia chief stride purposefully toward them. Each had his own thoughts about the American.

Hassan Rafat, the young Iranian smuggler, fought down an involuntary giggle as he wondered whether the uncouth American gangster would have anything to say about the spies whose murders he had contrived.

Emil Oltu, stocky, hard-bitten Turkish opium exporter, hoped the meeting wouldn't last too long. There was always too much work to be done to allow time to be wasted in talking—and also, his feet hurt.

Alfonzo Bonifacio, the short, heavily muscled, brilliant Corsican heroin producer, gave Carini credit for plenty of balls, taking on this crowd of abattoir experts.

Claude Thibault, the French narcotics entrepreneur for Europe, quaked as he watched the Mafia chief approach. He knew Carini would demand faster progress toward doubling the quota of heroin consumed on the Continent. Thibault had already overbought, out of fear of the American.

Wahji Ghandhouri, clearinghouse for illicit traffic through the Mediterranean funnel of Beirut, eyed Carini speculatively as the American strode across the lawn. Ghandhouri decided to give himself better than house odds that he'd cut away from the Americans a bigger share than they intended him to have.

Something about the warm Mediterranean afternoon and the tranquil garden setting made Big Lou Carini feel fine. Expansively, he flashed a toothy, gold-embellished smile as he greeted his committee, five of the world's most dangerous men. He shook hands with each in turn, calling them by their first names. Carini then invited the group to join him at a glass-topped, ornate wrought iron table that he'd had set out for their meeting. Large beach umbrellas posed like colorful mushrooms around the table, available for those preferring shade to sun. On the table at each place a leather-bound folder of notepaper rested, together with a gold pen. Alongside each of the leather folders a small, transparent plastic cube had been placed. Each of the cubes contained, visibly embedded in its center, a burnished brass wood screw.

The white-jacketed servants stood discreetly nearby, ready to attend to any wants of the conferring group. Carini called for whiskey and ice, and moved to the head of the table. He waited as the other five made their choice of seats. In a silent toast Carini hoisted his glass, then took a generous swallow from it. "Gentlemen," he began, "it's good to see you together again. We are going to have a good meeting today. I have some news that you'll all enjoy hearing. I hope you people have something profitable to say as well." He glanced around the table as though to emphasize his last sentence. In doing so he noted that the small plastic cubes had attracted everyone's curiosity. The cubes had been picked up and glanced at by all five of the men.

Leaning forward, Carini put down his drink and rested an elbow on the table. "I want each man, including myself, to speak his piece today. You will tell the rest of us what's been going on in your jurisdiction since the last time we met." Carini smiled as he looked at the others. He picked up the little plastic cube from the table in front of himself and said, "I see you've all noticed the little paperweights. I think you'll all remember what they signify. We'll be talking about that later on, so don't throw the cubes away. For now, let's get busy with the important stuff. After I've made my report I'll just call on you, one at a time. I'll start the ball rolling since what I've got to say comes down to the guts of this project."

With that, Carini proceeded to announce in general outline the success of his meeting with the Chinese at the encounter in Albania. He told the five men that this success represented removal of the last principal uncertainty in the preliminary growth of their plans, and that from this time on they could expect to be tested by a heavy increase in the flow of illegal narcotics and weaponry through their system.

Carini was pleased to note an assortment of smiles appearing with his announcement. He added, "The beauty of our outlook may be clear to you, but I'm going to touch on a couple of details anyway. There are two things I want to be goddamned sure you understand." He poked one finger in the air. "The first thing is, everyone of us is going to grab huge profits out of this project, and before very long we'll be operating the whole action on somebody else's money." Another finger joined the first one. "The second thing, and by God the most important, is that this whole, fat scheme will blow sky high if anybody at this table allows any screwup in his department!" With this statement, Carini's voice grew harsh and vicious. He glared at the faces around the table. "Now, I want to hear what you have to say. We'll start at the front and work backwards." The Mafia chief had abandoned any pretense of friendliness. "How about it, Bonifacio?"

The Corsican turned his broad, scarred face toward Carini and, with unemotional calm, said, "You bring us the morphine, we sell you back the heroin. It is of no consequence how much you want. We can handle any amount."

Carini knew this was true. He grunted and turned to the next step in the chain. "All right, Thibault, it's your turn. Bonifacio can handle all the morphine we dump on him. The problem is getting rid of the horse, and that means you. I'm already committed, for the US, with cash, to double the quantity we bought from Bonifacio a year ago. When in hell are you going to double your lousy little quota for Europe?"

The handsome, stylishly long-haired Frenchman studied his polished fingernails, his pallid face betraying the outward show of composure. "We are doing quite well, Monsieur Carini. I have in my possession documented pledges for amounts well in excess of the doubled quantity you refer to." Carini suddenly slammed a fist down on the glass-topped table and exploded out of his chair. "*Pledges my ass, Thibault!*" he roared. "You show us nothing but hard cash in this game! If you like pledges, *you* keep them! Or better yet, you try paying Bonifacio with your lousy pledges!"

Eyes swung to Bonifacio. The massive Corsican looked at Thibault, a lethal smile on his face, and ever so gently shook his head.

Carini seated himself again, his eyes still on the pale Frenchman. "What about the rest of your story, Thibault? What good have you done in Prague?"

Thibault struggled to control himself. Carini enraged him. Claude Thibault, who had, himself, ordered throats cut without compunction, was frightened for his own physical safety for the first time in his life. The ghastly threat visible in the eyes of Carini and Bonifacio terrified him. Behind his fear and his Gallic fury, however, hung the hypnotizing allurement of the huge sums of cash proffered by this association. He dared not back out.

Thibault, tight-lipped and hoping to sting the American, said, "You speak of cash, Monsieur Carini. The contact in Prague has advised me, two days ago, that the armaments in the quantities specified will be ready for shipment to the Near East exactly in accordance with the schedules of time and place that we have demanded. They in turn demand cash payment within the next fortnight. That will require just under five million dollars."

Carini grunted, unimpressed. "They'll get the money. That's the easy part." He turned abruptly away from the Frenchman. "Ghandhouri! How is every little thing down at the crossroads, friend?"

The Lebanese-Palestinian, Wahji Ghandhouri, felt anything but friendship for the American Mafia chief. Ghandhouri's glistening black eyes slid to look at the sunlamp tan of the American's face and, in a habit that he knew was an irritation to Carini, raised a slender hand and wafted a scented handkerchief under his nose. He said, "I am, of course, quite ready. After all, you are introducing nothing new to me. It is simply a difference in quantities. Weapons from the north and east, channeled to the Arabs and to the Israelis. Narcotics—opium, morphine—and hashish, moving through my hands from east to west. Quite routine. Quite routine, sir. This is an elementary exercise for my organization, my dear Mr. Carini."

Carini, with a hard, sarcastic smile, directed a stony look at the Lebanese. He decided to keep Ghandhouri in his place and to publicly remind him of his own limitations. "*My dear* Mr. Ghandhouri," he began in a mocking voice, "there is only one other man at this table besides myself who can actually handle this deal without straining his milk. That man is *not* you, Ghandhouri; it happens to be Alfonzo Bonifacio. What you've been running through your dirty little funnel is the garbage left over after all the big boys got through eating, now isn't it?"

Outraged but concealing it, the Lebanese kept his voice flat. "Mr. Carini. I have said this to you before. Such shipments as these are only a pitiful few of the many enterprises under my direct control. They certainly do not comprise my sustaining income."

Carini laughed into the man's face. "Wahji, try to remember who the hell it is you are talking to! Whether you like it or not, friend, I know your secret balance sheet as well as you do! On paper, you're the richest man in this meeting. In actual fact you can't even get your hands on enough hard scratch to buy yourself a clean Lebanese passport!"

Carini had struck hard. Ghandhouri, having been apprehended publicly for smuggling weapons of war through Beirut to Israel, was actually under sentence into exile from nominally Arab Lebanon. During the three years since that sentence had been handed down, he had quietly spent a fortune in bribes, trying to arrange a full exoneration. The best he had accomplished was a permissive waiver of exile that allowed him Lebanese residence and entry, provided he absent himself from the country for ninety-six hours of each month.

The Palestinian-born Lebanese did not wish to have the subject pursued, and remained silent. Carini however, had more to say. "The point I'm going to get across to you is, forget the sucker talk at these meetings! You're on thin ice financially these days, Ghandhouri, and I know it. You've skinned those oil-rich ragheads from Kuwait and Saudi Arabia just once too often. Your sheikhs are pissed off with you, Wahji Baby. One little slip from you and they'll be asking for all their invested money back. When that happens, it won't matter if you're exiled from Lebanon or not, because you'll have to run for your life anyway!"

Although Ghandhouri kept his rage under control, he could not conceal the venomous hatred visible in his glistening black eyes. He snapped, "Am I to remain the principal subject of discussion for this meeting?"

"Definitely not," Carini said crisply. "You're in a key spot in this operation. We need you, but no more nor less than we need anybody else that's here today. By God, though, you damn well need us, Ghandhouri, one helluva lot more than we'll ever need you!" After a momentary, charged interval, Carini changed the subject, still glaring at the Lebanese. "Now, friend, let's get back to business. That wheat you've been stealing from the US Food For Peace program. Those tinhorn ten-percenters you've been hiring in Washington are screwing you blind, Ghandhouri. You should be making ten times as much out of that gambit. With the muscle I can give you at that end, it will be a breeze. This association could use that juicy pad to help pay for the rest of this action, so I suggest we work out a split. The deal I'm offering you is this: I help you put the thing on its proper paying basis. I guarantee to you *double* the money you made in your best year in that program. The rest of the profit goes into funding for this committee's project. What do you say?"

Ghandhouri's rage slipped away at the thought of this hard cash windfall. The American had surprised him unpleasantly with his apparent familiarity with the details of Ghandhouri's tampering with US Public Law 480's foreign aid food shipments. The Lebanese made lightning calculations in his head and decided he could realize much more profit from Carini's offer than Carini might expect. He answered abruptly. "I accept your offer."

Lou Carini eased back in his chair, smiling, and looked around the table. He made no comment but was pleased to notice one or two heads nodding in satisfaction with this new contribution to their respective pockets. Carini picked up the gold pen from the table in front of him and pointed with it to Emil Oltu, the Turk. "Emil, it's your turn! How's everything in the poppy fields?"

The dour Turk, speaking with a heavy accent, answered, "The crop, it will be a big one this year. Even the government, after it takes her share, there will be left plenty more for us than usual. The new opium, now coming from Iran, I have fixed with the Syrians to process into morphine, also with the Turkish. We must help them making many new secret factories. It is much work. Five of the government snooper Syrians who we pay, they got too hungry with the new shipments news." Oltu paused, groping for the right words, then added unemotionally, "We killed dead those Syrian noses of pigs. The guns coming out of Czechoslovakia now, it is good. Now the trucks have both ways good loads, from when we ship to Bonifacio Bey the morphine overland. It is only much work. This meeting is soon over, I hope so, to get back to the work, yes?"

Carini laughed delightedly, tickled by the flinty old Turk's jumbled English, and pleased with his unpretentious bluntness. "Emil, we'll all get back to work as soon as possible. You're absolutely right; there is much to do. And Emil, we may need your help later on, moving the war junk the Chinamen want to ship."

Oltu simply nodded his head.

One member of the committee remained to speak. Hassan Rafat. The young Iranian had posed himself importantly, anticipating his moment at the center of attention. Carini swung his gaze out over the sea, appearing to be lost in thought. The gold pen was still in his hand, and he tapped it absently against the notepad in front of him. In a minute, he turned his face back to the group of men. "Some of you think you've heard tough talk from me today. If you don't like that, I'm going to tell you something else you won't like. Figure it this way, gentlemen. The only time you're going to hear tough talk from me is when you goddamn well deserve it! And don't forget, you're making the worst mistake of your life if you kid yourself into thinking Big Lou Carini is the only one you've got to worry about. When I get tough, it's because somebody is on the verge of screwing up. When somebody screws up, he's going to have *five* people getting tough, not just me! There's not a man at this table who will laugh it off if this project gets crapped on just because one damn fool tries to get cute, or gets too big for his drawers, or decides not to cooperate. Think about that, gentlemen. One bad move out of anybody at this table, and the world won't be big enough to hide in! The rest of us will track you down like a dog. You'll be a walking dead man the minute you step out of line!"

Hassan Rafat, worried and peeved that he might not be called on, had only half-listened to the first part of the American's words. Halfway through the speech he suddenly realized that Carini's hard stare was fixed unmovingly on him. He heard quite clearly the last of Carini's rasping statement.

Keeping his eyes on the young Iranian, Carini said, "Rafat, what have you done lately to get this project moving?"

The young man, dismissing the faint uneasiness that had suddenly swept into him, tilted nonchalantly back in his chair, waiting until he was sure he had captured everyone's attention. His eyes danced wildly from the excitement surging through his brain. He launched confidently into his speech. "As you have said, Mr. Carini, I am the beginning link in this chain. I am sure you know how reliable the Rafat organization is by now. Iranian opium is now moving smoothly into Syria in our vehicles. All the preparations are also in complete order in Afghanistan, and we have begun, on schedule, to move the Chinese materials west, by air and by surface transport." Hassan

Rafat, wearing an inordinate grin on his face, waited expectantly for Carini's acknowledgment and praise.

Carini's response was not in keeping with the young Iranian's anticipation. With no change of expression, Carini asked, "What else have you done, Rafat?"

To the complete astonishment of all the men, Hassan Rafat burst into almost hysterical laughter. Carini, his face a grim mask, continued to stare ominously at the Iranian, who fought to control himself. Finally the young man gasped, "I see what you mean, I see what you mean!" After a high pitched giggle, he continued, "You want me to tell these men about the spies!"

Carini sat rocklike, saying nothing. The other four men had all leaned forward, their attention now riveted on Rafat. A wide, fatuous smile grew on the Iranian's narrow face. He looked slyly at each of the men in turn, then said, "The Rafat organization has important friends throughout the Middle East, gentlemen. We learned, from high sources in Iraq and Syria, the identities of certain people suspected of espionage against our Palestinian customers. I saw clearly that these people would stand in the way of this project." At this utterance the young man had to stifle another fit of laughter. He went on, "Gentlemen, those people will never bother us now!" With his finishing statement, Rafat threw his head back and shrieked with laughter.

Luigi Carini waited for Rafat to calm down. The other four men, exchanging looks among themselves, began to realize some unpleasant implications in what they had just heard.

Carini's voice was lethally quiet and toneless when he spoke. "I will finish your report, Rafat." He swung his eyes in a quick circle around the table. "What our Iranian representative is telling us, gentlemen, is that he took it on himself to murder a few intelligence agents in the Middle East. Top agents from both Russia and the US! CIA and NKVD! I'm not positive of the count, but it's near a half dozen, minimum. Probably more."

Silence settled over the group. All eyes fixed on Rafat. Carini let the silence endure, waiting to see who would speak. To his surprise, it was Emil Oltu who disturbed the deadly quiet. The old Turk leaned to one side and spat loudly through blackened teeth into the grass. His badly phrased English was no longer amusing. With venomous contempt he growled, "So!

What we get is this, from the laughing, *merkep* jackass who, so young, is still pissing full his own boots!"

But it was Bonifacio who said what was on everyone's mind. "So, what we get, Emil, is the American CIA on our ass! Not to mention the filthy Russians!" Bonifacio had not taken his eyes from Rafat's face.

The young Iranian, his face now contorted with annoyance by the bitter response, opened his mouth to speak. Carini cut him off with a roar. "*Rafat*! Keep your mouth shut! You're already standing in your own coffin, little friend! You'll be lying in it soon, if you're not very, very careful!" In a quieter voice, Carini demanded, "How much of this does your father know about, Rafat?"

Hassan replied in a tense, haughty voice, "My father studies the profits I produce for him. I am the legs of that crippled old man. I do not bother him with unimportant details."

Carini looked at the Iranian in utter disgust. "You are that crippled old man's butt! It's too bad you didn't inherit more from his other end." He turned his attention to the other men at the table. "This may not be as bad as it sounds. We're in the clear for the big move coming from the Chinamen. After that, we'll hold things down and take a reading for a while." He gestured at Hassan Rafat. "I'll personally go talk to this damned fool's father and make sure this kind of crap never happens again."

Carini, despite the senseless blunder committed by the young Iranian, remained anxious to keep the powerful Rafat organization in the system. He decided to try to placate the others, and to try to divert them by changing the subject. He said, "Old man Rafat may be crippled but I'll guarantee you, he'll handle this young shit better than we can. All we could do is quietly murder the punk. His old man will make him wish we had!"

Then Carini, with elaborate deliberation, picked up the small plastic cube from the table in front of him and held it up to view. "Now, let's talk about a different kind of 'screwup.' " He smiled at his own play on words. "As you can see, gentlemen, inside your little cube you find one of the special brass screws we have previously agreed to use as part of our association scheme. I have had these made up as little souvenirs, and as reminders of this meeting. These are the only six of these little paperweights in the entire world. The screws, represented by the samples we have here, are now in full use. We get them made specially in China and in Czechoslovakia. I am going to review for you their purpose and significance."

The five men at the table, with varying degrees of interest showing on their faces, picked up their plastic cubes and examined them. Luigi Carini proceeded with his commentary. "At first glance these seem to be ordinary, run-of-the-mill, one-inch brass wood screws. On closer examination, of course, a person discovers that there is an unusual difference. The slot in the head of the screw will not accept an ordinary screwdriver. A special tool must be used to drive or remove these screws, due to the S-shaped slot in the screwhead. Gentlemen, the heads of these screws represent the secret trademark of this association: a circle, divided in half by an S-shaped curve. More important than their symbolism, though—these screws will play a practical and important role in our day-to-day operations."

Carini paused, appearing to study the plastic cube in his hand. "First of all," he went on, "the singular design of the screw serves as an identification mark. In your shipments, it will usually be that crates of contraband goods will be mixed among crates containing legitimate, harmless materials. These screws will always provide a simple yet almost invisible means of sorting between the two."

Lou Carini twisted the cube. "Secondly, since these screws are, for all practical purposes, indestructible, they will continue to supply identification in the event of unexpected destruction of a shipment. That is, the screws will survive damage from such things as fire or immersion in seawater. We will know if our materials are involved. Finally, they are easily removed if it turns out to be advantageous that we eliminate our markings in a hurry. The screws will not be used in the construction of the shipping crates. They will only be added to the finished, loaded crate, with no more than one for each surface marked. I repeat, they are for identification only."

Carini looked around the table, seeking comments or questions. There were none, so he rose to his feet and looked at his watch. "Well, gentlemen, as our friend Emil says, there is much work to be done. Let's adjourn this meeting. You all know the scheduled time and place for our next conference. If anything else important turns up in the meantime, you'll hear about it."

John Maxton
Beirut, Lebanon
APRIL 1966

The "Fasten Seat Belt—Attachez Votre Ceinture" sign came on. Jefferson Ryder turned to look resignedly at the rumpled lump occupying the window seat next to him. The lump, covered completely by a blanket, snored violently. Ryder reached overhead and pulled the "Stewardess Call" button. He watched as, in a moment, a rangy, heavy-breasted stewardess emerged from the forward lounge and swung her sensational legs briskly down the aisle. She wore a stern look on her pretty face as she stopped at Ryder's seat and reached up to switch off the call light. She looked at Ryder and started to deliver a rehearsed lecture on the importance to passengers of observing instructions given by the seat belt sign.

Ryder held up a hand, interrupting the speech. "Okay. I understand," he said good-humoredly. "When that sign comes on, everybody has to strap himself in, including you crew people. But there is a problem here," he poked a finger into the rumpled, snoring mound next to him, "which I think will take both of us to solve."

She studied the shapeless bundle. A smile tugged the corners of her mouth, but she made her face remain stern. "He has to have his seat belt fastened, and I must return to my position up front. We'll be landing at Beirut in about twenty minutes, and the captain expects rough air as we descend. If you can't help your friend then I will, but it must be taken care of right now."

Ryder nodded and smiled wryly. "Well, you're right, I do have a friend inside that noisy rag pile somewhere. And yes, something must be done about him immediately. First, though, before I ruin his dreams, how about a little assist from you? After all, it was your generosity that put him to sleep!" Ryder pointed to the bulging seat pocket in front of the snoring mound. It was stuffed with assorted empty highball glasses.

The girl smiled. "All right, how do I help?"

Ryder tilted his head toward Maxton. "First I ll find him in there. Then I'll need to get a cup of hot coffee into him. You get me that coffee, and I'll do the rest, including the seat belt. Okay?"

"Okay," she smiled. "It's against the rules, but okay." She headed forward and disappeared into the galley alcove.

Ryder admired the swing of her hips as she walked away, then pulled the blanket off Maxton's inert form and proceeded to awaken him.

The friendship between John Maxton and Jeff Ryder had been cementing itself together by bits and fragments over nearly two decades. In unguided growth the companionship between the two men had weathered the inevitable gamut of minor and major assaults, and had securely survived. Now no longer contending with one another, they enjoyed contending with the rest of the world together.

John Maxton couldn't have articulated his feelings about Ryder. They were just there. To Maxton, Ryder's presence was a comfortable thing, like shrugging on the old hunting mackinaw when the winter day was raw.

In physical build and appearance, Maxton was virtually Ryder's opposite. Against Ryder's long-legged, sinewy linearity, Maxton, half a head shorter, carried the powerful, blocklike torso of a wrestler, balanced on legs proportioned like oak stumps. He wore a pair of arms that seemed a little too long. Above an 18-inch collar size, Maxton's crew-cut head thrust up from massive shoulders like the business end of an artillery shell.

In contrast to the sharply chiseled angularity of Ryder's features, Maxton's face seemed made up of weathered lumps centered on a broken, misshapen nose. Easily the most outstanding features of that face, however, were John Maxton's eyes. Wide set under great bushes of tangled eyebrow and framed by crow's foot crinkles, the clear, Nordic blue of those eyes was almost startling.

Maxton's heavily masculine, homely face, seamed by the tools of time, openly displayed to the world a phlegmatic view of life. Maxton's interest in women was specific and emphatic. It was for the most part a bluntly physical matter. He had never married and was, at age forty-five, content with that status quo.

By the time the airplane had begun to level out from its long descent toward Beirut, Maxton was awake and upright, buckled into his seat, and imbued with a predictably foul humor. The last of the day's light had faded, and below, Beirut's lights stretched across the night in a sparkling crescent, delineated in black sharpness on one side by an invisible shoreline. As the big jet swung gently over the sea into a turn toward the city, Ryder watched the jeweled panorama of lights drift across the window alongside Maxton. Ryder commented, "Home away from home, Max. From here it doesn't look so bad."

"Bullshit," Maxton grunted without a glance at the window.

Ryder grinned at his sour friend, "Someday maybe you'll learn to appreciate the finer things of life."

Maxton said "bullshit" again, and closed his eyes.

The airliner hurtled over the runway threshold and flattened out its glide, losing the last of its lift. The pilot eased back on the control wheel, feeling for the concrete under the landing gear. Through the seat of his pants, Ryder followed the pilot's management of the landing, judging the rate of descent and the speed by looking out the window. "Now!" The involuntary thought became an audible one as Ryder sensed the touchdown an instant before the airplane bumped onto the runway. "Overshot a little," he observed to himself. His criticism was immediately borne out by the thunder of maximum reverse thrust and the shuddering deceleration of heavy braking.

Maxton was thoroughly awakened by the hard landing, and sufficiently annoyed to issue his own, very audible, criticism. "Jesus! They've got a trained ape flying this thing!" Maxton groaned and looked out the window, watching the blue boundary lights slide by along the taxiway as the airplane now rolled slowly toward the terminal building.

Ryder stood up and retrieved his and Maxton's jackets from the overhead shelf. "Here, amigo, let's try to get through this arrival madhouse ahead of some of these tourist types. I've got the baggage tags and the mad money." Ryder handed Maxton his jacket, then fished through a worn billfold stuffed with paper currency from a dozen countries. He extracted a small stack of very dirty Lebanese livres.

True to Ryder's prediction, the arrival area of the terminal presented a scene of unmanageably chaotic humanity. A number of other recently arrived jets had disgorged their loads of passengers, and the inadequate entry gates were mobbed. Ryder eyed the churning congestion ahead and swore in disgust. He turned to Maxton. "Let's pull rank and bypass that convention of nitwits." He started walking back in the direction of the ramp. Reaching the outside door he paused, searching among the faces of airline personnel working on the ramp. Maxton stood alongside, doing the same. It was Maxton who found what they were looking for. "There's one!" he said, pointing. "Just coming out of the VIP lounge. That's De Vilbiss of TWA, isn't it?"

Ryder swung around, his eyes focusing in the direction of Maxton's pointing finger. "Good shot, Max. Come on, let's get him!" They started walking rapidly toward their quarry. To run would be to attract attention from some of the armed and uniformed Lebanese sentries, who for no apparent purpose always patrolled the commercial flight line of Beirut's airport. Ryder and Maxton overtook their man just as he stuck a leg into TWA's ramp jeep. "Hey, Ralph!" Ryder called as he and Maxton came up to the jeep.

De Vilbiss turned, squinting his eyes against the glare of floodlights that bathed the ramp area. As the two figures approached he finally recognized them and smiled, stepping back out of the jeep. "Hi, strangers! You guys are supposed to brownnose the Mahogany Row types, not us slobs!" De Vilbiss was happily remembering a number of epochal sprees he'd been treated to by Maxton, on Max's expense account.

Wise to this, Ryder let Maxton step in. Maxton proclaimed heartily, "What we're trying to do right now is to avoid slobs, all right, but I sure as hell don't mean you, Ralphie Boy!" He jabbed a thumb back toward the arrival area. "There are a thousand unwashed nincompoops back there, all trying to get through that two-holer check-in gate at the same time. Get us out from behind this peasant uprising, De Vilbiss, and Ryder and me'll tell Mahogany Row how indispensable you actually are!"

De Vilbiss was delighted. He had already begun to think up excuses for a night out without his wife. He genuinely liked Ryder and Maxton, although Ryder awed him a little. He grinned and said, "No sweat, men, follow me. We'll just goose through the VIP side. I can get your passports stamped, easy." De Vilbiss had grabbed Maxton's arm fraternally as he spoke, and the three men moved toward the doorway from which De Vilbiss had emerged earlier.

Despite their avoidance of the visa and quarantine tedium, Ryder and Maxton had still to recover their baggage. De Vilbiss was powerless to help with this problem, although he offered to stay while they waited for the bags. Ryder and Maxton sent him back to his work, however, content with Maxton's suggestion that the two of them get together for an evening out.

They finally secured their baggage, and located a porter. They allowed the porter to serve as a battering ram to penetrate the inevitable stubborn throng of Lebanese well-wishers waiting to greet arriving relatives and friends.

At length, they succeeded in pushing through the tightly packed crowd of sweating people, and emerged into the cool night air. A nondescript taxi blattered up to the stand and their bags were loaded aboard. Ryder tipped the porter with two of the pound notes and said, "Phoenicia Hotel," to the taxi driver. He and Maxton climbed in, and the taxi rattled away toward the city.

Bogart Schuyler III
Beirut, Lebanon
APRIL 1966

The aged doorman at the Phoenicia Hotel, resplendent in traditional Lebanese costume topped by a red-felt, black-tassled tarboosh, stood waiting for the taxi to pull up to the hotel entrance. Short in stature, the doorman had the frame of a great bear. Huge shoulders surmounted an equally huge belly. The old doorman, now in his sixties, had once held Lebanon's wrestling championship. His strong, jovial face suddenly illuminated with a great smile of pleasure as he opened the taxi door and recognized Jefferson Ryder, "*Ahlan wa sahlan! Ahlan wa sahlan*, Mr. Ryder!" The old man's Arabic welcome was as genuine as it was enthusiastic.

Ryder grinned back at the smiling, bowing old doorman and extended his hand. "*Marhaba*, Joseph! *Keef halak*, old friend?" Ryder seized a huge hand in his own and proceeded to squeeze with all his strength in the handshake. This little ritual always delighted the old wrestler, who could, even now, crush the bones of an ordinary man's hand in his powerful grip.

Upon hearing Ryder's name called by the doorman, a covey of the Phoenicia's young bellboys came scampering to the scene, each calling, "*Ahlan wa sahlan*, Mr. Ryder!" They seized the luggage and sped into the hotel. Ryder paid the taxi driver, then he and Maxton entered the hotel and rode the escalator to the mezzanine reception level. Their arrival had been announced by the bellboys, and the two Americans were met at the head of the escalator by the senior reception clerk, the bell captain, and a costumed attendant who offered them demitasse cups of Arabic coffee. Cordial greetings were once again offered.

Through all this and while they registered into the hotel, Ryder and Maxton remained unaware of the middle-aged, stockily built, sandy-haired American who idled inconspicuously nearby and intently watched the entire arrival episode.

Escorted by two of the bellboys, they rode the elevator to the tenth floor and headed for their adjoining rooms. By Beirut standards the evening was young. The two Americans decided to meet in the lobby cocktail lounge later after unpacking and freshening up. Maxton sorted out his own two bags and disappeared into his room. Ryder followed one of the bellboys farther along the corridor and into the next room, tipped the departing boy, and began unpacking. The telephone rang. Mildly annoyed, Ryder tossed a handful of socks back into the open suitcase and went over to the telephone. He picked it up and said, "Hello," then swore when the line went dead in his ear. He punched the instrument back onto its cradle. Although thoroughly accustomed to Beirut's erratic telephone service, Ryder nevertheless was invariably galled by it. He returned to the business of emptying his suitcase.

Ryder was stowing the empty bag in a closet when he heard a knock on the door of his room. He found Bogart Schuyler waiting when he answered, and invited him in, studying the first secretary and wondering at this unusual visit.

Bogart Schuyler looked to be older than his years. At age forty-three he had lost control of his weight, and his torso had sagged into flabbiness. Schuyler's face displayed an overpreoccupation with sophistication, through vertical lines of cold, anxious haughtiness. In correction of nearsightedness, he chose to wear a style of rimless eyeglasses that contributed to an aged appearance. Ryder knew, however, that Schuyler was gifted with a clever mind and an exceptionally retentive memory. In amused tolerance, he disregarded Schuyler's habitually supercilious manner. Ryder said, "Well, Boge, this is a pleasant surprise! You must have finally hooked onto the Lebanese grapevine! I'm just barely here!"

Schuyler, feeling guilty of an etiquette breach, reddened slightly. "Jeff, I know this is a terrible time to disturb you, and I certainly wouldn't have come here unannounced if it hadn't been necessary. But there is a matter of some urgency that I must take up with you." To Ryder's mounting puzzlement, Schuyler had taken a light hold on his arm and was gesturing toward the outside balcony beyond sliding glass doors at the end of the room. The doors were already opened to the warm Mediterranean night air. The two men stepped out onto the balcony, overlooking the lighted turquoise oval of a large swimming pool ten floors below.

To Bogart Schuyler III, Jefferson Ryder represented an intimidating entity. To begin with the sense of hard physical capacity about Ryder was heavily repugnant to Schuyler, even frightening. Schuyler considered cultured and scholarly demeanor an epitomic rule of human conduct. It was Schuyler's cherished view that physical aptitudes and proclivities in a man are, in the main, directly associated with mental sloth and brutish intellect. The unmistakable presence of an intelligent brain in Ryder's head made, to Schuyler, the man's disdain of behavioral niceties all the more aggravating. It was vexing to observe enviable accomplishments performed by a man to whom Schuyler's cultivated code was inconsequential. To add to his frustration with Ryder, Schuyler knew irrefutably that his own success as a career diplomat demanded the capacity to cope readily with every manner of personality. It was invariably irksome to Schuyler to sense the unease that would persistently underrun his composure in Ryder's presence.

Ryder turned to Schuyler and asked with a smile, "What's this all about, Boge? You're out after hours!" Any humor intended in Ryder's remark was utterly lost on Schuyler. The CIA matter burdened his thoughts, and Ryder's offhand manner affronted him. He answered stiffly, "Actually, this is important, and it concerns you, not me. We should keep our voices down because, as you know, rooms are frequently bugged in this city. What I have to tell you is confidential. There is a man whom the ambassador would like to have you meet with tonight if at all possible. You know that you wouldn't be asked to do something like this if it weren't truly urgent."

Ryder digested Schuyler's remarks for a moment. "Okay, Boge. Then, what's the rest? Where do I go, and when?"

Schuyler replied, "As soon as you're ready to go, I'll drive you. You know my car, the blue Mercedes. I've parked it up the hill by some excavations they're doing. You'll have to walk a block or so, and I'll watch for you."

Ryder could only tolerate a certain amount of melodrama, and felt this was all forming up like a comic opera. "I guess you know, I wouldn't do this for just anybody, Boge old pal. But since it's you, let's press on. I'll meet you at your car in about"—he glanced at his watch—"ten minutes. I have to undo a small drinking date I've laid on with Maxton."

Schuyler hurried out. Ryder picked up the telephone and asked for Maxton's room. There was no answer so Ryder shrugged into his jacket and headed for the elevator.

He found Maxton seated at the lobby bar, engaged in lively discussion with the Lebanese bartender. They seemed to be arguing over the merits of arak, the Lebanese aperitif, as an aid both to digestion and to masculine potency. As Ryder approached, Maxton started to climb off the barstool, expecting to move to a table. Ryder waved him back. "Stay where you are, Max. As usual, the telephone started ringing the minute I got in the room. I've got to go take care of a little business right now, so carry on. I'll look for you around here whenever I get back, but don't wait up for me."

Maxton eased back onto the stool, happy enough that he wasn't to be involved with Ryder's chores. He nodded and hoisted his martini glass in mock salute. "Hurry back, or this stuff will all be gone!" Ryder waved as he walked away, thinking wryly that Max might indeed drink the bar dry with no one there to slow him down.

Ryder made his way out of the hotel. He hiked briskly up the dimly lit street until he found Schuyler's car. As Ryder seated himself in the sedan, Schuyler started the engine and switched on the headlights, then eased the car out of its parking place. They drove for a few moments in silence. Schuyler finally said, "Jeff, there isn't anything I can tell you ahead of time. I'm afraid you'll have to wait until we get to the embassy." He paused, then ventured to add, "I hope you're not overly tired, because I think you'll want to stay as alert as you can."

By this time everything about the episode began to seem peculiar to Ryder. Schuyler never risked driving his prized Mercedes in the frenzied traffic of Beirut, preferring to pay taxi fares, especially at night. Then, Schuyler's usual professional haughtiness had given way to a tense overlayer of what looked to Ryder like anxiety. Ryder shrugged off these puzzles phlegmatically. It was evident that he wouldn't learn more about the situation until they had reached their destination.

Beirut's Wednesday evening street traffic had achieved its normal state of inching bedlam, and ten minutes went by before Bogart Schuyler managed to drive the very short distance from the hotel to the US Embassy. With a sigh of relief he finally maneuvered the blue Mercedes sedan into the embassy driveway. He stopped the car under a lighted portico at the building's main entrance.

As the two men climbed the steps to the embassy lobby Ryder remarked lightly, "I'm suspicious of this VIP treatment, Boge! Any other time we would've walked—and got here quicker at that!"

Schuyler, hurrying up the sweeping front stairs, made no comment other than to mutter something about deference to Ryder's travel fatigue. He spoke briefly to the marine guard at a reception desk, who then busied himself with the telephone switchboard. Ryder followed Schuyler past the guard and into the embassy's small elevator. They rode up two flights, then, still without conversation, Schuyler led the way out of the elevator and down a lighted corridor past the ambassador's suite of offices. He stopped and rapped briefly on a door nearby. The door swung open almost immediately and Ryder heard a man's voice say, "Please come in, gentlemen." He followed Schuyler into a large, brightly lighted conference room, then stood watching as the door was closed behind them by a thick-framed, sandy-haired man in a business suit. The room was otherwise unoccupied.

The stockily built man smiled as he came over to them. He extended his hand. "I'm Jim Crawford, Mr. Ryder. You can blame me for this bizarre evening." Ryder shook Crawford's hand but made no comment.

Crawford turned and greeted Schuyler, then waved an arm toward the conference table filling the center of the room. "We can sit and talk here at the table, gentlemen. Please make yourselves comfortable."

Ryder saw that one of the chairs on the far side of the table had been moved back, and that a plain manila folder lay beside a briefcase on the table there. He presumed that Crawford had occupied the chair, so moved toward a place opposite. Schuyler took a seat beside Ryder.

James Crawford studied Ryder closely. He was accustomed to the appraisal of men, and to the selection of those with the capacity to function efficiently under stress. He had, earlier in the evening, started liking what he saw as Ryder, unaware of the scrutiny, had walked into the Phoenicia Hotel on arrival from the airport. The CIA man had studied the disarmingly relaxed appearance in Ryder's walk—the slack-muscled, energy-conserving, loose efficiency of an animal's movements.

Now, in a closer inspection, Crawford resumed his assessment. He watched the shuttle of Ryder's eyes as they scoured the surroundings. Crawford watched himself be visually dissected, judged, and categorized. He searched out the natural athlete's qualities in Ryder. Bunched muscles piled under the jacket across wide shoulders. Lean, flat abdomen. Powerful grip from hard hands and strong fingers. Hands that hung loosely, but ready. Steady hands that didn't fidget or try to hide themselves.

He studied Ryder's face, appraising the evidence there of experience, will, and character. He noted the erect head and the level, challenging gaze. He saw lean, firm flesh, weathered and marked from sun and wind. He cataloged the good-humored seams of self-confidence, crossed with lines of thought and concentration, and an ample scatter of tracings left by trial and crisis. Violence had left its register too, in the diagonally scarred left cheek.

Crawford decided that on the outside, Ryder looked just fine. It now remained to have a look at the inside.

Crawford moved around the table and stood facing the other two men. He looked at Ryder and asked, "Mr. Schuyler has agreed to let me host for the evening. Before we start our discussions, maybe you'd like some coffee or a drink, Mr. Ryder?"

Ryder shrugged. "Sure. Scotch and water would go good."

Schuyler, who thought Ryder should have asked for coffee, sent a disapproving glance in Ryder's direction and asked for coffee for himself.

Crawford deduced Schuyler's reaction and wore a small smile as he headed for a small adjoining pantry. Schuyler was proving uniformly predictable. At the same time, the small incident suggested that Ryder was pretty much his own man.

A clinking of china and glassware emanated briefly from the pantry doorway, then Crawford reappeared carrying a serving tray with their drinks. He had mixed a Scotch and water for himself. The bottle of Scotch and a pitcher of water were on the tray too, together with a bowl of ice cubes. He set the tray on the table and distributed the three drinks, then sat facing Ryder and Schuyler.

Crawford lifted his glass in an unspoken toast, and each man sipped his drink. Crawford then spoke, addressing himself to Ryder. "It's about time we do away with some of the mystery for you, Mr. Ryder. Let me lead off with a quick summary of what this is all about. I am with the Central Intelligence Agency. Certain developments in this part of the world dictate that we go after a category of information not now readily acquired. We are talking about matters of vital importance to the United States, Mr. Ryder. We think you can help us. My purpose in being here is to ask you if you are willing and able to engage in doing so." Crawford paused and took a swallow of his drink, watching Ryder's reactions.

Despite the bluntly stated and unexpected nature of Crawford's words, the singular events of the earlier evening diminished the impact of these remarks upon Ryder. He turned to Schuyler. "No wonder you've been so tight-lipped tonight! Are you a spy too?"

Crawford was amused, pleased with the way Ryder had neatly sidestepped the purposely direct thrust of that opening statement. Crawford also noticed that Ryder had unconsciously run a finger along the white line of the diagonal scar on his cheek as he listened.

Schuyler, slightly piqued, retorted defensively, "I'm almost as new to this as you are, Jeff. Frankly, I don't know what, exactly, the CIA wants you to do. No, I'm not a spy. At least, not yet," he added in evident disquiet.

Crawford resumed speaking. "Now, let me elaborate a little. The sort of work we are talking about is detailed. It deals with fragments, very important fragments, of bigger things. You have fought a war, Mr. Ryder, and I'm sure you've learned the importance to a campaign of the many separate actions that comprise it. This is the essence of what we will be doing. It is tactical, not strategic. It is important, of course, that you understand the strategic goal to which you are contributing. You will be kept aware of those goals." Crawford remained silent momentarily, then continued. "Right now, the United States finds herself facing simultaneously a formidable number of such goals in this part of the world. To be honest about it, Mr. Ryder, circumstances have arisen that leave us rather poorly equipped for the scope of things that have more or less suddenly become visible out here. The executive branch of our government has directed that this state of affairs be remedied at once." Crawford stopped speaking and took a swallow of his drink.

Ryder, leaning comfortably back in his chair, had listened intently to Crawford's words. He remained silent, however, joining Crawford in tasting the Scotch and water.

Crawford looked at Ryder and began again. "I'm sure, with the kind of work you do, that you keep yourself well informed on international events that pertain to this region. Between reports available in the press and the observations you make yourself in the course of your travels, I suspect that you already know a great deal about some of the adverse trends we are concerned with. There are others that you probably know nothing about. What you also could not know is that the cadence of events comprising these several ominous trends is being stepped up. These are deliberate actions, contrived by masters, carefully timed, and highly complex. They must be dealt with in kind. Our conversation tonight constitutes a step in that direction." Crawford stopped speaking and leaned back.

The three men sat silently for a time, each with his own thoughts. Ryder looked at the CIA man. "You said you think I can help. What does that mean, Mr. Crawford?"

Crawford toyed with the glass in his hand for a moment. "Before I try to answer you, Mr. Ryder, I must tell you that there is a chicken-and-egg problem in this conversation that we will be up against very soon. That is, there is a point beyond which I cannot go in being explicit with you until you have committed yourself to accepting participation. On the other hand, you will understandably be reluctant to make a decision until you are satisfied on some of the details. With that in mind, then, let's continue. Oversimplified, what I mean is this. The kinds of information we want must come from places to which you routinely travel. Access to that information can for the most part only be achieved through freedom of activity among people with whom your contacts are commonplace. Then, the intervals of time between your trips into the area actually serve advantageously. So you see, you possess a remarkably unique set of attributes in our eyes, Mr. Ryder."

Ryder studied Crawford. "That could be a tall order. Let's say I do decide to go along with you. How do you figure I can do what you want and still do justice to my normal job? I'm not of a mind to short-sheet my company. After all, they pay my salary. And, as a matter of fact, I like my job."

Crawford shook his head. "We do not propose that you do anything that will interfere significantly with your normal job performance. Quite the contrary. Any such interference would immediately invite suspicion, and we would be defeating our own purposes. As you know very well, we are dealing among people with whom suspicion is a way of life. Their forebears probably invented devious intrigue. And, there is another thing you should be told. This arrangement will be made known to the chairman of the board of your company. This kind of arrangement will not be unprecedented with him."

Ryder thought for a moment, then said, "Well, so far so good. Another question. People out here tend to take a pretty dim view of anybody who comes poking into their private playpens. They can play pretty rough. Do I do all this on my own, or do I get help?"

"You act alone, Mr. Ryder," Crawford answered bluntly. "Arrangements will be made through Mr. Schuyler to provide a communications channel. Otherwise, you will be on your own."

Ryder considered Crawford's reply, then commented, "Okay. Getting right down to it, I guess I'd rather have it that way." He paused, then went on. "So far you haven't given me any good excuse for turning you down. Maybe the best way to find out if this scheme will work would be to try it out once. Have you got an easy one to test me with?"

Crawford nodded. With this suggestion Ryder had anticipated the intended CIA plan. "You're quite right. That is the best approach. In fact, your full participation would have to be conditional on the success of a trial period, for the benefit of both parties. As to your question, Mr. Ryder, I'm sorry to say that there are no easy ones."

Ryder grinned. "I guess I'd have been insulted if you hadn't put it that way." Ryder gestured questioningly with his hands. "Well, it's still 'so far, so good'—where do we go from here, Mr. Crawford?"

Crawford did not return Ryder's grin. He fixed a penetrating look on Ryder's face and said, "Before we go anywhere from here, and before you can make up your mind, there is one more important piece of background information you need. One that might supply the excuse that will cause you to turn me down." Crawford paused to let that sink in. He then went on, "One of the reasons we need your help, Mr. Ryder, is that three of CIA's Middle East agents have recently died. They were killed."

Ryder's eyes blinked and widened momentarily. He sat silently, digesting this harsh pronouncement for a drawn-out, frowning interval. Crawford said nothing more. He simply waited, watching Ryder's face.

At length Ryder drew in a large breath. He spoke in a sobered tone. "Well. That one's not so easy to laugh off!"

James Crawford said, "No, it certainly isn't." Then, continuing to speak, Crawford busied himself in returning the manila folder to his briefcase. "And now I think we've done all we should for tonight. I would like to ask you, Mr. Ryder, to think over this conversation during the next twenty-four hours. I propose that we then meet here again, at some appropriate time tomorrow, if that is suitable to you."

Ryder said, "That sounds all right. I'll have my business affairs wound up by three o'clock tomorrow. Anytime after that will suit me."

Crawford nodded, then turned to Schuyler. "Will it be convenient for you, Mr. Schuyler, to meet again tomorrow?" Schuyler, under orders to monitor the CIA affair, replied without hesitation, "Certainly."

Crawford looked back at Ryder. "It is essential that we keep our acquaintance under wraps, Mr. Ryder. I believe the reasons for this are self-evident. Beirut is a small community. Familiar figures in this city such as yourself cannot expect their movements to go unobserved. Strangers here, people like me, are the subject of even more lively scrutiny. At least, they remain so until the extraordinary local curiosity is satisfied. Fortunately your visits to the embassy are routine. We will, however, want to avoid meeting in public."

The CIA man stood then, smiling cordially. "Well, let's plan to meet here at, say, three thirty tomorrow afternoon. How would that do?"

Ryder and the first secretary got to their feet. Ryder looked at Crawford and shrugged slightly. "Okay by me. I'll be here." He turned to Schuyler and added, "See you tomorrow, Boge. I'll hike myself back to the Phoenicia."

Crawford extended his hand. Ryder smiled and shook hands briefly with the CIA man, then headed out of the conference room, on his way back to the hotel.

On Board
Beirut, Lebanon
APRIL 1966

Jefferson Ryder stepped out of the embassy elevator and into the high-ceilinged corridor. He headed for the conference room adjoining the ambassador's office suite. The corridor echoed as he walked, seeming to emphasize the quiet. Ryder glanced at his watch. It read 3:25 PM.

At Ryder's knock the conference room door was promptly opened. Bogart Schuyler peered out at Ryder momentarily, then, sounding official and formal, invited him in. Ryder entered and the CIA man, James Crawford, stepped up, his hand extended in greeting.

Crawford's manner was affable and friendly as they shook hands. "You're right on time, Mr. Ryder." He indicated the conference table where two partially consumed cups of coffee rested. "Can I pour you a cup?"

Ryder acknowledged the man's greeting with a smile. He said, "Sure. Black, please."

While Crawford went after the coffee, Schuyler and Ryder seated themselves. Ryder settled himself comfortably and then made conversation. "How'd your day go, Boge?"

Schuyler fiddled with his glasses, slightly unsettled by Ryder's offhandedness in the face of what seemed to Schuyler to be a crucial occasion. "Oh. Well. Today was fairly routine, actually. We're busy these days watching the Lebanese political scene. As you probably know, their prime minister, Karami, is about to resign. Ambassador Harte keeps asking me who Karami's likely successor will be." He paused. "You can imagine how difficult that question is to answer!"

Ryder chuckled. "Yes, I certainly can! Predicting Lebanese politics is about like slipping pantyhose onto an octopus!"

Crawford, returning from the pantry, listened with amused interest to Ryder's remark. He handed Ryder's coffee across the table and sat down, commenting, "I've heard politics described by experts, but never more accurately nor as colorfully!" The CIA man lifted his coffee cup in a mock toast, and Ryder followed suit, smilingly acknowledging the salute.

Schuyler took an unceremonious sip of his coffee too, and changed the subject, "Well, Mr. Crawford, Ambassador Harte would never forgive me for making you listen to embassy gossip. Certainly not in the presence of your important mission here."

A shadow of amusement stayed on Crawford's face as he turned his gaze to Schuyler and nodded his assent. "Thank you for your concern, Mr. Schuyler. And you're quite right; we do have serious problems to solve here, and not much time. So, we might as well get at them." This direct statement by Crawford was then followed, perversely, by an oblique one. He asked, "Do either of you gentlemen have questions or comments not concerning Mr. Ryder's proposed assistance to the CIA?"

There was an interval of silence. Ryder waited, watching to see whether Schuyler meant to speak. Schuyler evidently did not, so Ryder turned to face Crawford and said, "Well, let's just get the suspense over with, Mr. Crawford. I've thought it all over and I've decided to go ahead and have a try at your game. However, I do have a couple of conditions to throw into the pot."

Crawford nodded noncommittally and remained silent. Ryder went on, "First of all, I'm taking it for granted that you do not intend exposing me to risky situations without first warning me. Also, I'll take it for granted that you will always take steps to lessen any such risks I have to take, at least when you know about them, in whatever ways you have sensibly available. Then, whatever I do for you, I want to do at my own pace. That's within reason, of course. If I see a serious cross-up with my business affairs, I want you to let me decide how to handle the overlap. And if that happens too often, and gets too awkward, I want freedom to opt out of the whole stunt. Now, in case those conditions don't sound so good to you, I'll also say that I don't want any pay for this. As far as I'm concerned, you asked me to do a favor. I'm saying I will."

Crawford leaned back in his chair, studying Ryder. At length he spoke. "Your conditions are not unreasonable, Mr. Ryder. Some of them are definitely irregular, though, even in this irregular business, and I will want to give them further consideration. However, I don't see anything to prevent our going ahead with a trial effort. My considerations of your conditions can be regarded as part of that exploratory period. And as to those risks—yes, you most assuredly may take it for granted that you will be guarded in every way possible within CIA's resources. Does that all sound agreeable to you?"

Ryder nodded. He said, "That sounds okay."

Crawford's expression relaxed. He let his voice and manner ease back to a less formal tone. "Believe me when I say that I am immensely pleased and relieved by your decision. I look forward to working with you, Mr. Ryder, and I think, altogether, we are going to get some important things accomplished out here." He turned to Bogart Schuyler. "That last is meant to include you, Mr. Schuyler. And now that Mr. Ryder has given us his decision, is there anything you'd like to say about our enterprise?"

Schuyler nodded soberly. "As a matter of fact, yes, Mr. Crawford. There is one question that has occurred to me. Jeff's aviation business affairs involve practically every one of the nearby countries. In truth, I'm not even sure that I know all of the ones that he covers. But we have embassies in each of them, of course, and I'd like to know what role we, here in Beirut, will occupy vis-à-vis all the other embassies concerned."

Crawford eased back in his chair. "It's helpful that you've mentioned this subject, Mr. Schuyler. I should have covered that matter earlier. In coping with this problem, we prefer to function from some kind of central, on-site location. We've chosen Beirut. This choice, by the way, was made in very close coordination with topside State Department. They want Ambassador Harte to pilot things connected with this project for them on the scene out here. Whatever other arrangements State may make with different embassies or consulates will of course be their decision. For our purposes, though, your Beirut embassy is the only one with which we will be in regular direct contact for this effort."

Schuyler didn't look satisfied, but he said, "Yes, I see." Crawford reached into his pocket and produced a notepad, a pen, and a map of the Middle East, which he unfolded and laid out on the table. "All right, let's get into a few details." He looked at Ryder. "I would like to know what you have planned as an itinerary for your present trip—places and dates."

Ryder nodded, then started into a recitation of his plans. "Okay, it'll go something like this. I'll leave Beirut day after tomorrow, on the Saturday night flight to Jeddah in Saudi Arabia. I'll be there until Wednesday the twentieth, then back here to Beirut. I'll overnight here and then take a morning flight to Amman, Jordan, on Thursday. Ought to finish there by Sunday night. Then, either Sunday night or Monday morning, I'll come back through Beirut again on my way to Teheran in Iran. A few days there, then a short call in Kabul, up in

Afghanistan, and then I'll be heading back to the States, unless some kind of delay develops along the way. In other words, I'll be done with this work trip somewhere in the first week of May, about three weeks from now."

Crawford took notes, following Ryder's announced itinerary with a finger on the map. He whistled lightly. "That's a lot of geography!" He looked up from his notepad. "But you've given me just what I wanted. So now let's talk a little about what you may do for us, both in general terms and in particular regard to the trip you're heading out on."

Crawford let the map and the opened notepad remain where they were on the table, and turned his attention fully to Ryder. "I'd like to start with a question, Mr. Ryder. What is your opinion as to the position occupied by the Palestinians now in Jordan—apart from those living in the refugee camps, I mean? In particular, what influence do you feel they bring to bear on Jordan's principal affairs, governmentally and businesswise?"

Ryder studied the question for an interval. He then began, "Well, that's kind of a sticky one, but I'll try to tell you how I see it. To start with, even though it might not seem so, there are some fairly basic differences between the Palestinians and the Jordanian people. The real Jordanian is a hard-nosed bedouin; he's a desert warrior and he's damn proud of it. They are honest-to-God, tough desert Arabs, like the Saudis were before the oil, and they generally don't let anybody shove them around." Ryder then pointed to the outline of Jordan on Crawford's map and said, "Now, look at where the Palestinians hail from." He moved his finger up and down the blue markings of the Mediterranean coastline, from the Sinai Peninsula on the south, up to Lebanon on the north. "These people, both the Palestinians and the Lebanese, have the instincts of waterfront Fagins. They're different from the bedouin Arabs. Their great-great-granddaddies were a combination of hairy, slope-shouldered pirates and gimlet-eyed traders, churning around in their biremes and triremes looking for somebody to sell the Brooklyn Bridge to." Ryder leaned back, smiling a little. "And as far as I'm concerned, they haven't changed much since."

Crawford also smiled, listening to Ryder's earthy account. "So, you see a difference from the Jordanians, stemming in part from history and the local geography."

Ryder nodded and ran a finger up and down the north-south line of the Jordan River. "Right. Pretty much sorted out by the Jordan. The Jordanians are mostly like the old-timers—nomad bedouins who lived east of the river in the desert. The Palestinians came from the easy side of the Jordan, to the west where things will grow in the ground, and where most of the commerce has always centered."

Ryder took a sip of his coffee, then said to Crawford, "I guess that doesn't really answer your question, though. Since '48, when the Palestinians were shoved inland by the UN to make room for Israel, they ended up mainly in Jordan. Since then, they haven't been wasting their time, and by now a whopping chunk of the top businessmen in Jordan are former Palestinian displacements. They're smart enough to keep their noses out of front-line Jordanian politics. They just keep wagging the local flag while they rifle the Jordanians' cash registers."

Crawford asked, "Then you don't feel the Palestinians have a very strong sense of allegiance to Jordan?"

Ryder shrugged. "Under their hides, I don't think any of them give a tinker's damn for Jordan's King Hussein. They'll dump him on his royal rump anytime they think it would help them get back to their easy beach. If you could get a Palestinian to level with you, you'd find out he figures the only things bedouins are good for is raising goats and body lice."

Crawford chuckled. "Well, that's succinct enough!"

Ryder held up a hand, "But don't get me wrong. It wouldn't balance to pile too much blame on the Palestinians. After all, they got a mighty shaky deal in 1948 when they were shoved out of their nests with no place to go."

Crawford, in a serious tone, said, "All that you've said is, in its own way, in line with what we see in Jordan. Right now one of our main sources of concern hinges around the organized Palestinians, particularly their guerrilla groupings such as Al Fatah. Far more scope is involved in this so-called guerrilla activity than is visible in the press. Far more than just border raids on Israel."

Crawford let this introductory statement penetrate, then went on. "The Palestinian guerrilla movements must be treated, in effect, separately from either of the nominal antagonists in the current Arab-Israeli confrontation. That is, while the Palestinians' allegiance is obviously and violently anti-Israel, it isn't at all automatically pro-Arab. You might oversimplify their position by regarding it as pro-Palestinian, and the devil take the bystanders. They have everything to gain out of an Arab-

Israeli war, and very little to lose. As such they possess an extremely ominous potential. They are intruding into the internal affairs, to one extent or another, in virtually every nearby Moslem country."

Bogart Schuyler listened avidly to Crawford's remarks, grudgingly according the CIA man a growing measure of respect. Schuyler commented, "They seem to be accumulating a considerable roster of backers too."

Crawford nodded agreement. "They're securing help from many directions. From the UAR, from Syria, Iraq, Russia, and from Communist China, to name a few. Incredibly enough, they are even receiving assistance from Cuba. Yet, they are actually not offering much of anything in return. These others are helping them because it serves their own various purposes of the moment. The Palestinians are perfectly well aware of that, I might add. One of these days these erstwhile benefactors may find they have outsmarted themselves, or find they've been outsmarted by the Palestinians, to the end detriment of both! In order to obviate open warfare out here, which is the overriding goal of our activity in the Middle East, these warmongering Palestinian splinter groups have to be checked. And if we must, we will pitch in and help some of these participants outsmart one another." The CIA man sat silently for a moment, then looked at Ryder. "That brings us to the basic nature of your problem, Mr. Ryder. To find out as much as you can about the Palestinian guerrillas. Information of any kind is useful. Who they are. Who their friends are. Who is helping them and in what ways. How they are funded. What their activities and plans are. The 'hows,' the 'whens,' and the 'wheres.' "

Ryder, listening to all this, began to look baffled. Crawford saw the look and interjected, "It's not as bad as it probably sounds from your present viewpoint. I'm not going to ask you for the moon, Mr. Ryder. On each of your business trips into this area, you will be asked to watch for no more than one or two specific items of interest. Whatever else you may come across will be a bonus. At this point, as a matter of fact, the best way to illustrate what you may come to expect hereafter will be for me to tell you what to look for during your forthcoming travels."

Ryder and Bogart Schuyler both stirred perceptibly, their attention heightened by Crawford's words. The CIA man looked at Ryder. He said. "My latest information out of Jordan mentions a man you probably know. His name is Abdallah

Rifai. The information suggests that he is prominently implicated in the affairs of Al Fatah. As you no doubt know, Al Fatah is the most lethal of the Palestinian terrorist groups."

Ryder's recognition of Rifai's name was easily read from his face. Crawford observed, "So. Then you do know Rifai."

Ryder nodded. "I do if we're talking about the same man. Abdallah Rifai is the name of one of the board members of the Jordanian airline. He is also a banker, and is into a lot of other businesses in Jordan. I've also been told he's a former Palestinian." Ryder paused, then volunteered, "I'm not actually acquainted with him. Rifai and I know one another by sight and to say hello, but no more than that."

Crawford said, "That's the man. And at the present time we know next to nothing about the nature and extent of his links with Al Fatah. It is safe to say, though, that whatever those links might be, Rifai has successfully kept them concealed from the Jordanian security people." Crawford's features coalesced into a stone-hard look. "The first and only mention of Abdallah Rifai's name reached me in the final message sent by our foremost agent in Amman. The next thing heard of that agent was the discovery of his corpse beside the road between Amman and the Jordanian village of Az Zarqa. He was found beside his car, shot to death from long range with a high-muzzle velocity rifle."

Bogart Schuyler gasped. Crawford finished his remarks with icy deliberation. "It is essential that we learn, and soon, whether or not Rifai was involved in the murder of that agent. The agent had only recently succeeded in penetrating Al Fatah as a guerrilla squad member."

Ryder blinked a few times in frowning thought. Then he said, "Well, I get the picture, but I'm still not sure that I see where I fit in."

"Now, just take your time on this. Don't rush it," Crawford cautioned. "Rifai is your subject. I suggest that you simply start by trying to find out as much as you can about Rifai, prudently and judiciously. Feel your way very slowly. You do not need to try getting any closer to him personally. In fact, that sort of overt thing could touch a raw nerve. If Rifai is privy to that removal of our agent, he is probably as jumpy as a cat right now. So I emphasize again—go slow! Feel this thing out at your own pace! Just don't forget, they play for keeps down there."

Ryder shrugged. "Okay. I'll just take it as it comes, without pushing. It won't be much of a trick for me in Amman to poke around and pick up lots of poop on Rifai without rousing the guard. Those Arabs love nothing better than to gossip about one another, if you can just get them started; a little whiskey goes a long way, since damn few of them can hold their liquor." Then, somewhat musingly, Ryder added, "In fact, this kind of thing will dovetail surprisingly well with my ordinary routines anyway!"

Ryder noticed the hint of a smile go by on Crawford's bland face. He paused and amended, ruefully, "Aha. I see! Not so surprising to *you*, eh? Well, okay. So now I do begin to see where I might fit in!"

Crawford looked his approval. "And keep it exactly as you just expressed it, dovetailed smoothly within your ordinary routines. I can't emphasize that enough."

Ryder had leaned forward, elbows resting on the table. He frowned in thought for a moment, then asked, "Okay, so far so good. Supposing that I do manage to dig up something worthwhile about Rifai, or about Al Fatah, or the Palestinians in general. What do I do with it?"

Crawford's reply was prompt. "Turn it over to Mr. Schuyler, in person and verbally, at your earliest next opportunity here in Beirut. Keep in mind that such meetings must continue to appear customary and casual. When he receives your reports, Mr. Schuyler will see to it that they are put into the right channels."

The first secretary seemed, by his expression, to be enjoying his moment in the limelight of this sinister apparatus. He did not, however, enter the conversation. Ryder went on, "And I suppose that as far as I'm concerned, judging from your remarks, the less written down the better."

The CIA man shook his head emphatically. "Don't write anything down that pertains to this effort. No notes. Nothing."

"All right, that's clear enough," Ryder agreed. "How about signals the other way around? Do you plan on trying to get in touch with me along the road?"

"Only under exceptional circumstances, but it undoubtedly will happen," Crawford said. "And when it does, you will be contacted by an agent, in person. Such contacts will be authenticated by an opening reference to a 'Mr. C. James,' an inversion of my name, of course. I might note here too that some of the agents are women, by the way."

Ryder grinned. "Well, hell. Maybe this job isn't *all* bad news!"

Crawford smiled back at Ryder. "There are some real temptresses among them too. But we also have a number of dragons. You'll just have to take pot luck." The CIA man returned to the subject. "It will help, too, if you will keep Mr. Schuyler up to date on the details of your itinerary. It may be that you will find me unexpectedly joining you on one or another of your flights, just for some conversation. Airplanes can be good places to meet."

Ryder shrugged. "Will do."

Conversation lapsed for a moment as Ryder pondered, then spoke again. "There is another angle to this thing that needs to be cleared up in my mind. On most of my trips out here I bring along a colleague, a man named John Maxton. He's an engineer and he helps with technical details and aircraft performance calculations. Max and I have been friends from clear back into World War II, when we first met in the old Army Air Corps. The point is, Mr. Crawford, that Maxton and I know one another like a book, and while I may be able to fool the Arabs about this extra business for you, old Max is going to smell a rat. My guess is that it won't take long, either." Ryder stopped and allowed the implied question to hang in midair.

Crawford regarded Ryder quizzically. "So you want to know what to do about him." It was a statement, not a question. "Let me say first," Crawford continued, "that we *do* know about Mr. Maxton's acquaintance with you. My view of him is that if approached properly, an arrangement can be made with him in which he could be trusted not to compromise your work for us."

Ryder interrupted bluntly. "If you can trust me, you can trust Maxton."

Crawford laconically continued his remarks. "I quite agree with that statement. Now, there are two ways to go with this, and I would like to hear your views as to the choice. There is no question but that Mr. Maxton will have to be told about your liaison with the CIA. He may then either be asked to accept that knowledge passively while keeping his silence, or else to actively participate with you, for the CIA, to one extent or another. I'd like to know, Mr. Ryder, which you think would work best. Bear in mind as you reply that Maxton appears to us to hit the bottle pretty hard. And that, of course, is a habit that mixes very poorly with this kind of work. I'd like to hear your comments on that as well."

"Okay," Ryder said. "This ought to be an easy one to settle. About the drinking—yes, Max is a rough old Irish cob who likes his booze a little too well. But: that's manageable, because the more he drinks the less he says, and he's a noncommittal old bastard to begin with. If that weren't true, I wouldn't be hauling him along with me, anyway, friend or no friend. Loose-mouthed bottle talk will wreck a business deal too, you know."

Crawford, listening to Ryder's frank response, squinted his eyes a little and suppressed a smile. Ryder went on, "As for the rest, if I know Max it will be almost impossible to keep him out of this once he gets the drift. He'll rear up like an old firehorse. As you might already know, he lived out here, in Jordan, for almost seven years, back in the fifties, and he knows the place inside out. He worked for the now-defunct Galaxy Airways when they had contracts to help some of the local Arab airlines get started. Max still knows droves of the natives on a first-name basis, and they really like him. He can understand a lot of Arabic too, although he speaks it like a talking dog. But he can get inside scuttlebutt and local poop they'd normally never spill to an infidel. Not even to me. He could be a big help, and he'll love every minute of it!"

Crawford let his gaze drop, and seemed to be contemplating the backs of his hands for a time. He then looked up again and said, "All right, it's settled then. I'm satisfied with your assessment of how Mr. Maxton can be fitted into our arrangements. I would want you to bear a certain amount of responsibility for his conduct, Mr. Ryder, and he will definitely have to accept a subordinate role to you. Do you see any problem there?"

Ryder shook his head. "No. That's no problem, since he's used to working as an assistant to me in our business doings."

Crawford sat back from the table. He rolled his pen back and forth between thumb and forefinger for a silent interval, then said, "Well, gentlemen. I think we've done all that we can for now. We might as well call it a day. I'm sorry this took so long; we seem to have talked away a good bit of the afternoon."

Ryder and Schuyler both reflexively glanced at their wristwatches. It was a quarter past five. Bogart Schuyler got to his feet and turned to the CIA man. "Mr. Crawford, if we're finished here for the day, I have some other problems I should attend to. Will you need any more help from me?"

Crawford, busy folding and putting away his Middle East map and notes, looked up and smiled, shaking his head, "No, we're all done here. Thanks for your help, Mr. Schuyler, and if you happen to see Ambassador Harte please tell him I'll stop by to see you both before I leave Beirut tomorrow."

Schuyler agreed, then excused himself to both men and left the conference room.

As the door closed behind Schuyler, the CIA man turned back to Ryder. He withdrew a small package from a pocket, and placed it on the table. "This might help make your new job feel official," he said jovially, inviting Ryder with a gesture to accept the package, "It's a Minox camera. I'm sure you'll find use for it. Full instructions are included inside the package, in case you're not familiar with its use."

Ryder, intrigued by anything mechanical, looked pleased as he accepted the package, and thanked Crawford. Ryder jokingly added as he dropped the small package into his pocket, "There's one reassuring thing about this. At least you didn't think I'd have to start out with a gun!"

Expressionlessly, the CIA man reached a hand inside his coat and brought out an ugly, businesslike, blue-black automatic pistol. "You don't start out with a gun," Crawford stated flatly, "because it would only be taken away from you by some airport customs inspector." He continued, holding the gun flat on his palm, displaying it to Ryder. "This is an eight-shot, nine-millimeter Smith & Wesson double-action automatic. An excellent and very lethal weapon. There is a shoulder holster to go with it. This handgun is yours, Mr. Ryder. It, and ammunition for it, will be in Mr. Schuyler's custody, although he doesn't yet know that. The time is not right, just yet, for you to have to carry the weapon. When that time comes, we will arrange suitable means for the gun to remain undetected. Meanwhile, I want you to thoroughly familiarize yourself with it as time permits here in Beirut. Mr. Schuyler will be advised of a location nearby to which you may be taken for expert instruction in the use and care of the gun, including access to an excellent target range."

PART 2: A CACHE

The unsynchronized shuddering and vibration in the aged Jordanian Airways propeller-driven DC-7 diminished noticeably as the pilot eased back on the power for the descent toward Amman. Ryder and Maxton cinched their seat belts and listened to the whine of hydraulic fluid shoving into the landing gear system, then felt the thud of the struts against their stops as the wheels extended. After completing his landing approach pattern the Jordanian captain put the old four-engined airliner down faultlessly onto the Amman airport runway.

As with virtually all commercial flights in the vicinity of Mecca, Saudi Arabia, during the Hadj season, this airplane had come to Amman from Beirut loaded to capacity with Hadjis making their holy pilgrimage. Rather than face the inevitable tedious struggle through the airport's overtaxed arrival facilities, Ryder and Maxton dawdled on the ramp outside the airplane in the warm sunlight, chatting briefly with the captain, Sami Yamut, about his smooth landing while they watched the crowd of passengers slowly melt into the arrival building. As Captain Yamut and his crew excused themselves and headed across the parking apron toward the terminal building, a khaki-colored jeep came tearing across the ramp. It skidded to a stop perilously close to the two Americans. Ryder saw that the driver was Hakim Rabahby, the director general of civil aviation for Jordan. This splendid old Arab, a former Jordanian Air Force general, was one of Ryder's favorite people.

The old general presented a striking appearance. Under a full thatch of almost white hair, his dark, chiseled features made a handsome contrast, further enhanced by the Arab prize of blue eyes, and a vast, RAF-style mustache—white too, but streaked with indelible yellow tobacco stains. A near lifetime of military service under the tutelage of British command had left an immutable stamp on the old Arab. Despite his seventy years, Hakim Rabahby carried himself smartly erect.

The old general sprang nimbly from the jeep, not bothering to shut off its engine, and strode briskly over to Ryder. His dark, hawklike face was seamed in a great, gold-toothed smile. He seized Ryder's hand, exclaiming, "Jeff! By Jove, it's very good to see you back again! Yamut has radioed us of your presence on his flight!"

Ryder returned the general's hearty handshake. Smiling back at the feisty old soldier, Ryder said, "Hakim, it's always good to come here! Now, how the hell are you? As usual, for an old battle camel, you look hale and hearty!"

The general laughed, shaking his gray head. "I am feeling fine, Jeff, for a *very* old battle camel! But look at what a diplomat you are! You do not compare me to a breeding camel now that I am so old that I can only service one cow per week!"

Ryder laughed in return. "General Rabahby, don't bait me with your false modesty! I have seen your winning ways with the girls at the clubs around town! They know and appreciate the experienced skills and talents of an old bull better than anybody. They won't bother to come around unless they can count on satisfaction, and those beauties swarm around you like bees on the jam pot!"

The general's smile flashed. He said, "Let's continue this argument over a drink." He turned to greet John Maxton, remembering him from Maxton's earlier years of residence in the Middle East, then gestured at the jeep. The three men climbed into the little vehicle. Rabahby tramped on the throttle, careening the jeep through a tire-screeching half circle, and drove it roaring across the concrete apron to the main building. He stopped in front of a wide glass door adjacent to the passenger arrival portal, and shut off the engine. Climbing out of the jeep, he said, "Here we are, my good friends. Come and join me for a few minutes."

Ryder and Maxton followed the general through the glass door and along a short hallway into a small but comfortably furnished room that had been set aside for off-duty flight crews. It was equipped with a tiny bar. Captain Yamut and the two stewardesses from his crew were in the room when the trio entered.

The general said to Yamut, "I have brought these Yankees with me for a welcoming drink! Sami, please serve our guests with whatever they wish. I will have Scotch, neat." The general waited while Yamut moved to the bar, then seated himself on the sofa between the two brightly smiling stewardesses. Ryder and Maxton sat on two of the tall stools in front of the little bar while Yamut poured Scotch for the general.

Ryder said, "Captain Yamut, it looks like you've been promoted from pilot to bartender. But that's the way it goes for us throttle jockeys, heroes one minute and bums the next! Anyway, I'd like a Scotch and water, please. And I think my friend here will go for that too." Maxton nodded, and Captain Yamut proceeded to fix their drinks.

The general, a pilot himself, on overhearing these remarks shouted, "Jeff! You've got that wrong. It's bums all the time, and once in a while, bloody heroes!"

As everyone laughed, Yamut delivered the neat Scotch to the general. The old soldier directed everyone to stand, announcing that he intended to sponsor a toast to his guests. Captain Yamut and the two girls retrieved their half-consumed drinks and stood, waiting. The general hoisted his glass, saying, "I propose this toast to our friends from Yankee land, Mr. Jeff Ryder and Mr. Johnny Maxton. May Allah be with them!" He took a hearty swallow of the straight Scotch.

Continuing to stand, Ryder demanded attention, and said, "Now, General, it's our turn to propose a toast." Raising his glass, Ryder said, "Here's to the good fellowship of all Flying Arabs, and to the charm and beauty of their stewardesses!" Amid pleased smiles from the Jordanians, everyone tasted their drinks.

Light conversation continued for a while, centered mainly on the general and the two girls. Then, Captain Yamut excused himself, explaining that he had yet to complete his post-flight reports. With Yamut's departure, General Rabahby instructed one of the stewardesses to attend to Ryder and Maxton's arrival formalities. He directed that their baggage be brought to the club room. Ryder and Maxton handed their passports and baggage claim checks to the girl. Both of the stewardesses then left, after courteously bidding the three men good-bye. The general, with a show of reluctance, let them depart.

Rabahby steered the two Americans back to their seats at the bar, then glanced at his watch and made a face. He said, "I'm afraid I must run along, my friends. Duty calls as usual. I am, regrettably, obliged to attend a business luncheon. I would far rather have enjoyed a lunch with you two Yankees today, but alas, there can be no escape. Since that is the case, though, I insist that you accompany me to the Dead Sea Club for a dinner and some amusements. Would tomorrow evening suit your plans?"

Ryder nodded and replied, "Couldn't be better, Hakim."

At that moment a porter stuck his head in the door and timidly asked a question in Arabic. The general stood and issued some loud commands in reply to the man's inquiry. The porter scrambled into the room and deposited Ryder and Maxton's luggage and their passports, then hastily backed out. Ryder tried to stop him long enough to accept a tip, but the porter only increased the speed of his departure.

General Rabahby shook hands warmly with Ryder and Maxton, apologizing again for having to leave. He promised to pick them up at their hotel on the following evening, then hurried out the club room door. Ryder and Maxton picked up their briefcases. They lagged along behind the general's disappearing figure, and looked around for a porter. The one who had brought their bags to the club room saw them and, now that the general was safely out of range, hurried over. Ryder told the porter to bring their bags to the taxi stand. He and Maxton proceeded on through the building and out into the bright daylight. The baggage arrived and was loaded into their taxi. This time, the porter happily accepted Ryder's tip. The two Americans entered the cab, and Ryder told the driver to take them to the Al Urdon Hotel.

The Dead Sea Club
Amman, Jordan
<u>APRIL 1966</u>

General Hakim Rabahby hurried into the small cocktail bar adjoining the main lobby of the Al Urdon hotel. It was nearly twenty minutes past eight. The general's note had said seven thirty. Earlier in the day, the general had left a message for Jeff Ryder, indicating that he would be by to pick up Ryder and Maxton for their dinner engagement at the Dead Sea Club.

The appointed hour had come and gone with no sign of Rabahby. Ryder and Maxton, having waited in the hotel lobby for a reasonable time, asked the desk clerk to watch for the general's arrival, and to tell him they would wait in the bar.

Rabahby saw the two Americans gesturing, and bustled over to their table, waving them back into their seats. He pulled another chair up and shouted for the waiter. The general ordered a double Scotch, neat, then apologized effusively for his tardiness. He explained vaguely that he had been delayed by "His Majesty."

The little bar was crowded, and resonated with the glottal staccato of animated Arabic conversation. The old general, widely known and liked in Amman, attracted a barrage of loud and friendly greetings from all sides. Once he had settled into his chair, extra rounds of drinks began appearing on the table, ordered by unidentified acquaintances of the garrulous old soldier. The convivial atmosphere of the little bar heightened with the presence of Hakim Rabahby. Reinforced by the free-flowing Scotch whiskey, the general's extroversion swept him into a series of happy exchanges with virtually everyone in the bar, including a few tourists with whom he had no previous acquaintance at all.

An hour slipped away without notice in the good-humored hubbub. Rabahby suddenly stared in disbelief at his wristwatch and rose abruptly from his chair. "Jeff! Max! I'm starving us all to death! Quickly! We must hurry on our way!" Making a scribbling motion in the air for the benefit of the bartender to indicate his intention to pay the bar bill, the general hastened Ryder and Maxton out of the bar amid handshakes and backslaps from among the crowd.

Ryder and Maxton followed the general's compact figure in amusement as he sped them through the lobby and out of the hotel, waving his arms and speaking to everyone he passed. The doorman, noticing the trio approaching, issued some sharp Arabic into a wall-mounted microphone, producing a booming summons into the night air of the parking lot. General Rabahby's new Chevrolet sedan was promptly delivered to the entrance, and the three men entered the car, Ryder joining the general in the front, while Maxton sat in the rear.

The route to the Dead Sea Club took them through Amman's city center. Predictably, nighttime traffic through the ancient, constricting streets held them to a crawling pace. The old general shouted and ranted violently at all other cars and drivers, while simultaneously blowing a steady tattoo on the Chevrolet's raucous horn. Neither measure produced the slightest visible effect. To a man, the competing drivers behaved in exactly the same way.

The snarl of traffic increased until the mainstream had traversed past the ruins of an amphitheater dating back to the Romans. Once beyond this point, the jam of vehicles quickly faded. The general's jovial mood returned as quickly as it had vanished. He waved a hand. "We've lost another ten minutes, thanks to that clutter of bloody rock apes! Well, no matter." He glanced at his watch. "It's right on nine thirty. We've twenty-five miles to go, and I'll make that in twenty-five minutes! We'll arrive in time for the floor show." With that, Rabahby tramped down on the accelerator and the car sped away from the lighted roads of the city and onto a narrow but well-paved and graded highway that stretched ahead into the desert night.

Conversation among the three men centered on airplanes and matters related to the Jordanian airline. Pursuing the airline subject, Ryder asked the general, "Hakim, how do you think the atmosphere is shaping up these days for the airline's plans to reequip their fleet? Do you think they'll be in a position to buy some new stuff soon?"

Rabahby smiled. "Aha! Jeff, are you trying to worm some inside info out of me while I'm tipsy?"

Ryder laughed. "No, but when I do, I'll have sense enough to wait until you're properly smashed!"

Rabahby chuckled too. "As to your question, Jeff, I can tell you that there will be no objections or delays coming from the government side."

Ryder clicked his tongue. "I wish everyone around here would hand out direct answers like that! Lately, Max and I feel like we've been talking to a wall!" He then added laughingly, "I sometimes think I've got a heavy enemy somewhere among those elegant Palestinian gents on your airline's board!"

Ryder, looking at Rabahby as he spoke, watched in surprise as the old man's face lost its pleasant expression. Warily, Ryder went on, "As you know, Hakim, we've been working with the airline for nearly a year now, putting in our bit on their comparative studies of the competing types of airplanes. Everything seemed to be racing along great guns until about two months ago. Since then, all of a sudden, we've been getting the *ba'ad bukra mish mish* treatment. 'Tomorrow, or the day after, or when the apricots bloom.' I had thought it might be due to second thoughts from the palace."

Silence prevailed for an uncomfortable interval. The general finally said, with uncharacteristic abruptness, "I am unable to speak for that board."

Ryder, puzzled by the oddly hostile reaction, decided to drop the subject of airline affairs. "Well, the hell with business! Hakim, what's going on out here at the club these days? Have you got a new show for us tonight?"

The General showed his relief at abandoning the previous conversation. He responded genially, "By Jove, yes! Two events of sterling consequence have happened since your last visit: We've got a heroic new chef at the club now, an Italiano chap. He's absolutely wizard in that kitchen! At least he is as long as we can keep him sober! Then, we have six cancan girlies in the show! I'm told they danced at the Moulin Rouge in Paris! They do smashing good things with their legs! And by the way, that wild oriental dancer from Cairo, Nadia, is still here."

Ryder nodded his head. "Well, well! Sounds like luck is running our way! I'm half starved, so I hope your fancy new chef is on his good behavior tonight."

The general's enthusiasm seemed to be returning. "I'm delighted to hear that your appetite is good! Tonight the menu should be excellent! New shipments of fresh beef and seafood were flown in yesterday. This Italiano's fish dishes are superb, by the way!"

Amiable conversation continued as they drove on through the night toward the Dead Sea Club. The club, built on a side road about a mile away from the main highway, represented one of the efforts of the Jordanian Ministry of Tourism to attract increased tourist travel into this ancient and biblically rich land. Grand plans had been laid for the club.

Visions had been advanced for the creation of a lavish resort atmosphere, exploiting the unique seaside merits of this northern extremity of the Dead Sea's coastline. A site had been selected and good roads built, positioning the club approximately halfway between the capital city of Amman and that unparalleled tourist attraction, the holy city of Jerusalem.

Funds for continuation of the club's construction had dwindled, however. Its buildings had never been fully completed. In its present form it comprised an austere, graceless structure sufficient to house a large dining room, a kitchen, office space, a small cocktail bar, and an unfinished gaming room. A paved expanse adjoined the rear of the building, overlooking the sea and the sand of a swimming beach. The club had served only meagerly in its intended role. As yet, it was no tourist magnet. It had become, however, a highly favored haunt for dining and drinking among those of the local populace who could afford it.

The general drove his Chevrolet smartly up to the brightly floodlit entrance. Stepping out of the car, he imperiously directed the doorman to have it parked, then waved Ryder and Maxton ahead of him. Walking away from the car, Ryder saw that the club's parking area was surprisingly crowded.

The three men proceeded into the club. They passed through an attractively decorated foyer flanked by a pair of untenanted cloak rooms, and entered the main dining salon. The room had been finished at modest expense, but was nevertheless tastefully and pleasantly done. The dining room was, however, almost unoccupied. Glass doors forming the back wall of the room stood open to the warm, dense air of the desert night. Beyond the doors, on the outside concrete patio overlooking the sea, dozens of busy tables surrounded a small, circular dance area. On the perimeter of the dance floor a four-piece rock band filled the air with howlingly amplified music. A cluster of sweating couples, gyrating elbows and knees in athletic interpretations of imported dance vogues, flapped and bounced wildly on the little dance floor.

A swarthy, perspiring steward clad in a wilting tuxedo rushed over to the three men as they emerged onto the patio. He effusively greeted the general. Rabahby demanded a certain table, and the steward scurried away. The general, strolling unhurriedly ahead, explained that he had chosen a somewhat inconspicuous table removed from the vicinity of the dance floor so that they might dine and converse more comfortably, and with fewer intrusions. Ryder, wincing from the din of the shrieking music, agreed emphatically.

The two Americans found themselves steered to a table situated somewhat apart from the outer fringe of the main patio dining area. The table rested on a raised step, affording an unobstructed view of the dance floor, yet offering a sense of privacy and a measure of quiet. The table was elaborately set with places for six.

As Ryder and Maxton seated themselves, the general fired a rapid paragraph of Arabic instructions to the steward. The man nodded and hurried away. In a very short time a uniformed waiter appeared, delivering a bottle of excellent Scotch whiskey, a seltzer bottle, and a supply of ice cubes. At the general's invitation, Ryder and Maxton helped themselves to drinks.

The three men chatted idly, surveying the crowded tables and the agitated dancing. Rabahby suggested, "If you gentlemen feel you will survive, I suggest we postpone our meal until after the floor show. It should be starting very soon." As he finished his sentence, a huge smile beamed across the general's face. He stood and waved happily toward a point somewhere behind Ryder and Maxton. Turning to look, the two Americans saw the club steward hustling toward their table, shepherding three gaily costumed cancan girls.

The general hurried to meet them, jauntily preening his mustache and shouting, "Welcome! Welcome, my little bonbons! Come, I want you to meet some fine friends of mine!" He seized one of the girls by the hand and trotted back to the table with her in tow. The other two girls followed, and the perspiring steward hurried away.

The general postured comically. "Now, mesdemoiselles, here are two handsome American gentlemen that you can practice your English on! This is Mr. Jeff Ryder, and this is Mr. Johnny Maxton." Turning to the men, he gestured gallantly. "Jeff and John, here are Nanette, and Danielle, and Claudine! Nanette is partial to me, so you must decide between yourselves which of these other two little French lovelies you will each entertain."

Rabahby escorted the blond, buxom Nanette to a seat beside his own, and sat down. Ryder turned to the other two girls. He spoke to the one introduced as Danielle, a broad-faced, dark-haired brunette who boldly returned his look. "Danielle, it's a pleasure to meet you! Do you speak American?"

The girl smiled enigmatically. "Not very well, but I can manage okay." The words were pronounced with a distinct French accent, but it was evident to Ryder that indeed Danielle could manage. He turned to the other girl and took her by the hand. "And you, Claudine. How is your English?" Ryder noticed that the auburn-haired Claudine had, under the heavy layers of makeup, a surprisingly attractive face. She hesitated, then answered, "*Je le comprend assez bien, mais je ne le parle pas beaucoup, Monsieur.*"

The taciturn Maxton eyed the two females with emphatic interest. Ryder said to him, "Max, I believe this brown-eyed beauty talks your language in every way. Why don't you take charge of Danielle's needs, and I will exercise my French with Claudine."

Maxton took Danielle's arm and held a chair for her next to his. She immediately focused her cool gaze on Maxton's face, a look that he returned with hard interest. Ryder turned back to the auburn-haired girl. "*Allons nous mettre une table,* Claudine." Her jade eyes widened in pleasant surprise. "Ah! *Vous parlez français, Monsieur!*" She smiled prettily as Ryder slid a chair aside for her. The other two girls looked alertly around at Ryder for an instant, hearing his well-spoken French.

The general's spirits were soaring. He poured ferocious quantities of the Scotch for Nanette and himself, handed the bottle to Maxton, and then waved to the waiter. The man hurried over and the general demanded an iced bottle of French champagne and more Scotch whiskey.

Rabahby's companion, Nanette, in addition to speaking better English than the other two girls, seemed to be in charge. She tugged on the general's sleeve. "I must remind you! You must remember, *mon Générale,* that we must soon appear in the show!"

The old general laughed and waved the problem aside. "The show will wait for you, bonbon! Just relax and enjoy a little refreshment! Then, after the show, you may return, and we will have a jolly time!"

As the general spoke, Maxton busily duplicated the extravagant measures of whiskey poured by the old soldier, for himself and the brown-eyed, bold Danielle, and succeeded in emptying the bottle just as the waiter returned with the new supply.

Ryder, inviting Claudine to have a drink, said, "*Avez vous soif, Claudine? Buvez quelque chose avec moi! Nous avons le Scotch ou, si vous le préféré, du champagne. Que voulez vous?"*

Claudine brightened visibly. Her eyes swung to the bottles of whiskey. *"Merci, Monsieur Jeff, J'ai bien soif! Je préfère le Scotch, s'il vous plait."* Ryder had expected her to ask for champagne.

The blond Nanette looked quickly across the table at Claudine. *"Ne pas sculpter une gueule de bois ce soir, ma chère."* Nanette did not smile. Ryder noted Nanette's sharp admonition to Claudine, not to "carve" a hangover, or get "wooden-faced" from drinking. He suspected there was good reason for the scolding tone and decided to go sparingly with the whiskey as he fixed Scotch and water for Claudine and himself.

General Rabahby reached a pinnacle of good humor. He loudly enjoyed himself in a running and ribald exchange with the quick-witted Nanette. Most of the attention of the group centered on that spirited conversation, and everyone was kept laughing by their banal chatter.

At length Nanette stood and announced firmly that it was time for the girls to head backstage. The general did not interfere with their departure, but did insist that Nanette promise they would return immediately after their performance for dinner, and later, as the general put it, for a jolly, jolly good time.

Danielle and Claudine hastily downed the remains of their drinks and prepared to leave with Nanette. Claudine smiled happily and said to Ryder, *"Nous serons ici dans une demi-heure, Monsieur Jeff,"* and hurried after her companions.

The General grinned at Maxton. "Johnny, how do you like my little bonbons?"

Maxton was obviously contented with the evening's prospects. He wagged his head. "I don't know how you two are doing, but that Danielle dolly is my speed! How long have these cookies been here, General, and how long are they staying?"

Rabahby chuckled. "These 'cookies' have been here long enough for me to enjoy some splendid French lessons, and they will be here long enough for you to take a lesson or two yourself!"

A subterranean sound of pleasure rumbled from Maxton.

The Cancan
Amman, Jordan
APRIL 1966

With a sudden blaze of spotlights, a loud fanfare blared from the bandstand. General Rabahby exclaimed happily, "*Mash'Allah*! The show will now begin!"

An immensely fat master of ceremonies, stuffed into a black tuxedo, bounced into the circle of light. His jovial face glistened with perspiration under the lights as he genially waved his arms for silence and introduced the first act of the show. A costumed Spanish couple bowed their way onstage and danced a creditable flamenco. Their spirited performance was well received by the crowd, and the sweating but happy couple was whistled and shouted into an encore.

The cheerful emcee then introduced a pair of ludicrously dressed Belgian comics, proclaiming them to be world-famous acrobats and jugglers. The two comics, one a tall and gangling man and the other exceptionally short and chubby, started their performance with an acrobatic routine. Each of their separate tumbling and acrobatic stunts appeared near calamity, owing to the seeming inebriation on the part of the tall clown.

The crowd presumed this to be a staged charade and laughed encouragement. As the act continued, however, it became evident that the inebriation was genuine. The short, cherubic clown was clearly angry with his partner, although trying desperately to salvage the performance. Inevitably the audience began ranting at the pair in caustic Arabic. The two Belgian comics continued to blunder through their performance despite the catcalls, while the anxious emcee hovered on the fringe of the spotlighted stage.

Their acrobatic routine called for the tall comic to flip his smaller partner into a backward somersault. The whiskey-soaked tall Belgian missed his timing disastrously, however, and the little round clown sailed awkwardly backward through the air and crashed heavily to the floor, flat on his back. The derisive spectators applauded raucously in merciless delight. The dazed little man, collecting himself from the floor, was too late to prevent the other from dragging onstage their table of juggling apparatus.

With a flourish from the band the two jugglers then began tossing assorted pieces of heavy china dinnerware back and forth between them. For a minute or two all went well. Plates, cups, saucers, bowls, and drinking glasses whirled through the air between the two men, in unbelievable numbers and in an incredible spectrum of trajectories. Suddenly, two of the larger pieces collided in midair and smashed into pieces on the floor. The tall man's resulting split second of hesitation brought catastrophe. In a wild effort to compensate for his pause, the tall man frantically, drunkenly, hurled a large bowl in the general direction of his disgusted partner. It sailed lazily over the little man's head, while an avalanche of china began raining to the floor around and between both jugglers. The flying bowl struck one of the spectators. The furious Arab seized the heavy bowl and heaved it back with deadly accuracy. It thudded against the drunken Belgian's head. This triggered a howl of approval from the hooting, jeering crowd who, in vast delight, proceeded to pelt the staggered juggler with a deluge of garbage and dirty dishes from the tables.

The two Belgians, driven from the floor, were unceremoniously seized by a covey of the club's waiters and hustled out of sight. The band struck into an unscheduled medley of tunes while the audience greeted with ringing applause a pair of sheepishly grinning workmen sent onstage to clean up the mess.

The general thought the calamitous performance hilarious and laughed himself into weakness and tears. He turned to Ryder and Maxton, wiping his eyes and gasping, "Those two fools are the hit of this show! Imagine it if they were both drunk! Those clumsy bastards have delayed our dinner, though. Never mind. We will have some more to drink!" He seized the bottle of Scotch and splashed great slugs into their three glasses. As he set the bottle back on the table, the unmistakable musical prelude to the cancan arose from the bandstand, and again the blazing spotlights flashed onto the stage. A great cheer swept from the audience and six cancan girls spun onstage, each in turn and each introducing herself with her own lively specialty stunt. The girls moved into a chorus line and swung wholeheartedly into their version of the rousing dance. The crowd entered into an unabated and wild cheering as the dance progressed, their shouts punctuated by shrill answering shrieks from the high-kicking dancers.

The general beamed ecstatically. He bobbed in his chair, keeping time with the stirring music with clapping hands, shouting encouragement to Nanette. Ryder and Maxton joined the enthusiasm for the lively and ably performed dance, enhanced by their more personal interest in three of the performers. They both entered into the rhythmic hand clapping and laughed along with the old general as they watched.

The dance and the music moved with increasing spirit toward the familiar and anticipated climax. Ryder, fully enjoying the moment, turned smilingly to watch the general's boundless gaiety. As he glanced at the general, he found himself watching for the second time that evening as the old soldier's face lost its amiable expression. In place of his uninhibited enjoyment, Rabahby's smile suddenly faded and he sat stiffly forward in his chair, directing a grim stare at some distant point in the crowd across the way.

Astonished, Ryder quickly looked away. He continued the rhythmic clapping while he scanned the crowd, trying to target whatever it was that had so disturbingly caught Rabahby's eye. Then, across the dance floor and just within the fringe of light from the spotlighted circle, Ryder saw the steward solicitously seating three newly arrived patrons. The newcomers took a table in the second row from the stage. Ryder recognized two of the men. They were members of the board of directors of the Jordanian airline. The third man looked vaguely familiar, but Ryder could not immediately place him. One of the two board members was Abdallah Rifai.

Ryder glanced back at the general. He saw that Rabahby remained tense while balefully watching the movements of the three men in that distant group. Abruptly the general stood. Scarcely taking his eyes from the object of his sudden and intense focus, he curtly excused himself and strode away in the direction of the exit. He disappeared through the glass doorway. Ryder immediately poked Maxton's arm and directed his friend's attention to the three men now seated at the far table. "Max, I know two of those men, of course, Issam Lahoud and Abdallah Rifai. But who is that third one?"

Maxton, unaware of what had transpired, studied the men and then answered, "I don't know either. What the hell is going on? Where'd Rabahby go in such a hurry?"

Ryder answered slowly, "I'm not sure. Something rotten seems to be in the wind, and it has to do with those three over there at that table. You saw the way Rabahby was carrying on! He was having the time of his life! Then all of a sudden he went sour. When he saw that trio show up. I don't know where he went, but I'm betting it wasn't to the latrine! Max, I've got the damnedest feeling I should know who that third guy is over there with Lahoud and Rifai. After Crawford's report on Rifai, it'll be worth noticing who he runs around with. Are you sure you can't place that man? He must be the cause of this strange behavior of Hakim's."

Maxton peered silently across the intervening space again, studying the face of the man in question. He shook his head. "Can't recognize him, but now that you've leaned on it, I've got the same funny feeling. I've seen that face before someplace too."

Ryder relaxed and leaned back in his chair. "Well, the hell with it for now. Maybe Hakim will come back in a while." He gestured toward the stage, where the cancan girls were now performing an encore that the crowd had demanded in a standing ovation. "Those gals put on a pretty classy show, don't they?"

Maxton's eyes swung back to the dance floor and a lopsided smile showed itself on his face. "Damned if they don't! And I was halfway expecting to get that Danielle cookie cornered somewhere tonight." Maxton shook his head, "There won't be any hanky-panky with any of those 'bonbons,' though, unless Papa Hakim decides to show up again. Those little hookers won't waste their talents on us fly-by-nights."

Ryder eyed Maxton. "Much as I hate to bow to your superior knowledge on the subject, I'm afraid you're right. If Hakim is as gone as I think he is for the night, so are our cancan girlies."

As if to confirm that last statement, conversation was interrupted by the arrival of the steward. He handed Ryder a sealed envelope. "General Rabahby asked me to give you this personally, sir." The steward turned to go, but Ryder detained him. "Steward, during the dance by the French girls I thought I saw my good friend Mr. Issam Lahoud from the airline come into the club. Did you happen to see him?"

The steward, anxious to assist the general's guests, replied earnestly, "Oh, yes, sir! Mr. Lahoud is sitting just over there"—the steward pointed across the dance floor—"with Mr. Rifai and Mr. Tabet."

Ryder shot a glance at Maxton, then thanked the steward, handing the man a generous tip. The steward smiled, and, bowing his gratitude, hastened away. Ryder turned to Maxton. "Max, did you hear that name?"

Maxton's bushy eyebrows were raised. "I heard it, and now I know why that guy's face has been bugging us! We've been looking at it in the local newspapers off and on for the past year! That son of a bitch is Yasser Arafat's number-one butcher boy!"

Ryder nodded. "Right! Asad Tabet! Mighty strange company for a couple of airline board members. And how does all this manage to louse up the general's evening so thoroughly?"

Ryder, as he spoke, tore open the envelope sent by Rabahby. He withdrew a terse, handwritten note from the general. He glanced at it silently for a moment, then reread it aloud to Maxton. " 'Jeff and Johnny. Kindly accept my apologies. An urgent matter has arisen unexpectedly, and I must immediately depart. Please enjoy yourselves and have a nice dinner. The steward will arrange a taxi for you. The tab is taken care of.' It's signed, 'Rabahby.' "

Maxton remarked, "The old stud didn't even say bye-bye to his bonbons! That's a sure sign he was shook up."

Ryder mused, "Uh-huh. I was thinking the same thing."

Engrossed in their speculations, Ryder and Maxton didn't notice the finish of the cancan performance. Their attention was drawn back to the stage, however, by the sudden throb of tambours and the peculiarly moving discords of Arabic music. The fat emcee waddled grinning into the center of the stage, spread his arms wide, and announced that Nadia, the Middle East's premier oriental dancer, would now present one of her memorable performances. The introduction was received with wild shouts and whistling from the enthusiastic crowd of men.

In a great drum crescendo, Nadia whirled to the center of the spotlights. She stood gracefully poised in midstep, an arm extended high, the other crossed in front above her full breasts. Slowly, almost imperceptibly, her hips began a sinuous undulation to the rhythm of the exotic music. The tantalizing chinking of her finger bells entered the pulse of sound, seemingly exciting that flowing pelvic swing into rising response. The girl's face remained impassively sultry, eyes heavily lidded, lips full and pouting. In a languorous pirouette, Nadia unwound a frothy, spectral veil from around her torso, revealing the heart-shaped contours of her smooth belly. Now, with small and gliding movement of foot and with arms gracefully arched above her head, she seemed to float across the floor. Voluptuous hips rolled, creamy thighs parted provokingly. The pulsating tempo gradually climbed. Nadia's body, with its quickening surge, seemed to murmur of her growing desire. Eyes nearly closed, moist lips parted, Nadia dreamily tilted her head back, relinquishing herself to the rapturous need described by her writhing body. A rising, seething fever seemed to take possession of those trembling thighs and that thrusting, heaving pubis. Arms stretched wide, Nadia began to whirl to the mounting frenzy of the throbbing music. Face and body, swinging arms and writhing legs, all glistened with hot perspiration. The crowd of male watchers roared hoarsely, urging the gyrating figure on, demanding more and more from the volcanic performance. Nadia swept wildly around the rim of the dance floor, gossamer skirt swinging against the ringside men, sweeping glasses from the tabletops as she spun. The dance reached a crescendo. Nadia erupted into a galvanic whirlwind. The musicians played like men possessed. The crowd stood, stamping and whistling and pounding, shouting themselves raw. The dance became a frenzied vortex of barbaric sensuality. Nadia leaped onto a table, writhing in sybaritic passion, showering the tumultuous spectators from her perspiring body. In a great, crashing climax, the dance came to an end. Amid a roaring bedlam of sound from the wildly shouting men, the gasping Nadia bowed herself limply from the stage.

Ryder and Maxton were swept into the wild enthusiasm with the rest of the men. As Nadia's performance ended they found themselves standing and applauding with the crowd. Ryder at length resumed his seat at the table, although the audience continued to demonstrate. Maxton sat down too, and proceeded to refill the Scotch glasses. He was still refreshing the drinks when their waiter, amidst the unrelenting pandemonium from the crowd, hustled up to their table and handed Maxton a folded piece of paper. Maxton grunted, tipped the man, and unfolded the note. He scanned the paper briefly, then in obvious disgust handed it to Ryder. "Well, do I know my hookers?" he asked.

The curt note, written in a fine feminine hand, read, "*Mes Cher Amis*—The show it takes extra time tonight and now we have not the time for the dinner with you. *À bientôt*, Nanette." Ryder chuckled as he wadded up the note and tossed it into an ashtray. He hoisted his glass in mock homage to Maxton, and took a swallow of the whiskey. He smiled and said, "Ah, well—win a few, lose a few. I'm damned if I want any big dinner now anyway. What do you say we just have some kind of a snack, and then get the hell out of here?"

The Warehouse
Amman, Jordan
APRIL 1966

After the late Friday night at the Dead Sea Club, Ryder had declared a sleep-in for the morning following. It was nearly 10 AM when he and Maxton met in the hotel snack bar for a late breakfast. After a desultory effort to cope with a stack of well-intentioned but rubbery imitations of "American-style pancakes," they loitered through an extra cup of coffee, and discussed the forthcoming afternoon's activities.

Ryder told Maxton, "Since we have to canvas the board members anyway to see what we can do about getting this equipment deal off dead center, let's start with those two we saw at the club last night. At least we know they're in town. And we might turn up something for Crawford too, who knows?"

Maxton glanced up from his coffee. "Don't forget, today is Saturday. Everybody will be trying to take the day off. Maybe we can snag Lahoud, though, at that big truck warehouse of his outside of town. He likes to loaf out there with a bunch of his cronies, away from the main uproar downtown. He takes the phone off the hook and they torch up a big hookah, then sit around drinking arak and bullshitting about their cocksmanship."

Ryder got up from the table, telling Maxton, "Stay put. Get me another cup of coffee while I see what I can do on the telephone." He headed for a battery of coin telephones ranked along the wall just outside the snack bar entrance.

He returned to the table a few minutes later, just as the waiter delivered two fresh cups of coffee. Ryder seated himself and waited until the waiter had departed. "No answer at all from Rifai's numbers. Home nor office. Lahoud's downtown office says he's not available today. I tried his trucking company number too. It rang, but I got no answer."

Ryder sipped his coffee thoughtfully, then put the cup down. "Hell, let's just grab a cab and head out to that truck place of Lahoud's. I've got a hunch you're right that he's there. If we catch him there, he can't very well slough us off. And we might even find him with his pals Rifai and Mr. Asad Tabet of the Dead Sea Club and Al Fatah!"

Maxton tilted his blunt head. "Your trouble is, you can't wait to get your nose into this double-oh-seven shenanigan! Don't forget what the man said. Take it slow!"

The two Americans signed their breakfast tabs and left the hotel, taking a taxi from the stand at the entrance. The early spring day sparkled bright and clear, and the two men watched the passing scenery in comfortable silence as they traveled through the small city's familiar environs.

The Al Urdon hotel was placed on the crown of a low hill—called a *jabal*—overlooking the central part of Amman. The capital city of Jordan is located amidst, and imposed upon, the ruins of thousands of years of human occupancy. The location was perhaps best known during its period as the ancient Macedonian city of Philadelphia. The city mushrooms on the floor of a rocky defile, with flat-roofed, cube-shaped block and plaster buildings scrambled in haphazard steps up the slopes on either side. The heaviest cluster of buildings, marking Amman's main commercial district, collects near the streambed, and presents the enigmatic paradox of losing the battle of appearances, with its raw, squared, graceless monotony of the recent failing against the unavoidably visible remnants of timeless past grandeur.

Their taxi followed much the same route through the city as they and the general had taken the night before, directly through the city's commercial center. The sidewalks bustled with people, at least half of them uniformed army men from the country's desert legions. Street traffic was a bedlam of outworn American and British automobiles, now for the most part in a terminating existence as taxicabs. Their horns and Klaxons were clearly prized, and kept in better repair than the tedious vital running parts.

Emerging from the thronged business section, the taxi made its way along rough streets paralleling Amman's railroad yards. Corrugated iron warehouses and small, unpainted industrial buildings lined both roadsides in drab, foreboding monotony. The area stood deserted on this Saturday morning, with only infrequent vehicular traffic, and no pedestrian activity whatever. At length the taxi drew up before a sprawling, silent, two-story building of vast extent. The building wore on its rust-streaked and weathered, almost windowless face the sign, "Lahoud Transport, Ltd." The forbidding mass of the structure was flanked on both sides by uninterrupted reaches of high, solid fencing constructed of corroding corrugated iron sheets.

That barrier was guarded along its ridge by a wicked arrangement of heavily barbed and rusted wire.

Ryder and Maxton climbed out of the taxi and silently surveyed the somehow intimidating tawdriness and odd quiet of the scene. Ryder turned to the watching taxi driver and asked him if he could wait for perhaps an hour. With surly reluctance, the driver negotiated himself into an outrageous fee for the service, then promptly leaned back and went to sleep.

During Ryder's harangue with the taxi driver, Maxton had walked over to a heavy, man-sized steel entrance door let into a huge, metal-sheathed sliding door on the front of the building. He found the small door unlocked, and signaled so to Ryder. He waited until Ryder joined him, then opened the door, and together they entered the warehouse's cavernous interior. The steel door clanged shut from its own weight with a startling suddenness, the sound booming through the building in eerie reverberations. The two men hesitated just inside the door, letting their eyes adjust to the gloom, and to see whether their noisy entrance would evoke any notice. Silence returned, and they found themselves in an open bay extending in height to the building's roof. Far overhead, dirt-stained skylights admitted vague illumination. The air within the building was chill, and smelled pungently of rust and diesel oil and rubber. The vast bay in which they stood was walled on both sides to a width sufficient to accommodate three massive enclosed trucks, which the two men could see parked side by side, obscurely visible toward the back of the building and facing away from the entrance. Ryder gauged the trucks to be about a hundred feet from where he stood. In front of the middle vehicle, another massive sliding door had been partially moved aside.

Along the right and near the trucks, an open wooden staircase slanted up the wall, leading to a closed door. In the feeble glow from a bare lightbulb mounted above the door, Ryder made out the word "Office" lettered in peeling paint just under the lamp. He consciously shrugged off a sense of uneasiness induced by the dim, chill, alien surroundings. He remarked in a subdued voice, "It's damned quiet in here for a place with the front door unlocked. Do you know the layout of this tomb? What's beyond that office sign over there, under that measly light?" He pointed toward the top of the wooden stairs.

Maxton shook his head. "All I can remember about this place is how easy it is to get lost in. But I do think that up there is where Lahoud used to hang his hat." Maxton looked at his watch. "You know, it's getting to be lunchtime. It could be that everybody's gone for some chow, or to face Mecca, or both."

Ryder stood silently for a moment, then said, "Well, let's see what we can find." He headed purposefully for the stairs, with Maxton following. The light tread of their footsteps on the concrete floor echoed in hollow, fading multiples. They trotted up the stairs to the door marked "Office," and finding it too unlocked, entered. The door led them into a long hallway, evidently in recent use since overhead lights burned along its length. They strode down the hall, peering into open doorways on both sides as they went. The rooms along the hallway appeared to be in use as storage deposits for cargo and for machine parts and supplies. All were dark and untenanted. They passed a large freight elevator and, adjacent to it, a descending stairwell. Low-wattage bulbs burned over the stairs.

Continuing along the corridor, they found near its end an office complex surrounded by partitions glassed above the half height. Lights were on in the main offices, but again, curiously, there was no sign of life. The corridor entry doors to the office areas were locked.

After rapping loudly on the main office entry door, and after peering through the glass panels into the various inner office spaces, Ryder commented in a puzzled tone, "Looks like we're still drawing a blank, Max. Lahoud, or somebody, must be around here someplace, since they've left all these lights burning. Let's head back down the hall and try that stairway back there by the elevator. Maybe somebody's down there."

They retraced their steps to the stairwell and proceeded down the steeply winding stairs. The staircase ended at a battered door, which hung ajar. Ryder stepped through the doorway, with Maxton following, into a narrow, sour-smelling passageway formed by what seemed to be solidly stacked tiers of wooden shipping crates piled ceiling high. Random electric bulbs covered with dust and grime hung from bare cords overhead, and offered only the most meager illumination as the two men moved tentatively forward. They immediately found themselves faced with a maze of choices in direction. The stacked cargo boxes created a massive confusion of poorly lit access passageways having no discernible pattern or order.

Ryder said, as they groped ahead through the dim chill of the acrid-smelling aisles, "Let's see if we can find our way to the rear of the building. This is getting ridiculous."

Maxton grunted. "Sure. Especially that last part." He then suddenly swore sharply and stamped his feet. Ryder, startled, halted and spun around. "What's wrong? What happened?"

Maxton settled down and made a disgusted gesture in the gloom. "Sorry. I didn't mean to make so much noise. But me and rats just don't get along, and I just found out this lousy place is crawling with them!"

Ryder stared into the shadowy reaches of the passageways, and confirmed with gross distaste that Maxton was right. He now saw that the dim corners of the alleys heaved and undulated in fat, shapeless, gray blurs. There were hordes of rats on all sides.

Ryder shuddered and shook his head. "Well, now it has sunk from ridiculous down to revolting. But damn it, we're this far, and we're going to see this through, rats and all."

He led off again, along a devious course, choosing any path that seemed to lead away from their point of entry and toward the rear. The confusion of alleyways seemed interminable. At length, however, plodding onward through trial and error they discovered that the room did not extend fully to the rear of the huge building. They had emerged into a long, continuous, foul-smelling aisle that reached across their chosen direction. It was blocked solidly with stacked crates on the side of the passage toward the back.

Ryder muttered in disgust, "Damn! Now we either turn around and find our way back through this rathole, or try this stinking tunnel that goes the wrong way! And I can't see giving up, so let's keep going."

Maxton sniffed and snorted, then added in a thoroughly sour tone, "Anything you say, Coach, only let's get the hell going before I throw up!"

Ryder led off to the right, down the murky reaches of the lateral alley. After some distance a break appeared in the solid stack of crates on their left. It led to a closed door. Ryder stepped into the gap and tried the door. It opened to his hand, and he found himself staring into the unlit and uninviting prospect of another, similar warren of passageways. He closed the door. "That's worse than this, if that's possible." They resumed traveling laterally. Presently another side exit appeared, and again Ryder tried this door. It too was unlocked. He opened the door a crack and light streamed into the gloom behind him. He gingerly stuck his head through the opening, then spoke softly to Maxton over his shoulder. "This is more like it. There are signs of life here."

Easing through the doorway, Ryder and Maxton entered a large, open, brightly floodlighted warehouse room. Orderly piles of packing cases outlined the room, stacked against the walls, leaving the main space open, except for a mass of large wooden shipping crates piled in disorder in the room's center. Hammers, crowbars, and other tools lay in a scatter on the floor among a litter of split and slivered wood stripped from opened crates. A small forklift tractor stood silently among the cases. No one was visible, and the room was silent, apparently empty of people.

Maxton remarked, "There's a door over there, open to the outside. I don't know about you, but I want to smell some fresh air. I'll go see what's going on out back." He headed off, picking his way diagonally across the littered floor toward the distant door he had indicated.

Ryder, not caring to startle any possible occupant of the large room, called "Hello!" a few times as he wandered over to the considerable pile of crates where the signs of recent activity were centered. There came no response. As he meandered among the huge boxes, he came across one that stood opened, with its heavy lid propped back. He stepped over and peered into the opened crate. Inside the great outer box was a second box of different wood, fitting closely into the outer shell. The lid of the inner box had also been pried loose, but rested closed on the ends of protruding nail points. In curiosity, Ryder leaned on a crowbar that had been left in position by whomever had opened the box.

Gazing into the box under the ample light from overhead flood lamps, he found himself staring into the unmistakable gleam of blued steel gunmetal. As nearly as he could tell the case was solidly packed with heavy automatic rifles, carefully racked and stored in preservative grease. Ryder felt a prickling in the hairs on the back of his neck, and unconsciously ran a finger down the scar on his face as he contemplated the contents of the box.

After easing the box lid back into place he hurriedly looked into other opened containers. He then made his way through the confusion of crates, trying to catch sight of Maxton. As he emerged into open floor space, he saw Maxton sauntering toward him, returning from the open rear door. Ryder gestured for Maxton to hurry, and continued his own rapid pace toward his friend. He waited until they had met before he spoke. Turning back toward the array of scattered boxes, and steering Maxton with a light grip on his arm, Ryder hastily told him, "Max, some and maybe all of these boxes are full of guns! I'll show you in a minute. What did you see out that door?"

Maxton answered, "Plenty! Of people, that is! There are a dozen or so peasants out back, lounging around smoking or snoozing or eating, on their lunch break, I figure. And somebody's got a transistor radio whining full blast. Lahoud's out there too, sitting on a packing crate across the yard and chewing the fat with our boy Rifai and with some other dude in a business suit. From the look of it, they've been unloading another one of those big truck rigs into a small shed over there near where they're parked."

"How far away from that door are they?" Ryder asked. Maxton answered, "I'd guess about fifty feet to the nearest of those laborers, and maybe a hundred to where Lahoud and Rifai are sitting. What the hell's this about guns?"

Conversing as they walked, Ryder had steered their course among the boxes and back to the opened crate he'd first seen. He told Maxton, "Here, take a look," and grabbed the pry bar again, lifting the lid of the inner container. Maxton stared inside and whistled. He said, "What we'd better get is our asses the hell out of here!"

Ryder said, "Right—except one thing first. Max, go back and keep an eye on Lahoud and his crew. I'm going to take some pictures of this stuff. It won't take more than a few minutes. I want to get some shots of the guns, and also the markings on some of these crates."

Maxton blinked once or twice, then, with a shrug, he turned to hurry back to the door. Ryder reached into his pocket and extracted the tiny Minox camera Crawford had given him, thankful that he had spent some time studying the instructions that had come with it.

He had been puzzled by the scatter of broken wood from the packing cases. Now, he thought he saw the answer. A quick inspection among the disarray of containers confirmed his idea. Each of the crates, as received, contained a second box. The outer wooden shells were being stripped away from the inner boxes, hence the litter of splintered wood. Ryder spent the next five minutes making a rapid succession of exposures with the small camera, using two complete film loads. He then moved to where he could beckon to Maxton, who had been dividing his time between looking out the door and uneasily watching as much as he could see of Ryder's progress. Maxton did not need a second invitation to abandon his post. He came at a lumbering trot to rejoin Ryder.

Glancing back as they hustled across the brightly lit room toward the exit door, Ryder said, "Here's hoping they're all out there behind us. It might get a trifle stuffy if somebody finds us prowling around among the kind of goodies Lahoud seems to be moving these days!"

Maxton, chugging along beside Ryder's long-legged strides, said, "I doubt if anybody'll catch up with us inside this next rat's nest of a room, providing we don't starve to death while we try to find our way out."

Leaving the floodlit cargo bay, they plunged into the miasmic gloom of the stacked labyrinth, closing the access door quietly behind themselves. They paused inside the door, listening for a moment and letting their eyes adjust to the poor light. The silence remained, somehow ominous in itself, and Ryder led off down the long lateral alley. In a low voice, he said, "Keep your ears open, Max. If anybody else comes in here, let's try to hear him before he hears us." Maxton grunted his assent.

Taking a guess as to their position, Ryder finally plunged to the left away from the long lateral and into the labyrinth of aisles traversing the main bulk of stacked containers. The two men groped and twisted and turned their way, edging forward as silently as possible. The confusing maze of passages now seemed darker and more airless than ever. Time seemed to drag into eternity. Then Ryder felt his senses collect. Somehow, suddenly he felt that they were nearing the stairwell exit. But in the next instant Ryder went hollow inside and froze in midstep. He reached back and seized Maxton's arm to alert him. They stood motionless in mute, nerve-wracking dismay, listening to a muffled pattern of footsteps descending the concrete stairs from the upper hallway. At Ryder's gesture, Maxton moved with him, and together they crowded into a dark recess among the crates. They waited, pressing against the rough wall of boxes. Unaccountably, the footsteps stopped. A prolonged interval of silence, broken only by the incessant rustlings of the rats around their feet, caused the two Americans an agony of uncertain suspense.

Then the noise made by the battered door being opened at the foot of the stairwell sounded absolutely thunderous. The sound seemed perilously close. With the door opened, the footsteps, now becoming deliberate and cautious, were disconcertingly clear. The unseen, threatening cause of these sounds headed unmistakably into passageways leading toward Ryder and Maxton. Ryder judged the sounds to be less than thirty feet away, and moving closer. He felt a race of adrenaline through his system. He moved tensely in the darkness, positioning himself for better freedom of action as he braced himself for discovery by the approaching interloper.

Ryder thought to himself that the odds could not get much worse against their remaining undetected, but in that instant they did. He was appalled to suddenly find himself watching flashes of light bouncing among the alleys, clearly emanating from a battery-powered lantern of some sort in the hands of the unseen person. The stalking footsteps and the moving flashes of light approached steadily, slowly forward, nearer. Ryder realized that the unknown one was purposefully searching, and he allowed a dart of bafflement to intrude on his tense concentration.

Then with startling abruptness the intruder stepped into view. The man was moving along an aisle parallel to the one Ryder and Maxton had followed. One of the countless and seemingly aimless cross aisles interrupted the wall of packing cases that separated the two Americans from the third man. He halted at the cross aisle, playing the beam of a powerful, multicelled flashlight down the cross aisle in the opposite direction. The man's momentary search of the far aisle gave Ryder the chance to see him clearly, backgrounded against the reflected light. Ryder's eyes were instantly drawn to the ugly silhouette of a machine pistol gripped in the man's right hand. The flashlight was in his left.

The man appeared to be wearing mechanic's coveralls, with a military-type fatigue cap tilted back on his head. Ryder's inspection of the searcher was rudely terminated when the man swung the flashlight's beam directly down the cross aisle toward the two apprehensive Americans. For an instant the beam of light struck directly at the shallow, four-cornered recess Ryder and Maxton were squeezed into. The searcher failed to notice anything unusual, however, and he continued to swing the flashlight's beam through random arcs along the rat-infested aisle. Then, with two careful steps ahead, the man took himself, his gun, and his flashlight past the cross aisle, and out of view. The sounds of the stranger and his search then unquestionably began to diminish as he gradually moved away toward the back of the labyrinth.

Ryder felt the tautness slacken from his muscles as he continued to wait. The sounds dwindled, at last weakening into bare audibility. Ryder finally muttered, "He's as good as gone now. I don't hear anybody else coming, so let's get the hell out of here if we can." He heard Maxton exhale an "Amen" as he led out from the shadowed alcove with quiet but rapid steps, and headed directly toward the point from which the sounds of the stranger's entrance had come. With Maxton on his heels, Ryder worked his way through the short remaining distance, and readily located the exit door. The two men hurried through the doorway and up the concrete stairs, pausing momentarily at the top to check the long hallway in both directions. They detected no evidence of activity, and hustled down the corridor to the door at its end, then down the diagonal flight of stairs. They trotted across the huge entry bay, and at last stepped out of the warehouse and into the welcome sunshine and fresh air. To their further relief they saw that their taxi remained where they'd left it. The driver sat behind the wheel with a cigarette dangling from his mouth, watching them with a strangely sullen expression on his face. Ryder noticed the man's changed demeanor, and, after directing the driver to return them to the Al Urdon, muttered to Maxton to hold the conversation down until they were out of the cab. Maxton glanced sideways at Ryder and ran a forefinger across his forehead, wiping away mock beads of perspiration. He rumbled his agreement, and they rode back to the Al Urdon in silence.

Back at the hotel, Ryder announced that he would regard a three-finger shot of whiskey, neat, as a suitable reward for their warehouse experience. Maxton of course emphatically sanctioned the idea, and they headed directly to the cozy atmosphere of the bar and a corner table. The waiter cheerfully supplied the two potent drinks, plus a bowl of salted peanuts. The two men silently toasted each other and took large swallows of the Scotch, then leaned back to consider the implications of their episode at Lahoud's truck depot.

At length Ryder said, in a somewhat somber tone, "I don't think we got home entirely free from that pinch we were in. It looks like that goon with the gun must have grilled the taxi driver. How else would he have been tipped off to look for someone?"

Maxton's eyebrows went up a fraction. "Jesus! So that's it! I never thought about that taxi angle!" Maxton paused, shaking his crew-cut head, then said, "What in the hell do you figure we got out of all that, besides our skins, I mean?"

Ryder replied, "Maybe not much. But maybe plenty. I think it's going to be mighty interesting for the likes of Crawford to see those pictures I took, supposing I didn't make any boo-boos with that camera. It sure looks to me like Lahoud's a big-time gunrunner, and I don't see a chance in hell for that artillery to be slated for delivery to Hussein's army. What the hell, Lahoud and Rifai were holding hands with Asad Tabet just last night. In my book, those guns go to Al Fatah!"

Maxton said, a little dubiously, "I guess that adds up. So what do we do next, Sherlock?"

Ryder toyed with his glass. "I've been wondering if maybe we should try Lahoud on the phone again, right away, now, to play innocent. But the more I think about that idea, the less I like it. That could also be the best way to stick ourselves right into large trouble. Let's leave it the way it is, and give it all up for the day. I've got a mess of paperwork to clean up anyway."

Maxton said, "Music to my ears. I might just look up a couple of my old drinking buddies this afternoon. Maybe I can turn up another line or two on Rifai or Lahoud." He eased his powerful bulk out of the chair, saying, "Sit still, I'll go get our keys." He headed for the reception desk, and a minute or two later returned and handed Ryder his room key. Ryder signed their bar chit, and headed for the elevator.

Al Fatah
Beirut, Lebanon
APRIL 1966

Wahji Ghandhouri glanced at the face of a gold desk clock, and then closed the red, leather-bound portfolio in front of him. He stood and moved from behind his vast, ornately carved desk, strolling pensively over to the glass wall of his penthouse office. He stared out at the brilliant blue of the Mediterranean. At three o'clock, five minutes away, his office door would open to admit one of the few men in the Middle East shrewd enough to command Ghandhouri's caution and respect.

Ghandhouri had long since learned that this visitor, contrary to Arab habit, would be precisely punctual. It was always safe to relinquish a specific appointment hour to Asad Tabet. Tabet would infallibly appear on time, and with equal infallibility would waste few words on anything less than relevant.

Wahji Ghandhouri was uneasy and puzzled over the forthcoming meeting. Uneasy because he could not discover a valid reason for Asad Tabet to pay this visit to Beirut. Puzzled, since Tabet risked his life whenever he left concealment, particularly in or around either Beirut or Cairo.

Ghandhouri had spent hours, and a sizeable sum of money, unearthing a collection of new, secret information concerning Asad Tabet and of Yasser Arafat, Tabet's chief, and of recent and planned doings of the Al Fatah guerrillas, in an attempt to anticipate Tabet's reason for coming. Among many other items of information that Ghandhouri had so gleaned, one was the probable location of Asad Tabet's currently favored hideaway. To learn this information was, in itself, a stroke of miraculous good fortune. Knowledge of Tabet's true whereabouts offered its owner vast trading power, if he knew how and where to use it. All this notwithstanding, for neither price nor cost of effort could Wahji Ghandhouri discover why Asad Tabet was taking the risk of paying him this call.

At precisely three o'clock, the door to Ghandhouri's private elevator slid aside, and two men entered the luxurious suite. In the lead, a foppishly dressed, slender young Lebanese named Nebil, on Ghandhouri's payroll as an aide, swayed gracefully into view. Behind Nebil shambled the bearded, cigar-smoking, slightly corpulent figure of Asad Tabet. Ghandhouri noted that Tabet had forsaken his favorite garb, the shapeless anonymity afforded by army fatigue coveralls. Ghandhouri thought, however, that Asad Tabet looked equally uncouth and slovenly in the ill-fitting black serge suit he now perspired in. How easy it is, Ghandhouri mused, to misjudge this man.

Ghandhouri let Nebil direct Asad Tabet to a comfortable chair facing the desk. He then dismissed the aide with a wave of his hand, and moved out to greet the phlegmatic second-in-command of the Al Fatah terrorists. Ghandhouri, displaying the flashing smile he was famous for, strode lithely up to the visitor with a slender hand extended. "My dear Asad, *ballit ilba'raki*!" he exclaimed, claiming in Arabic a blessing from Tabet's visit.

Asad Tabet smiled around his cigar and accepted the limp handclasp. He replied in Arabic, *"Jit lahza ta shufak,* Wahji." (I have come to see you for a moment).

As he spoke, Tabet's military eyes slid to glance at the fat figure of Ghandhouri's bodyguard, who seemed to be asleep in an upholstered chair in a far corner of the office. Ghandhouri noticed Tabet's appraisal of the bodyguard. Walking with his peculiar bouncing step, Ghandhouri returned to the throne-like confines of the chair behind his desk. He said gaily, "Asad, you know I always indulge myself with the comforting presence of a personal attendant." He flaunted a perfumed handkerchief in the general direction of the somnolent fat man slumped in the corner. "Please do not concern yourself with him. We shall speak in English, which he cannot understand." Ghandhouri laughed facetiously. "The poor dolt can scarcely understand his *own* language!"

Asad Tabet glanced at the fat one in the corner, evidently asleep with his mouth open. Tabet said drily, "He's like my soldiers, Wahji. Nothing matters, as long as he's alive and can shoot straight."

Ghandhouri's unsmiling eyes swung to Tabet's face. Still wearing the famous smile on his lips, he said, "Ah, yes, my dear Asad. How are your brave soldiers, and how are things with Al Fatah?" Ghandhouri's effeminate hand, heavy with expensive finger rings, wafted gently onto the red, leather-bound portfolio on his desk. "In anticipation of your welcome visit, I have acquainted myself with the current status of Al Fatah's accounts. I must say, my dear Asad, it is a wonder to me how well funded you manage to remain!"

Asad Tabet leaned his head back and slowly blew a cloud of cigar smoke toward the Chinese red of the ceiling. "Yes, Wahji. It is a vast comfort to find one's self well funded in this uncertain world. What a compliment it is, though, to hear such words from a man who must be known as one of the richest on earth! The poor sums attributable to my beloved Al Fatah are surely like *bakshish* to one such as Wahji Ghandhouri!"

Ghandhouri kept the wide smile stretched across his angular features while an ominous chill swept through him. He did not like the temper of Tabet's words. Ghandhouri swung the scented silk of his handkerchief idly past his face. "It is a privilege to listen to your compliments, Asad, however unlike you it may be to consume time with such trivia."

Tabet's teeth showed around the cigar. He looked squarely into Wahji Ghandhouri's cold eyes. "It has a bearing, Wahji, it has a bearing." Again Ghandhouri sensed a threat. He watched as Asad Tabet withdrew a sealed, unmarked envelope from the pocket inside his jacket. Tabet rested the envelope on his lap. He tapped it with a dirty fingernail. "Al Fatah may elect to spend a considerable sum of its money in the very near future, Wahji. If so, it will be essential that our drafts be backed and honored with ready cash, on very short notice."

Ghandhouri felt a rapier of alarm pierce his thoughts. His mind raced, wondering what the sealed envelope might contain. With a fine gambler's instinct, however, he considered that Tabet might be running a bluff. Coolly, he said, "Of course, Asad. That is business as usual, *n'est ce pas?* Naturally, if you are referring to something extraordinary, I will appreciate some small advance warning."

To Ghandhouri's inner annoyance, he watched as Asad Tabet calmly returned the sealed envelope to his inner pocket. Tabet then said bluntly, "Al Fatah has religiously provided you with advance notice of anticipated expenditures. The consequences of that have not been comfortable for us, Wahji. From time to time, certain opponents of ours have learned in advance of our intention to spend. With that information, they have managed to thwart some of our plans. Worse than that, we have occasionally been embarrassed by angry suppliers, who have found themselves holding drafts from us which are not immediately negotiable."

Ghandhouri sat stiffly forward in his chair, a picture of outrage. He exclaimed, "Asad! It is unthinkable that you might suspect me of leaking such information!"

The Palestinian leader studied the cold end of his defunct cigar, then tossed it accurately into a wastebasket. He bit the end from a fresh one and spat tobacco fragments onto Ghandhouri's rich carpet. "While you choose to present yourself otherwise, Wahji, you are a displaced Palestinian peasant like the rest of us. No, I do not suspect that you would leak Al Fatah's private information." Relief showed on Ghandhouri's face momentarily. Then, however, Asad Tabet added, "You might *sell* it, though."

Wahji Ghandhouri stared frigidly. "Am I, then, the only possible outlet for such leaks? Obviously not!"

Asad Tabet looked calmly at the financier. "There are a few other possible candidates. We will know, very soon, exactly who is responsible."

Asad Tabet lit the fresh cigar. He then said, "But as I mentioned before, Wahji, that is not Al Fatah's main concern. What is important is that we would like to put, forever, an end to these reproofs from our suppliers. We have the money with which to pay. They no longer believe that we do."

Ghandhouri flicked his handkerchief in annoyance. "I cannot understand how such things could happen! Believe me, it will never again occur, not if there is a fault somewhere in my organization. It may easily be that clerical errors have taken place. You know that we are now employing electronic computers in our accounting system. I will make a personal investigation of this!"

Asad Tabet smiled sarcastically. "Oh, yes. I know about your computers. I've been sent around the grand tour of Ghandhouri's facilities, with one of those shaved-groin pretty boys of yours leading me by the wrist! But isn't it a little beneath you, Wahji, to blame a box of wires?"

Ghandhouri drew himself up in his chair. He looked impassively back at the Palestinian guerrilla leader. "You have my abject apologies for those inexcusable errors of the past. If our management of your finances is unsatisfactory, obviously you have every right to consider moving your account elsewhere. I would deeply regret such an eventuality, however."

Asad Tabet chewed placidly on his cigar for a time, then said, "Al Fatah does not thrive on popularity. Unlike our more amicable brethren in the PLO, we refuse to conciliate. It becomes a way of life very easily, that inflexible attitude. It is appalling to discover how successful one can be with a program of merciless intimidation! Of course I think you know that quite well already. In fact, you serve as one of the most encouraging symbols to me, Wahji, of how wealth can be accumulated through employment of intimidation and impenitent conduct in one's business affairs. Al Fatah, in its detested role, does not easily attract unsolicited fiscal donations. As you have already noted, however, we do remain well funded."

Ghandhouri spat acidly, "I congratulate you for that impassioned speech. What has it to do with the business at hand?"

A hard smile appeared on Asad Tabet's face. "We have considered removing our account from your care, Wahji. We would regret having to do so. You and your organization are peculiarly fitting as a partner of sorts to Al Fatah. The sealed envelope you watched me handle a while ago contains a handsome contribution to Al Fatah. It comes from some Kuwaiti friends of ours."

Wahji Ghandhouri leaned slightly forward, his interest instantly restored. Asad Tabet produced the sealed envelope from his pocket for the second time. He raised it in his hand. "This is a draft, representing cash, made out to Al Fatah. It is in the amount of one million pounds sterling. In this conversation you and I are having, a decision will be made whether or not this draft is to be placed on deposit with you, or with someone else."

Wahji Ghandhouri laced his fingers together and leaned back in his chair. He fixed saurian eyes on Asad Tabet. "By all means, then, let us proceed with the decision. It seems you have something further in mind to say."

The guerrilla leader had to admire Ghandhouri's poise. Tabet pressed relentlessly nevertheless against his disadvantaged host. "If Al Fatah stays with you, we will insist first that the scales be balanced. You have abused us by misuse of our money and of our reputation. In turn we consider it just that you endure a mild period of retribution."

Ghandhouri inquired icily, "While I do not acknowledge the abuses you allege, I will ask what form of retribution you have in mind."

Asad Tabet replied unemotionally, "Here is what I propose to you, Wahji. I believe Al Fatah has clearly established its fiscal responsibility with you by now. Therefore, I propose that you issue to us a line of credit equal to an overdraft of *double* our existing balance of deposits. You will be secured against risk by this note for one million pounds sterling. That is my proposition, plus one or two conditions."

Ghandhouri's face remained impassive. "And what would those conditions be?"

Asad Tabet pointed with his cigar at the sealed envelope. "We would hand this draft over to you now. It requires two signatures before it is rendered negotiable—that of Yasser Arafat, plus my own. Arafat's signature has already been affixed. Mine has not. Six months from now, if we remain satisfied with your continued management of our account, I will then sign the draft."

Ghandhouri asked, "There are other conditions?"

Tabet nodded gravely. "One modest addition. You will guarantee, in writing, that any draft against our account will be paid, in acceptable currency, within no more than seventy-two hours of its presentation to you. That will include drafts for any amount up to the overdraft limit I have mentioned."

Ghandhouri, externally calm, felt pressure rising against him. The proposition represented very little more than normal demand. Yet it required the one thing he could least afford, a liquid reserve of available cash. He looked at the guerrilla leader. "On the surface, Asad, your conditions seem reasonable. They portray, however, a clear lack of confidence in me. That could be ruinous, were those conditions to be publicized. Also there is another undesirable aspect. Forgive my heartless candor, but what am I to do with that collateral draft in the unhappy event of your death?"

Asad Tabet smiled. "Provisions have been made for overcoming that latter problem, should it arise. If I die during the next six months, Wahji, the million-pound note will then be signed, instead, by one of our Kuwaiti benefactors. That is, one of the people whose money we will be using. As to the risk that the terms and conditions of our agreement might unethically be revealed, you will simply have to trust us, as we have trusted you with our advance notice of withdrawals."

Ghandhouri, inwardly smarting, asked, "May I know the name of this Kuwaiti benefactor?"

Asad Tabet solemnly shook his head. "Not until I die, Wahji. Not unless he, or one of his fellow benefactors, otherwise chooses to come forward on their own. It is possible that they will; who knows? But for reasons that these Kuwaitis have not confided, they too speak these days of uneasiness over deposits made with you. I would not be surprised to see their concern vanish, were they to witness the prolonged success of this proposed agreement between Al Fatah and yourself!"

Wahji Ghandhouri felt as though a trap had snapped shut on him. He was appalled at the potential validity of Asad Tabet's blackmailing offer. With a total of more that a quarter-billion dollars in Ghandhouri assets, more than a third were derived through Kuwaiti deposits. Tabet was threatening him with a potential withdrawal by the Kuwaitis of nearly eighty million dollars in cash.

Wahji Ghandhouri studied the bearded Palestinian with hatred. He silently vowed that this man would, when the time was right, meet with an abrupt, unexpected, unpleasant death. He said, "I see that you had anticipated my objections. With those now disposed of, I see no remaining barrier to my acceptance of your proposal. I presume you came prepared with the necessary documents?"

Asad Tabet smiled kindly and nodded, then reached for his battered briefcase. "Oh yes, Wahji, I brought them along."

The Code
Beirut, Lebanon
<u>APRIL 1966</u>

Noon was approaching by the time Ryder and Maxton, after an uneventful flight from Amman, finished checking into the Phoenicia Hotel in Beirut and headed for their rooms. Ryder drudged through the repetitious tedium of unpacking, then looked at his watch. Five minutes past one. He picked up the telephone and called the US Embassy. Ryder was informed by the embassy's switchboard operator that Mr. Schuyler was not in the office today. Ryder asked to speak to the ambassador. A moment later Marge Mackenzie, the ambassador's secretary, came on the line.

Ryder heard Marge's low voice and smiled. "Hello, Marge. This is Jeff Ryder. It's a treat to hear that voice of yours again!"

Marge's voice came back sounding pleased and surprised. "Well, how nice! Or are you just currying favor with this office, Mr. Ryder?"

Ryder encouraged the banter. "Marge, it would be a better world if you would call me Jeff. And if I'm currying favor, ma'am, I'm speaking with the party of the first part!"

Marge said candidly, "This sounds like a conversation that might deserve different surroundings. What can I do for you in the meanwhile, Jeff?"

Ryder responded, "Well, I understand Boge isn't around today. If there's no way to reach him, I guess I'll have to try for a session with your boss instead."

A shadow of humor came into Marge's voice. "Yes, I'm sorry to say that Bogart is out, ill. He's at home with an upset tummy. It may be best if you don't disturb him."

Ryder smiled to himself. Aloud, he said, "Hmm . . . King Tut's revenge, perhaps. Yes, that definitely excuses poor old Boge from the problem. Marge, what can you do about squeezing me in to see Ambassador Harte? Any chance this afternoon?"

Marge answered, "As usual, Jeff, he has an awful load, but I think in this case we'd better let him be the judge. I'll ask him as soon as I can. May I call you right back?"

Ryder said, "Sure, Marge, I'll stand by for your call. I'm in 1108 at the Phoenicia. Thanks." He hung up the telephone and reached for a paperback Western. He had barely found his place in the book when the telephone rang. It was Marge.

She told him, "Jeff, Ambassador Harte suggests that you just come over right now if you can. You might have to wait a few minutes, but he will be pleased to see you as soon as he is able to finish with his present visitors."

Ryder responded, "Okay, Marge, I'll hustle right over. See you swiftly."

The US Embassy was only about a ten-minute walk from the Phoenicia Hotel, and the April afternoon was glorious, so Ryder set out on foot. As he walked along the narrow byways he speculated to himself about Beirut's strange network of streets. He wondered idly how it had come about that none of this city's streets seemed to travel any respectable distance without either bending, or angling, or not infrequently simply ending suddenly. It seemed unworthy to blame such confusion on the impeccable Roman engineers. Someone else must have been responsible—or irresponsible. Maybe the streets simply lay on top of goat and cattle trails, in keeping with the laissez-faire attitude of these coastal inhabitants. And now, Ryder thought, adding neo-perpetuity to the tangle, the soaring population growth of automobiles had driven Beirut's city fathers to superimpose upon the cow-path maze a pattern of one-way streets! The combined consequence called for the patience of Job and the genius of da Vinci to navigate a simple crosstown trip on wheels.

Ryder's contemplations faded as he arrived at the embassy. He checked in with the marine guard's desk in the lobby, then headed upstairs to Ambassador Harte's suite of offices.

Marge Mackenzie greeted him genially and told him, "You'll be able to go right in, Jeff. Our other visitors have finished and gone since your call." She escorted Ryder into the ambassador's office.

The two men shook hands, and the ambassador invited Ryder to sit down. Julius Harte had met Ryder casually on two or three occasions in the past, but never under close, private circumstances. He studied his visitor with poignant interest now. Paying secondary attention to the man's physical attributes, Harte looked for signs of Ryder's inner person. It seemed to the ambassador, in this superficial inspection, that he detected a strange and almost fascinating admixture. He liked the firm handshake and the direct, open look from those almost black eyes. He liked the appearance of lurking humor in the face, modified though it seemed to be by edges of flinty cynicism. He found, looking into Ryder's eyes, the surface signs of deep mental capacity. He sensed an aura of friendliness, and what seemed to be a purposely veiled faculty for compassion. In ostensible contradiction, though, Harte also saw in Ryder, however controlled, a latent ferocity. He was reminded of the old motto, "Don't tread on me."

The ambassador opened the conversation. "It is unfortunate that Boge has been taken ill. He would want to be here. On the other hand, I've been looking forward to a chance to improve my acquaintance with you, Mr. Ryder, so we might as well look at the bright side of the situation."

Ryder smiled. "The pleasure is mine, Mr. Ambassador. I'll try to keep this brief, because I feel like I've barged in on your schedule."

Harte made a deprecatory gesture. "I believe you're just in from Amman. Anything associated with Mr. Crawford's program takes a very high priority with me, Mr. Ryder. I would appreciate it if you will give me a quick summary of what you wish to discuss. After that we will be better able to decide how to arrange our time."

Ryder, admiring the ambassador's forthright manner, launched into the requested summary. "Well, it'll be embarrassingly brief, Ambassador Harte. During my three days' stay in Amman I've come across something that seems worth reporting. I believe I've come across a flow of contraband arms into Jordan, apparently destined for delivery to Al Fatah."

During his terse commentary, Ryder had taken the Minox film cartridges from his pocket and placed them on the desk in front of the ambassador. "If my efforts with the new camera Crawford gave me aren't hay-bag, we might find some interesting things to study on these rolls of film, sir. If my photos are okay, we will have some shots of some of those weapons."

The ambassador picked up the two tiny film cartridges. He studied Ryder's face as he digested the substance of the oversimplified statements. At length Harte said, "You and I must discuss your findings in detail. I think it can wait, however, until these films are developed for us. Can you return here this evening? Say, at eight o'clock sharp? I'll meet you in my conference room. The photos will be ready by then."

Ryder nodded. "I'll be here at eight, Mr. Ambassador." Harte stood, and Ryder got up from his chair. The ambassador smiled and shook hands with Ryder. With concern tempering his voice, he said, "Mr. Ryder, you are engaged in a difficult undertaking for us. Your efforts are deeply appreciated. I do not profess to be well schooled in the arts of Mr. Crawford's field, and I only hope that, as another amateur, I can do my part as well as you appear to be doing with yours."

Ryder, standing there facing this US ambassador, sensed the great worth of the man. He detected genuine sincerity behind the wiry little ambassador's words, and liked him for it. In the same moment he felt a vague sense of apprehension. Looking directly into the ambassador's eyes, he said, "Mr. Ambassador, it seems to me that there is a limit to how far you should let yourself become personally involved. If you don't mind my saying so, this kind of taffy pull is out of your league, sir." Ryder's voice had turned almost scolding.

A smile moved onto Harte's long face. He stepped around his desk and put his hand on Ryder's shoulder, gently urging him toward the door. "That's partly true, I suppose. But then, you wouldn't deny me a chance now and then, would you, to do something a little more exhilarating than helping frightened tourists locate their misplaced passports?"

Ryder paused at the door and grinned back at the feisty little ambassador. "No, sir. See you tonight, sir." Ryder left the ambassador's office. Strolling back to his desk and smiling to himself, Julius Harte thought, "And *I'm* trying to take care of *him*!"

The conference room at the embassy seemed familiar to Ryder now, yet somehow different with Ambassador Harte there to meet him instead of Crawford. Ryder seated himself alongside the ambassador and picked up the plain manila envelope that Harte had placed on the conference table. "I can't stand the suspense, Ambassador Harte! Tell me, did I get pictures on that film?"

Harte smiled and answered, "Yes, indeed! Your photos are excellent, as nearly as I'm able to judge. Everyone of your exposures came out. I've brought along a magnifying glass to use in studying them. It's inside the envelope, with the enlargements." He pointed to the envelope in Ryder's hand.

Ryder opened the manila envelope and withdrew the photo enlargements and the magnifying glass. The photos were clipped together in two separate stacks. Harte held one of the stacks in his hand. "These have been sorted into two groups, one for each of the two rolls of film you used. In each of these two piles, the photos are arranged in the sequence in which the pictures were taken."

Ryder picked up the second stack and removed its clip. He proceeded to spread the photos out in rows on the table. The photographs had come out sharp and clear. Ryder then gave the ambassador a verbal summary of the events that had led to the photographic episode in Lahoud's warehouse.

Harte asked, "You say this man's name is Issam Lahoud? The person who owns this warehouse and trucking firm?"

At Ryder's affirmative reply Harte wrote the name down. Then, to confirm further notes he had made, he inquired, "And he's a member of the airline's board of directors, as well as an acquaintance of Asad Tabet. And the other board member seen with Tabet and Lahoud is named Abdallah Rifai?"

"That's right, sir," Ryder affirmed.

Harte put down his pen and notebook. "All right, let's go on."

Ryder selected the first four photographs from the array on the table and handed them to the ambassador. "These show pretty well what's in one of the boxes at Lahoud's, sir."

Harte studied the easily visible automatic rifles, stacked in orderly profusion within the huge crate. After examining each of the four pictures he said soberly, "There's not much doubt about the nature of this cargo, is there?" He looked up. "What's next?"

Ryder had continued to spread photos out on the table, carefully maintaining their sequence. "From here on, we're kind of on our own, sir. I was playing a hunch when I made the rest of these shots. As you can see, they're just pictures of boxes. From a mighty hasty look at those markings on the crates, I got to thinking that somebody who could read Arabic might find a clue or two about where the boxes came from, or maybe even who sent them, or who they sent them to. I can read Arabic numbers, but that's the end of it for me."

The ambassador selected one of the photos, a close-up showing a line of Arabic script painted onto one of the boxes. "For a year or so now, whenever I've had the time, I've been trying to learn to read the Arabic calligraphy. I can manage fairly well with the spoken Arabic word. So let's see whether or not my reading lessons are doing me any good." Using the magnifying glass, he began studying the script.

Still peering through the glass, Harte said, "I make out four words and a number. There doesn't seem to be any sense to the way it reads, though. Here, you write these down as I read them." He handed Ryder a piece of heavy paper that had been inserted into the manila envelope as a stiffener. Ryder took out his pen and waited.

Harte, studying the photo, read, "*Kal'a*. That means castle, or fortress. Next, *turuk*. *Turuk* means roads, or streets. Then, the number four. The next word is *kadim*. That would mean very old, or ancient. The last word seems to be *wast*, which means center, or middle."

Ryder had written:

Castle; Roads; 4; Ancient; Center

He put the heavy paper down, and both men stared silently at the words. Harte finally spoke. "Whatever this may mean, we'll need more than this to go on. Let's check some others."

Together, the two men examined the photographs. They selected additional clear examples of the markings. With Harte reading, and Ryder noting down the word sequences, they emerged with a list:

Photo #1: Castle; Four Roads; Ancient; Center
Photo #2: River; Metal; Center
Photo #3: Castle, Four Roads; Three Hills; Center
Photo #4: Deep Valley; Four Roads; Wheat; Center; Sea

Together, they stared at the four cryptic collections of words and numbers. Ryder muttered, "It doesn't make much sense yet, but at least we're beginning to get some common denominators. All four of them have 'center' in them, and three have 'four roads,' for instance."

Harte agreed. "I was thinking that too. It suggests that there's a pattern here. If this same exercise were done for every box that can be read in those photos, it might produce enough from which to work out something meaningful. I'm pretty sure, though, that you and I won't solve that mystery this evening. This is a job for experts, and I'm sure that Mr. Crawford has access to plenty of those. What about your other roll of film?"

Ryder pointed at the photos they had been studying. "Ambassador Harte, before we put this first bunch away, I'd like to mention one other thing." He sorted through the distributed photos for a moment, then found the one he wanted. He picked it up and placed it in front of the ambassador. "There is a peculiar detail I noticed about those boxes that may not mean a thing. I'd like to call your attention to it anyway, though." Ryder bent over the selected photo and carefully pointed with his pen. "If you'll take that glass, sir, and look closely right here above where I'm pointing, you'll see the head of a brass wood screw that has been driven into the outside of this box."

Harte peered through the magnifying glass. After a moment he muttered, "Yes. I believe I see the screw head."

Ryder instructed, "Now, sir, just study it carefully. You'll see that it doesn't have the usual screwdriver slot. The slot on that screw is curved, like an 'S', not a simple, straight, conventional slot."

Harte bent closer to the photo and worked with the glass, then straightened up and put the glass on the table. He looked at Ryder and exclaimed, "Why, you're perfectly right! I've never seen nor heard of such a thing before, and my hobby is woodwork!"

Ryder shook his head. "Neither have I, and I'm supposed to be an engineer. On top of that, there's only one of those screws on each face of each box. I looked over a bunch of the boxes carefully, and in that one respect, they all seemed alike."

Harte started staring through the magnifying glass again, at other photographs. "Yes! Now that I look for them, I can see that one little screwhead on every box that appears!"

Ryder said, "As a matter of fact, sir, it was the presence of those peculiar wood screws that got me going on the second roll of film."

Ryder restacked the first set of pictures, clipped them together, and set them aside. He then spread the second set of photos out on the table. He selected one of them and handed it to Harte. "Here's a close-up of one of those brass screwheads."

Harte looked through the glass at the photo, but made no comment. He then picked up one of the other pictures and studied it under the glass. "Yes. I see. But now, let's have a look at some more of these Arabic markings." The ambassador turned his attention to the photographs. "Write these down on our list, Jeff." He again began translating Arabic words. "Metal. Center. Sea. Here's a second one: Metal. Caravan. Here's a third: Metal. Water-spring. All of those can be seen in this one view, and there are several repeats of each of them. An interesting thing about these is that they all seem to have the word 'metal' first." Harte's eyes shifted to the list Ryder had been filling out. It now read:

Photo #1: Castle; Four Roads; Ancient; Center
Photo #2: River; Metal; Center
Photo #3: Castle; Four Roads; Three Hills; Center
Photo #4: Deep Valley; Four Roads; Wheat; Center
Photo #5: Metal; Center; Sea
Photo #6: Metal; Caravan
Photo #7: Metal; Water-spring

Harte frowned at the tabulation for a moment, then said, "Well, there's still no magic solution, although I'm sure that all this can be puzzled out. Let's put this aside and plan on letting Crawford decipher whatever is to be learned from it. Now, is there something else related to these photos, Jeff?"

Ryder nodded, "Two more items. First, we have only been looking at the outer boxes, as they arrived at Lahoud's. In that first stack of pictures, the last string of shots shows the *inner* boxes, the ones stripped out at Lahoud's."

Ryder shuffled through the first stack of shots again, and separated several from the bottom. He handed them to Harte. "These inside boxes don't have the same kinds of Arabic markings. These are Arabic too, all right, but they're different. They look stenciled and more uniform, for one thing."

Harte studied the photos Ryder had handed him. After a time he said, "These are quite ordinary markings." Peering through the glass, Harte painstakingly read the inscriptions. "This one simply says, 'This side up.' This one is, 'Open here.' As best I can tell, each of these boxes also shows its gross and tare weights." Harte was silent for a moment, still studying the photos. He then looked up. "That's all I can find on these inner boxes, except to note that they also carry those wood screws!"

Ryder remarked, "Well, those inner markings don't sound fishy. They sound like they're meant for public viewing."

Harte put down the photos and the magnifying glass. "I agree, and I believe we might as well leave it at that. What was your other item, Jeff?"

Ryder reached into a pocket and produced three Al Urdon Hotel stationery envelopes. The envelopes were sealed. He rested them on the table and said, "I've probably read too many Hercule Poirot whodunits, but anyway, I picked up some splintered wood from those crates. I figured there might be a chance somebody could dope out where the wood came from. There are some nails in there too, and a couple of those odd wood screws I found on the floor at Lahoud's. The envelope marked #1 came from the outside crates. The inside crates seemed to be one or the other of two different kinds, so I took slivers and nails from both sorts. They're in the #2 and #3 envelopes."

Harte said, "You needn't minimize your 'Poirot' idea. These slivers could turn out to be the best source of information of all!" He paused, collecting the photos and replacing them in the manila envelope, together with the notes Ryder had been taking and the samples of wood.

The ambassador leaned back in his chair. "Let me summarize our discussion, to be sure I'm not leaving out anything important. I have the following main elements in my mind. We have positive evidence of clandestine, and massive, shipments of arms into Jordan. We have the name of one man definitely involved in those shipments, Issam Lahoud, and the name of another quite probably also implicated, Rifai. The arms shipments give every appearance of being destined for Yasser Arafat's Al Fatah terrorist guerrillas, thanks to the presence in this scene of Asad Tabet, Arafat's chief subordinate. These arms shipments evidently reached Jordan by overland transport, although air and sea transport could also be involved. We have found, in those unusual screwheads, what appears to be a consistently used identifying mark on all the shipping containers involved. The weapons are apparently transshipped somewhere en route, at a place, or places, where their original shipping containers are masked within a second, outer container. In transshipment, the outer containers are marked with coded symbols in Arabic, perhaps to specify routing." Harte paused, then asked, "Does that agree with your thinking, Jeff? Have I omitted anything significant?"

Ryder, immensely impressed with Harte's accurate and concise summary, answered. "Mr. Ambassador, as far as I'm concerned, you've covered it perfectly. You'd have made a great engineer!"

Harte smiled. "Believe me, there are times when I'd rather be an engineer! Since I'm not, though, I think we'd better head our separate ways now. I must get this on its way to Crawford immediately, and that means tonight!"

Wahji Ghandhouri
Beirut, Lebanon
APRIL 1966

ahji Ghandhouri's obese bodyguard grunted heavily as he shifted his seated bulk into a more comfortable slump, moving to reposition the holstered automatic pistol that chafed the rolls of fat beneath his arm. He glanced furtively up from the *Playboy* magazine on his lap, momentarily concerned that his unintentional grunt might have disturbed the man across the room. The boss's temper was violent and unnervingly unpredictable. Apparently not guilty, the fat guard returned avidly to his lascivious study of the American magazine that he could not read, but whose erotic pictures and cartoons invariably caused him a pulsing erection. Such was the case at the moment.

Across the spacious, luxurious room, beyond his magnificent, hand-carved desk, Wahji Ghandhouri stood motionless, his slender, almost feminine figure facing a vast expanse of double-paned, bulletproof glass that formed one wall of the penthouse office. He stared across the rooftops of Beirut. From this tenth-floor level, the city looked almost attractive. Ghandhouri did not see Beirut, however, nor its rooftops. His vision was turned inward. He stood engrossed in the resolution of matters of crucial consequence to himself, matters that could, and should, lead to a huge windfall of cash. Ghandhouri set about formulating a decision.

In an all but ceremonial ritual, whenever Ghandhouri faced decisions deemed sufficiently vital, he would command for himself absolute isolation—always excepting, of course, the twenty-four-hour-a-day presence of an armed personal bodyguard. These sequestered contemplations occurred only rarely, in diametric contradiction to Ghandhouri's customary hyperactive conduct. Famed for flamboyant snap judgments involving literally millions of dollars, in his normal routines Ghandhouri kept himself constantly attended by harried aides-de-camp at whom he habitually raved and stormed in petulant, theatrical tyranny.

To Wahji Ghandhouri, in the presence of his already enormous personal power, there remained only one stimulus sufficient to seduce him away from his cherished limelight: the prospect of seizing immediate, desperately needed hard cash.

Silently gazing across the city in his ritual introspection, Ghandhouri urged a flood of sequestered thoughts into his consciousness. He let himself remember that he had been born the bastard son of an ignorant sixteen-year-old Palestinian village girl. He singled out in vicious detail a mental parade of despicable events from the history of his own successful rise, through commerce in vice and corruption, from novice to overlord.

Ghandhouri punished himself deliberately. He writhed inwardly, purposely, in his own sordid past. He bathed himself again in the acid wash of scorn, contempt, and disgust he had borne from the eyes of others for too many years. He let himself remember, in vivid clarity, what he really was.

Then he slammed closed those doors again. He returned his mind to now, and in grim relish contemplated not what he really was, but what, to his now world, he seemed to be.

Abruptly, to the startled hearing of his seated protector across the room, Ghandhouri began to laugh aloud. The laughter rose into shrieks. Ghandhouri stamped the floor; he rocked from side to side shouting and gasping, tears of laughter streaming down his face. He clapped his hands, gesticulated wildly with his arms, and pirouetted dizzily.

The fat bodyguard, head down and mouth agape, sat paralyzed in dumb, blind focus on the magazine in his lap, trying desperately to ignore the demoniac spectacle. Ghandhouri danced wildly across the room. He hurled a volume of the Koran through the opened glass doorway, arching it out over the parapet to fall on the city below. He seized priceless porcelain objets d'art from their niches and smashed them onto the imported tiles of the floor. He ripped a Prussian dueling saber from its mountings and slashed to shreds an authentic medieval tapestry.

At last exhausted, Ghandhouri flung himself full length upon the floor, face upward, choking with repressed giggles as he slowly quieted himself. The terrified guard continued staring into his magazine, trying to wish his own quivering, sweating bulk into invisibility.

Silence returned to the room. Minutes passed. Finally, Ghandhouri sprang nimbly to his feet, causing the fat bodyguard to jump convulsively in his chair. With calm, sure strides Ghandhouri exited from the room through an arched doorway leading to a small adjoining boudoir. Thirty minutes later he returned, having bathed and groomed himself, and having changed his entire ensemble. He ignored the agonized bodyguard, and briskly seated himself at his desk. He proceeded, with pencil and notepad, to concentrate on a lengthy string of calculations.

Wahji Ghandhouri had, out of his ritual machinations, evolved a perilous idea. He had decided it would be feasible to steal from the American Mafia through its recently organized international smuggling association.

His decision had, thus far, simply amounted to a weighing of the certain, awesome risk against the immense potential gain. In the gambler's mind of Wahji Ghandhouri, the temptations presented by quick access to huge sums of cash had won over against the sobering appraisal of the ghastly hazards involved. Ghandhouri stood in desperate need of liquid assets, and after all, hadn't his rise to the heights been the product of just such winning gambles?

Now, with his interest wholly aroused, Ghandhouri put his mind to the details. Heroin. Heroin, in splendid, magnificent quantities. Heroin, the golden powder, the touchstone of Midas. To steal, say, just one hundred-kilo container. To do it soon, while this Mafia scheme remained new and green. Tap off a private supply now, early, before procedures firmed into hard practice. Better yet, be clever enough to arrange that respectably sized bits continue, automatically and invisibly, to divert themselves out of the intended mainstream and into the Ghandhouri coffers!

But for now, just one box. One hundred kilos! Say, forty-five thousand addict-sized packets per kilo. Sold at US street prices, that would bring in about $250,000 per kilo. One hundred kilos, at a quarter of a million dollars each! *Twenty-five million dollars!*

But of course, there would be heavy expenses and risks. So be generous. Reduce the net expectations to, say, half of that, per year? Four or five major US cities, perhaps. Half of $25 million is only $12 million, though. *Only?* But perhaps the actual net from this will be even less. Costs will inevitably run high. But how high? One or maybe two million dollars more per year? That would leave, say, $10 million. Yes. A nice round number. Entirely acceptable. Quite good enough.

Now, a look at the difficulties. This first heroin must be moved rapidly. Sell it fast, then get out. Get out before the Mafia suspects. My people in New York will do that. Arrange everything in advance. Assure that the sale and disposal are made and waiting!

One serious problem. Where, and by whom, will the morphine be converted to heroin? By that Corsican cutthroat Bonifacio? Never! It can be done in Spain. Or in Cairo. Or by the Syrians. But the Syrians cannot be trusted. They will sell the information. The Egyptians will demand too much in return. Probably Spain, then. This will require careful research. The rest is perfectly feasible. Perfectly feasible!

Ghandhouri concluded that as he chose, it all could indeed be done!

Palmer Tuxford Lane
Beirut, Lebanon
<u>APRIL 1966</u>

It was an hour before midnight by the time Ryder strode into the lobby of the Phoenicia, returning from his embassy meeting with Ambassador Julius Harte. The hotel night clerk handed Ryder a message slip along with his room key. Ryder opened the message and glanced at it as he strolled through the quiet lobby toward the elevators.

The message advised him that an overseas telephone call had come for him from New York City during his absence. It requested that he return the call as soon as possible, and it was marked "Urgent." Written into the space for the caller's name was "Vice President P. Tuxford Lane."

Ryder glared witheringly at the message form in his hand as he entered the elevator, and swore aloud. From the date of their first company encounter ten years past, Ryder had found himself viewing P. T. Lane as an incredible embodiment of everything Ryder considered detestable. He detested Lane's pallid, flaccid face, his pulpy physique, his wooden stance, the mincing, uncoordinated walk, the nasal, whining voice, the prissy mannerisms, and as a binder to all these, Lane's fawning, back-slashing, ruthless ambitions. And above all, Ryder wholly and actively distrusted the man.

Numerous occasions began to collect wherein Ryder bluntly and emphatically expressed his dislike for Lane to the man's face, and he finally decided to simply stay away from him. This had proven not to be too difficult, since Lane's driving ambitions led him unerringly into the US domestic marketing scene. Here, the huge commitments of such as United Airlines, Pan Am, TWA, American Airlines, Delta, National, Northwest, Continental, Western, and the rest, generally governed the company's fate. To avoid Lane, Ryder had directed himself single-mindedly toward the international market arena, the arena that he preferred anyway.

With the passage of time, P. T. Lane's ambitions, guile, talents, and maneuverings, devious or not, served him well, however. In a recent and to Ryder an appalling move only months old now, the company had elevated Lane into a dual, expanded role. P. T. Lane now managed both domestic and international marketing. Suddenly Lane had become Ryder's boss.

In his room, Ryder seated himself alongside the telephone. He glanced at his watch and made a quick calculation. It would be around four in the afternoon in New York City. He dialed the overseas operator and placed a call to Lane. Ten minutes later the call went through to the company's New York office. The office secretary came on the line, a girl Ryder knew and liked. She said, "Hello?"

Ryder said, "Hi, sexpot! Jeff Ryder here. Got your message. I guess you know you're getting me out of bed in the middle of the night!"

The girl laughed. "That'll be the day! Should be the other way around!"

Ryder grinned. "One of these days, one of these days! But aside from this budding romance, what's this urgent thing from Lane?"

The humor went out of the girl's voice. "Jeff, I don't have the faintest. He's been in the inner sanctum alone all day, going through all our files. He's still in there, and won't let anyone else in. He told me over the squawk box to get you on the phone. That's all I know, Sugar."

Ryder said, "Okay, thanks. Let's get it over with. Put me through, will you?"

The telephone went silent. Ryder waited. A minute passed, then another, and Ryder began studying his watch. Another minute. Periodically, Ryder began saying "Hello" into the telephone to forestall intermediate operators from breaking the transatlantic connection. Five minutes had gone when Lane came on the line. Lane's voice said, "Hello, is that you, Ryder?"

Ryder said, "This is Ryder."

Lane said, "Too bad you had that wait. I've had a roomful of Pan Am VIPs on my hands all afternoon, and had to get rid of them when you finally returned my call. Where have you been, out on the town, Ryder?"

Ryder listened to Lane's perjury as to the Pan Am VIPs, and answered in disgust, "That's right. Nothing but fun and games out here in this paradise."

Lane answered sarcastically, "I wouldn't be surprised, judging from a look I've had at your expense accounts. Other than the night life, though, it must be hell working where you do."

Ryder answered sourly, "I can think of worse, Lane."

Lane said abruptly, "All right, Ryder, let's get down to business. This call is costing money. I have had reason to examine all of the agreements you have established in your territory covering the hire of local sales agents. I'm not satisfied with them."

After a moment's silence while Ryder quashed his mounting annoyance, he said, "There's always room for improvement, I suppose. Some of those agents of mine aren't too bad, though. I've sold a shade over a hundred million bucks worth of our airplanes with their help! Did you have reason to notice that?"

Lane's voice whined, "That's hardly the point. The point is, maybe that should have been *five hundred* million. Your competition is selling some out there too, you know."

Ryder lost interest in curbing his irritation. He snapped, "Lane, maybe you ought to come on out here on some kind of a maiden visit and show me how a real pro swaps beads with these natives."

Lane purred, "That's part of your trouble, Ryder. You really don't know how to handle this kind of thing. You try to work from the bottom up. You waste your time with unimportant underlings. This is big business, Ryder. It has to be managed from the absolute top."

Ryder shook his head to clear the exasperation. "Listen, Lane, it's pretty clear you're leading up to something that stinks. Why don't you just forget all this horseshit about big business and spit out what you have to say?"

Lane ignored the hard insolence. "I've noticed that a number of your agency agreements pertaining to some of your prime airline prospects are falling due for renewal. Fortunately, I will be able to offer you an improvement for them. Yours will not be renewed."

Ryder visualized the work of years heading for the trash can. He asked icily, "And exactly which ones are you talking about, Lane?"

Lane answered smoothly, "That isn't important right now. What is important is this. I have been approached by one of the most influential financiers in the world, who happens also to be prominent in your area. He has offered us a most generous arrangement, under which he will *guarantee* the sale of our aircraft in no less than *eight* countries within your territory! What have you got to say about that?"

Ryder's voice rose in incredulous disgust. "Lane, you've got to be kidding! The Prophet Mohammed couldn't issue a guarantee like that! And by the way, this conversation is getting far too goddamned proprietary! They bug telephones in this place as a matter of routine!"

Land replied condescendingly, "That is the kind of thing that strikes you as important, Ryder, when actually it is trivial. The man I'm referring to is immune to interference from the kind of people who must resort to listening in on telephone calls."

Ryder snapped, "Okay, Lane, just don't forget that I warned you. Blurt out whatever you like."

Unperturbed, Lane said, "I intend to. Now listen carefully, Ryder. I want you to drop everything else and make immediate contact with this man. He has advised me that he will be in Beirut, at his headquarters there, for two days starting tomorrow. When you meet him, he will tell you what to do."

Ryder, unable to believe his ears or to control his temper, raged, "No, Lane! No bloodsucking agent is ever going to tell me what to do! I tell them what to do, my friend! And I don't care if you think you've got Moses on commission! Man, you are talking a line that will make this company the laughingstock of this underprivileged world out here, and Buster, no Son of Islam buys anything from somebody he's laughing at! Not unless he's flaying the victim alive in the process!"

Lane replied dryly, "That is no more than another expression of shortsightedness, Ryder. You will perhaps understand better once you've met this man."

Ryder rasped, "And what is this genius's name? Aladdin?"

Lane said, "His name is Mr. Wahji Ghandhouri. His Beirut headquarters are located at one of his many corporations. It is called 'The Near East Board of Trade, Ltd.' "

Ryder was stunned. He finally exclaimed, "My God, man! You can't mean it! You could have scoured this area for fifty years and not found a worse son of a bitch to represent the company than Ghandhouri! He is, hands down, the most universally despised con man in the Middle East! He's as crooked as a snake's cradle!"

Lane laughed sarcastically into Ryder's ear. "*All* powerful people are hated, Ryder. Just go and see him tomorrow. We'll discuss this further when you return to California. That's all. Good-bye." Lane hung up the telephone.

Ryder stared mutely at the silent telephone in his hand. It was a full minute before he dropped the instrument into place. Then all of a sudden, late though it was, Ryder discovered that he couldn't stand the four walls of his room. He grabbed his jacket and stormed out, heading for the lobby bar. He discovered Maxton there, and climbed onto the barstool next to him. Ryder contained his seething anger while he looked closely at Maxton to see what shape he was in. His friend seemed to be surprisingly sober, so Ryder ordered a drink and then turned to face Maxton. "Answer a question for me, old friend. If you were assigned to purposely pick the worst bastard you could find in the Middle East for an agent, who would you choose?"

Maxton's bushy eyebrows rose slightly. With a mildly thick tongue, but with scarcely a moment's hesitation, he answered. "I'd pick that head-hunting superpimp Ghandhouri, of course. How come the dumb questions tonight, old buddy?"

Listening to his moderately inebriated friend, Ryder immediately began to rid himself of his bile. He took a generous swallow of Scotch, then asked Maxton, "Here's another one for you, then. And be careful before you answer, because this one is a beaut!"

Maxton nodded and watched Ryder with curiosity. "The question is, Mr. Maxton, who the hell do you think is about to become our new agent for this whole damned scene?"

Maxton frowned and blinked. Gradually the incredible suggestion dawned on him. He peered at Ryder. "For the love of Christ, Ryder, you're not seriously suggesting we're getting into a deal with Ghandhouri? Your trolley's off!"

Ryder glumly swirled the Scotch around in his glass. "Max, you'll have a hard time believing this, but here's the story." Ryder described in detail his telephone conversation with P. Tuxford Lane.

Maxton sat in silent thought for a while, sobered by consequences he read into the Lane mandate. At length he remarked, "If that asshole Lane actually sticks us with this, we might as well throw in our jocks. If he was dumb enough to blab all that on the telephone, the word will be out in about two days. Then it'll take about a month, and after that, you and I will be as welcome with our Arab pals as a carload of pig fat!"

Ryder nodded morosely into his glass and said, "Nevertheless, that's the way it is. I suppose we'll know the worst of it after I get in to see Ghandhouri tomorrow." Ryder looked at his watch. He pushed his glass aside and said, "Speaking of tomorrow, amigo, I'm heading for the pad."

At ten o'clock the following morning, Ryder telephoned the Near East Board of Trade, Ltd. He was mildly surprised to find his call expected and, although Wahji Ghandhouri himself did not take part in the telephone conversation, Ryder experienced no difficulty in securing an appointment to meet with Ghandhouri in the afternoon. He was surprised again when he was advised by the female voice on the telephone that a car would be sent to pick him up for the meeting.

The Penthouse
Beirut, Lebanon
<u>APRIL 1966</u>

Jefferson Ryder stepped out of the private elevator that had carried him to Ghandhouri's penthouse office. He found himself viewing the spacious, lavish room with mixed impressions. Unquestionably, a small fortune had been invested in the room's furnishings and embellishments. In clashing contrast to the treasure of art objects, paintings, wall hangings, statuary, ceramics, and wood carvings, however, was an overpowering garishness in the color scheme someone had selected for the room. Apart from an end section of elegant, red Spanish tile, the entire floor was covered in a brilliant, electric shade of deep-pile blue carpeting. The ceiling had been painted Chinese red. While the room's walls were generously interspersed with rich sections of mahogany paneling, all exposed plaster surfaces had been painted gold. Ryder was struck with the cynical notion that in an attempt to achieve Napoleonesque grandeur, someone had managed instead to create an atmosphere reminiscent of a high-priced whorehouse—complete, he noticed, with a heavy scent of perfume.

Ryder paced alongside the foppishly dressed aide who had escorted him from the ground-floor reception desk as they strolled into Ghandhouri's capacious business suite. They approached a massive desk that confronted the room like a throne. There was no one else visibly present. The aide stepped to the desk and rested his hand on a corner. Ryder decided that the man had touched a concealed signal button, since shortly a door slid open along one of the walls, and two men entered.

The first, a swarthy, pear-shaped fat man having almost no forehead, gave Ryder a hard, unsmiling scrutiny, then shambled over toward an upholstered chair in one corner of the room. Ryder took amused but interested notice that the unmistakable shape of a concealed holster stood clearly outlined by the dark sweat stain spread beneath the armpit of the fat man's tight-fitting suit.

The second man was Wahji Ghandhouri. Ryder found the notorious figure mildly repugnant from that first moment. He watched as Ghandhouri's glistening black eyes flicked over him—close-set, reptilian eyes that remained cold and hostile despite the smile on the face beneath. Ryder wondered at the man's dainty steps, springing slightly from the balls of absurdly small feet. He felt disgust after the nerveless, frigid handshake, as though he'd lifted the desiccated hand of a dead man. He noticed with distaste that Ghandhouri flaunted an unfolded, heavily perfumed silk handkerchief from the fingers of his left hand.

Ghandhouri, having acknowledged Ryder's introduction by the escort, spoke in French to the aide. He told him, "Remain here Nebil, until I tell you to leave." Ghandhouri watched Ryder's face as he spoke, but saw no indication that Ryder had understood the French words. He then said, in English, "Ah, yes. Mr. Ryder, is it? You must forgive me for sometimes not using your language. You see, unlike you sensible Americans, we foreigners are obliged to master several languages in order to get along with our neighbors."

In a purposeful drawl, Ryder replied, "Why, you just go right ahead and think nothing of it, Mr. Ghandhouri. I'm used to being around folks that speak languages I can't understand."

Ghandhouri smiled and wafted the scented silk toward a baroque chair for Ryder, as he glided into the massive seat behind his desk. The aide seated himself in a chair nearby. Ghandhouri said, "Mr. Ryder, you come to me very highly recommended by your superior, the vice president Lane."

Ryder said, "Well, that's nice of him if he spoke kindly of me to you, Mr. Ghandhouri." Ryder noticed that evidently no mention was going to be made of the armed fat man in the corner.

Ghandhouri continued, "Yes, I think we will make very, very much money for your company, Mr. Ryder. It is as though you will be selling your marvelous airplanes to me, you see, since among my many other interests it is my good fortune to be more or less the owner of practically all the foremost aviation companies in this little part of the world."

Ryder thought, *this must be part of the "big business" pitch that Lane went for*. He said, "That's mighty interesting, Mr. Ghandhouri. I guess that must mean you own more than half of the stock in all those airlines. Is that right?"

Ghandhouri's eyes narrowed slightly. He smiled coldly. "In effect, that is right, Mr. Ryder."

As their conversation proceeded, Ryder continued to study Ghandhouri. He scanned the man himself, and the appurtenances Ghandhouri had chosen to display, compiling clues to the man's personal characteristics. Ryder noted a great flourish of gold in the scatter of accessories on the desk: a miniature world globe in gold; a golden calendar pad; golden pens in a gold desk set; a gold barometer; a battery of gold clocks displaying the hour of the day for half a dozen major cities around the world; a gold letter opener; a gold cigarette box; a gold carafe; and even a gold-embellished French-style telephone.

Ryder decided that Ghandhouri was inordinately anxious to announce his wealth to the world. He saw that the man habitually fingered a massive diamond set into a tie tack that was matched by an identical pair of diamonds in his cuff links. Ryder's attention moved from the cuff links to the man's slender, fragile hands. He looked at the impeccably manicured, faintly tinted fingernails; he counted the jewel-studded finger rings, some of gold, some evidently of platinum, three on each hand. Ryder's eyes shifted to the lustrous gold watch on Ghandhouri's left wrist, then to the heavy, gold-linked identification bracelet on the right.

Ryder brought his thoughts back to the thread of the conversation. He spoke to Ghandhouri. "From the sound of it, whatever you said to Mr. Lane must have made a big impression. He told me on the telephone that we might be doing business together, but I have to admit I don't know any of the details."

Ghandhouri's eyes glittered. "Yes, yes, Mr. Ryder. Of course, your superior and I discussed many aspects of the arrangements that will be made. No doubt they are of little interest to you now however. We must, of course, commence immediately with steps to remove any obstacles to the entry of my extensive services on behalf of your company. Mr. Lane advises me that you will see to the termination of a number of unsatisfactory existing arrangements that would conflict with ours."

Ryder said, "That's pretty much what he said to me too." Ghandhouri, slightly vexed at that point, turned to the silent aide and spoke rapidly in French, "Nebil, this *sans culotte* is evidently too thick headed to appreciate what he sees and hears. I am going to send him with you. Take him on the limited tour of the building. He is the sort who swills that moronic American television rubbish. He will be impressed by our communications room, the map room, and the computers. *Comprenez?*"

The aide's face remained expressionless. He simply inclined his head in affirmative reply.

Ghandhouri again excused himself to Ryder for resorting to French. He explained, "I have asked Nebil to show you some of our superb facilities. I am anxious that he shows you all that is important. Everything you will see is later to be placed at your complete disposal, Mr. Ryder, as soon as our companies have concluded negotiations."

Ryder smiled, "That will suit me fine, Mr. Ghandhouri. I'd like to learn as much as I possibly can about how you operate."

For a brief moment Ghandhouri looked suspiciously at Ryder's bland face, but then he smiled fatuously. "Ah, yes. You are already planning to enjoy life once you are under our wing in this tedious part of the world, no?" Ghandhouri, smiling grandly while his eyes remained cold, rose to his feet. Ryder and the aide followed suit. Ghandhouri said, "Well, then. Let Nebil guide you through our establishment, Mr. Ryder." He waved the perfumed kerchief. "I would be pleased to conduct you myself, but unhappily I must put through an important telephone call to New York. You see, I am buying a building in Manhattan as part of my current expansion program. You will learn more about that with Nebil. Perhaps on the next time we meet, my dear Mr. Ryder, we will have the pleasure of commencing active business relations."

Ryder said, "Perhaps we will, Mr. Ghandhouri." After another of Ghandhouri's lifeless handshakes Ryder, with the aide Nebil leading the way, headed for the elevator. Wahji Ghandhouri wasn't sure exactly why, but the meeting with the barbaric American had left him vaguely uneasy.

Later, while returning in the limousine to the Phoenicia, Ryder mentally summed up his session with Ghandhouri. He dismissed the episode as little more than a badly staged theatrical display, and concluded that P. T. Lane was inviting nothing but disastrous results for the company in any formal affiliation with Wahji Ghandhouri.

PART 3: A CARAVAN

Ali Boubahri
Teheran, Iran
APRIL 1966

The city of Teheran sweeps away from the foothills of Iran's snow-capped Elburz Mountains in a flaring, curving slant to the south, undulating at its edges like the skirt of a whirling houri. High on the city's northern perimeter, where the hem of her skirt brushes against the upthrusting mountain chain, Teheran hides from the Caspian Sea. Here, elegant homes and landed estates of the very wealthy dot the rim of the tipped plane of the land, overlooking the vast city below. Central among them, and grandest, rests the summer palace of Iran's imperial ruler, Shah Mohammad Reza Pahlavi.

Far below that exalted aerie Jefferson Ryder and John Maxton were greeted at Teheran's Mehrabad International Airport by a chill spring rain that sluiced down through the night. The wet weather inspired a session of grousing between the two Americans, a register of their disgust with the immediate prospect of a storm-drenched taxi ride across the city through nighttime Iranian traffic, invariably chaotic but tending toward berserk with rain-slickened streets.

Very few Teheran passengers deplaned, and Ryder and Maxton made their way to the passport inspection counters with little delay. Ryder was relieved to note the swarthy personage of his Iranian business agent and longtime friend, Ali Boubahri, waving and smiling in greeting beyond the entry gate. Ryder remarked to Maxton, "Bless his cotton socks and his comfy Cadillac! Our pal Ali is here to rescue us from the elements!"

The two Americans finally made their way through the entry port, and greeted and shook hands with the diminutive, good-natured agent. Ali Boubahri asked them for their baggage claim checks, and handed the checks to his uniformed driver. He directed the man to retrieve the luggage for the Americans. The three men chatted until the driver returned, then followed the man out to Boubahri's waiting Cadillac sedan.

The Cadillac swung out of the airport drive, and as it splashed through the driving rain toward the city, the three friends exchanged small talk, settling themselves for the long ride to the Teheran Hilton Hotel.

Ali Boubahri, a small, amiable man in his early forties, dearly loved anything on wheels. He owned a vast and growing wholesale distributorship for automotive parts and supplies that extended throughout Iran, in addition to his aviation business efforts in Ryder's behalf. Boubahri's business had flourished in direct ratio to Iran's burgeoning population of automobiles, and also served in support of that country's heavy construction equipment operators. Ali Boubahri, while unpretentious and soft spoken, was a considerably wealthy man. He was well able to afford indulgence of his passion for automobiles of any and all kinds, and Jeff Ryder enjoyed bantering with him over the fleet of vehicles the likable Iranian had accumulated.

Ryder said, "Okay, Ali, let's have a status report on your stable of wheels. It's been almost two months since I've seen you. What automotive extravagances have you committed this time?"

A wide smile flashed across Ali Boubahri's dark, mustached face. Looking back at Ryder from the front seat, Boubahri hinted, "As a matter of fact, Jeff, I *do* have a little surprise to show you!"

Ryder grinned. "Aha! I knew it! Well now, let me see. If you've gone and bought another one, that would make"—he started counting on his fingers as he listed Boubahri's autos—"one, this Cadillac; two, your wife's little Fiat; three, the Rolls; four, that cream-puff 1930 Duesenberg; five, your 250 GT Ferrari red bomb; six, the old Bugatti 43; and seven, the Alfa. A new one would make eight, right?"

Ali Boubahri, smiling wider than ever, nodded his head. Then Ryder exclaimed, "I think I've got it! I'll bet you've got that Aston Martin you've been pining for like a sick calf!"

Boubahri laughed in delight, his head bobbing in confirmation. "It's the DB4 GT, Jeff!"

Ryder wagged his head. "So! The DB4, with that measly 240 horsepower wasn't enough. You had to get the GT! If I remember right, that GT crowds 300, doesn't it?"

The Iranian said happily, "The book says 302, Jeff. It drives beautifully. It's a natural for these high elevations. I have had it for more than a month now, so I have had a good workout in it. Therefore I don't mind if you would like to try it before you leave!"

Ryder rubbed his hands together. "Just name the day and let me at it, Ali!" Jefferson Ryder was an enthusiastic auto buff himself, having done a share of amateur race driving in his own aging Jaguar coupe. At one time or another during their acquaintance, Ali Boubahri had let Ryder drive each of his marvelously maintained automobiles. Boubahri himself loved to race, and was a daring and skillful driver.

The avid automobile talk drifted on, into detailed pro and con discussions of various cars and engines. Engrossed in the conversation, Ryder was surprised when he glanced out and discovered that the Cadillac was already making its way up the long, straight incline of Pahlavi Boulevard that reached, with its wide, tree-lined length, up the slope to serve the summer palace of the Shah, and, lower down, the Hilton Hotel. Ryder and Maxton had arrived in Teheran at the beginning of No Ruz, the springtime festival of welcome for the Iranian New Year. The second day following their arrival would be a declared holiday, and the two Americans accepted an invitation from Ali Boubahri to join him with his wife, Anna, at the Boubahri family estate in the country. They were invited to spend the day and to attend a Boubahri cocktail party in the evening. Ryder accepted enthusiastically. He had enjoyed previous visits to that grand old villa situated high on the slopes overlooking Teheran, and within a mile of the Shah's palace. Ryder knew that Ali Boubahri kept his beloved fleet of automobiles stabled in an immense garage at the country place. Furthermore, he knew that Ali had constructed a very creditable two-mile course on his property, which he used for practice driving of his sports cars. Ryder began hoping he might get his hands on the new DB4 GT.

On the morning of the holiday Boubahri sent his Cadillac and driver to pick up the two Americans at the Hilton. As they were driven up to the splendid old villa, they found Ali outside waiting for them. The inclement weather had vanished, and in deference to the warm spring sunlight, Ali greeted them in his shirtsleeves. With a sly look, the Iranian said to Ryder, "Jeff, I know that you won't bring the subject up, and I also know that you can think of nothing else, so let's talk about the DB4!"

"GT!" Ryder added, and smiled.

Maxton groaned. "Sweet Jesus, here we go again! Listen, Ali, if you two guys are going to spend the day having hard-ons over those damned cars, I'm going to spend the day making passes at Anna!"

Unnoticed by Maxton, Anna, Boubahri's buxom, vivacious wife, had stepped onto the veranda from within the house. She had emerged just in time to hear Maxton's entire speech. She giggled delightedly as she hurried over to Maxton and seized his big arm. "That's the nicest promise I could possibly have hoped for today, Johnny Maxton! In fact I am constantly jealous of those dreadful automobiles of Ali's; I believe I will flirt right back at you!"

Maxton's face had gone awash in crimson embarrassment. Smiling sheepishly, he let his massive bulk be led into the house by the triumphantly smiling Anna.

Ali and Ryder laughed as they watched the diminutive Anna maneuver Maxton's lumbering bulk through the door. Ali asked, "What will it be first, Jeff, a drink, and then the Aston Martin, or first the Aston Martin?"

Ryder looked tentatively at the house, then smilingly said, "I'd hate to interrupt that emerging romance in there. Let's go have a look in the garage, Ali." They stepped off the veranda and headed along a graveled path leading around the house.

The path followed a winding course, meandering across an elegantly tended lawn and bordered by a profusion of newly set out plants that would soon bloom into a riot of floral color. Ali Boubahri, true to Persian tradition, loved his flower gardens, and kept a full-time gardener at work on the lovely landscaping surrounding the old estate.

Ryder commented as he crunched along the gravel path, "Ali, this country place of yours has a terrible influence on me. It makes me want a rural hideout of my own. A country spot, maybe just one of those cars of yours, a good horse, and a damned good woman, and I'd think I was in Paradise ahead of time!"

Boubahri smiled and said speculatively, "I wonder if there is a significance to the sequence of your list?"

Ryder chuckled. "The truth is, Ali, I doubt if I'd bother with the rest of that list if I couldn't find that good woman first!"

Ali trudged along in amused silence for a moment, then said, "Jeff, you sound like a Persian. Now, explain something to me. You know, of course, I am born and raised a million miles from your country, so it is supposed that I think differently. It seems I do, since there is something I have much trouble understanding; it is all this I am reading from your country these days about the way your women seem to be talking. Why do they seem to want to be like men?"

Ryder laughed. He answered, "Ali, you give me too much credit. What makes you think I understand what goes on inside a woman's head?"

Ali waved a hand expansively. "When I want to know something I go to an expert. About you, I listen to Anna. Anna says you have a good instinct about women. Then she says thank Allah that *my* such instincts are not as good as yours!"

Smiling, the two men continued their amble along the curved garden path. Ryder looked at his Iranian friend. "Ali, I'll say this about *your* instincts—they're always in the right ballpark. Every time you and I get to talking, it's either about women, cars, booze, or food. And one of these days, I'm going to get you fired up on horses!"

Boubahri chuckled and said, "It is not so different. In my garage I have something like 1500 horses already! Now, Jeff, tell me about your American women."

Ryder said, "You're talking about this 'Women's Lib' stuff that's all over the American press these days. Ali, I'm damned if I can tell you what it really is that's got our girls so worked up. I've got my own notions on what a woman is supposed to be, but that doesn't answer your question. And don't forget, I belong to the wrong generation, anyway, to even try to explain that situation!"

Boubahri shrugged. "Okay . . . but since women are such interesting things to talk about, tell me those notions of yours."

"Sure, Ali, just don't go around quoting your source," Ryder quipped. He pondered his words, and then went on, "It may be tough to admit, but the fact is, the ladies are important. Maybe you could say that a man is kind of like one of your great race car engines. All by itself it's damn fine and wins a lot of the time. But, if you just add an eight-pound supercharger, it turns into a world-beater and wins all the time! Doesn't Anna kind of do that for you, Boubahri?"

Ali nodded, smiling. "Yes, Anna surely does! But like you, I too do not wish to be quoted!"

Ryder laughingly added, "It wouldn't matter with Anna. She knows it damned well already! Your Persian gals are wise. They know how big they really are in the scheme, and they relax and enjoy being 200 percent woman. I don't know what the hell's the matter with some of our gals back home, the ones who seem to want to grow hair on their chests. It seems to me they're just going to turn sex into something about as interesting as chewing gum."

Boubahri chortled. "From that answer to my question, I certainly hope we do not import that idea into Iran! Now, I believe we should shift gears from women to cars for a while! Here is the garage." He took out a ring of keys and unlocked a side door, which admitted the two men into a small office. Spread across a desk was an assortment of folders and technical pamphlets on the Aston Martin that Ali had been studying. He led Ryder on across the office and through a glass-paned door that stood open to the gloom of the garage's cavernous interior. Ali reached alongside the doorway and flipped a switch, flooding the garage interior with lights from overhead.

Ryder's admiring voice echoed in the huge room. "Boubahri's motor pool! Lord, look at those lovely brutes!" With the exception of the Cadillac, all of Boubahri's cars were there, parked side by side and gleaming under the lights. Nearest in the line, wearing a lustrous metallic blue finish, rested the sleek new Aston Marten DB4 GT two-seater.

Boubahri walked over to the front wall of the garage and pressed a switch to open the garage door in front of the new car. The door slid upwards, letting sunlight reach in to dance on the bright chrome spokes of the Aston Martin's wire wheels.

Ali watched as Ryder circled the beautiful new machine, admiring its details. During Ryder's silent inspection, Ali mentioned a few of the car's vital statistics. "Three point six liters, Jeff. Aluminum block and head, and twin overhead cams. Seven bearings on the crankshaft. Four-wheel disc brakes."

Ryder asked, "In the dumb-question department, Ali, what's the 'DB' stand for?"

Boubahri smiled and replied, "No glamour in it, Jeff . . . 'DB' stands for David Brown. He is the owner of the Aston Martin Company, and—of all things—is a tractor manufacturer too!" Boubahri walked over and climbed in behind the wheel. He said, "Come on, Jeff, let's take her for a spin." Ryder rubbed his palms together and clambered in next to his friend. Ali started the powerful engine.

Boubahri eased the throbbing car out into the sunlight and let the engine idle long enough to warm itself up. He drove across the wide concrete apron in front of the garage, and into a narrow, graveled drive leading to his closed-circuit track, which curved through the woodlands and fields of the estate. Ali raced the fiery car expertly around the track, then stopped and traded places with Ryder.

Ryder drove the circuit then, holding the Aston Martin to a modest pace while he accustomed himself to the steering and to the feel of the clutch and the brakes and the gear ratios, and to the tremendous power available under his foot. Ali Boubahri offered a few coaching comments, and then, back at the driveway to the garage, he got out of the car. Leaning in the door, he said, "Go play with it, Jeff. You'll get more out of it alone, and besides, I've got to put a new set of plugs in the little Fiat for Anna."

Ryder grinned and said, "This is too much, Ali! And the best is yet to come!"

Boubahri grinned back and started to close the car door. He paused, then poked his head back in again. "Listen, Jeff, my track is great except that it has no decent straightaway. If you want to see what she'll do flat out, take her out the gate down on the south end, where the track runs next to the highway. There is a well-graded, three-mile straight run to the east from there, with good visibility and no side roads, other than private driveways. Beyond that, the road winds up the mountain. Just one thing. If you try the road, look out for my neighbors next door on the east. We don't really get along too well. Two of the brothers are racing nuts. They've seen me in the DB4, and are trying to catch me on the road, to race. Anyway, keep your eyes open for a bright yellow Lamborghini or a black Porsche Spyder. They belong to the Rafats. Hassan, the older one, drives the Lamborghini. Ishmail drives the Porsche. Jeff, they play dirty."

Boubahri closed the car door then, and, leaning down and smiling, saluted as Ryder eased out the clutch pedal and drove away.

The Race
Teheran, Iran
<u>**APRIL 1966**</u>

Despite the recent rains, after the third circuit of the track the Aston Martin began raising a billow of dust in its wake from the hard-rolled but unpaved surface. A light breeze blowing from the east kept the dust drifting away from the track, however, and Ryder kept going. He edged the Aston Martin's speed up with each round as he gained familiarity with the powerful car's driving characteristics.

The east wind, while helping move the dust aside, also brought a less pleasant reminder of its presence. Ryder began to notice that each time he reached one particular tight curve that sliced through a dense stand of oak and elm trees, a heavy, putrid odor had drifted in, overpowering the rain-freshened spring scent of the air. The unpleasant stench became distracting enough, finally, to cause Ryder to think more about the smell ahead than about his driving each time he approached that particular turn. Annoyed, he decided to follow Boubahri's suggestion and abandon the track to give the straightaway on the main road a try.

He continued around the course to its south edge, then out through a gated opening to the main road. Ryder closed and latched the gate behind himself, then headed the Aston Martin eastward along the graded, unpaved avenue, letting the car accelerate steadily. He kept an eye on the climbing tachometer and speedometer needles, and had just watched his speed creep through 80 miles an hour when he noticed, ahead and coming from the left, a heavy plume of dust racing down a crossroad toward the road he was on. Watching the progress of the dust cloud, he realized that it would come close to intercepting him as it reached the main road. Ryder guessed it would be someone from the neighboring Rafat place that Ali had mentioned, coming out to challenge him to race.

Ryder took his foot from the accelerator pedal and let the Aston Martin slow itself. As he approached the point of intercept with the dust cloud he saw its cause ahead of it, the yellow splash of the Lamborghini that Ali Boubahri had described. Beyond and alongside the Lamborghini, the black Porsche Spyder paced abreast of it.

The two sleek sports cars roared into the road ahead of Ryder and stopped, each facing on opposite diagonals away from the Aston Martin, with their tails close together near the center of the road. The roadway was effectively blocked by the positions of the two cars. Ryder saw the door come open on the driver's side of the Lamborghini, and presumed that whoever was driving the yellow car intended to have something to say. Accordingly, he halted the Aston Martin a few feet behind the two idling sports cars, and rolled down his window. The driver of the Lamborghini, visible to Ryder only as a dark silhouette, drew quickly back into the low-slung yellow car, and pulled its door shut. Immediately, both the Lamborghini and the Porsche began revving their engines in bursts of power. The result, as intended, was to send up a choking cloud of fine yellow dust raised by the blasting exhausts. Helped by the light breeze, the dust enveloped the Aston Martin completely in a blinding ochre fog.

Ryder swore, and hastily rolled up the side window. Disgusted, he recalled Boubahri's precautionary remark to expect these people to "play dirty." The dirty play was now a literal reality. Ryder's thoughts spun aggressively. The maneuvers of the other two, to all appearances, were well rehearsed. Ryder saw that the logical move, the one they probably anticipated, would be for the Aston Martin to reverse its course and flee back the way it had come. He shoved the gearshift into reverse and spun the steering wheel to the right, backing the car through a sharp swing out of the gagging dust. He stamped on the brakes, stopping the car at right angles to the roadway, apparently prepared to wheel to the left, back toward Boubahri's place. Ryder held the clutch pedal down, slid the Aston Martin into first gear, and watched as the yellow Lamborghini and the black Porsche charged into new positions. As he had expected, the other two drivers executed a precise maneuver. The Porsche moved first, backing violently in an arc exactly parallel to Ryder's auto, and sliding to a stop alongside and to the right of the Aston Martin. The yellow Lamborghini, as soon as the Porsche had cleared past its rear, reversed with equal violence and slammed to a stop facing out of the side road from which it had come. Ryder watched the Porsche driver next to him through the haze of dust, and as he'd hoped and expected, saw the man begin to crank the steering wheel to the left, prepared to stay as close as possible to Ryder's Aston Martin as it tried to escape back to Boubahri's. Ryder couldn't see the yellow Lamborghini's driver across the road through the dust, but he was sure that the yellow car was likewise preparing for the chase back to the west. In the instant it took for the Porsche driver to start his front wheels angling to the left, Ryder engaged the Aston Martin's clutch and punched down on the throttle, whipping the blue car through a wild, roaring takeoff to the right, eastward, between his two antagonists. He caught both of the other two drivers in flat-footed surprise as he put the DB4 into that screaming acceleration to the right instead of to the left.

Ryder had the eminent satisfaction of watching a huge rooster tail of flying dust and gravel explode all over the other two cars behind the Aston Martin's churning rear wheels. Intent now on the race he'd been forced into, Ryder put the Aston Martin smartly through its gears, letting the sleek car have all the power it was designed to use. Meanwhile he kept an eye on the mileage as it rapidly rolled up on the odometer. Ryder knew his present advantage would disappear when the three miles of straightaway were gone. The other drivers would be familiar with the road's winding mountain climb that Ali said lay ahead, while Ryder would have to take it as it came.

He watched the tachometer needle wind past 5,000, and began straining his eyes into the distance ahead, trying to detect evidence of the last of the straight stretch. The terrain rose gradually, and Ryder finally made out a sweeping turn to the left, beginning about a half mile away. He stared into the rearview mirror, searching through his own trailing dust for the pursuing racers.

He saw the yellow glint of the Lamborghini. It seemed to be five or six hundred yards behind. Ryder was unable to see any sign of the black Porsche. As he roared down on the approaching turn he eased off the throttle and downshifted, then let the revs wind up above 5,000 as he tore screaming through that first turn, finding it gentle and well banked. The next bend, to the right, was much tighter, and although Ryder braked and shifted down through two gears, he still drifted with all four wheels through the turn. From that point on the road became a nightmare of unpredictability. Ryder enjoyed himself immensely, although he was sweating from head to foot, and his nerves were taut as bowstrings.

Whenever he could find an instant's opportunity he glanced into the mirrors, checking on the Lamborghini. He gauged that the pursuing yellow car might have closed the gap between them by a very small margin, but Ryder was pleased to find that he was giving the other driver a fair bone to chew, along with a continual fog of dust and flying gravel.

As the wild, roaring race hurtled on up the mountain it began to seem pointless to Ryder. Unwilling to simply abandon the race by pulling over to a stop, nor caring to trust the Lamborghini driver, Ryder began watching for a chance to make a quick turnaround. He finally found what he wanted at a blind, hair-raisingly tight switchback. He entered the blind turn somewhat too fast, and since he found himself obliged to let the Aston Martin slide broadside toward the wide, firm outside shoulder anyway, he purposely oversteered. He let the car reverse its own direction in a sliding, turning stop. Ryder then slid the gearshift into reverse, and backed well out of the way of the Lamborghini. He put the Aston Martin into first gear and waited. An instant later the yellow Lamborghini came howling into the hairpin turn. Its driver, knowing the tight turn was in store, managed a fully controlled slide through it, and ended up perfectly positioned for a thundering acceleration on up the slope. But the blue Aston Martin changed all that. The Lamborghini driver was literally helpless to alter his car's course, even though, as his high-speed, sliding turn developed, he saw that Ryder had tricked him. Ryder simply tramped on the throttle, and the Aston Martin shot back downhill behind the yellow car, leaving the Lamborghini floundering in another dense cloud of dust and gravel. Ryder got a momentary glimpse at the yellow car as he flashed away behind it, and saw that its right rear quarter was crunched and bent. He grinned to himself as the DB4 howled down the mountain, reasonably sure that the dents in the Lamborghini had been delivered by its own stablemate, the black Porsche Spyder.

Ryder felt a greater sense of confidence on the road as he retraced it, and pressed his driving skills to the limit racing through the downgrade curves. When he reached the homebound straightaway Ryder floored the accelerator pedal. He roared past the private drive leading into the Rafat estate with the speedometer needle resting quietly on 120 miles per hour, and watched a group of figures scatter wildly out of his way as the Aston Martin screamed past the black Porsche Spyder. It stood immobilized in the road with its left front fender collapsed tightly against a flat tire. The yellow Lamborghini was a plume of dust following distantly behind.

Goat Hides
Teheran, Iran
APRIL 1966

The warm spring sunshine had inspired Anna Boubahri to serve lunch outside. She joined her husband and their guests, Ryder and Maxton, at a comfortable, umbrella-shaded patio table. The four chatted amiably. Nearby, on its own low bench, a beautifully ornate and polished copper samovar steamed quietly. Anna had declared a moratorium on the serving of hard liquor during the half hour or so just before lunch, insisting that the men take, instead, a cup of her fragrant tea. When Ali made a wry face about this she indignantly announced that her dictum would not seriously inconvenience Ali nor any other determined intemperate who might be present, since, she informed the men, her luncheon menu was to feature Iranian blinis with Golden Imperial caviar, and all the vodka anyone cared to consume. Anna's announcement was greeted with a contented smile from her husband, an enthusiastic vote of approval from Jeff Ryder, and a great bear hug from John Maxton, who had been sampling the vodka all morning anyway.

With the tea served, Ali happily insisted that Ryder tell again, for Anna's benefit, his morning's episode in the Aston Martin against the Rafats and their now-dented pair of sports cars. Anna Boubahri clapped her hands and giggled with delight as she listened to Jeff Ryder's account of the event, and Ali sailed into convulsions of laughter for the second time.

After Ryder had satisfied Ali Boubahri's final barrage of jubilant, detailed questions regarding the Rafats' misadventures of the morning, he asked Boubahri, "Ali, you and Anna are people who get along with everybody. What's the rub with these Rafats?"

Boubahri sipped his tea, then replied, "It isn't that we have any serious disagreement with them, Jeff. In fact, they are invited to our cocktail party tonight, and will almost certainly be here. Especially after your automobile happening," he added with a chortle. "There are certain things about the Rafats and their business affairs and methods that we do not admire particularly. They are, in their own way, very powerful people in this country. As neighbors, we try to get along with them."

Anna, giving Ali a reproachful look, said, "Why don't you say what you mean, Mr. Boubahri?" Turning to Jeff, she said, "The fact is, those Rafats are nothing but a pack of evil thieves, and they are very dangerous as enemies. They are arrogant and very rude, and some of them are unbalanced mentally."

Boubahri protested. "Anna! Jeff and John are not interested in the gossip that goes around."

Anna smiled complacently, then said, "It is not gossip, it is fact! But you are right, Ali, the Rafats do not represent a pleasant subject of conversation."

Boubahri simply waved his arms in demonstration of his sense of futility with Anna.

Ryder, while amused by the Boubahris' friendly bickering, thought nevertheless that a change of subject was a good idea. He said, "By the way, Ali, what in the devil is causing that stench coming out of the woods over there on the east side of your track? It smells as though you've got a runaway batch of Limburger out there!"

Ali Boubahri smiled, puzzled. "Are you joking with me, Jeff?"

Ryder answered, "Not at all! On the east side run of your track, about three quarters of the way back, there's a nasty curve that eases through a thick stand of trees." Boubahri nodded. Ryder went on. "That's the smelly spot. I didn't notice anything until the breeze came up. If it hadn't been for that foul stink, though, I probably wouldn't have gone out onto the main road."

Anna interrupted. "If you men are going to continue discussing such unwholesome ideas, I shall refuse to cook the blinis!"

Ali, still with a puzzled look on his face, said, "The blinis come first! We will take a little ride after lunch, though, and see if we can solve Jeff's mystery."

Anna accepted this as a signal to serve lunch. She went into the house, and returned carrying a large silver tray on which were arrayed a tempting variety of delicacies. She placed the tray on the table and invited the men to start helping themselves. Anna busied herself cooking the blinis. She served the delicate, wafer-thin pancakes hot, along with a choice of yoghurt sauce or caviar. Among the delicacies on the large tray there rested a bowl heaped with Golden Imperial caviar, accompanied by dishes of chopped onion, lemon slices, and chopped whites and yolks of boiled egg.

Savoring the delicious caviar, Ryder asked, "Anna, this is a rare privilege! I thought this type of caviar was strictly the private property of the Shah. Isn't that so?"

Anna smiled conspiratorially. "Jeff, you are quite correct! Ali has discovered, though, a lovely black market source for the Golden Imperial, and we give ourselves this treat once in a while!"

Ali had produced a huge bottle of vodka, which he proceeded to pour generously into the glasses on the table. The group fell to, and with gusto demolished Anna's delicious lunch.

Sated with the rich food, everyone leaned back from the table and sipped coffee. Boubahri, holding his stomach and groaning, contentedly said, "I think your mystery expedition will be a welcome exercise, Jeff. After so much to eat I need to move around a little. Anna is trying to make me fat so that all the other women will cease desiring me so fiercely!"

Anna turned down the corners of her mouth. "Mr. Boubahri, it is you who should see to it that all those women you speak of become fat and ugly, since it is you who has all those fierce desires!"

Boubahri smiled at his wife, "I confess, dear Anna, that I do delight in studying the loveliness of the female form when it passes before me. However, since I am spent to the utmost in accommodating your vigorous demands on my body, what can I offer these passing damsels but a vacant promise?"

Anna's face went pink, and in mock outrage, she swept up the silver tray and bustled into the house, wriggling her rounded bottom provocatively.

Ali smiled at Anna's retreating form. Then he turned to Ryder. "Now we should go take a little auto ride, before Anna decides how she will get even with me!" He got up from his chair. Ryder stood too, asking, "How about it, Max. Coming along?"

Maxton studied the half-full tumbler of vodka in his hand, then shook his head. "I'm not swapping good booze for a bad smell. You guys can tell me all about it when you get back."

Ryder followed Ali to the concrete apron in front of the vast garage. The little Fiat sedan stood there where Ali had left it that morning after installing new spark plugs. They got into the car, with Boubahri driving, and headed out to the practice course. Boubahri drove onto the track, and when they came up to the turn through the grove of trees, Boubahri stopped the Fiat, and the two men left the car on foot. Although the light breeze had faded, the foul smell still filled the air.

Boubahri looked puzzled. He wrinkled his nose and said, "Something very large must be very dead near here!" He wandered into the wooded grove, and Ryder followed. The two men walked along in silence, using the increasingly heavy stench to guide them as they navigated through the thick stand of trees. They found themselves moving in an easterly direction, and Ali said, "Very soon now we will reach the edge of my property." He smiled at Ryder. "Perhaps the bad smell is owned by my neighbors, the Rafats."

Peering ahead through the trees as they walked, Ryder saw a stone fence stretching across their path. Boubahri told him, "That fence marks my property line, Jeff. For whatever it may be worth, it is not my land that stinks."

They came up to the rock barrier, which stood almost five feet high, and looked across it into the shaded gloom of the continuing forest beyond. Boubahri shrugged. "Well, we've come this far, and we might as well keep going. I'm curious now." The peculiar stench had grown to acrid strength.

Ali clambered over the piled fieldstone fence, and Ryder followed suit. They continued to tramp across the carpet of fallen leaves into Rafat woodlands. After traveling several minutes through the trees they came to a small clearing occupied by a stone building secluded by the tall surrounding trees, and situated at the end of a narrow dirt road that disappeared into the forest to the east. Boubahri pointed to a great stack of animal hides piled in front of the stone structure. "So, there's the mysterious stench! Goat hides! What in the world would the elegant Rafats want with a pile of stinking goat hides?"

Ryder found his attention focused elsewhere. The stone building, seen from the front, turned out to be an open-fronted shed, once a stable. The interior of the old stable was filled, as high as they could be stacked, with cargo crates. Ryder ran his finger speculatively over the scar on his cheek. The cargo boxes and their markings appeared identical to those he had seen in Jordan, including the strange brass screws.

Jeff Ryder wondered if somehow he could manage to get photographs of the stored crates without Boubahri's notice. Then Ali solved the problem for him. The Iranian excused himself, making a joke by referring to an Iranian phrase that, translated, meant "the reply of the tea," and disappeared behind the corner of the stone shed. Ryder hastily extracted the Minox from his pocket, adjusted the little camera, and rapidly snapped a number of exposures. The Minox was safely back in his pocket when Ali Boubahri reappeared.

Bitter Cocktails
Teheran, Iran
APRIL 1966

Anna Boubahri had assigned Ryder and Maxton the use of a large, comfortable room on the second floor of the Boubahris' huge old villa. Their room, situated on the front of the house, offered a panoramic view of the artfully lighted circular drive leading up to the house, and to its porte cochere at the entry. Early guests were beginning to arrive for the Boubahri cocktail soirée. Jeff Ryder stood at one of the front windows, inserting his cufflinks and watching expensive limousines deliver elegantly dressed couples to the entrance below. Maxton lay sprawled on one of the beds in the room, clad in underwear and socks, and trying with poor success to drink from a glass of beer without moving from his prone position.

Ryder had described to Maxton the old stone shed and the piles of goat hides and cargo containers he and Boubahri had discovered that afternoon. He commented, "Ali tells me that the old stable on the Rafat spread has stood there empty and deserted for as long as he can remember. He says when he was a kid he used to play around there with the Rafat brats."

Maxton grunted. "So you've got this big notion that the boys next door are bad guys."

Ryder shrugged. "Hell, I don't know. But they've got those shipping crates over there, and ten to one they're just like the ones at Lahoud's. Also, as far as I'm concerned, whoever put the stuff in that shed is trying to keep it out of sight."

Maxton remarked, "But not out of smell. If that stuff's bad loot, then why the stinking goat hides?"

Ryder turned away from the window. "Maybe to cover up the rest of the stuff from would-be snoopers. Who'd want to stick his nose and hands into a putrid pile like that?"

Maxton raised bushy eyebrows. "Yeah, I guess that could figure." Then, to needle Ryder, he added, "Tell you what—if your racing buddy, Rafat, shows up tonight, I'll ask him what the hell that garbage is doing in his stone shed."

Ryder rose to the bait. "Like hell you will! I've already got Ali convinced there's no point in us telling Rafat we were poking around on his property!"

Maxton chuckled. "Okay, Charlie Chan. Just trying to be helpful."

Ryder walked over to his open suitcase and pulled out a black knit tie. "If you're so damned anxious to help, get your pants on. Some of the airline brass will be in that crowd down there tonight. Some of your old friends. You can help by being nice to them."

Maxton belched and rolled into a sitting position on the edge of the bed. "No problem. I'll be glad to help for about an hour. Then I'm going to get quietly snockered. Gimme them pants."

By the time Ryder and Maxton came down to join the party a dozen or so couples had already arrived, and were collected around the room in assorted groups, quietly conversing. Ali Boubahri was busy at the door greeting a steady flow of new arrivals, while Anna moved around the great living room in animated pleasure, pausing at each of the clusters of people to chat for a moment. Ryder and Maxton headed over to the bar and stood there looking over the scene while the red-jacketed barman poured them a pair of Scotches with water. As new people drifted into the room, the two Americans moved away from the bar and stood to one side, out of the flow of casual movement.

Anna Boubahri, plump and buxom above, possessed a striking pair of legs, and had them displayed to full advantage for the occasion beneath the straight black sheath of a miniskirted cocktail dress. Ryder and Maxton watched her in fond amusement, bouncing gaily around the room, spreading a wake of smiles and happy atmosphere. She spied the two Americans standing alone and sped toward them, shaking an accusing finger.

Coming up to them, she scolded, "Jeff and John! I cannot permit two such handsome and eligible males to escape from my ladies!" She linked her arm around Maxton's massive bicep. "There is someone I especially want *you* to meet, John. One of my lovely acquaintances has inquired about you this evening. She thought you might be an oil man, because you look so strong! She *loves* big, strong men. Both of her husbands have been big and strong! Unfortunately, neither of them are still living, however, and she is quite lonely."

Maxton, looking demoralized, shook his head violently in protest. "No! Look, Anna, I'll just get tongue-tied! I don't know how to talk to real girls! Anyway, I don't savvy the lingo."

Anna poked her nose up. "Well! I like that, Mr. John Maxton! Am *I* not a real girl? You most certainly know how to speak to *me*! As to your other silly excuse, Olga speaks English every bit as well as I!" Anna pivoted around, still clinging firmly to Maxton's arm. Her eyes darted around the room. Then, pointing delicately but triumphantly, she declared, "There! Over there, John, standing beside the piano. That is my friend Olga—the girl in the white dress."

Maxton and Ryder both looked across the room and saw Olga. Even at a distance it was evident that Olga was an exceptionally attractive woman. Raven black hair swept back from her oval face, and tumbled luxuriantly over her shoulders. Her slender, sensuous figure was admirably affirmed by a clinging, short-skirted white silken dress. She stood gracefully alongside the grand piano, listening attentively to conversation from an aged, gray-haired Iranian man.

Olga's face swung toward Anna, and to John Maxton's vast dismay, Anna beckoned vigorously to the lovely woman. The trio watched as Olga spoke briefly to her elderly companion. The old gentleman smiled and bowed slightly as Olga departed.

Ryder grinned, alternately glancing at the disconcerted Maxton's perspiring face, and watching the graceful swing of Olga's handsome form as she moved nearer. Anna continued to clutch Maxton's arm fiercely. She turned to Ryder. "I'll see to you next, Mr. Jeff Ryder, so stop looking jealous. In the meanwhile, though, you may wish to have a word with General Tajodod. I just noticed Ali escorting him in."

Ryder, admiring Anna's superb awareness, mentally thanked again the good fortune that had led him to this Boubahri couple. He glanced in the direction Anna had indicated by a slight nod of her head. He saw General Omar Tajodod, chairman of Iran Air, strolling into the room with his wife on his arm. Ryder excused himself hastily, and strode away before Olga had arrived.

Jeff Ryder enjoyed a warm and reciprocal friendship of long standing with the dignified old chairman. He found himself greeted with genuine feeling by both General Tajodod and by his gentle, soft-spoken wife. Ryder had served as host to the fine old couple during a week's visit they had paid to California, and although Mrs. Tajodod spoke very little English, he had succeeded in making their experience unforgettably pleasant.

Ryder led the Iranian couple to a comfortable grouping of easy chairs in a relatively quiet corner of the thronged room, and the three seated themselves. Ryder visited with the general and his wife for about half an hour, mixing a useful share of business conversation in with sociable pleasantries and reminiscences. He was watching for an opportunity to make a courteous exit when Ali Boubahri appeared at his side. Ali affably greeted the Tajodods again and chatted for a moment, then said to Ryder, "Jeff, there is someone I'd like you to meet, whenever General Tajodod will excuse you." General Tajodod voiced his pleasure in visiting with Ryder. Ryder stood, and after shaking hands with the general and paying his respects to Mrs. Tajodod, departed with Ali.

Boubahri, speaking quietly to Ryder as they walked away, said, "Hassan Rafat has arrived. He scarcely had the courtesy to say hello before he began probing me about the auto episode. He is in a vicious mood and already partly drunk. If you don't mind, I wish you would speak with him, Jeff. If you do not, I'm afraid he will destroy my party."

Ryder smiled at Boubahri. "We can't let anybody spoil a good bash like this one, Ali! Lead me to him."

Boubahri moved through the crowded room, followed by Ryder, searching for his neighbor and guest, Hassan Rafat. Ali finally spotted him and paused, pointing him out. Ryder looked Rafat over. He saw a slender young man of medium height wearing a Van Dyke beard and pencil-thin mustache. His thick head of black hair hung at an extreme length. Rafat was dressed in a bright purple corduroy suit. His shirt front and cuffs were embellished with fluffing riffles of white lace, and he wore an absurdly immense lavender silk bow at his throat. He was shod in glistening yellow pumps.

Rafat stood posed, with a full martini glass in his hand, talking to a tall, astonishingly dressed young woman. In contrast with the fashionable elegance of the rest of the women in the room, the girl's costume was outrageous. She wore a pair of wildly patterned pants, skintight at the hips and thighs, and flaring at the knee into immensely belled, floor-sweeping bottoms. Reaching barely to her hips, the pants were cut low to hang well below her bared umbilicus in front, and revealed the upper portion of the cleavage between her buttocks in back. In lieu of a top, the girl wore a tiered, beaded fringe across her chest that hung, parted, over her naked breasts. Several waist-length strands of heavy glass beads hung around her neck, and her ears supported huge, golden, hooped earrings.

Ryder muttered to Boubahri, "For Christ's sake, Ali, what's Anna got to say about that getup?"

Boubahri winced, whispering, "I don't even want to think about it, Jeff! No one else in this room would have the effrontery to bring such a sight as that into this home. No one but a Rafat."

Hassan Rafat pretended not to notice Boubahri and Ryder's presence until Ali Boubahri touched him on the arm. He turned his narrow head and stared rudely at his host for a moment. Without smiling he said, "What do you want, Boubahri?"

Ali smiled and calmly said, "Hassan, I believe you told me you would like to meet the driver of the Aston Martin who beat you in your race this morning. This is the man. Mr. Jeff Ryder. Jeff, this is Mr. Hassan Rafat."

The pupils of Rafat's eyes suddenly began to dance from side to side as he glared at Boubahri. Without acknowledging the introduction or even glancing at Ryder, Rafat snarled, "Your man Ryder did not beat me in anything, Boubahri! I don't know what he has told you, but what he did was become frightened by the first turn of the road and then abandon the run entirely!" Rafat's eyes, still flicking back and forth in wild oscillation, slid his gaze to Ryder. He added scornfully, "Sports car racing is not for old men who frighten so easily."

Ryder stared coolly back into Rafat's wild, agitated eyes. He drawled, "It's interesting to meet you face to face, Mr. Rafat. I didn't see much of you this morning on the road, except in my rearview mirror."

Rafat's voice grew suddenly shrill. He shouted, "You will never again enjoy that view of me, American! The next time, with your cowardly driving, you will eat my dirt! I will drive you to *death*!"

Ryder smiled. He quietly replied, "Every driver in a race usually finds some part of it he's unhappy about afterward. I didn't care much for the way ours started, Mr. Rafat. You didn't like the way it ended. I'd say that makes us about even. "

The blood drained from Rafat's face. In pure rage his voice flattened metallically. "You will regret having met me, American. We are not even. There is a debt you will pay me, and I will find a way to collect!"

Ryder did not like the turn the conversation had taken. He saw that flecks of white froth had appeared in the corners of Hassan Rafat's mouth. The Iranian's hands were quivering uncontrollably, and, unnoticed by the enraged young man, the contents of the glass he held were dribbling down the front of his purple corduroy suit. Ryder was abruptly relieved of the need for finding a way to end the discussion. Rafat suddenly hurled his martini glass smashing to the floor, and charged blindly out of the room, rudely shouldering men and women guests alike out of his way. The tastelessly dressed girl fled in frantic pursuit behind him.

Ryder turned to Ali Boubahri. He saw that his friend was badly shaken by the episode. Ryder put a hand on Boubahri's arm. "Ali, I'm sorry I caused that blowup. I didn't know how short that punk's fuse was."

Boubahri shook his head. In a quiet voice he said, "There's nothing for you to apologize for, Jeff. Truthfully, it is as Anna said. Hassan Rafat is not in full control of his senses, particularly when he becomes angry. I should have been honest and warned you. Unfortunately, he angers too easily." Ali looked into Ryder's eyes. "Jeff, that fool means what he says. You must keep away from him."

At that moment Anna hurried up to the two men, wearing a look of mixed concern and puzzled amusement on her face. She came close to them and whispered, "I'm so pleased that you've driven away that dreadful girl! But what in heaven is wrong with the nasty Mr. Rafat?"

As Ali quietly explained the situation to his wife, Ryder glanced around at the nearby faces of other guests. He saw that some showed serious concern while others appeared amused and pleased over Rafat's discomfiture. A few of the men, total strangers to Ryder, actually smiled and nodded to him, in unspoken applause.

Ali and Anna Boubahri excused themselves and went off in separate directions, circulating among their guests to try to remedy the disturbed amiability of the gathering.

The Moment of Truth
Teheran, Iran
APRIL 1966

On the morning following Ali Boubahri's cocktail party, Jeff Ryder and John Maxton were driven back to the Hilton Hotel by Ali's chauffeur. The two Americans spent the day in an exhausting succession of business meetings with segments of the Iranian airline's staff and with appropriate Iranian governmental offices. Both men were bone weary by the time their taxi made its way up the curving drive to the hotel's entrance at the end of the day. Chatting wearily as they walked through the sprawling lobby toward the reception desk to pick up their room keys, they agreed they would nap for an hour or so before meeting for dinner.

Ryder entered his room and draped his jacket over the back of a chair. He sat on the bed and loosened his tie, then removed his shoes and stretched out on the bed with a sigh of relief. Then the telephone rang. Ryder swore heartily and stared at the instrument, letting it ring a second time. Resignedly, he picked it up and growled, "Hello."

A familiar sounding male voice said, "This is C. James. I'd like to get together with you as soon as it's convenient." Ryder puzzled momentarily over the terse sentence, then remembered. The CIA. The caller had to be Jim Crawford or someone sent by him. Sighing tiredly to himself, Ryder said, "Okay. Where and when?"

The voice said, "I'm in the Hunt Bar, next to the lobby. Right now would be fine. I'll catch you when you come down."

Ryder said, "Give me five minutes," and hung up the telephone. Grumbling to himself, Ryder jammed his feet back into his brogans and tied the laces, then straightened his tie. He went to the bathroom sink and splashed a little water on his face, toweled dry, and combed his hair. He grabbed his jacket from the chair and strode out of the room.

Leaving the elevator, Ryder started across the lobby toward the Hunt Bar, searching faces as he walked.

He saw James Crawford seated alone on one of the large sofas, watching. The CIA man, satisfied that he had been seen by Ryder, rose from the sofa and turned toward a spiral staircase winding down to the lower-level patio deck of the hotel. Ryder, half the lobby's length behind Crawford, followed him down the stairs and outside.

Fair afternoon weather had brought out a contingent of sun worshipers and tennis players from among the hotel's guests. Diehard laggards from this group were congregated near the outside cocktail bar, clinging to the late-afternoon warmth. Crawford moved to an empty end of the bar and signaled for the bartender. Ryder came up to the bar and stood a few feet away from Crawford, deciding to let the CIA man take the next step. When the bartender had finished taking Crawford's drink order, he stopped by to take Ryder's. Ryder asked for a Bloody Mary, and the bartender left to assemble the two drinks.

Crawford looked at Ryder and casually said, "I'd like to buy your drink."

Ryder answered, "Thanks. I accept." He moved over, nearer to Crawford. Out of earshot of other bar customers, Crawford said, "Let's get the drinks and move over to one of those umbrella tables. We'll make ourselves look like a couple of lonely American traveling salesmen."

Ryder smiled and said, "That won't be a hard act for me to put on. The description fits me like a glove, if you just add being a shade played out at the moment."

James Crawford smiled back. "Hard day, eh? Well, I'm sorry, Jeff, but there's not much choice of timing in this business."

The bartender returned with the two drinks. Crawford paid in cash, and the two men carried their drinks casually to a table adjacent to the unoccupied swimming pool.

Jeff Ryder leaned back in his deck chair, and with a sigh stretched his legs out. He took a sip of his drink, and looked over at Crawford. "You are a long way from home."

Crawford lounged comfortably with his back to the pool. He nodded and said, "I'm beginning to think this project of ours is going to ruin my per diem budget. The only reason I'm here is to intercept you, and you're not an easy man to catch."

Ryder eyed the CIA man. "Okay, so I'm flattered. But I've also got the feeling I'd better brace myself for what comes next."

Crawford's tone turned businesslike. "Jeff, it certainly didn't take you long to get your feet wet in this thing. On my way out here I stopped for a chat with Ambassador Harte about his report of your Jordan episode. He went over the results of our look into that stuff you pulled out of Amman. It has already helped us significantly. In fact, the material you've turned up was sufficiently worthwhile to bring me out here for some conversation with you."

Ryder shrugged. "Well, I'm glad we're not wasting anybody's time so far. Can you tell me where that Jordan stuff fits in with the big picture?"

Crawford looked lazily around, checking the idle crowd circulating near the bar. "That's the main reason I'm here. I want to fill in a lot of blanks for you, to keep you from spinning your wheels. We're on the trail of a pattern to these contraband operations. Your material has plugged some important holes in the picture. It now looks as though the pattern is far more extensive than we'd previously figured."

Ryder peered thoughtfully into Crawford's face. "Before you go on about that pattern, maybe you ought to let me tell you about something I ran across yesterday, here in Teheran."

Crawford's eyebrows lifted a fraction of an inch. He looked keenly at Ryder. "By all means! Go ahead!"

Ryder, reminding himself to try to look casual for the benefit of any watching eyes, began, "It looks as though I might have stumbled across the trail of those shipping crates again. It seems like a rare coincidence, but there it is." Ryder dug in his pocket and took out the tiny Minox film cartridge of exposures he had made at the Rafat stone stable. He laid it on the table and pushed it across to Crawford. "Here's some more Oscar-winning photography for you." Ryder then related briefly the story of his discovery of the stone stable, the wooden crates it housed, and the goat hides on the land of the Rafat family. He described in detail the whereabouts of the site. He added, "Those crates at Rafat's have the same-looking Arabic markings, and they have some of those weird wood screws in them too."

The sound of Crawford's voice betrayed the intensity of his interest. "Was there any clue to the contents of those boxes?"

Ryder shook his head. "None at all. They were all intact, unopened. New looking, in fact."

Crawford asked, "Did you see any sign of shipping documents, or manifests, or other paperwork possibly fastened to any of the crates?"

Again, Ryder shook his head in the negative.

James Crawford gazed into the distance for an interval, thinking. He turned to Ryder and remarked, "This is a vital piece of news. It is imperative that we learn, if we can, the contents of those crates before they disappear from that location."

Ryder remained silent, considering Crawford's words. A sudden disturbing suspicion had flashed into his mind, and once surfaced, it now grew into focus. He stared at the CIA man and declared, "Crawford, I don't think any of this Rafat affair is much of a surprise to you!"

Crawford's eyes were impenetrable. He eased back in the deck chair and returned Ryder's intense look. Seconds dragged by, and then Crawford spoke. "I once told you, Jeff, that you are exceptionally well suited to this problem. Your long-standing association with Boubahri is an important part of that. Boubahri himself has nothing whatever to do with the problem. He does, however, have the misfortune to own that land adjacent to the Rafats, and those people occupy our attention very considerably!"

Ryder shook his head, on the edge of anger, then turned his gaze off into the distance. He said in a low, strained voice, more or less to himself, "God help Ali Boubahri with this filthy mess on his doorstep." He swung his head back to direct a hard stare at the impassive CIA man. "Listen, Crawford, Boubahri's got to be warned. I won't allow any of this dirty business to rub off on him! He's my friend!"

Crawford watched, and gauged the level of Ryder's temper. He said calmly, "If Boubahri faces any hazards from his neighbors, it has nothing whatever to do with you. Nor will it represent any particular news to him. The illicit history, past and present, of the Rafat family is certainly no mystery to his next-door neighbors."

Ryder was forced to recall the veiled exchanges between Ali and Anna Boubahri whenever the Rafats were discussed. He lost a little of his anger, but none of his concern. He said to Crawford, "Well, I've got to warn Ali somehow. I'll just tell him to keep Anna and himself the hell away from that estate until this mess blows over. They can just stay in their townhouse in Teheran." Ryder swung around on Crawford. "You weren't going to tell me you'd ever heard of Rafat, were you?" he demanded.

Crawford just looked blandly back at him. "No. It would have served no useful purpose. It would only have led you to worry about Boubahri, as you are now doing. Above all, the Rafats must not be allowed to suspect we are anywhere nearly this close on their heels." Crawford continued his bland study of Ryder as he went on. "Now that you do know about the Rafats, I cannot prevent you from saying something ill advised to Boubahri. But the hard facts are, Jeff, that the more Boubahri is told about details, the greater the peril will be to him and to his family from the Rafats. And they are very, very dangerous people. If you want to help him, you will say nothing at all about this to him. And after all, what is there really for you to tell? He already knows about the stinking hides, as he was with you when you found them. And even you and I don't yet know what is really inside those crates, do we?" Crawford stopped talking.

Reluctantly, Ryder admitted to himself the hard truth in what the CIA man was saying. He looked down at the table, and shook his head again with the unhappy dilemma.

Crawford spoke gently. "There is a great deal more that you and I have yet to discuss tonight, things that will shed more light on this for you. I think you will be in a much better position to see where you are after we have finished. Let's go on with the rest of it now, and come back to this, if you want to, later."

Ryder abruptly moved his shoulders, seeming to shrug off his burden of unease. He said decisively to Crawford, "Right. Let's get on with it. You were saying we need to find out what's in those crates. Do you want me to try to have a look?"

Crawford's face relaxed. "No, Jeff, that won't be necessary. At least, I hope not. We'll be trying another way."

Ryder's eyes squinted in concern. "I gather you'll be sending somebody up there to poke into those crates. Well, whomever you send, tell him to walk on eggs. That Rafat is every bit as dangerous as you labeled him. If I've ever seen murder in a man's eyes, it's in Hassan Rafat's! He strikes me as the type who'll shoot first, and the hell with the questions. I think he's a homicidal nut!"

For a fraction of a second, Ryder also saw murder in Jim Crawford's face, a flash of malevolent intent more spine chilling in its own way than Rafat's deranged menace. The CIA man nodded stiffly without smiling. He spoke in a toneless voice, "Mr. Rafat's homicidal inclinations just might get him chewed to ribbons one day soon." Crawford stared into his glass as he swirled the ice cubes. After a moment he looked up at Ryder. He asked, with restored calm, "How's your itinerary coming? How much longer do you plan to stay here in Teheran? And then what?"

Ryder answered, "I've got one more day's business to do here tomorrow. Then, day after tomorrow in the morning, if all goes well, it's up to Kabul for a few days. When I'm through in Afghanistan I'll be heading back to LA. But I'm going to stop off in Beirut for one, maybe two days." Crawford made no comment, and Ryder added in an idle aside, "I'm hoping I can sidetrack a budding company involvement there. A Lebanese high roller named Ghandhouri, whom I don't trust, is trying to elbow into the airplane business out here." Ryder casually sampled his drink.

For the second time in the conversation, Ryder discovered he had aroused Crawford's full attention, this time unexpectedly. The CIA man asked, "Did you say this Lebanese is named Ghandhouri?"

Ryder raised his eyebrows as he replied, "That's right."

Crawford asked another question. "And this interest by him is a recent development?"

Now Ryder's interest and puzzlement were piqued. "Yes. Very recent. It sounds like *you* are acquainted with the shady Mr. Ghandhouri too!"

Crawford ignored Ryder's last, leading remark. He pursued his inquiry. "Jeff, do you know how your company became aware of Ghandhouri? Who initiated that action?"

Ryder shrugged. "The first I knew of any business with Ghandhouri was when I came back to Beirut from Amman last month. I got a telephone call in Beirut from a highly placed genius in the company. I was ordered, over strenuous objections, to meet with Ghandhouri for preliminary business conversations. I did, the next day."

Crawford asked, "Then you don't have any idea how this liaison originated?"

Ryder spread his hands speculatively. "I think I know. I think Ghandhouri made the first move. I think he dazzled this genius of ours with his footwork, probably at some extravagant bash in New York. This genius I'm talking about has never set foot east of Paris."

Crawford nodded and said, "All right, let's talk about your 'genius.' What is his name?"

Ryder answered in a slightly cautious tone. "As you might have gathered, I can't stand the man. And he's now my boss, at that—at least for the present. His name is Lane. P. T. Lane. He is executive vice president for marketing."

Crawford then inquired thoughtfully, "And how well do you know Ghandhouri?"

Ryder shook his head. "Mostly by reputation, which is all bad in the circles I trade in. I've met him personally just that once, up in his penthouse on top of a Mickey-Mouse, ten-story skyscraper he owns in downtown Beirut."

Crawford sat in silent thought. Ryder took the opportunity to register his own curiosity. "Are you going to tell me what causes *your* interest in Ghandhouri?"

The CIA man gave Ryder a quizzical look. His answer was evasive. "At the moment there isn't much to tell, Jeff. Sufficient to say, perhaps, that the man normally plays in a different league from your company. I am surprised at their interest."

Then, with an abrupt change of subject, Crawford said, "Let's talk about your report from Jordan. We've had our eye on your board members, Lahoud and Rifai, for a while before your warehouse visit. We know they've been receiving a fortune in payments for helping Al Fatah and the Palestinians."

Ryder asked, "And those Arabic words on the crates. Do they add up to anything?"

Crawford nodded his head. "Yes, you and Ambassador Harte were on the right track." The CIA man drew a folded piece of paper from his pocket and handed it to Ryder. "Here is a copy of what we've doped out about the code they're using. It applies to their shipping routes. We sorted this code out using your photos together with data we've collected elsewhere."

While Ryder glanced over the material Crawford had handed him, the CIA man went on, "We've analyzed the wood fragments you picked up too. The wood from the outer boxes is local. That is, those boxes are built in either Lebanon or in Syria, depending on their routing. On the other hand, the inner boxes are of two separate types. In one, the wood comes from the Balkans, and the other type comes from the Hindu Kush, eastern Afghanistan." Crawford tasted the contents of his glass, letting his eyes drift over the nearby vicinity.

Ryder, intrigued by Crawford's recitation, asked, "Do those weird wood screws mean something?"

Crawford looked back at Ryder. "Those weird wood screws of yours add up to what may be the most important item of information of all. They are entirely singular. Our supposition is that someone has cleverly designed them as a means of identifying these shipments, apart from any other marks."

Conversation lapsed. Crawford let Ryder mull over the new information, then he resumed. "Jeff, I think you can see how much you have helped. Now I have to emphasize to you that all of a sudden, you've gotten yourself very close to some extremely dangerous people. If you continue to work with us on this, the risk will be high." Crawford watched Ryder's face.

Ryder tilted his head quizzically. "Look, I took it for granted in the beginning that this might be bad news for my insurance man. You must be telling me the heat is hotter."

Crawford responded, "You've managed to push your nose right into the steam already. You have alerted Lahoud's suspicions, and much worse, probably Tabet's as well. And if Tabet suspects you, sooner or later so will the Rafats. Yes, Jeff, the heat is considerably hotter."

Ryder gave Crawford's reply an interval of sober thought. Then he asked, "When you gave me that Minox, you mentioned other toys I could have, when and if. Well, if these people are going to start getting rotten, maybe it's time you let me have that Smith & Wesson equalizer you showed me."

Crawford's answer was prompt. "I brought it along. I will see to it that one of our people here at this hotel places it in your luggage, in your room, soon after we finish this chat."

Ryder leaned back in his chair, smiling somewhat wryly at the CIA man. "*That* felt like the moment of truth! I guess I was expecting it all to come down to this, but never quite faced up to it. Now that it's in the open, it's almost like a relief!"

Crawford couldn't help smiling slightly at Ryder's flat candor. He observed, "Well, you lay it on the line." Crawford returned to the immediate problem, saying, "There isn't too much else we need to discuss right now. Just bear in mind that you're on the right track, and because of that you're going to have to watch yourself. Now, I'd like to see you again tomorrow night, after I arrange a look into those boxes at the Rafat place. Also, while it's on my mind, the Rafats' business affairs extend into Afghanistan, so don't relax up there either."

Crawford looked over at the bar, then noted, "I see that the bartender is beginning to turn on lights. It's getting late and I've got quite a bit to do tonight, so I'd better get busy. Unless I have to call you tonight for one reason or another, let's plan to meet down here again tomorrow evening at the same time. I'll tell you then the outcome of our search into those crates. Is that agreeable to you?"

Ryder nodded his head. Crawford got up from his chair smiling, leaned over, and formally shook hands with Ryder. In a quiet voice he said, "It will be better if we leave separately. Stay a while and have a few more swallows from that empty glass of yours. I'll be seeing you." The CIA man turned and walked toward the hotel.

Morphine
Teheran, Iran
April 1966

With Crawford's departure, Ryder looked at his watch. He saw that he wasn't going to get any nap. He wandered back up the winding stairs to the hotel lobby. With very little time remaining until Maxton was due to appear, he entered the dim elegance of the Hunt Bar and seated himself on one of the barstools. He thought about the advisability of going easy on the hard booze, then decided he couldn't face another Bloody Mary, and asked for a vodka martini. An attractive, young, harem-costumed girl with immense dark eyes wheeled a serving cart up, and supplied Ryder with a snack plate of caviar and several little triangles of toast.

Ryder was halfway through his drink and the snack when John Maxton ambled in and moved onto the adjoining stool. Maxton silently inspected Ryder's glass of vodka and the portion of caviar, then signaled for the same. Ryder decided against a second drink, and as Maxton worked on his vodka, Ryder described his unexpected conversation with Crawford. Maxton offered, "If you have to head up the hill tonight to tamper with Rafat's loot, I'll come along and stamp on the bogeymen if you want."

Ryder chuckled. "Thanks, but no thanks. You're too goddam big and clumsy. Rafat will think there's a gorilla loose in his barn. Anyway, Crawford says he'll be getting the job done by somebody else."

After the drinks, Ryder and Maxton decided their hard day's work had earned them a fancy meal. They headed for the luxurious supper club in the hotel. While extravagantly priced, it offered a splendid gourmet menu and a good floor show.

Ryder had just begun to demolish his serving of Chicken Kiev when the headwaiter came up to their table carrying a telephone. He placed the phone on the table, advising Ryder that there was a call for him, then bent down and inserted the telephone jack into a conveniently placed plug.

Ryder tipped the headwaiter, then said "Hello" into the telephone. Crawford's voice said, "C. James here. It seems I need a partner for the big game tonight."

Ryder let the surprise sink in, then responded, "Well, well! Okay, coach, if I'll do, count me in. Where and when?"

"I'll pick you up in front of the Miami Club in thirty minutes. The dress is informal, so no white shirts," Crawford replied, then hung up.

Ryder put down the telephone and looked ruefully at the Chicken Kiev, then at John Maxton. He said, "Looks like the signals are on for me. I hate to eat and run, amigo, but the coach just gave me the nod. Get some sleep for me, will you?"

Maxton looked into Ryder's face and rumbled, "Take care," as Ryder left the table.

In his room, Ryder hurriedly got out of the olive green gabardine suit he'd worn all day and hung it up. Then, heeding Crawford's "white shirt" hint, he went to his suitcase for a navy blue turtleneck pullover and a pair of charcoal sports slacks. He pulled the dark shirt out of the bag and tossed it on the bed, then undid the fasteners on the center divider of the suitcase and flipped it over to get at the slacks. Under the divider and neatly arranged on top of his clothes, Ryder was startled to find the blue-black steel automatic pistol and shoulder holster Crawford had promised, along with two spare clips of ammunition.

Ryder slipped the gun out of its holster and hefted it for a moment, then set it down and studied the rigging of the holster. After one false start he solved how to wear the harness. He pulled the turtleneck sweater on, then buckled the holster and straps over it. He slipped into the dark slacks, then pushed the nine-millimeter automatic into its holster snuggled under his left arm. He shrugged into a dark gray sports jacket, then couldn't resist having a look in the mirror to see if the unaccustomed lump of the gun was as obvious as it felt.

A five-minute taxi ride brought Ryder to the curb in front of the Miami Club. He paid the driver, then strolled over to stand on the walkway in front of the club, to one side of the entrance path. After he waited only a minute or so, a black sedan eased to a stop across the wide span of Pahlavi Boulevard, and honked its horn. Ryder trotted across the road, dodging the speeding night traffic. He approached the automobile in the darkness, peering to try to see the driver. Crawford's voice came out of the gloom. "Hop in, Jeff. This is the right chariot."

Ryder hustled around behind the car and got in on the far side. Crawford shoved the car into gear and tramped on the accelerator, maneuvering the car expertly into an open space in the headlong downhill traffic. He continued down the road for a quarter mile, then made a brisk U-turn. Neither man spoke until the car had swept back past the Miami Club, heading up Pahlavi Boulevard's grade. Settled on their way, Crawford opened the conversation. "I'm sorry I had to call on you tonight. The truth is, the Iranian I was counting on for this is in the hospital. Got himself into an auto accident just this afternoon. The accident must have been at about the same time as you and I were talking. He came out of it with a broken arm."

Ryder looked over at the CIA man in a sudden realization. "You intended to be in on this yourself all along, didn't you?"

Crawford took his eyes off the road for an instant and glanced at Ryder. He smiled a little and said, "Don't sound so surprised! You're hurting my feelings!"

Ryder declared, "Well, I'll be damned! I was sure you must have high-powered help oozing out of the woodwork around here!"

Cryptically, Crawford remarked, "The good ones come and go." He then crisply changed the subject. "Jeff, let's get into the details of this deal tonight. There is a black valise on the floor in back. See if you can pull it up here in front, on the seat between us."

Ryder leaned an arm over the seat rest behind, and grabbed the valise by its handle. He found the bag quite heavy, and it took an effort to hoist it to the front. With the bag finally situated between them, Crawford instructed, "Open it up, Jeff. I want to acquaint you with the equipment in there, and give you an idea of how we're going to proceed."

Ryder opened the bag. Crawford handed him a pencil flashlight, saying, "There are three large pieces of equipment in there, on top. Let's take them one at a time. I think you'll recognize the first item."

Ryder, with the aid of the little flashlight, lifted the first item, a plastic-wrapped bundle, from the bag, and placed it on his lap. He saw through the clear plastic that he was holding a dismantled submachine gun. Crawford told him, "Unwrap the gun and put it together now, Jeff. It's in three pieces. All you have to do is screw the barrel into place. Keep turning it until you feel it click . . . then, snap the cartridge magazine into its slot on the left side. After that, slide the wire stock back until it pops into place."

Ryder, following Crawford's verbal instructions, found the weapon simple to assemble. When the gun was intact, Crawford said, "It's as easy to shoot as it is to put together. Hold onto the clip with your left hand, and the pistol grip with your right. Under your right thumb, you'll feel a square safety latch. You will push it down to release it. The clip holds thirty cartridges of nine-millimeter ammo."

Ryder leaned forward, and, pointing the gun at the floor, held it in firing position against his shoulder. Its operation and use seemed straightforward.

Crawford asked, "Any problems?"

Ryder said, "Nope. I've run a tommy gun before. This can't be much worse."

Crawford continued, "Okay. Put the gun on the backseat, then, and hope we never get a chance to use it." Ryder did as instructed. Then Crawford told him, "Now let's get into the stuff we *will* use. The other two big items in the bag are a battery-powered drill and a metal detector. Under them are a few ordinary tools: pliers, wrenches, screwdrivers, a bow saw, a nail saw, a pair of small crowbars, a claw hammer, chisels, wire cutters, files, and stuff like that." Crawford paused, then interjected, "By the way, did you find the Smith & Wesson in your room?"

Ryder patted the lump on his left side. "It's right here, rubbing a couple of places raw on my ribs."

Crawford nodded. "Okay, then let's get back to the details. You won't especially need to know all about the other equipment, because if we're interfered with, we won't be using it anyway. Meanwhile, if everything goes quietly, I'll be doing the tricky stuff. Now, correct me if I'm wrong. Your friend Boubahri has a chauffeur and a gardener, and either or both of them might be at his place out here, apart from Boubahri himself and his wife. There are no children involved."

Ryder confirmed, "That's right. Those are the only ones I know of. Boubahri and his wife, and the chauffeur, normally spend their time in the Boubahri's downtown place. They only head out to the villa on weekends or holidays. Odds are nobody will be there at all tonight, except the gardener. I don't know if he has a wife."

Crawford said, "And if I've got it all straight, we should be able to get where we're going, onto that race track, without disturbing the Boubahri villa anyway."

Ryder again nodded. "Right. If we go in through the east gate, right onto the driving track, we'll never go near the house."

Crawford was quiet for a moment, thinking. Then he said, "That only leaves three possible big problems. Guards, dogs, or alarm systems."

Ryder speculated, "I've never seen any guards at Ali's villa. Anna has a small poodle that stays in town, but there are no other dogs on the place. But of course I have no idea what we might run across on the Rafat property. Nothing bothered Ali and I when we poked around there, though."

Crawford turned to look at Ryder. "If we're discovered by guards, they may have to be eliminated. If so, it will have to be done as silently as possible. That means chloroform, the knife, or a garotte. I have silencers for the handguns, but we'd be better off using one of the other ways. Are you up to it?"

Ryder felt the hairs on the back of his neck bristle. He said slowly, "It's been a long time, but I've done it before, so I can do it again."

Crawford reached into a pocket. He withdrew a cylindrical object, which he handed across to Ryder. He said, "Here's a silencer for your automatic. We'll plan on my doing the elimination of any interference, unless it comes to a bad pinch. If you have to get involved, use the silenced gun."

They drove on through the night, and as their route departed from the main avenues, traffic diminished drastically. Finally, having reached the unpaved roads of the rural highlands, they found themselves driving quite alone. Crawford reached to the dashboard and turned off the car's headlights, remarking, "Let's practice running without lights. There's a quarter moon, and we should be able to make out all right. How much farther do we have to go?"

Ryder thought for a moment. "I'd guess another two or three miles, straight ahead." The road in front of them, without lights, showed well enough as a pale ribbon against darker surroundings. Stone walls and fencing were faintly visible, bordering along the roadway. They drove slowly past the main turnoff leading into the Boubahri villa, and onward until they came to the track gate. At Ryder's signal, Crawford stopped the car. He handed one of the pencil flashlights to Ryder, who left the car and walked over to the gate. There was no lock. Ryder unlatched the gate and swung it open. As Crawford eased the car through the opening, he told Ryder to close the gate behind them.

They made a slow circuit along the track, finding the visibility poorer than on the main road. Finally, the blacker darkness of the grove of trees loomed ahead, and Ryder called for Crawford to stop the car. Leaving the engine running, the two men got out, and with the occasional aid of the small flashlights, found a place where the car could be turned around. Crawford climbed back into the automobile, and with Ryder guiding from the outside, backed it around to face toward the direction of their entry. He shut off the engine.

They left the car then, with Ryder carrying the heavy valise and Crawford carrying the submachine gun. Ryder led the way, making as little sound as possible as he picked his way slowly through the almost total blackness of the wooded grove. He tried to go sparingly with his use of the flashlight. The still night air was filled heavily with the rank stench of the hides. The eeriness of the total silence made the inevitable rustling and crackling sounds from underfoot seem earsplitting, adding to the tension.

The two men arrived at the high fieldstone fence marking Boubahri's property line. Ryder heaved the valise onto the top of the barrier, then, glumly visualizing what all this might be doing to one of his favorite outfits of clothes, he climbed over the wall. Crawford eased over behind him, and they moved on through the heavy darkness among the trees. Ryder made a random guess that they had traveled about halfway to the stone stable from the wall, and began moving more cautiously and quietly. After what seemed like far too long, and just as Ryder was beginning to worry about having gone past the stable, he made out the structure's vague outline to his left. He stopped and waited until Crawford edged up beside him. He swung his arm to indicate the position of the stone stable, and saw Crawford nod his head. Crawford gripped Ryder's forearm, then moved ahead, indicating his intention to lead for the rest of the distance.

Ryder followed Crawford, inching forward through the blackness, one silent step at a time. The putrid stench from the hides was almost overpowering in the dense night air. Within a few yards of the stable, Crawford motioned for Ryder to set the valise down. He patted the bulge under Ryder's left arm. Ryder drew the pistol. Crawford, satisfied, signaled for Ryder to stay put, and moved silently away into the gloom. As quietly as he could, Ryder injected a cartridge into the chamber of the automatic, then made certain the safety catch was off, and the gun ready for use. He stood tensely, straining to hear any sound of activity. Then, with chagrin, he remembered the silencer Crawford had given him. Hastily, he fished the attachment from his pocket and fumbled to fit it to the barrel of the gun. With the silencer installed, he resumed his vigil, thinking extraneously that now, the gun wouldn't fit into the holster, and that he would have to stick it under his belt.

Minutes crept by. The silence remained unbroken. Thoughts of what might happen cascaded through Ryder's mind as he waited. He tried to sort them into orderly alternatives. He decided he should act as Crawford's ace in the hole. If sounds of a scuffle occurred, he would move to assist. He wondered how he could avoid having Crawford mistake him for foe, not friend, and decided he'd just have to rely on Crawford. Finally, and above all, Ryder reminded himself that he must not allow himself to be taken by surprise. These tense thoughts vanished suddenly as, hearing a sound, he shifted his eyes and saw a faint stutter of signals flash from Crawford's light. He watched the CIA man's vague form move toward him.

Crawford came up to Ryder, and in a low voice said, "Not a sign of life. Bring the valise." Crawford turned, and, less carefully now, moved around to the front of the open shed. Ryder tucked the pistol into his waistband and picked up the bag, then followed Crawford. With the help of the small flashlights, the two men made a quick inspection of the shed and its stored contents. As nearly as Ryder could tell, nothing had been changed since his previous visit. He said as much to Crawford. Crawford rested the submachine gun on one of the crates and said, "I'll take the equipment and get to work. You can stay out here in front and stand guard over those stinking hides. If you see or hear anything, rap a couple of times on one of these boxes. Which way leads to the Rafat house?"

Ryder pointed, and Crawford said, "Ten to one any problems will come from that direction, but *don't count on it*! Now, here's what I'm going to do. First of all, I'm going to make a scan with the metal detector. When that's done, and before I do anything else, I'll check back with you."

Ryder moved a few feet away from the front of the shed to a large log that lay fallen among the dew-covered, foot-entangling spring weeds and wild grass. He decided he could watch and listen as well while sitting, and sat down on the old log, holding the automatic pistol on his lap. Meanwhile, Crawford disappeared into the shed's blackness.

The better part of ten minutes went by, seeming like an hour to Ryder, as he perched on the log. Through the ominous stillness of the night air, he listened to small sounds issuing from the stable where Crawford was working, and tried to forget the choking miasma from the nearby pile of hides. Occasional rustling noises and a few cries from night birds disturbed the pressing silence of the dark woods.

Crawford came quietly out of the night and over to Ryder's log. He sat next to Ryder, and speaking low said, "This is a little baffling. I get no sensible reaction from the metal detector. I know the detector is working; I tested it on the submachine gun and on my pistol. I'm not anxious to rip open any of these boxes unless we absolutely have to. I'm going to probe a box or two with the drill and see what might turn up. I can use some help for that project." Crawford got up and Ryder followed him, back to where the valise stood open, resting on one of the shipping boxes.

Crawford removed the compact electric hand drill from the valise. He fitted a 12-inch length of small diameter bit into the drill chuck. As he worked, he described the intended procedure to Ryder. "We'll drill diagonally into a corner of the box, toward the center. Once we get the hole through the wood, we'll fit extra lengths onto the bit. With the bit extensions I have, we can reach as far as three feet into the box if necessary. The idea is to find out as much as we can about the contents without leaving external evidence of our tampering. Particles of whatever is in there will collect in the drill bit grooves." Laconically, he added, "It could be embarrassing if the box is filled with TNT."

Crawford wrapped a heavy piece of chamois skin around the body of the drill to muffle its sound. He went to work on the first box right in front of them. Ryder was surprised at how little noise escaped from the muffled drill even though, from its whine, he could tell it operated at an unusually high rpm. He held one of the penlights, directing its beam onto the drill's point of entry. The drill bit penetrated the wood swiftly. The two men watched shavings tumbling out behind the shank of the spinning bit. The drill's sound changed suddenly as the point of the bit passed through and beyond the wood of the box. A moment later, crystalline granules emerged from the hole instead of wood fragments. Crawford withdrew the drill and shut it off, saying, "Looks like we're hitting pay dirt. I'll put an extension on."

Ryder turned and stared into the gloom, uneasy with the return of total silence. He cursed inwardly, realizing that he had let his night vision suffer by staring at the light while Crawford worked. Crawford finally said, "All set. I've run Vaseline into the bit to help collect some of those tailings. That stuff we saw could be anti-moisture crystals inside the box. We'll find out this time. Now, take this other piece of chamois and wrap it around the middle of the bit. It's two feet long now, and I don't want it to start whipping. Hold your hand lightly around it while I'm drilling, and use the chamois to protect your fingers."

The drill assembly was awkward now, due to the extreme length of the fine bit. Crawford and Ryder maneuvered into position, and Crawford asked, "Ready?" Ryder grunted an assent, and the drilling resumed. With Ryder steadying the drill shaft, Crawford drove the long bit into the box. Using an old pilot's trick, Ryder kept one eye closed this time, to preserve at least half of his night vision. A small cascade of the crystalline substance continued to emerge from around the bit's point of entry. Crawford drove the entire length of the bit into the box, then withdrew it, and turned off the drill. With the flashlight, he studied the bit's grooves. Crawford moistened the tip of a finger, picked up some of the granules, and tasted a tiny sample. He spat and said, "Whatever it is, it doesn't taste very good."

Ryder asked, "Have you got any guesses?" There was a moment's hesitation, then Crawford said, "Yes. I've got more than a guess. I think this stuff might have come from somebody's poppy garden." The full implications of Crawford's curt reply weren't obvious to Ryder. He remained silent, pondering, and watched Crawford collect a sample of the material in a small plastic sack from the valise. Crawford removed the lengthening extension from the drill bit, then said to Ryder, "I'm going to do some random sampling of other boxes in this stack. You watch out front until I'm through." He picked up the drill and moved into the black-shadowed interior of the shed. Ryder returned to his post at the log. Several minutes passed. Ryder could hear the faint, high-pitched whine of the drill from time to time. Then suddenly, Ryder froze. A deep throated, vicious growl rumbled out of the surrounding night, ominously nearby. Ryder's stomach contracted. He hesitated before risking a sweep of the darkness with his flashlight, and then it was too late. With no further warning, one hundred pounds of savage canine fury came hurtling out of the blackness, striking Ryder full on the chest. He went down hard under the crashing impact, slammed backward into the tangle of wet weeds. Ryder instinctively rolled as he struck the ground, covering his face with his arms. The massive German shepherd ferociously attacked his fallen quarry, its slashing teeth seeking Ryder's throat. Ryder clung desperately to the pistol in his hand as he rolled back and forth, warding off the raging dog's fangs with his arms. He felt the animal's jaws clamp hard on his left forearm. He locked the dog's hindquarters between his knees, then rolled hard to the left, throwing his right arm and shoulder over the dog's neck. He pinned the slavering, thrashing beast under his own weight. Momentarily, he had control of the dog. With his right arm free, he pressed the muzzle of the silenced automatic against the dog's spine and pulled the trigger three times. The powerful body heaved wildly under him, then the dog's strength faded into spasmodic jerking.

Ryder felt his own strength drain away, and he let himself lay limply on top of the furred, quivering body. His ears rang with a surf of sound from his own pounding pulse. Through the rushing sound in his ears he heard Crawford's quiet, concerned voice, and felt a strong hand grip his shoulder. Ryder shook his head, then struggled to disentangle himself from the twitching animal beneath him. He found that the dog's teeth still were clamped on his left arm. With Ryder up onto his knees, supporting the rest of his weight on his right arm, Crawford slid his hand under Ryder. Ryder saw the glint of a steel blade. With one powerful stroke, Crawford cut the dog's throat. The gripping jaws relaxed, and Ryder, freeing himself, sat back on his heels. Perspiration dripped from his face. He did a strange thing. He stroked the furry body of the dog, and said, "Sorry, fellow."

Crawford squatted down beside him, and in a low voice asked, "How bad is it, Jeff?"

Ryder's chest heaved as he tried to regain his breath. Between breaths he said, "The son of a bitch got me pretty good, I think, on the left arm. Otherwise, I'm okay."

Crawford rose from his squat. "Let's see if you can stand up."

Ryder came up unsteadily, annoyed to find his knees shaking. Crawford kept a hand on Ryder's shoulder. Ryder said, "If my goddamned knees will settle down, we can get on with it. How much noise did me and Fido make?"

Crawford answered, "Not as much as you probably think. It might have been too much, though." Still holding Ryder by the shoulder, he took a cursory look with his flashlight at the bloodstained left sleeve of Ryder's jacket, then said, "Stay put for a minute while I collect our gear, then we'll get out of here." He took his hand away, watched Ryder for a moment, then turned on his heel and strode away in the darkness back to the shed. Ryder's left arm began to throb with excruciating pain, and he could feel that the left sleeve of his jacket was heavily soaked with his blood. He tried to force his thoughts away from his injuries, and remembered the gun. He knelt down and retrieved it. In doing so he noticed the gleam of the little chromed penlight resting in the grass a few feet away, and picked it up as well. Using the light in a quick inspection of himself, he saw that both sleeves of his jacket were ripped and torn. The left sleeve trailed in sodden, tattered shreds. Under the light he could see that his left forearm was leaking a steady run of blood.

Crawford returned from the shed, carrying the valise and the submachine gun. He spoke crisply. "Let's get to the car. I'll have a better look at your arm then."

Ryder told him, "I'm leaking, and I'll leave a helluva trail. How about giving me some of that chamois to wrap around this mess."

Crawford quickly snapped open the valise and grabbed the chamois skins, handing them to Ryder. As Crawford closed the valise, Ryder wound the soft hides around his left forearm, grimacing with the stabbing pain. Holding the arm against his middle to keep the temporary bandage in place, he grated, "Let's go."

They retraced their steps through the thick darkness. With a few muttered profanities at the throbbing in his arm, Ryder clambered over the stone wall, following Crawford. The two men finally emerged from the forested grove, back at the automobile. Crawford opened the trunk of the car, and placed the valise in it. He helped Ryder work himself out of the ruined sports jacket. Together, they studied the torn places in Ryder's arms.

Both arms were lacerated with wicked gashes, the left forearm and hand in particular. On close inspection, none of the wounds appeared immediately critical, however, with the possible exception of one very deep slash, almost an inch in length, on the underside of Ryder's left arm. This wound stubbornly continued to bleed profusely. Crawford opened the valise and withdrew a small first-aid packet. He doused the deep wound with tincture of Merthiolate, sprinkled it with sulfa powder, then tightly bandaged a large gauze compress into place. He handed the medical kit to Ryder and said, "We've got to keep moving. I'm going back to the shed and try to hide the dog's carcass before anybody else gets there, and I'll do what I can to cover our trail. While I'm doing that, you can patch up some of those other cuts." Ryder watched Crawford disappear into the night, back toward the stone stable.

Half an hour later, the two men were driving back toward Teheran. Apart from the pulsing ache in his arms, Ryder felt much better, now that there had been time to attend to his wounds. His arms were a patchwork of white adhesive bandages, and felt strange whenever he moved, owing to the stiffening crusts of coagulated blood on his skin.

With a chance to relax a little now, Ryder said, "Crawford, you owe me an expensive sport coat and a new pair of pants, and if I get rabies, I'm going to sue you."

The CIA man glanced at Ryder. In the faint glow from the dashboard lights, Ryder saw a small smile. Crawford said, "Let's just say, I owe you."

Ryder nodded in the dark, knowing Crawford was watching, and said, "How the hell am I going to get into the hotel without scaring everybody in the place to death with the way I look?"

Crawford answered, "We're going to stop on the way first, and get a certain doctor out of bed. After that we'll head for the Hilton. We'll fix you up so nobody will know the difference."

Ryder, satisfied, said, "Okay. So much for that. Now, what the hell does this 'poppy garden' business amount to?"

Crawford drove on, silent for a minute or two, then admitted, "Jeff, I certainly don't know all the answers yet. Unless I'm badly mistaken, though, we've found the Rosetta stone tonight. If I'm right, what this adds up to is that some of the same people who are shipping contraband arms into the Arab-Israeli confrontation are also moving illicit narcotics, and in large quantities. We'll know for sure tomorrow, after I have these samples analyzed."

Mondo Cat
Kabul, Afghanistan
MAY 1966

The venerable DC-6B's four great propellers drew the old airliner along, droning across Afghanistan's mountainous heartland. Jefferson Ryder leaned against an aching arm while he looked out one of the rectangular windows, staring down at the wildly broken upheaval of the earth's crust below. John Maxton slept soundly aft in the last seat row of the sparsely occupied passenger compartment.

As he watched Afghanistan roll by beneath, Ryder thought irrelevantly that a town with a tongue-teasing name like Timbuktu ought to be somewhere here, in Afghanistan, instead of in the desolations of flat West Africa. If people wanted to think of the ends of the earth when they heard someone say "Timbuktu," likely they'd want to think of a sterile-looking, vertically pitched fastness of inhospitable rock such as this. All the more so, maybe, once they'd walked among the rugged, fiercely capable people of this remote place.

Ryder liked the Afghanis. He admired their hearty, ingrained stamina and respected the phlegmatic humor with which they endured one of the world's most pitiless environments. Ryder watched as the edges of jagged stone ridges clawed higher, seeming to grasp at the lonely eastbound airplane. Formidable mountain ranges wearing names befitting their hard, exotic character: Band-i-Baba, Band-i-Baian, Koh-i-Baba, and finally, the towering Hindu Kush, Killer of Hindus. Ryder watched the lower peaks of the western reaches thrusting up to 12,000 feet. Distantly, ahead and to the north, majestic challengers rose to 24,000 feet, marking the barbaric eastern recesses of the country.

A hell of an unlikely place, Ryder thought, to have served so often as a crossroads for wandering conquerors. Who, in his right mind, Ryder wondered, would choose a place like this to wander through? But they had. Alexander, Tamerlane, Genghis Khan, the Persian hosts, the Moslem Arabs, the Seljuk Turks, and others—even the British. But the tributes go as well to the Afghanis themselves, as to their restless, transient masters of bygone days, Ryder thought. While you may persuade an Afghani to tolerate your presence, you do not conquer him.

With such thoughts in his mind, Ryder felt all the more acutely his sense of distaste for the youth apparently asleep in the opposite window seat on the airplane. Ryder glanced sourly at the slovenly figure. The pimple-faced young man was unpardonably filthy, emanating a foul stench compounded of rancid accumulations of his own excreta. Head and face were all but hidden under greasy mats of unkempt, pale brown hair and beard. Crusts clung in the mustache under his nose. A sweat-stained, beaded leather headband stretched across his forehead. One ear supported a gold earring. Strands of dirty, multicolored beads hung from his neck, together with a braided thong carrying a heavy metallic medallion. He wore a stained, heavily fringed leather coat mottled with dark permeations of grease and grime. Heavy serge pants, once the lower half of some military uniform from some unidentified army, were indistinguishable as to original color under layers of caked and embedded dirt. His feet were shod in knee-length, fringed, laced buckskin moccasins. The young man's baggage consisted of a rucksack and, inevitably, a guitar.

Over recent years, Ryder had watched as a considerable tide of these bizarrely caparisoned young people had surged, cultlike, onto the traveled byways of the world, seeking some nonexistent Shangri-la. Brimming with ecstatic, idealistic zeal, youthful dissenters of a dozen affluent nationalities launched themselves on passionate pilgrimages toward a succession of rumored seats of The Real Truth.

The presence of this category of traveler on an airplane no longer aroused any particular stir or notice among veteran airline passengers or employees. Jaded border officials had even ceased to be moved, much beyond disgusted exercise of particular thoroughness in their customs inspections.

As Ryder's glance swept over the recumbent figure of the unclean young man, his gaze caught on the streamered, bedecked guitar resting on the aisle seat. He studied the psychedelically emblazoned instrument in idle curiosity. The words "Mondo Cat" were painted across its face. Ryder presumed that this must be what the young man liked to call himself. Ryder's eyes roved over the musical instrument, noting the painted patterns, fringings, beads, and other adornments with which the guitar was laden. Then, at the top of the guitar's neck between the two sets of string tuners, Ryder saw a row of brass studs. They were the polished heads of wood screws, featuring an S-curved slot!

Ryder's thoughts came flashing back to his CIA problem. Suddenly, he was conscious of the aching in the raw wounds on his arms. Illegal morphine. That was what Crawford said was in the boxes on the Rafat property. Morphine, destined for conversion into heroin, in all likelihood. Morphine, packed in great wooden boxes, and hidden in the Iranian boondocks by a snotty young Persian with lethal madness in his eyes. Great combination: a verging madman like Hassan Rafat, and now this sloppy-looking mess across the aisle, hauling a guitar around like a security blanket. With that one little ingredient added—those nasty, brassy, funny-headed wood screws—the filthy, crumpled sprawl across the aisle had become an ominous presence rather than a dismissible, piteous slob. Ryder turned his eyes back to the window. Afghanistan now looked even more inhospitable.

Kabul
Afghanistan
MAY 1966

Jefferson Ryder lay in his bed wide awake and staring, yet it was only five thirty in the morning. Annoyed, he remained in the bed for a while, watching the dawn light creep into the room, and wondering why it was that whenever he came to Kabul, this same thing seemed to happen. This exasperating business of waking too early. Maybe something about the 6,000-foot elevation. Possibly the collection of unusual early morning sounds penetrating into his room from the streets of central Kabul, which surrounded the relatively modern and well-built Springer Hotel.

Ryder finally gave up and climbed out of bed. He showered and shaved, dressed, and headed for the hotel's coffee shop. The expatriate Bulgarian who managed the Springer recognized Ryder from previous visits, and, welcoming a chance for some gossip from the West, wheedled an invitation to join him. While Ryder ate a light breakfast, the amiable Bulgarian drank black coffee and chatted enthusiastically in his very bad English. Ryder learned that Maxton and himself were, at the moment, the only new arrivals registered at the Springer. Ryder hadn't really expected to find the soiled owner of the "Mondo Cat" guitar staying at this hotel, but had maneuvered the conversation to find out for sure.

Ryder finished his early breakfast, and decided to consume some time with a stroll outside. He enjoyed walking, and especially enjoyed ambling through the streets of this ancient and exotic place. Ryder bid the Bulgarian a cordial good morning, and stepped out of the hotel into the brisk, clear, early-morning air of this more-than-mile-high city. Daily life in Afghanistan starts with sunrise, and Ryder found the early-hour streets of Kabul already lively with streams of Afghanis bicycling to work in swarms around the occasional Russian-built trucks and even fewer autos moving on the roads.

Ryder headed off at an easy pace among the picturesque and colorfully dressed pedestrians. He selected at random a direction away from the commercial center, and within five minutes was strolling among the city's traditional open-air sidewalk shops, watching the Afghani merchants industriously arranging displays of their wares while the first of the day's customers began haranguing those proprietors in lusty bargaining sessions. The narrow, unpaved side streets were thick with slow-moving foot traffic. Turbaned men, men in shagged fur coats and caps, veiled women rendered faceless and shapeless in their traditional *chadri* costume, horse-drawn carts, occasional heavily burdened yaks, all moved patiently along the street, threading their respective ways toward morning destinations, each contributing to the unique sound, sight, and smells of this distant place.

Ryder found himself the object of lively scrutiny as he trudged along with the crowd. His western clothes set him apart as an obvious stranger. He stopped at a stand that offered a display of lambswool caps, and proceeded to discuss a possible purchase with the proprietor. He had scarcely begun when he found himself the center of an audience of swarthy, grinning faces from the pedestrian crowd. Ryder launched into a good-humored, arm-waving exchange with the hat merchant, delighting the watching Afghani tribesmen with his mixed scraps of Arabic, Farsi, English, and sign language as the bargaining narrowed down. At last he made the purchase, aware of many heads being shaken to indicate that the merchant had made by far the best of the deal. Ryder donned the curly wool cap, smiled at the watchers, and moved on down the street.

Making his way among the shoppers, Ryder sensed that someone seemed to be following immediately on his heels. He moved to the side, stopped, and turned around. He found a young Afghani standing a few feet away, looking embarrassedly at him. Ryder smiled and nodded. He said, "Hello!"

The dark, slender young man of about eighteen immediately smiled happily in return. "Hello, sir! I am named Abdul Azzam. Excuse me please, for disturbing you." The young man's English was spoken carefully and with hesitation as he groped for correct words.

Ryder saw only innocent candor in the young man's face. He extended his hand and told the youth, "My name is Ryder, Jeff Ryder. I am American. You are not disturbing me at all, Abdul Azzam." Ryder spoke slowly and distinctly.

Young Abdul shook Ryder's hand energetically. "It was my hope that you were American, Mr. Ryder. In school, I am learning your language. My father says that I should talk with every English-speaking person I am able to meet."

Ryder replied gravely, "Your father advises you well, Abdul; and it is to his credit that he has raised a son with the courage to try, as you are doing."

Abdul Azzam was immensely pleased by the praise. He offered, "It is not my wish to delay you, sir. Will it be acceptable that I walk with you a short distance?"

Ryder smiled. "I would welcome your company." The two men resumed walking. Abdul Azzam's confidence had soared, and with it, his loquaciousness. Ryder used the opportunity to ask many detailed questions of Abdul regarding the passing people, and concerning items of interest nearby.

The narrow street soon intersected with a considerably wider, dustier, and noisier one, and Ryder saw that here the bordering ranks of open-fronted stalls and shops were occupied by craftsmen rather than merchants. A leatherworker's table, covered with newly made boots and shoes; a furniture maker's shop, with beautifully hand-carved and inlaid pieces in assembly; a brassworker's forge; a gunsmith. Ryder stopped in front of the gun shop to look over the weapons on display. He found young Abdul Azzam's interest in the weapons as keen as his own, and that the young man was surprisingly knowledgeable of firearms. With the aged gunsmith standing attentively by, Ryder examined admiringly a long-barreled, muzzle-loading flintlock rifle in perfect operating condition. A plate on the flintlock mechanism was inscribed with the date 1802, and with the initials of the venerable East India Company. As he studied the old gun, Ryder felt a light touch on his arm. He looked up inquiringly to find Abdul Azzam pointing up the street. Ryder turned to see a long procession of heavily laden camels approaching ploddingly down the center of the roadway, under the charge of dusty, fierce-looking cameleers on foot. Ryder returned the flintlock rifle to the old gunsmith, thanking him, then silently watched the spectacle of the caravan moving slowly past. When the last camel in the train had shambled by, Ryder had counted seventeen of the great beasts of burden. He and the young Afghani sauntered along, keeping pace with the rear of the caravan. Abdul Azzam, with eager animation, plied Ryder with facts about the massive, double-humped Bactrians. Ryder learned that if well loaded, each camel would be carrying around six hundred pounds, or forty *seer*; that a day's march for a caravan would cover about twelve miles, and that along traditional caravan routes, ancient caravanserais still stood, spaced a day's march apart. Abdul said that even now, distances in Afghanistan were apt to be described in *serais*.

The young Afghani pointed at the animals' humps and explained that a fully grown camel, weighing perhaps half a ton, could have as much as two hundred pounds of fat stored in those humps, and could survive for weeks without food. He told Ryder that although the camels were terribly bad tempered and sadly lacking in intelligence, they provided their owner with food from their milk, warm cloth woven from their fur, and with an immense capacity to work. Referring to the caravan, he pointed out that in Afghanistan, a tribesman who owned seventeen camels was a wealthy and prosperous person.

Ryder asked what manner of load might be expected, brought in by such a caravan. Abdul told him the camels might be carrying many different things, but that these were of the Kyrgyz, from the north in the Pamir Mountains, hence would probably be carrying tallow or felt, or hides, to be traded for items unobtainable in the northern region. Having answered Ryder's question, Abdul Azzam glanced at the angle of the morning sun, and announced that he must, regrettably, hurry away to his school. He thanked Ryder profusely for permitting him to exchange conversation, then reluctantly headed back in the direction from which they'd come.

The young Afghani's evident overstay reminded Ryder of his own obligations, and he looked at his watch. Owing to his early awakening, however, he found no need to discontinue his stroll, and resumed the leisurely pace behind the slowly progressing camel caravan. As Ryder walked along, idly studying the load lashings on the last camel in the file, he caught sight of an unmistakably familiar figure. There, walking abreast of that last beast and on its far side, was the guitar-carrying, unwashed young man from the airplane, Mondo Cat. Ryder saw that the young man was engrossed in a gesticulating conversation with one of the tribesmen in the caravan. The two were waving paper documents at one another in seeming argument. Warily, Ryder slowed his pace, screening himself from the direct view of that strangely mismatched pair. He decided to try to discover where the caravan—or at least where Mondo Cat—might be headed. Ryder followed the plodding line of camels, taking care to keep Mondo Cat in sight while trying to keep himself inconspicuous. After nearly ten minutes of this singular pursuit, Ryder was relieved to see that the caravan had evidently reached its destination. The lead animal had turned through a great gated opening in a vast mud-brick wall that paralleled the far side of the roadway. At a discreet distance from that gate, Ryder stopped and watched the succession of animals and drovers file slowly through the opening. Satisfied that Mondo Cat had also disappeared through the gate, still arguing with the dusty tribesman, Ryder crossed the street and approached the opening himself. He had just time to see, through the gateway, that the wall continued around to form a huge enclosure. The camels were being circled in preparation for a halt. Then, with creaking protests from rusted hinges, massive gates were swung closed by two straining, cursing men.

Ryder started walking slowly back along the side of the road, musing over the evident association between the caravan and the bizarre figure of Mondo Cat. Strolling along in his contemplations, he gradually became aware that he was walking beside a considerable bustle of noisy industry. Ranked along the outer foot of the high wall enclosing the caravanserai, a platoon of Afghani carpenters busily labored. The air was filled with the sour-sweet tang of freshly cut wood. In a quick scan of the work in progress, Ryder brought himself to an abrupt alert. The men were constructing large shipping crates with a very familiar look.

Ryder kept his leisurely pace while he studied details of the work under way beside him. The Afghani carpenters paid little heed to the solitary American figure strolling past. At last, Ryder found what he had been searching for—a wooden keg filled with the peculiarly designed brass wood screws. Alongside the keg rested an open box containing a number of new screwdrivers, adapted for driving the S-curved screwheads.

Two Afghani craftsmen were working together at the end of the shipping crate assembly line, installing the wood screws in nearly completed boxes. Ryder paused to watch them. With this neatly dressed foreigner as an audience, the two workers reacted by adding extra flourish and zeal to their efforts. Each began barking officious commands and instructions to the other. They rapidly finished with the box in hand, and together shoved the heavy container aside. The two Afghanis then marched briskly down the line of toiling carpenters, shouting for another unfinished box.

Jefferson Ryder watched the backs of the pair as they moved away. Then, hoping the other carpenters were too busy to notice, he knelt hastily down and seized one of the new screwdrivers and a handful of the brass screws. He pocketed the hardware, then leisurely stood and gazed over the scene. He watched idly for another few moments, reassuring himself that his theft had not been noticed, then turned and merged with the morning traffic of the street, and headed back toward the hotel. As he strode along, Ryder made a mental calculation. Seventeen camels, each carrying six hundred pounds, could deliver a total load of around five tons. Five tons of tallow, or felt, or hides. Or, five tons of morphine, or of Chinese or Russian guns and war matériel.

By the time he had reached his hotel room, Ryder decided that James Crawford should be told soon about the camel caravan and its five tons, and about the youth with the Mondo Cat guitar. Ryder took the handful of brass screws from his pocket and dropped them into his shaving kit, then shoved the screwdriver under a pile of shirts in his suitcase. He then headed down to the coffee shop, where he found John Maxton seated alone at a table, wolfing down a huge breakfast. Ryder asked a waiter to bring him coffee, then sat down with Maxton. Maxton looked up, chewing on a great mouthful of breakfast. "These Bulgarian pancakes are pretty good! Why don't you try some? How's your arm?"

Ryder flexed his left arm and shrugged. "I still know I've been in a dogfight. It's okay, though. And I've already had breakfast." He then recounted his morning's experience with the camel caravan, and its apparent connection with Mondo Cat.

Maxton listened while he continued to work on his Bulgarian pancakes. When Ryder finished his story, Maxton muttered, "If I get this straight, it sounds like that punk who smells like he sleeps with a dead halibut is running errands for your pal Rafat."

Ryder nodded his head. "That's the way I think it goes, Max. On our way out to see the airline this morning, I'm going to stop at the embassy here, and send a message to Schuyler to meet us in Teheran. Crawford seemed to be really worked up about this poppy powder development, and I think he ought to get the word on this caravan deal ASAP."

A chuckle rumbled from Maxton. "I'd give a paycheck to see Schuyler's face when you haul him that far into this deal! Ryder, you're going to scare that poor old cold-nose so bad he'll piss his bloomers!" Maxton sampled his coffee, then added, "Speaking of the airline, I ought to spend some time with the ops guys out at the airport today. How about me going out there while you're making points with the VIPs downtown?"

Ryder agreed. "Good idea, Max. We'll get more done, and sooner, that way. I'd like to get back to Teheran by dinnertime tomorrow, if we can."

Forty-five minutes later Ryder and Maxton emerged from the American Embassy in Kabul, and set out, each to face the business of the day. Ryder had sent the message to Bogart Schuyler III in Beirut.

Anna Boubahri
Teheran, Iran
MAY 1966

Ryder looked at his watch as he and John Maxton climbed out of the taxi at the entrance to the Teheran Hilton. It was nearly seven thirty in the evening. There had been a departure delay of almost an hour on their flight from Kabul. Ryder wondered whether Bogart Schuyler was already in the hotel, waiting for them. He asked Maxton to supervise the transfer of their baggage into the hotel, and went ahead to the reception desk. After accepting the clerk's cordial welcome, he asked about Schuyler. The clerk checked his register. He told Ryder that a reservation was being held for Mr. Schuyler, but that the gentleman had not as yet arrived.

Ryder proceeded to register into the hotel, and Maxton joined him at the counter. The two men completed the usual formalities, then headed for the elevators. As they moved through the crowded lobby, one of the hotel's assistant managers hurried to intercept them. With a knowing smile on his face, he handed Ryder a sealed message. "Mr. Ryder, a lady has telephoned for you several times during your absence. She asked that you be given this message."

Ryder thanked the man, then opened the message. It was from Anna Boubahri, and read, "Jeff. Urgent that I see you immediately. Please telephone me, no matter what the hour. Anna."

Ryder frowned as he handed the message to Maxton. "Max, that's not like Anna. Something must be seriously wrong."

Maxton pondered over the brief wording, and nodded soberly. "This sounds like the panic button."

The two men entered an elevator and went up to their floor. Maxton saw to the sorting of their baggage, then came into Ryder's room and listened as Ryder placed a telephone call to the Boubahri's town number. Anna Boubahri answered after the first ring.

Ryder said into the telephone, "Anna, this is Jeff Ryder. Max and I just got here, and the people at the hotel gave me your message."

Anna Boubahri's voice immediately became excited. "Jeff! Thank heaven you're here!" Ryder heard her take a breath, then she continued, "Jeff, something is dreadfully wrong! I don't know where Ali is! Please help me!" Anna's voice quavered.

Still mystified, Ryder looked over at Maxton and shook his head. He said into the phone, "Of course we'll help you, Anna Doll. Just stay where you are. Max and I will get there as fast as we can, right now." Ryder put down the telephone. He gave Maxton a verbatim account of the brief conversation, then said, "She's really shook up. Let's get the hell over there." They headed immediately back to the elevator.

Passing through the lobby, Ryder gave the reception clerk a message for Bogart Schuyler to the effect that Ryder would contact him immediately upon return to the hotel. Ryder and Maxton strode out the hotel's main entry doors and signaled for a taxi.

Within twenty minutes Ryder was knocking on the door of the Boubahri residence. Anna Boubahri opened the door, and in her relief at seeing them, burst into a flood of tears and flung herself into Ryder's arms. Maxton edged past them, and after Ryder had soothingly urged the weeping Anna into the house, closed the door behind them.

Ryder patted Anna's shaking shoulders, then took her streaming face between his hands, and gently tilted it so he could look into her moist eyes. "Come on, Anna Doll, let's go sit down somewhere. You can cry all you want to, but first you have to tell us what's upset you so badly." He put an arm around Anna, and tenderly held her while he steered her toward the living room.

A middle-aged, frightened Iranian maid stepped hesitantly into view, wringing her hands. She hovered near the living room's entrance, wordlessly watching Jefferson Ryder help her weeping mistress to a chair. Maxton noticed the distraught maid, and made the time-honored, elbow-bending signal requesting that she bring drinks. The woman, desperately wanting to help, bobbed her head vigorously to indicate her understanding. She bustled across the room to a corner liquor cabinet.

Ryder held Anna's hand comfortingly as she tried to quiet herself. Maxton intercepted the worried maid and relieved her of the large silver tray loaded with bottles of liquor, glasses, and ice. Maxton poured a glass of sherry and handed it to Ryder. Ryder urged Anna to sip the sherry, and presently she regained her composure. In a halting, strained voice, Anna Boubahri started to explain. With her dark, moist eyes fastened on Ryder's face, she began, "Jeff, you surely remember the scene that Hassan Rafat made, out at the villa on Friday night?"

Ryder nodded without speaking. "Well," Anna continued, "Ali explained about it to me afterward that night, and he also mentioned the bad smell on the racetrack and his discovery, with you, of those dead skins on the Rafat land. He made a joke of it to cheer me up, and to cure my annoyance with Hassan."

Anna, pale but calm now, looked away and shook her head at her own thoughts. "Ali should know better," she said, and turned back to Ryder. "The next day, Saturday, we came into town because, as you know, Ali had to work with you for a while in the morning. After he left you, he had an appointment with someone in the petroleum ministry. While he was waiting there, he told me later, Hassan Rafat happened by. Ali said they talked together about little things, and then, thinking to make a joke, Ali teased Hassan about the smelly hides."

Ryder shot a quick glance at Maxton. Anna noticed, and with widened eyes she said, "What is it, Jeff?"

Ryder patted her hand. "Nothing important, Anna. What is important is for you to tell us the rest. Please go on."

Staring into Ryder's eyes and clutching his hand, Anna resumed her account. "Ali told me that, to his astonishment, Hassan went into one of his strange fits of anger, the kind that makes his eyes go back and forth so fast. Hassan didn't say another word to Ali! He turned his back and walked out without even meeting his appointment!"

Ryder asked, "And that was Saturday morning, four days ago, Anna?"

She nodded quickly. "Yes, just before midday, because after Ali finished at the ministry, he came home, and we had lunch together here at home. That was when he told me of Hassan's strange behavior about those skins."

Anna sipped a little of her sherry, then went on. "It was the next day that the really strange things happened, Jeff. That was Sunday." She looked downward, away from Ryder's face. "Ali wanted to do some work on the cars, as he always does on weekends when we have planned nothing else. I was having my monthly woman problem, and didn't feel at all well, so I stayed here, and Ali went out to the villa alone." Anna's eyes came back to Ryder's face. "Then, Jeff, on Sunday afternoon, Ali telephoned me. In the strangest voice, he told me he was going to test one of the cars on the mountain roads. He said he would be driving up to the ski lodge that we go to. You've been there with us, Jeff."

Ryder affirmed, "Sure, I remember the place, Anna. Did Ali say which car he was going to test?"

Anna thought for a moment. "Why, yes, he did, Jeff. He said the new Aston."

"What happened then, Anna?" Ryder asked.

Anna Boubahri's eyes suddenly filled with tears again. She gripped Ryder's hand as she spoke. "Jeff, something terrible has happened to Ali! I just know it! I haven't seen him or heard from him since then!" Anna's voice broke, and she started sobbing.

Ryder pressed her hand and asked, "Anna, did Ali say anything else on the telephone?"

In a quavering voice, Anna replied, "Yes, he said for me not to worry if he didn't get back for a day or two. He said some sports car people would be at the lodge, and that they were thinking of holding an informal rally. Ali said he might participate."

Ryder asked, "Is that unusual, Anna?"

Anna broke into heavy sobs. Through her weeping, she told him, "Jeff, he has never, ever gone away for days at a time like this! Not without planning ahead of time. And, Jeff, Ali likes to race his cars, but he really doesn't like sports car rallies at all. When he does take part in one, he always takes me along." She put her face in her hands, and cried uncontrollably.

Ryder tried to console her. He patted her hand and said, "Look, Anna, Ali's probably got himself stuck, off on some rotten road somewhere. I'll tell you what we'll do. Tomorrow morning, first thing, Max and I will get a car and go on up to the lodge. We'll find that rascal and bring him home to you." Feeling helpless, Ryder looked over at Maxton as Anna continued to shake with sobs. Maxton, trying to help, happened to say just the right thing. He growled, "Ali's probably trapped himself a blond bunny up in some shack in the hills."

Anna's tearstained face came around as she momentarily overcame her grief. She indignantly exclaimed, "John Maxton! Don't you dare even think such a thing; if Ali strays from home, it will *not* be with a *blond*!"

Ryder couldn't suppress a small chuckle as he watched Maxton's stolid face, and then Anna smiled a little too. The tension was relieved, and Anna turned back to Ryder.

"There is more I must tell you, Jeff. I have tried to find out about Ali by telephoning the lodge. I have been unable to get an answer. Also, there is something else, more important and more frightening." She got up from the sofa and went over to a small lamp table. She opened a drawer in the table, and took out a small, ragged piece of grease-stained paper. Returning, she sat down and handed it to Ryder. "Sunday evening, hours after Ali's call from the villa, our old gardener, Abdul, came here to the house. Jeff, it is unheard of for Abdul to do such a thing! That dear old man has spent his entire life on that country land of Ali's family. He cannot drive, and he is afraid of the city and of telephones, so you can see how unusual it was! Part of the way old Abdul rode on a bus, but the poor man had to walk for miles, getting here. He came all that distance to bring me this piece of paper." Anna indicated the dirty scrap in Ryder's hand.

Ryder held the slip of paper under a lamp. Written on it, in English, were the words, "Jeff—Aston." Ryder handed the slip to Maxton without comment.

Anna Boubahri stared pleadingly into Ryder's face. She said, "What does it mean, Jeff? Ali wrote your name. That is why I have come to you for help. It is Hassan Rafat that I am frightened of, Jeff. Old Abdul told me that Hassan, with some peculiar young foreigner, came to the villa while Ali was working on his cars. Abdul was setting out more new flowers by the garage. He said that Ali and Hassan drove away in one of Ali's cars, and that the foreigner followed in Hassan's car. Abdul says that just before Ali left with Hassan, he turned toward Abdul and said my name, then dropped this scrap of paper on the pavement at his feet. Abdul thinks Ali was concealing the piece of paper from the other two."

Ryder felt his stomach contract. He said quietly, "Anna, you are a brave girl. If Ali is in some kind of trouble, we will find him, and get him out of it. Please try not to worry any more. Max and I will fix everything."

Ryder and Maxton headed back to the hotel by taxi. They left Anna Boubahri enveloped by the mothering care of the maid. Anna, while still visibly overwhelmed with anxiety, was for the moment relieved by Ryder's brisk and active sharing of her burden of worry.

En route to the hotel, Ryder and Maxton discussed the problem. Ryder's face felt stiff as he said, "Max, I've got bad weevils in my guts about this. That pinch-headed Persian son of a bitch Rafat is capable of anything. The worst of it is, poor Ali is innocent of everything but a bad joke. If it hadn't been for me, he wouldn't be in this mess."

Maxton grunted. "Knock that off, Ryder. Don't try to take credit for the blame."

Ryder leaned back in the darkness. "I guess you're right. Moaning like that damn sure won't help Ali and Anna. What we've got to do is decide how we're going to find Ali and get him back."

Maxton said, "Like you told Anna. Tomorrow we'll make like a two-man posse."

With concern leaking into his voice, Ryder muttered, "Right, Max."

As the two Americans made their way through the evening crowd in the lobby of the Hilton, Bogart Schuyler came hurrying anxiously toward them. His face looked more wan and severe than usual. Ryder mentally ascribed this to Schuyler's bout with diarrhea, but he also suspected that the intrusion of this Teheran trip into Schuyler's customarily ordered routine was upsetting to the man.

Ryder moved to meet Schuyler. He extended his hand. "It's good to see you're back on your feet again, Boge."

Schuyler hastily shook hands with Ryder and said, "Hello, Jeff. Where have you been? Where can we go to talk? Ambassador Harte wants me to call him as soon as I find out about your message. I've got to get back to Beirut, you know."

Ryder studied Schuyler's face for an interval. An edge of impatience crept into his voice. "Boge, don't rush off just yet. Do you know John Maxton?" Ryder half-turned toward his friend.

Schuyler, taken slightly aback by the manner of Ryder's response, extended a limp hand to Maxton.

Maxton rumbled, "We've met," and shook hands distastefully with Schuyler.

Ryder pointed toward the spiral stairs winding down to the patio level. "Let's go sit outside and talk. It's not too chilly out yet."

The three men descended the stairs in silence and made their way out to the patio deck. Ryder steered them to the same table he and James Crawford had occupied four days before. A waiter followed them to the table and took their drink orders. Ryder watched the departing waiter head toward the bar, then said to Schuyler, "Boge, Max and I just got back from

Kabul a little while ago. Our flight was an hour later than scheduled. It's a good thing you didn't get here on time either, because we walked into another can of worms the minute we got here to the hotel. All of this has to do with the Crawford deal."

Schuyler sat tensely in his chair with a handkerchief in his hand, nervously polishing the lenses of his glasses. "I was late getting away from a tea held for some visiting UNESCO people. Then my taxi had a flat tire on the way to the airport, and I missed my flight. Luckily, I was able to find a seat on the very next airplane to Teheran."

Ryder wondered whether Ambassador Harte had issued priority to the UNESCO tea over this CIA effort. He said shortly, "The important thing is, Boge, you're here now, and we've made connections, so let's get with it. Here's the story." Ryder then gave Bogart Schuyler a detailed account of the incident with the camel caravan in Kabul, and of the apparent involvement of the long-haired youth, Mondo Cat, in some kind of transaction between the Rafats in Teheran and the Afghani caravan cameleers. Ryder then described the episode he and Maxton had just experienced with Anna Boubahri. He told Schuyler of their plans to search for Ali Boubahri on the following day. Ryder concluded by saying, "I'm sure you know, Boge, that Crawford and I have found that the Rafats are busy smuggling morphine as well as weapons."

Officiously, Schuyler said, "Oh, yes. Mr. Crawford provided the ambassador and me with a full briefing following his visit with you here in Teheran. By the way, how are your injuries from that dog?"

Ryder shrugged, "They hurt." He changed the subject. "Boge, you've got all the details now, and you can make your report to Harte. Before you leave town, I'll give you those wood screws and the screwdriver I swiped. That's all I can contribute for you, unless you want to hang around and see how this Boubahri thing comes out."

Bogart Schuyler showed his sudden discomfort. He swallowed, and his voice came out unevenly. "Is . . . is there some way you want me to help tomorrow?"

Seeing Schuyler's struggle with himself, Ryder adopted a less severe tone. "We want all the help we can get, Boge. If you can see your way clear to stick around, just for the day tomorrow, what we need is somebody to stand by here at the hotel, who can holler for help if we get into a deep jam. I'd like you to do that if you can, Boge."

The low level of involvement was a relief to Schuyler, and he readily complied, "Why yes, Jeff, I believe Ambassador Harte would want me to help. Yes, I'll stay. I'll help in any way I can!"

Ryder said, "Okay." He turned to Maxton. "I was afraid we'd have to count on Anna for our backup. Now we've got Schuyler."

Cynically, Maxton answered, "Like you said, we need all the help we can get."

The Red Ferrari
Teheran, Iran
<u>MAY 1966</u>

Daylight arrived reluctantly, hampered by a monotonous layer of pulpy clouds. Jeff Ryder, driving a rented sedan en route to the Boubahri estate, commented on the sky. "That's all we'd need. A damned rainstorm."

Maxton glanced at the clouds. "Looks like fairly thin stuff. Maybe it'll hold off."

Ryder said, "We turn off into Ali's villa in about half a mile. If it's going to rain, I hope it starts before we get too far out into the boondocks. That mountain road will be bad news in the wet."

Ryder slowed the car and turned in at the main gate to the Boubahris' villa. Driving slowly up the graveled lane to the house, he peered through the gloomy dawn light, watching for signs of the aged gardener Abdul. The villa grounds seemed deserted. Ryder drove across the curved parking area in front of the main house, and steered the car into the side lane leading to Ali's big garage. He honked the car's horn as he parked it on the concrete apron alongside Ali's Cadillac. No one responded to the sound of the car's horn.

The garage doors all stood open, revealing Ali's fleet of polished automobiles parked within. Ryder noticed immediately that the blue Aston Martin was there, occupying its place in the lineup. The Aston's hood stood open. There was an empty space in the line of cars where Ali's red Ferrari should have been parked. Ryder spoke to Maxton as they climbed out of the rented sedan, "Ali told Anna he was going to drive the DB4 up the hill, but there it stands. He must have changed his mind for some reason. It looks like he took the Ferrari instead."

Maxton grunted something unintelligible, then added, "Since when does Boubahri leave the doors open while he's gone?"

The two men walked slowly across the paved apron toward the garage. Both were looking around and listening for signs of life. The place seemed deserted. Ryder's voice was flat. "Ali *never* leaves this place wide open—not unless he's here." He headed for the raised hood of the Aston Martin. Ryder leaned across the front fender of the blue car, and peered under the hood. He saw no sign of work in progress on the engine. Mechanically, everything appeared undisturbed. He opened the car door on the driver's side, and climbed into the seat. The key was in the ignition lock. Ryder tried to start the engine. The starter spun the engine energetically, but the cylinders wouldn't fire. The gas gauge showed the tank to be three-quarters full.

John Maxton anticipated Ryder's next move. He picked up a long-handled screwdriver from Ali's toolbox, which stood on a castered dolly next to the Aston Martin. He signaled for Ryder to try the starter again. As Ryder spun the engine, Maxton leaned under the hood and tried shorting out the spark plugs with the screwdriver. He came out from under the hood, and walked around to Ryder, shaking his head. "No spark. I tried them all."

Ryder climbed out of the car and went back to look at its engine. He leaned in and undid the fasteners on the cap of the Lucas ignition distributor. He lifted the cap off. Maxton heard Ryder mutter something, then watched as Ryder withdrew himself from under the hood. Ryder held a small scrap of folded paper in his fingers. "This was stuck between the points. Ali must have put it there."

Ryder climbed back into the car and tried its starter again. The engine roared into life. He switched off the ignition and got back out of the car. He stared at the greasy scrap of paper in his hand. "This hunk of paper has a familiar look. Like the one Anna had."

Ryder went over to the garage wall switch and turned on the overhead lights, then opened the folded piece of paper and studied it. On the scrap of paper, Ali Boubahri had scribbled, "R—crazy—threat Anna—mtn race."

Ryder handed the paper to Maxton. "What does this say to you, Max?"

Maxton read the note. Still frowning down at the scrap of paper in his hand, he said, "Ali wrote this in a helluva hurry, but I think the 'R' is for Rafat, not Ryder. Sounds like that prick Rafat nabbed Ali by threatening to hurt Anna!"

Ryder nodded. "That's how I see it too. I think, there at the end"—he pointed at the words "mtn race"—"he means my mountain race with Rafat. Ali maybe got wind of the idea that Rafat was taking him back up that same road. Anyway, I think that's where we better look first, so let's get going."

Maxton lifted his eyes from the scrap of paper, and was on the verge of speaking when suddenly he froze. Looking past

Ryder, he muttered, "Uh, oh! Hold still, Jeff! We got a closer problem."

Ryder looked at Maxton, and saw that Maxton's eyes were focused steadily on a point somewhere to Ryder's rear. Ryder casually turned and looked in that direction. He found himself looking at the figure of the old gardener Abdul, standing fifty feet away at the front corner of the garage, and silently pointing an ancient double-barreled shotgun at the two Americans.

Ryder's thoughts raced. He decided that until he had switched on the overhead lights, old Abdul probably could not have recognized him. Gambling that the old man could now see him well enough, that he would recognize him, and not pull the shotgun's trigger, Ryder sent a friendly wave in the gardener's direction. In a low voice he said to Maxton, "I'm afraid you'll have to string out this gamble with me, Max. There's no telling what that old barbarian is apt to do. If we split up, he might panic. Walk along with me."

Ryder then started walking toward the aged gardener, smiling and talking steadily while gesturing exaggeratedly with his hands. He stayed under the bright overhead light. The fifty-foot distance looked and felt like fifty miles. Feeling hollow inside, Ryder continued smiling and talking and gesturing as he approached the old man, although he knew that Abdul understood no English. The distance narrowed to a few yards, and to point-blank range. The muzzle of the shotgun hadn't wavered in the old man's hands. Wondering how near he dared go, Ryder began injecting Ali and Anna's names frequently into his spoken sentences, waving his arms in gestures of uncertainty. As he spoke of the Boubahris, he let his face display his worry.

Ryder was within ten feet of the gardener when the old man abruptly lowered the barrel of the gun. Tears trickled down the seamed old face as the gardener hung his head. Ryder went up to the old man, and gently gripped his shoulder. He continued talking and stepped past the old man. He kneeled at the edge of the concrete ramp, and picked up a small twig. In the soft soil, Ryder used the twig to mark an outline representing the area of the garage and the main house. The old gardener watched Ryder's crude sketch develop. Suddenly he understood. He moved to Ryder and squatted down beside him, gesturing eagerly for the twig. Ryder handed it to him. The old man reached toward the diagram, and with firm strokes, drew in an accurate outline of the graveled lane leading into the villa from the main road. He anxiously handed the twig back to Ryder.

Ryder nodded, then drew small blocks in front of the garage outline. He pointed to the Cadillac and the rented sedan. He then repeated inquiringly, "Ali Boubahri? Ali Boubahri?" while moving the point of the twig from the garage to the main road on the dirt diagram. At the intersection of the main road, he indicated uncertainty as to the direction taken by the imaginary automobile, left or right. The old man excitedly seized the twig from Ryder's fingers. He made a quick trace with the twig from the garage to the main gate, then in a sweeping gesture, indicated that the car had turned left out the gate, and headed eastward. As he demonstrated with the twig, the old gardener spoke in his native tongue. His words repeatedly included his master's name, "Ali Boubahri" Ryder nodded his understanding. Then the old man, looking grimly into Ryder's face, slowly repeated another sentence in Farsi. Ryder understood only two words, "Hassan Rafat." The gardener, ending his sentence, made a contemptuous face, and spat on the ground.

Ryder got to his feet, and with elaborate arm motions, pretended to explain to Maxton the information given by the old gardener. Ryder pointed at the cars, pointed at Maxton and to himself, and waved toward the east. He was careful to include frequent mention of Ali Boubahri's name, and one or two repetitions of the name Hassan Rafat. The old gardener watched intently. Ryder finished speaking to Maxton, who indicated understanding with an exaggerated nod of his head.

The old man reached out and touched Ryder's arm. Ryder turned to look at the gardener. Extending his arms, the old man earnestly offered his ancient shotgun to Jeff Ryder. Ryder hesitated, then decided it would be unwise not to accept the old man's offer. He took the shotgun, and soberly nodding his head, thanked him. Ryder turned to Maxton. "Now, let's get the hell out of here while he's still on our side. We'll take the Aston Martin, in case we get caught in another driving contest with somebody."

Waving the shotgun and nodding his head, Ryder again thanked the old gardener, and walked briskly away. Maxton followed alongside. They went directly to the blue Aston Martin, climbed in, and Ryder started the engine. He ran the car out of the garage, and across the concrete apron. He and

Maxton waved to the tense old gardener, who stood watching their departure.

Ryder drove the Aston Martin easily for the first few minutes, letting the powerful engine thoroughly warm itself up. He pointed out the entrance to Rafat's land to Maxton as they passed by the place. There was no visible evidence of activity there. Daylight had brightened measurably, and although the threat of rain remained, the road was dry and dusty. Ryder headed up the first curves of the climb into the mountains. He glanced at Maxton. "Max, I don't know exactly what we're looking for, but from now on, keep your eyes open for anything that might give us a clue to Ali's whereabouts. The main thing is the Ferrari. If it's up here, it shouldn't be hard to spot with that red paint job. Other than that, let's watch for things like recent tire tracks on any turnoffs we might pass."

Ryder drove slowly up the winding mountain road. He and Maxton rode along in silence, concentrating their attention on their search. At the slow speed their progress up the road seemed interminable. They finally passed the hairpin turn where Ryder had reversed direction in the earlier contest with Hassan Rafat. From that point on, the road became entirely unfamiliar to both men.

Ryder continued to ease the Aston Martin up the narrow, winding track. Half an hour went by. The two men continued to strain their eyes in the difficult search. As time wore on, their seemingly fruitless efforts grew more discouraging. The Aston Martin climbed steadily higher and deeper into the mountains. Now and then, partly to break the monotony, Ryder stopped the car at wide places in the road. He and Maxton would get out of the car and study the ground for meaningful tire marks.

High on the mountain the roadway became a narrow ledge, hacked out of the sheer rock slope. The outer edge of the slender road fell away in a perilous drop into deep, boulder-strewn canyons below. Ryder was obliged to concentrate on his driving, following the snaking curves of the road. The car climbed toward the lowering gray bulk of the cloud level. Daylight waned again beneath the thickening overcast.

The Aston Martin eased around a sharp granite shoulder of the mountain. Ahead, the road curved through a tight reversal, and could be seen, looking directly across the deep chasm, angling upward in the opposite direction. Steering through the tight turn, Ryder noted that a wide turnout had been left at the turn's apex. Following the turn through its nearly 180 degrees, Ryder headed the car up a long, straight climb. With the Aston Martin moving slowly up the grade, he scanned the plunging ravine below. Abruptly, Ryder stopped the car. Maxton, surprised, asked, "What's up?"

Ryder stared fixedly down into the abyss. "Max, I see a patch of red down there." He swung his eyes up and backed the Aston Martin away from the edge of the road, then set the emergency brake, and shut off the engine. Both men climbed out of the car and walked over to the rim. Ryder pointed down into the yawning gorge. About three hundred feet below, and almost directly beneath the sharp turn in the road, the precipitous slope was interrupted by a massive rock outcropping. The upper surface of the stone ledge was almost obscured by an overgrowth of brush and a straggle of small, stunted trees. In the midst of the dark foliage there shone, unmistakably, a patch of bright red.

Maxton grunted, "That looks like bad news."

Ryder nodded grimly as he studied the terrain above the ledge and below the road. He pointed again. "Just below that last turn, Max. It looks to me like it won't be too hard to climb down from there."

Maxton's eyes followed the direction of Ryder's pointing finger. "Yeah, I see what you mean. If you angle off there a little toward the left, it looks like you'd have decent footing most of the way down."

The two men clambered back into the Aston Martin, and Ryder backed the car downhill until he reached the wide place in the road at the turn. He swung the car around and parked it facing downhill, alongside the rock face of the steep mountainside. They left the car, and walked across the road to its edge. Studying the ground as he walked, Ryder said, "Max, I missed seeing this as we drove past here." He pointed down at the wide shoulder bordering the outer edge of the roadway. "There's tire marks all over the place."

Together they studied the marks in the dirt. Neither man spoke. They looked at one another soberly. One set of deep-treaded tire prints led straight off the edge of the cliff. They stood at the edge, and stared down into the ravine. From their position, the red splash of color couldn't be seen. Ryder said grimly, "Well, let's go down there, Max." He led off, following a steep ledge angling downward from the road and off to the right. As nearly as Ryder could tell, this followed the direction he had noted from across the canyon, permitting descent to the great rock shelf further down.

Loose soil had collected on the narrow ledge the two men followed as they edged down the face of the precipitous rock wall. It provided reasonably secure footing. They had traveled a short distance down the ledge when Ryder stopped. He pointed to the ledge in front of himself. "Look, Max. Someone's been down here ahead of us."

Maxton edged up alongside Ryder. "Let me get by and take a look." He squeezed his thick torso past Ryder, and moved down the ledge another few feet. He knelt down and looked closely at the disturbed surface of the soil. Turning his head, he looked back at Ryder. "*Two* somebodies have been down here ahead of us. And I'm a pimple on a crab's ass if one of 'em isn't leaving tracks like an Indian!"

Ryder moved up and leaned over Maxton's shoulder. There, ahead of Maxton's pointing finger, he saw two clear footprints, one in front of the other. One of the prints had been made by a man's ordinary shoe. The second was the soft outline of a moccasin. Ryder noted, "Could be that hippie son of a bitch, Max."

Maxton grunted as he got up from his crouched position. "Could be. Could be."

With Maxton now in the lead, the two men continued their careful descent. Ryder commented, "Ten to one these prints go right where we're trying to get."

Maxton muttered, "Yep, and by the way, I see that the tracks go both ways. The two jokers who came down here came back up."

They continued the tedious downward hike, now and then obliged to assist themselves by taking handholds on protruding roots and stunted shrubs. Their range of vision remained limited by dense scatters of stubborn brush that somehow managed to thrive on the face of the weathered canyon walls.

The two men worked down the slope in silence, concentrating on the steep descent. At length Maxton paused and said, over his shoulder, "There's a flat spot here, just ahead." He waited until Ryder caught up with him, then together they pushed through a screen of wiry scrub onto a small, level table of bare rock. Ryder moved out to the edge overlooking the deep ravine. Below, about two hundred feet away and slightly to the left, he saw the rear quarter of Ali Boubahri's red Ferrari. The car had come crashing to rest in a heavy thicket of brush that rooted itself on the top of a huge rock promontory. From their present vantage point, only the rear right-side portion of the car was visible. The rest of the Ferrari was hidden by the dark foliage.

Scanning the intervening slope, Ryder saw that by working down a slant to the left of their position, the remaining descent could be accomplished with comparative ease. Maxton stood beside Ryder, staring down at the silent wreckage. Ryder said quietly, "We've got to take a close look, no matter what." Maxton nodded without speaking.

Ryder moved back from the rock edge. He pointed toward the brush that screened the avenue of descent he had seen. "This way looks best to me."

Maxton growled, "That's the way those other footprints go too." They pushed their way through snagging branches on a nearly level bench for several yards before the steep downward slant resumed. They headed down the last of the pitched rock wall leading to the wrecked Ferrari, now with their disheartening goal remaining in full view below. Ryder reached the level surface of the wide, brush-covered bench, and waited until Maxton joined him. Together they pushed across the last ten yards through the undergrowth to the Ferrari.

The car appeared to have crashed into the table of rock in a slightly nose-down angle, but upright. The rear fenders and wheels, and the rear portion of the chassis, remained exposed, thrusting out of the dense tangle of brushwood. The after-portion of the car appeared virtually unmarked by the terrible plunge the Ferrari had taken. The forward three-quarters of the machine were buried from view by the heavy thicket. Ryder said, "Well, here goes the worst part," and he plunged into the wiry entanglement of brambles and leaves, working his way forward along one side of the wreck. Maxton went around to the opposite side, and moved along parallel to Ryder.

Ali Boubahri was dead inside the wreck. While the front of the Ferrari was badly smashed and bent, it seemed miraculous to Ryder that the car had remained as intact as it had after the terrific impact it had sustained. Boubahri's body rested, crushed and broken, within the crumpled steel shroud of the cockpit. The door on Ryder's side of the car was mangled and twisted into an accordioned crumple. He saw no possibility for access to the corpse. He called, "Max, I can barely see in from this side, let alone try to get Ali out of there. How's it from your side?"

Maxton, thrashing around in the thicket, answered, "We got a maybe over here. This door's not too bad, but she's warped tight and I can't budge it. No way to get him out the window. He's wedged in too tight."

Ryder scrambled out, and pushed through the thicket to Maxton's side. He leaned down beside the wreckage, and looked in at the remains of his Iranian friend. The sight was ugly. Ali's broken body slumped in a grotesquely implausible posture. The corpse and the interior of the wreckage were mottled with black patches of dried blood. Ants and flies crawled over the body. Boubahri's head was turned to the side facing Ryder, eyes closed, resting against a ruptured steel section of the coaming beneath the shattered windshield. The side of the head had been crushed inward by impact with the rending steel. Ali Boubahri's lifeless face had, improbably, emerged unmarked by the hurtling crash.

Ryder looked away, sickened. Maxton asked quietly, "Jeff, wouldn't it be better to leave this mess the way it is right now, and see about getting some kind of hoist to haul the whole thing out?"

Ryder shook his head. "That's probably the right way to go at it, but I can't stomach the idea of leaving Ali to those goddamned flies and ants. How could we explain that to Anna? Maybe we can't get him out of there anyway, but by God, I want to give it a try."

Maxton said, "Let's do it."

Ryder studied the problem. He picked up a rock and broke away what was left of the window in the door, to make room for handholds. Combining their strength, he and Maxton strained and yanked on the jammed door. They could feel it give, but their efforts were not enough to open it. Ryder stopped pulling finally, breathing hard from the unavailing try. He turned to Maxton. "It will be a cinch if we have a pry bar of some kind. Max, stand by here. I'm going up to the car. I'll bring down the jack handle and whatever tools are there, and a blanket to put Ali in."

Maxton offered no argument. Ryder headed back up the precipitous trail. The climb was difficult and tedious. Ryder clambered slowly, using hands as well as feet, up the steep and uncertain footing. He climbed steadily, and at length approached the thicket surrounding the level shelf of rock halfway up. He began to realize that it might be impossible for him and Maxton to ever make this climb while encumbered with Ali Boubahri's body.

Nearing the dense brush cover of the shelf, Ryder suddenly halted and poised, listening. Over his own labored breathing, he heard the high whine of a powerful automobile engine reverberating through the canyon. He looked down at Maxton. Maxton, standing in the waist-deep thicket, was alternately waving his arms, then cupping his hands behind his ears. Ryder waved back, signaling his understanding.

Ryder moved ahead, closer to the screen of brush, and rested as he listened to the engine sound grow nearer. Unmistakably, a car was approaching up the road from the direction of the villa. Ryder stared down the canyon wall and into the distance, trying unsuccessfully to discover some visible part of the winding road. He decided there was little to do but wait and watch. The sound of the approaching engine rose and fell, intermittently muffled by intervening terrain as the unseen car followed the tortuous turns of the mountainside road. Ryder watched the rim of the roadway above him. Finally, he saw dust rising as the invisible automobile roared toward the sharp turn where the Aston Martin stood. The unseen car slowed, then stopped. The engine sound abruptly ceased.

Ryder instinctively crouched, then crawled into the thicket surrounding the small rock ledge. He moved part way toward the exposed ledge, then cautiously raised his head through the brush to watch the edge of the road above. Two men, visible from the waist up, moved into Ryder's view and stood peering down into the canyon. From one hundred feet away, Ryder easily recognized the faces of Hassan Rafat and Mondo Cat. Each carried a rifle mounted with telescopic sights. As Ryder watched from the concealment of the underbrush, Hassan Rafat raised the rifle to his shoulder, and, using the sighting scope, scanned the sloped hillside below. Ryder ducked his head. His heart pounded. He worried desperately about Maxton, hoping his friend had stayed put, out of sight of the road. A silent minute passed, and Ryder cautiously raised his head through the brush. He saw the two men as they started making their way down the steep slope toward him. Hassan Rafat followed behind Mondo Cat. Ryder had time to think. Crouched in the thick shrubbery, he thought about the pathetically torn and broken figure of Ali Boubahri. Ali Boubahri, the amiable, harmless human being, the good friend, lying uselessly mutilated and dead in his own automobile on the cold stone below. Ryder ceased fearing for himself. An implacable rage swept through him. With deliberate motions he took the nine-millimeter Smith & Wesson pistol from the holster under his arm, and injected a cartridge into its chamber. He crept carefully ahead through the brush, closer to the open point of rock, and across to the side away from the view of the wreck. Ryder then waited for the two intruders to reach the natural stopping place in front of him.

The sounds of the descending pair began to carry near. Ryder looked down at the cocked pistol in his hand and thought that if he could, he would disarm the two men and take them captive. Tensely, Ryder watched through the dense screen of foliage as first the unclean caricature, Mondo Cat, moved onto the open rock shelf. Behind him, with lithe, stealthy movements, Hassan Rafat followed. Once on the level surface, Rafat reached out and hooked the stock of his rifle roughly around the chest of the shaggy-haired youth, and shoved him aside. The Iranian pushed past Mondo Cat out to the point of the rock, and peered intently down at the wrecked Ferrari. Ryder felt his muscles tighten as Rafat raised the rifle to his shoulder again. He saw that the bolt was cocked. Rafat was scanning the slopes below through the scope, and Max was somewhere down there. That rifle was ready to fire.

Ten feet away from the two men, Ryder suddenly rose through the shrubbery to a standing position, and sighted his pistol on Hassan Rafat's head. He commanded sharply, "Throw those guns on the ground, both of you!!" Ryder watched Rafat jump at the sudden, unexpected sound. The Iranian stood immobile, frozen in position, the rifle still at his shoulder. Mondo Cat's rifle immediately clattered to the rock surface at his feet. The startled young man stood staring at Ryder, his mouth hanging open and eyes bulging.

Ryder roared, "*Rafat*! Throw that goddamned gun down!" The Smith & Wesson automatic in Ryder's hand remained steady, aimed at Rafat's left ear.

Hassan Rafat slowly lowered the rifle to waist level, its muzzle angled downward. Trembling visibly, he turned a malevolent, twitching face toward Ryder. Rafat's crazed eyes danced wildly. Without moving, Rafat suddenly shrieked at the quaking Hondo Cat behind him, "Pick up that rifle, you brainless fool! He can't shoot both of us! Pick up your gun! Pick up your gun and shoot him!!" Rafat was screaming in insane, quivering rage.

Jefferson Ryder stood without moving, eyes leveled across the sights of the black automatic, staring with deadly intensity into Hassan Rafat's convulsed features. He saw the Iranian's mouth working uncontrollably, flecks of white froth forming at the corners. Ryder watched Rafat's eyes shuttle erratically as the Iranian sent sidelong glances at the petrified Mondo Cat.

With feline suddenness, Rafat whirled to face his shaking, pallid, terror-stricken companion. He kept the muzzle of his rifle carefully lowered as he spun. Rafat screamed at Mondo Cat, "Listen to me! Do what I tell you, you stinking, sniveling idiot!"

The cowering youth stared ashen faced at the maniacal look on Hassan Rafat's slavering face. Ryder saw the young man tense. Then, as suddenly as Rafat had turned, Mondo Cat broke and ran, scrambling wildly away, clawing at the rough rock wall with his fingernails, and sobbing in hysterical fear. Rafat lifted the muzzle of the rifle and fired into the small of the youth's back, fifteen feet away. The magnum-powered, soft-nosed slug smashed through the young man's body, ripping his vitals, and sending him crashing face first against the stone cliff. Having fired, Rafat instantly worked the rifle's bolt, injecting another cartridge into firing position. Without a glance at Ryder, Rafat put the rifle to his shoulder and took deliberate aim at the writhing, screaming figure on the ground in front of him. He shot the youth a second time where he lay.

Ryder witnessed the cold-blooded execution unstirred. Remorselessly, his total focus remained concentrated on keeping the nine-millimeter pistol trained surely on Hassan Rafat's head. Rafat worked the bolt of his rifle again, then slowly turned his face back to Ryder. Ryder saw that Rafat had calmed, and now faced him with savage deliberation. Ryder said flatly, "For the last time, you son of a bitch, I'm telling you to drop that gun!" Ryder watched the remaining color drain from Hassan Rafat's face. He saw the muscles in Rafat's neck tighten into corded ridges, and knew that Rafat would try.

Hassan Rafat sprang into motion. He bounded violently to the side, jerking the muzzle of the rifle through an arc toward Ryder. Rafat never pulled the trigger. Ryder coolly moved the pistol to follow Rafat's wild leap, swinging its sights unerringly with the movement of Rafat's head. He squeezed the trigger, and the pistol bucked against his hand. He instantly brought the sights back and fired again. Ryder's first shot made a blue hole through Hassan Rafat's forehead, then blew off the back of the Iranian's head. The second shot tore the jaw loose from one side of Rafat's face.

Inbound
Beirut, Lebanon
MAY 1966

Jefferson Ryder noted the time as he felt the Swissair jet lift off into Teheran's crisp morning air. The Teheran-to-Beirut flight was on its way, and the punctilious Swiss had managed, as usual, to get their airliner off exactly on schedule. Ryder settled back in his seat, sighing to himself, and feeling utterly depressed. He knew that his low spirits were due in no small part to submerged aftereffects from his violent showdown with Hassan Rafat on the mountain only yesterday. Too, he held himself responsible for the grievous circumstances into which Anna Boubahri had so suddenly been plunged. Leaving Teheran while so much remained unresolved and bewildering for Anna made him feel like a fugitive.

Ryder looked at John Maxton sitting next to him by the window. He decided to air his troubles at Maxton's expense. "Max, I feel lousy. Say something to cheer me up."

John Maxton turned a phlegmatic face to Ryder. "If you think *you've* got problems, how do you think old buddy Schuyler feels right about now?"

Ryder shook his head, but couldn't help a small smile. "You *would* bring that up! The poor sod. I don't envy him. We get to ride in the parade, and he gets to sweep up the droppings!"

Maxton stated laconically, "Don't waste your sympathy. Bogart the Third *needs* to get a little shit on his shoes."

Ryder said, "Maybe so, but we left him with one helluva wire-walk! He's got to cope with the Persian cops, keep the State Department out of the mess, pretend he's never heard of the CIA, please Harte, soothe Anna Boubahri, and also steer clear of the rest of the Rafat family!"

Maxton just shrugged. "What the hell, he's a *diplomat*, isn't he? All that stuff is right up his alley. And anyway, there wasn't any choice. Harte and Crawford ordered us to haul ass!"

Despite all that had remained unsaid, Ryder felt better for the conversation. He tilted his head against the seat back and absently observed, "For a change, it's good to be heading for home."

Maxton looked speculatively at his friend for a moment. "You know what? Something tells me what you need is to spend some time with a decent dame. Like for instance that little redhead Marge Mackenzie, who you always talk about when you're drunk and lonely."

Ryder looked sideways at Maxton, surprised. Between themselves, out of long, unspoken practice, he and Maxton rarely spoke of personal things. Ryder decided that his friend was pursuing the effort to cheer him up. He smiled and admitted, "Not a bad thought."

Maxton refused to let himself get caught in too much serious discussion. "And now that I think about it, I do believe I've got dames on my mind too."

Ryder chuckled. "You're probably dreaming of Anna Boubahri's pal Olga!"

Maxton brightened. "Now you're talking! I've got a guaranteed date with that gorgeous piece anytime I'm in town!" In a contented voice, Maxton added, "And she may not look it, but she's as by-God horny as I am!"

The conversation was interrupted by a comely Swiss hostess who asked for their breakfast orders. Ryder ordered a light snack. Maxton ordered everything on the breakfast menu. A while later the food was served and Ryder watched as Maxton devoured the huge breakfast, and then leaned back and promptly dozed off as usual.

On arrival in Beirut, Ryder and Maxton checked into the Phoenicia Hotel. They confirmed their onward flight reservations to the United States, for departure from Beirut on the following day. The intervening afternoon and evening of uncommitted time offered an inviting opportunity to do absolutely nothing for a few hours. Ryder held in check the temptation to relax, having one remaining voluntary chore to complete. He telephoned the American Embassy and secured an appointment with Ambassador Julius Harte.

At the embassy, Ryder was warmly greeted by Harte's secretary, Marge Mackenzie. He looked admiringly at her and said, "Marge, the real reason I keep calling on Ambassador Harte these days is to give me an excuse for some conversation with you!"

Marge smiled a little, and looked briefly down at the papers on her desk. Then she removed her glasses, and with wide-set green eyes fixed squarely on Ryder's face, she quietly said in her low voice, "The ambassador thinks very highly of you, and as a matter of fact, Jeff, so do I. I don't think you'll ever have trouble speaking with either one of us."

Taken by surprise by Marge's direct sincerity, Ryder was fumbling for a response when the door to the ambassador's office opened. Julius Harte strode out, preoccupied and frowning down at some papers in his hand. He said, "Marge, put these in the safe for me, please." As he spoke, the ambassador looked up. Discovering Jefferson Ryder standing there, the frown vanished from Harte's homely, elongated face. It was instantly replaced by a wide, beaming smile. Harte placed his papers on Marge's desk, and came over to Ryder, his hand extended in greeting. "Mr. Ryder! Jeff! I'm certainly pleased to see you!" The ambassador's hearty handshake gave Ryder a sharp reminder that his forearms were still sore from his foray with Rafat's dog.

Ryder smiled back at Harte. "Thanks for the compliment, sir."

The ambassador waved genially toward his office. "Please come on in, Jeff. I'm anxious to talk to you."

Harte urged Ryder to precede him into the office. Speaking back over his shoulder to Marge, the ambassador asked her to see that he and Ryder were not disturbed for the next half hour or so. The two men seated themselves, and Ambassador Harte opened the conversation. In a serious tone, he said, "Bogart Schuyler has kept me constantly advised of the situation since he arrived in Teheran, Jeff. I am terribly sad about the death of your friend Mr. Boubahri. I know how you must feel, and I know it was difficult for you to leave Teheran so abruptly, in the presence of Mrs. Boubahri's grief-stricken state of mind. I hope you will understand that Mr. Crawford and I asked you to come away from Teheran only because we could see no safe alternative."

Ryder nodded briefly. "I understand that, Mr. Ambassador. I just hope Anna Boubahri does too."

Julius Harte said earnestly, "Believe me, Jeff, while you may not think it to look at him, Bogart Schuyler will be very good with this kind of problem. He's a sympathetic and understanding person."

The ambassador leaned back in his chair. After a moment's pause, he introduced a change in the subject. "Now, since you're here I want to pass along to you some recent developments. It has been quite positively established that those weapons shipments you came across, into Jordan, are part of a much larger and very complex apparatus." Harte unconsciously picked up a pencil, and tapped its point on the top of his desk as he continued. "While the connection seems improbable at first glance, the movement of arms and the shipments of narcotics through Afghanistan and Iran are each parts of a greater overall operation. I cannot explain it all to you since we simply do not know the whole story. One thing is certain, however. The entire sordid, dangerous scheme operates directly against the United States."

Ryder studied the ambassador for a moment. "It sounds like you're telling me there'll be more before this is over with."

Ambassador Harte looked solemn. "We are facing an incredibly deadly and far-reaching intrigue, Jeff. Among the several vicious motives underlying this traffic, millions upon millions of dollars are at stake. It will not be simply nor quickly undone. In the meanwhile, as you have good reason to know, personal risk will run very high. It will increase for you as time goes on. So remember, you are perfectly free to withdraw. No one will think an ounce less of you if you do."

Jefferson Ryder shook his head slightly. "Ambassador Harte, I'm not going to pretend I haven't been scared silly a couple of times in this mess. But after the Boubahri thing, it's reached the point where it's kind of personal now. I'm not ready to quit."

The ambassador digested Ryder's statement for a while in silence. He looked at Ryder and said, "Jim Crawford will be very pleased to learn that you intend continuing in this effort. For my part, however, I will confess to mixed emotions. Your assignment is a vital one. You have already accomplished much in it, and it is rewarding to have a person of your competence on this urgent task. Nevertheless, Jeff, I dread the thought of your further exposure to the personal dangers involved. My inclination is to urge that you withdraw."

Ryder ran his right hand over his left forearm, where the stitched wound was healing. With a rueful smile, he said, "That's probably the best advice I've ever had, Ambassador Harte. Somehow, though, I wouldn't feel right if I didn't see this thing through."

Julius Harte nodded. With a note of resignation in his voice, he said, "I rather thought you'd feel that way. But it was worth discussing." The ambassador's manner changed abruptly. "Now, there are one or two other items I want to mention to you. Mr. Crawford has made elaborate arrangements to track the movements of that morphine shipment you found on the Rafat land in Teheran. That shipment was removed from there while you were in Kabul, probably coincident with the timing of Mr. Boubahri's death. If Crawford's effort is successful, and he is able to follow that shipment, point by point, to its ultimate destination, he believes he will know enough to halt the entire scheme. In the meanwhile, he is virtually certain that someone very powerfully placed here in Beirut occupies a keystone position in the major structure of this alien operation. Crawford believes that this Beirut link is their point of greatest vulnerability. As soon as the morphine shipment trace is completed, he intends to apply concentrated effort here."

The ambassador sat silently for a moment, holding Ryder's attention with his eyes. At length he spoke. "Jeff, I frankly don't know whether or not the CIA people will reveal all this to you. As far as I'm concerned, though, you need to know as much as possible for your own protection."

Jefferson Ryder looked at the ambassador with new respect, reasonably certain that the man had exercised a freedom that tested the limits of his authority by making those disclosures. Harte had evidently done so solely out of concern for Ryder. Ryder said, "I'll put that information to good use, sir, when the time comes. For now, as I guess you already know, I'm heading for home. In case Crawford wonders, I won't be stopping along the way. I'm going straight on through to LA via London and JFK."

Julius Harte stood and moved out from behind his desk. Ryder accepted this as a signal to leave. He rose and thanked the ambassador for his help. The two men shook hands, and Ryder turned toward the door. The ambassador walked to the door with him. Harte said, "I will expect James Crawford to keep me informed during your absence, Jeff. I'm sure he will advise me when you plan to return. In any event, please plan to see me and Schuyler when you next come back to Beirut."

Ryder smiled. "You can count on that, sir." He stepped out of the ambassador's office, and closed the door.

Marge looked up at Ryder as he emerged from Harte's office. He went over to her desk, smiling into her lovely, expectant face. "Miss Mackenzie, as I recall we were interrupted a little while ago in the middle of an important conversation. What I'd like to do is continue that conversation from where we left off tonight over dinner. How do you feel about that idea?"

Ryder saw a hint of added color come into Marge's smiling face as she looked up at him and said, "I feel just fine about that idea, Mr. Ryder!"

Ryder said, "Marge, just give me your telephone number. I'll call you at eight, and you can tell me how to find you." Marge Mackenzie wrote her number down, and, still wearing a rosy glow, handed the slip of paper to Jeff Ryder. He pocketed the telephone number, and with a parting wave of the hand, headed out of the embassy.

PART 4: A TRIPLICITY

Dimitri's
Beirut, Lebanon
MAY 1966

Ryder's taxi stopped in front of the address he had given the driver. It belonged to a new-looking apartment building overlooking the Corniche, Beirut's seashore drive, and was situated about a quarter of a mile away from the US Embassy. Ryder asked the driver to wait, then entered the lobby of the building and stepped into the automatic elevator. He rode the elevator to the fifth floor and glanced at his watch, noting that it said eight thirty, and that he was right on time. Ryder knocked on Marge Mackenzie's apartment door.

The door opened a little, then Marge unfastened the chain latch and opened the door wide. She smiled handsomely, and greeted Ryder warmly. "Good evening, Jeff! Please come in."

Ryder stood at the door for a moment, staring at a Marjorie Mackenzie that he hadn't realized existed. She looked stunning. Ryder emitted a low whistle. He said, "Marge, I'm spellbound! Where is that efficient little girl in the quiet tailored suits that used to be Marge Mackenzie?" Ryder stepped past Marge, and after she had closed the door behind him, he took her gravely by the hand, and gently spun her around as he looked at her from head to foot.

Marge wore a form-fitting white silk dress with a deep V-neck, and with a dropped waistline low around her hips. The short, pleated skirt swirled above her knees, displaying an admirable length of Marge's lovely legs. Her outfit was classic in its simplicity. Marge wore a single strand of pearls, which hung enticingly over the shadow of cleavage between her full, rounded breasts. With small pearl earrings, and wearing white, high-heeled pumps, she was a picture of elegant grace. The white outfit seemed to send burnished highlights into the cloud of her deep auburn hair.

Jefferson Ryder refused to release Marge's hand, or to take his eyes from her. She scolded, "Jeff! I believe you've been away from girls too long lately! Now, come and have a quick Scotch with me." Marge led Ryder by the hand to a comfortable-looking couch, then went into her tiny kitchen, where a bottle of Scotch and a pair of tumblers and some ice waited. She called, "With water or soda, Jeff?"

Ryder answered, "A splash of water, please." He watched her through the kitchen doorway, busily working at the counter, and tried to sort out the intensity of his reactions since Marge had opened the door.

She brought the two glasses back, and seated herself next to Ryder. She handed him his drink, then held her glass up for a toast. Ryder clinked his glass against Marge's, and she said with a smile, "Here's to an auspicious occasion!"

Ryder looked into Marge's wide green eyes, and said, "Truer words were never spoken, Miss Mackenzie!" They each tasted their drinks. Ryder leaned back, and comfortably swung his ankle across his knee. He studied Marge critically, and said, "I'm trying to decide whether you look like a big eater or not. I've got a zillion things to find out about you. So far, all I know is you're intelligent, you're efficient, you have a nice voice, you like Scotch whiskey, and you're impossibly beautiful."

Marge laughed a little, then made a quizzical face. "Dreadfully transparent flattery, Mr. Ryder! I will shatter your grand illusions when you discover that I am absolutely voracious at the dinner table!"

Ryder lightly slapped his knee. "Sorry to disappoint you, but the truth is, I don't care for ladies with dainty appetites. Tonight, I'd like to take you to my favorite hideaway in Beirut for dinner. Do you know Dimitri's?"

Marge thought a moment, then, to Ryder's pleased surprise, shook her head. He stood and said, "That makes it perfect. Dimitri is a little old Greek who, as far as I'm concerned, is the best cook in the whole world!"

Marge said solemnly, as she rose from the couch, "For future reference, Mr. Jefferson Ryder, I consider that statement something of a challenge. I'm pretty wicked with the pots and pans myself!"

Ryder chuckled. He glanced at Marge's drink, and saw that a swallow remained. He said, "Okay, Miss Challenger! Bottoms up! Let's proceed with the first half of this grudge match between you and Dimitri." They drained their glasses and set about leaving Marge's apartment.

Dimitri, a wizened old Greek who had learned his masterful culinary talents in the kitchens of Greece's royalty, had come to Beirut to retire. He operated his tiny Beirut restaurant in a completely unique manner. To begin with, his establishment had no sign in front, and consequently was little known, and difficult to find. Then Dimitri, relying on word of mouth for his trade, reserved the right to accept only those guests whom it pleased him to serve. He rarely allowed more than five couples to dine on his food in a given evening. Dimitri's restaurant occupied space once relegated to basement service. Its uneven brick floor rested three steps down from street level. The low-ceilinged space had, under Dimitri's direction, been irregularly divided into a miniature honeycomb of intimate alcoves, separated by low brick walls of varying height. Vines and ferns seemed to thrive in strategically accidental gaps in the erratic masonry, and a trio of miniature fireplaces sent their flickering light dancing into the dim dining niches. Amber candlelight provided the only other illumination. During Dimitri's dinner hours, the atmosphere of his little cave would fill with delectable gourmet aromas.

It was Marge Mackenzie who was spellbound this time. She kept gasping in astonished delight as Jeff Ryder, following the bent figure of the chuckling old Greek, led her carefully through the shadowy, cozy recesses of Dimitri's tiny labyrinth. Nothing pleased the old chef more than this, the delight of a beautiful woman. He led them to their low table, set before a deep, curved stone bench piled with fat cushions. Soft music emanated from some invisible source. Dimitri waited patiently as they settled themselves into the pillowed comfort behind the table. He then produced champagne on ice, poured their glasses, and bowed himself out of sight.

Marge, bursting with things she wanted to exclaim, could scarcely wait for the old chef to disappear. In her delighted enthusiasm, while Dimitri opened the champagne and poured, Marge unconsciously hugged herself against Jeff Ryder's arm. As soon as the old Greek had moved out of view, she spun her head and turned her sparkling eyes into Ryder's face. She exclaimed breathlessly, "Jeff! This place is a treasure! And that dear old man is priceless! How did you ever find your way here?"

Ryder smiled into her eyes, "Marge, you're right . . . Dimitri's *is* incredible tonight. The funny thing is, it has never looked nearly this good before! Anyway, I don't want you to pass final judgment until you've had your dinner."

Marge impulsively reached for her champagne glass. She raised it and said, "It's your turn to propose a toast, Jeff!" Ryder picked up his glass, and suddenly he was serious.

He touched his glass to hers. "Listen, Marge. I don't know what the hell has been happening to me since sometime this afternoon, but I do know this. Great little moments like this one only happen a few times in anybody's life. So, pretty Marge, here's to this moment!"

Ryder sipped his champagne, continuing to look into Marge's eyes as he drank. To his astonishment, he saw her eyes fill with tears. Ryder put his glass down, but Marge did not look away. He looked questioningly into her brimming eyes, and said, "Hey, pretty lady, I aim to keep you happy tonight! Did I say something I shouldn't have?

Marge blinked back the tears, then shook her head and smiled. She said, quietly, "No, Jeff. On the contrary. What you said was beautifully true. You see, you are making me happy tonight. Happier than I've been for a very long time." Marge then laughed a little, and added, "Now you know one more thing about me. I cry when I'm happy!" Her smile faded away, and Marge looked down at her hands. In a very low voice, almost to herself, she said, "I'm afraid to be this happy."

Jeff Ryder, watching Marge's face, wondered at her quiet statement. He resolved that the evening's gala beginning was well worth saving. He cupped his hand gently under Marge's chin, and lifted her face. He said, "I'm very tolerant with honest displays of emotion, young lady, but I have to warn you that my friend Dimitri is not! He may pop out of the shadows at any moment, and refuse to serve you your soup! He'll do that if he thinks you'll let salty tears fall into it and spoil its taste!"

Marge couldn't help giggling a little. She said, with spirit, "Well, I'm darned if he's going to cheat me out of my soup! I'll fix my face so he'll never know the difference!" She rummaged in her diminutive evening bag, then proceeded, with the help of a few articles from the purse, to make good on her word.

As though on cue, Dimitri emerged from the shadowed aisle, bearing a tureen of soup and their plates. Ryder pulled a face and looked sideways at Marge. She failed in her efforts to keep a straight face, and tried to smother her laughter with both hands. The old Greek, smiling indulgently, ladled generous servings of deliciously aromatic soup into their plates. He then produced a fine Rhine wine, and, after Ryder had sampled it, filled two glasses for them, then bowed himself out. Her spirits fully restored, Marge made pleased sounds as she tasted the savory dish.

With flawless timing, old Dimitri kept their table laden with one delicious dish after another. The soup was followed by oysters on the half shell. Then came a crisply fresh green salad, with dressing abundantly thick with crumbled chunks of Roquefort cheese and crisp bits of bacon. Freshly baked bread hot from the oven was set beside their dinner plates of steak au poivre, potatoes au gratin, and generous portions of giant, tender asparagus tips.

Each course was accompanied by its separate, elegant wine. Ryder had ordered his favorite, a vintage year of Châteauneuf-du-Pape, as a companion to the steaks. For dessert, Dimitri prepared tiny crepes on an alcohol stove that he wheeled in beside their table. The crepes were covered with a hot brandy sauce that, with a flourish, Dimitri set ablaze as he served them.

Finally, with the table cleared and with coffee and a superb brandy to sip on, Jeff Ryder and Marge leaned in sated comfort against the pillowed backrest.

Marge sighed contentedly, her head leaning back against the cushion behind her. She turned her face toward Ryder, and smiled. Her eyes looked drowsy and warm. In her low voice, she said, "It must be sinful to feel so good! You are a diabolical man, Mr. Ryder!"

Jeff looked good naturedly back at her. He said, "It is a conspiracy between myself and Dimitri. That's only for tonight, of course. After tonight, Dimitri has stated that he will never let me return unless you're with me."

Marge laughed her throaty laugh. She said, "And *that*, Mr. Jeff Ryder, is the result of a conspiracy between *me* and Dimitri," and they both laughed. Then Ryder looked into his brandy glass, and said, "Marge, I've been coming out to the Middle East for years now. Tomorrow, when I head back to the States, will be the first time that I've gone away from here leaving something personally important behind."

Marge put her hand on Ryder's. She said, "I'll admit something too, Jeff." She looked into his eyes. "This may be foolish to say, but I've already started missing you." Marge looked aside then, and, sounding far away, said, "I want you to be safe, though. Away from here."

Ryder, wondering at Marge's words, said, "As far as I know, the only danger I'm near is you, pretty lady, and that I like!"

Marge looked at Ryder, her eyes showing concern. She shook her head and said, "Jeff, don't forget where I work. You must know that I'm aware of what you're doing . . . at least part of it, anyway." She tugged his left sleeve back until she had uncovered some of the angry scars on his arm. She looked up at him, and said, "Think how much worse that might have been!"

Ryder was quiet for a moment. Then he looked at Marge. He said gently to her, "Marge, you're over here, thousands of miles away from home, and among strange people, doing something you know is important, something you like to do, and are good at. I think everyone tries to get himself set up that way. Like you, I'm one of the lucky ones. I'm doing a job of work that I like, and I'm pretty good at. So, I'll make a bargain with you, pretty lady. I'll go ahead and let you worry some about me, if you'll let me worry about you too."

Marge took one of Ryder's hands in both of hers. Her eyes had misted. She said, "Darn you, Jeff Ryder! You've gone and made me happy again!"

Feeling the warmth of her hands on his, and catching the fragrant scent of her hair, Jeff Ryder looked into the depths of Marge's moist eyes. He leaned toward her, and said softly, "I think I'll take advantage of that," and he put his lips against hers. He heard a small, urgent sound in her throat, then felt her arms around his neck. He held her gently to him, and felt the warm softness of her breasts pressing against him while they kissed.

Marge shook her head and put her hands to her cheeks, which she knew were glowing. She said, "It's that old brandy! A girl doesn't have a chance against a combination like this! Napoleon, Dimitri, and *you*!" She leaned her head happily against Ryder's shoulder, and hugged his arm.

Ryder smiled and said into her hair, "Then I'd better take you home, pretty lady, before any more terrible plots are hatched around here."

Marge held firmly to Ryder's arm while they rode the elevator up to her floor. He said, "Now, Miss Mackenzie, if you will unearth your key from that little bag of mysteries you're carrying, I'll be a gentleman and open your door for you."

Marge found the key in her purse, but didn't release Ryder's arm. She handed the key to him as the elevator arrived. They stepped to her door, and Ryder opened it. Marge held one of his hands, and turned to face him. She asked, "Jeff, how long will you be away?"

Ryder looked into her lovely eyes. He said, "I told Dimitri to write 'Marge and Jeff' on that brandy bottle we didn't finish. We've got to go back soon."

Marge came close to Ryder, and looked up into his face. She said softly, "Marge and Jeff. That sounds corny, doesn't it?"

Ryder said, "Not to me, it doesn't," and he put his arms around her and kissed her hard. He felt her lips part, and felt his own heart pounding. Marge, her arms thrown around his neck, pressed herself trembling against him. A warm pressure surged through his loins. They parted from the kiss. Her breath catching, Marge took Ryder's hand. She stepped back through the doorway a little, and purposefully slipped out of her shoes. She looked into his eyes, and pulled him by the hand. In a small voice, she said, "Good night, Jeff, darling," and closed the door with him inside.

Port of Monaco
Riviera, France
MAY 1966

The cream Cadillac convertible, with its top folded down, moved sedately away from the seaside heliport, and headed toward the northern arm of the stone jetty that guards Monaco's tiny harbor. Enthroned in the rear seat behind the driver and his own bodyguard, Luigi Carini puffed contentedly on a fine Havana cigar, and adjusted his new, narrow-brimmed straw hat with its bright, peacock-blue band. He stared out at the unreal loveliness in the blend of colors surrounding him. Monaco, drenched in balmy warmth under its cloudless blue May skies, looked and sounded and felt too good to be true.

Carini, feeling superior and important behind his dark sunglasses, surveyed a row of gleaming yachts riding at anchor in extravagant idleness as the Cadillac eased along Monaco's Quai des Etats Unis. He watched denim-trousered, white-shirted crewmen attentively at work grooming their immaculate charges. Ahead, Carini recognized Alfonzo Bonifacio's magnificent, thirty-meter yacht. He nodded in unconscious self-satisfaction as the Cadillac slowed and confirmed his observation. Now that his meeting with the Corsican, Bonifacio, was about to take place, Luigi Carini let himself wonder again, for a moment, what might have prompted Bonifacio to call for this extraordinary private rendezvous.

The Cadillac's driver hurried to open the car door for Carini. At the same time, a white-uniformed steward from Bonifacio's boat seemed to appear magically as Carini stepped out of the car. The steward saluted him courteously, then, with the driver's help, removed the Mafia chief's suitcases and attaché case from the luggage compartment of the Cadillac. With the uniformed steward leading the way, and with his bodyguard pacing alongside, Carini headed for Alfonzo Bonifacio's yacht. He smiled to himself as he noticed the gilt letters on the prow of the sleek boat. They proclaimed the name of Bonifacio's yacht, *Le Cheval d'Or.*

Horse, the vernacular nickname for heroin, Carini thought to himself. *It would take someone with Bonifacio's brand of brute guts to name his huge goddamned boat "The Golden Horse," when he'd bought the thing with heroin profits!*

Two natty crewmen saluted Carini as the trio stepped aboard. Leisurely following the steward, Carini glanced back, and noticed that the two sailors had whisked away the gangplank behind him, and other crewmen were busily singling up the mooring lines in readiness for casting off. The steward led Carini aft, to a lounge deck on the fantail of the boat.

The burly, short-legged figure of Alfonzo Bonifacio emerged from a cabin companionway as Carini approached. The Corsican, unintentionally accentuating his own thick torso, wore a blue and white, barrel-striped pullover jersey. A battered yachting cap rested in a tilt on the back of his head, leaving a curly tangle of thick, iron-gray hair showing under its peak. Bonifacio jerked his thumb over his shoulder at the steward, then smiled and shook hands with Big Lou Carini. The steward obediently disappeared down the cabin companionway, carrying Carini's luggage. Carini's bodyguard, at a signal from his boss, followed the steward.

Bonifacio said, "We'll be under way in a couple of minutes, Lou. Let's save the business talk until later. Right now, there are probably a hundred pairs of binoculars trained on us."

Carini grimaced contemptuously as he glanced toward Monaco's multitude of seaward-facing windows. He waved his cigar in a disparaging gesture, and said, "It's too nice a day to let a few grubbing, shitting civil servants bother us." In further derision he added, "Those poor fools must grind their teeth every time they see the name of this boat! 'The Golden Horse'!" Carini laughed at the joke, which was anything but new to Bonifacio. Still chortling, Carini added, "I think I'll get a boat too. I'll call mine 'The *Brass* Horse'!" He continued chuckling in tribute to his own cleverness, and asked, "Alfonzo, how would you put that in French?"

Bonifacio smiled, and answered, "*Le Cheval de Cuivre.*" Carini tried to repeat the French phrase, but made the last word sound like "queever." He grinned foolishly at himself.

Bonifacio pointed toward some deck chairs. "Well, what's your pleasure, Lou? It's after eleven. You want to take it easy and have a drink now, or would you rather go get rid of that necktie?"

Carini looked down at his rumpled Palm Beach suit, then at his host's casual outfit. He declared, "I feel like a Miami kike in this straitjacket. I'm going to go change clothes." He tossed his cigar overboard. The steward reappeared at that moment, and came toward them. Bonifacio introduced him.

"Lou, this is my chief steward, Tony. He'll see that you get anything you want, anytime you want it." The Corsican turned to the steward. "Tony, show Mr. Carini his cabin."

The steward gestured politely for Carini to precede him down the companionway, and as they headed into the boat's cool interior, Carini felt the deck begin to thrum gently under the soles of his shoes as power was applied to the engines.

Half an hour later Carini returned to the lounge deck, clad in a lightweight, red nylon sport shirt and white duck slacks. He wore a pair of canvas deck shoes over socks that matched the red of his shirt. As he emerged into the shaded sunlight of the canopied afterdeck and donned his sunglasses, he found the scene changed. Silverware and crystal stemware gleamed on the white linen of a luncheon table set for four. Champagne stood chilling in silver buckets by the table. A sideboard displaying a mouth-watering variety of delicious foods had been set out, attended by a white-aproned Negro in a tall chef's hat. A barman wearing a purple, brass-buttoned mess jacket stood alongside a liquor cart. White-jacketed mess stewards waited inconspicuously in the background. The boat was under way and now, seen from this more removed vantage point, Monaco presented herself as a cluster of beige gems resting against a soft green pillow.

Lou Carini absorbed the transformed surroundings with a complacent glance, then focused his attention approvingly on one other attraction that had been added during his absence. Two stunningly lovely, fashionably dressed young women lounged gracefully in deck chairs, one on each side of Alfonzo Bonifacio. An empty chair stood invitingly nearby. Carini guessed the two girls to be thirtyish—"just right," he thought to himself—and thanks to Bonifacio's sagacious judgment in such things, the physical desirability of the two women was heightened by the simple fact that, here on a yacht at sea, they were fully clothed. *Better than bikinis . . . and a better place to start from*, Carini thought. Both of the girls wore modish hairdos, expensive-looking, short-skirted sports ensembles, high heels, and nylon stockings.

The two women, taking notice of Carini's arrival, looked pleasantly in his direction as they continued chatting with Bonifacio. Carini moved toward the seated trio. The burly Corsican, smiling broadly, stood as the Mafia chief approached. He introduced Carini. "Lou, I'm sure you'll be happy to meet these two charming friends of mine. This is Mlle. Nicole

Simonet." He gestured to a dark haired girl on his right. "And this is Mlle. Jeanne Leveque." The pretty blond girl seated on Bonifacio's left looked up and smiled. Bonifacio turned to the women. "Ladies, this is Mr. Lou Carini. Mr. Carini is an American businessman, and a close acquaintance. You have my permission to be nice to him."

Carini preened himself, and shook hands with each of the girls, then seated himself in the empty deck chair. This placed him nearest to the brunette girl, Nicole. Bonifacio signaled to the barman, then said to Carini, "Lou, Nicole and Jeanne will lunch with us. Then, since you and I have a few dull business things to discuss, the ladies will occupy themselves elsewhere for a while. Later this afternoon, after we have disposed of our affairs of business, they will rejoin us, and help us enjoy the balance of this very nice day."

The waiting barman took drink orders from the foursome. Luigi Carini ran his eyes hungrily over Nicole's figure, lingering on the admirable swell of her breasts under the loose, open-necked blouse, her narrow waist, and the shapeliness of her long, nylon-encased legs that rested, comfortably crossed, almost touching him. Carini began to think enthusiastically of the way he would spend the later afternoon.

Le Cheval d'Or cruised smoothly through the tranquil blue of the Mediterranean while the foursome enjoyed a delectable lunch. The luncheon ended in high spirits, and Luigi Carini, with a great show of reluctance, watched as Nicole and Jeanne waved teasingly, then disappeared into the cabin passageway.

Still smiling, Carini stood for a moment, staring after the women. Then he turned to the seated Corsican. Alfonzo Bonifacio, his face already businesslike, said, "Okay, Lou. Why don't you sit down? What I have to tell you is not pleasant."

Carini sat as suggested. A puzzled frown settled over his face as he waited for the Corsican to continue.

Bonifacio, watching the Mafia chief's face, said, "Lou, we're missing one hundred kilos of the Chinese 'M.' It never reached Marseille."

All traces of preoccupation vanished from Carini's face. He sat up rigidly in his chair, and stared at Bonifacio. After a moment of stunned silence, Carini's voice rasped, "Let's take this slow, Al. Tell me the whole story."

The Corsican, slouched in his chair, said, "In the half of the first move that came over by the Alpha route, overland by truck, there were one too many crates of hides, and one too few of the 'M.' The Beta shipment, off the boat, tallied perfectly."

Carini's mind raced. The suspicion crossed his mind that Bonifacio might, himself, be lying about the miscount. Carini immediately dismissed that idea as preposterous. He frowned, unhappy with the number of possibilities that presented themselves. He asked, "Were all the Alpha crates marked correctly?"

Bonifacio smiled grimly, admiring Carini's quick incision into the problem. "No. We didn't discover the problem until the crates were opened. One of the crates of hides incorrectly carried a properly placed set of the brass screws. It was made to look like a morphine box."

The Corsican's answer to his question brought Carini's thoughts around to three principal likelihoods that might explain this unpleasant development. For the moment, he kept the thoughts to himself. He looked at Bonifacio. "What are your ideas on this?"

Bonifacio's scarred face remained impassive. He said, "You haven't heard everything yet, Lou. That young fool Hassan Rafat is dead. His body was found in the hills back of Teheran, shot twice through the head."

Lou Carini's jaw dropped. Icy fingers of fear closed his throat momentarily. He thrust his head toward Bonifacio, and said hoarsely, "Why wasn't I informed? When in hell did this happen?"

The Corsican answered evenly, "I only got the confirmation and details this morning. Old man Rafat has kept a lid on it. He's not sure that it wasn't *us* who murdered that punk. As best I can tell, Rafat was shot on the fifth of this month, about a week ago."

Carini's mind was thrown into new confusion. He got up from his chair and walked to the railing at the stern of the boat, shaking his head as he stared at the foaming wake. He thought about some of the implications of Bonifacio's grim revelations. One hundred kilos. The equivalent, converted to salable heroin, of $25 million! A totally unacceptable loss anytime, but disastrously painful now, so early in this fledgling program. Impossible to explain in New York. No! Unmentionable in New York! The missing morphine must be recovered, and quickly!

Carini came back and sat down heavily in the deck chair. Leaning forward, he stared down at the deck between his feet while anger rose in him. With his growing temper, Carini began to feel like his old self again. He snapped his head up and narrowed his eyes as he looked at Bonifacio. His voice filled with menace as he spoke. "Alfonzo, you've given me a lot to swallow in one dose! Let's go back to where we were a few minutes ago. You've had a little time to think about this ungodly mess. Tell me what you think."

Bonifacio understood the appeal in Carini's words. He also understood the lethal promise in Carini's tone. He said, "Lou, as it stands, I see either a stupid mistake, or an inside job. There are other possibilities, but this looks a little too cute to be coming from the outside." The Corsican then added meditatively, "You know, the funny thing is, if it hadn't been the first shipment, we probably wouldn't have discovered the problem until too late to ever be sure. I handle a lot of morphine, Lou. The missing amount would have been buried in the system. If this is deliberate, whoever pulled it off could have gotten away with it, if he'd just been a little patient."

Carini, his eyes now keenly fixed on Bonifacio's face, nodded. "I had it boiled down to three big probables until you tossed me that curve about Rafat. I'm ruling out the idea of a mistake. It's either inside, or else somebody goddamned smart, like the lousy CIA, for instance, has got his finger up our ass. But, I'm damned if I can see how they could have wised up this fast, not after Rafat lopped off all their feelers. They might have cut Rafat down, but that doesn't have to tie in with this other crap, this disappearing morphine! I vote for the inside job." Carini began to feel better. The problem had started to shrink toward more familiar dimensions.

The Corsican nodded his agreement with Carini's logic. He said, "Let's play it out that way for a minute. Who could pull it off?" He held up a hairy hand, fingers extended, then began to eliminate possibilities by closing fingers down, one by one, into his fist. "There's you and I. Assuming you agree that I didn't steal the 'M,' I eliminate both of us at once." He closed his thumb. "The Rafat murder, plus a lot of obvious logic, pretty well eliminates the Rafat organization." He folded his little finger away. "Then, what about old Emil Oltu, the tattered-ass Turk? I'd say not in a million years. Emil had all he wanted before we even came along."

Carini broke in, shaking his head. "Forget the old Turk. We've got him busier than a one-legged man at an ass-kicking contest. He wouldn't have time or inclination to pull this kind of stunt."

Bonifacio closed his ring finger to indicate elimination of the Turk. Two fingers remained. The Corsican waggled the two fingers. He said. "Thibault or Ghandhouri. The Frenchman or the Lebanese. They're both hungry enough. They're both smart enough. And they both had plenty of opportunity. In fact," Bonifacio mused, "they could have worked together!"

Carini removed his dark glasses and leaned back in his chair, gazing vacantly into space as he considered Bonifacio's analysis. He pondered silently, oblivious of time. Alfonzo Bonifacio waited patiently while the Mafia chief contemplated the problem. The Corsican knew intimately the terrible proportions of the dilemma facing Carini.

At length Carini's eyes swung to a focus on Bonifacio's watchful face. The Mafia chief balled his hand into a fist, and brought it down hard on the arm of his deck chair. He said, "Okay, Alfonzo. I'll take it from here. You have helped me more than you had to, and I won't be forgetting that. I'm satisfied I know what to do. The association deal will stand as agreed. I will personally make good any losses that might result from this mess. In the meanwhile, I would appreciate it if you will keep quiet about what has happened." Carini leaned forward, his face fixed with murderous determination. "I will tell you, though, Alfonzo, that I don't think it's going to cost me a cent!"

The Corsican looked back at Carini, then nodded slightly. He said quietly, "That's good enough for me. I'll help if I can. "

Carini relaxed and leaned back in his chair. He smiled thinly as he tore the wrapper from a fresh cigar. He said, "Alfonzo, there are two things I need real bad from you right now. The first is a goddamned drink, and the second is a chance to pull the pants off of that gorgeous chick Nicole!"

Bonifacio smiled and said, "*Fait accompli!*"

Friday the 13th
Beirut, Lebanon
MAY 1966

After a routine and uneventful trip from Los Angeles by way of New York and London, Jefferson Ryder and John Maxton made their way wearily to their rooms in Beirut's Phoenicia Hotel. They left the elevator and followed the bellboys down the corridor. Ryder said, "Jet lag or no jet lag, I can't sleep now. After I let Ghandhouri know we're in town, and call Harte at the embassy, I'm going down to park myself beside the pool, and guzzle a beer or two."

Maxton brightened. "That sounds better than sacking out. I'm with you. Maybe we can get a good afternoon drunk started!" They arrived at Ryder's room, and stopped at the door. Ryder said, "After I make these calls I'll give you a holler."

Maxton nodded and went on to his own room. Ryder tipped the bellboy, then proceeded with his unpacking. He finished stowing away his clothes, then stretched out on the bed, and picked up the telephone. He dialed the number for the Near East Board of Trade, Wahji Ghandhouri's Beirut headquarters. Finally getting Ghandhouri's secretary on the line, Ryder gave her his name. The secretary told him that Mr. Ghandhouri was not in the office, but had left a message for Ryder. Tomorrow, Saturday, the message said, Mr. Ghandhouri would be pleased if Mr. Ryder would join him for luncheon and business discussions at Mr. Ghandhouri's summer residence, twenty minutes' drive from Beirut. Mr. Ghandhouri had instructed that a chauffeured limousine be put at Mr. Ryder's disposal.

Ryder thanked the secretary, and asked for the limousine at eleven o'clock the following morning. Ryder finished the conversation, then called the US Embassy and asked for connection to the ambassador's office. Marge Mackenzie's husky voice came through the receiver. Ryder said quietly, "Hi, pretty lady. This is Jeff. I've come back to see if Dimitri is taking good care of our bottle of brandy!"

Ryder was rewarded with incredulous, delighted surprise in Marge's voice. "Jeff! I don't believe my ears!"

Ryder chuckled. "Max and I just pulled in, Marge." Marge said excitedly, "Oh, Jeff! This is too good to be true!"

Ryder leaned back on the bed. "Well! I can see that my whole world has changed! Never have I been welcomed to Beirut like *this* before!"

Marge said, low into the telephone, "Jeff, dear, this is nothing like the welcome you'll get when we're alone!"

Ryder cleared his throat purposefully. "You're taking my mind off my work, ma'am. First I have a few little business items to clear up. How's chances for talking to the boss?"

Marge reverted to a businesslike tone. "For you, they're pretty good, Mr. Ryder! Hold on a minute," The line was quiet for a while, then Marge's voice returned. "He'll be available for a call in about five minutes or so. Can I call you back, Jeff?"

Ryder said, "Okay, I'm in 1026, Marge. Now listen. It's been a whole week since I've had dinner at Dimitri's. If you're game, pretty lady, I'd like to try for a return engagement tomorrow night."

In a pert voice, Marge declared, "It's not Dimitri's turn, it's mine! *I'm* making the dinner for tomorrow night!"

Ryder grinned, and said into the telephone, "I accept! What shall I bring?"

Marge answered brightly, "Just bring yourself and your appetite, Mr. Ryder. Say at eight o'clock?"

Jeff Ryder said, "Me and my appetite, we'll be there at eight."

Marge closed the conversation by promising to call back as soon as Ambassador Harte was free.

A few minutes later Ryder's telephone rang back. He picked up the instrument, said, "Ryder here," and heard Julius Harte's voice.

"Welcome back, Jeff! I've been expecting your call. Jeff, I'm truly sorry but I have an unusually heavy schedule today, and it is unlikely that I'll be able to meet with you. If it is agreeable, I'd like to have you chat with Boge Schuyler, though."

Ryder presumed that the ambassador wanted to convey a message of some importance to him. "My pleasure, sir. Just say where and when."

The ambassador replied, "If you'll be at your hotel, I'll ask Boge to stop by. Would right away be too soon?"

Ryder answered, "Be fine with me, Ambassador Harte. I'll be here waiting."

Julius Harte then spoke in a slow, serious voice. "All right, Jeff. I'll be wishing you success with your efforts. Please take care of yourself. Godspeed and good-bye for now." The ambassador rang off. As he put down the telephone, Ryder ran a finger along the scar on his cheek, and wondered what message Schuyler might be bringing.

Ryder picked up the telephone again, and asked for John Maxton's room. Maxton's voice sounded sleepy. Ryder said, "Wake up, you oaf! I'm going downstairs to find myself an umbrella by the pool. Bogart Schuyler will be here in a few minutes for some palaver. Want to join in?"

Maxton growled, "Until you said that, I was all set to charge. What the hell did you invite old Black Bloomers for?"

Ryder grinned, "Max, it's all part of this fascinating business."

Maxton rumbled, "Well, *you* are the fascinating half of this dog-and-pony show. Tell me what happened after."

Ryder said, "Okay. I'll roust you later. Pleasant dreams." He put the telephone back on its cradle, and headed for the pool.

Ryder left a message at the reception desk for Bogart Schuyler, then located an unoccupied umbrella table on the outdoor patio, well out of range of the noisy and enthusiastic splashing from around the swimming pool. He slouched comfortably into one of the canvas folding chairs, and, inspired by a tray of Planter's Punches being delivered nearby, ordered one for himself. The busy waiter took considerable time before he returned with Ryder's drink, and just as the man hurried up, Ryder spotted Bogart Schuyler emerging from the lobby's patio door at the opposite end of the pool. The first secretary moved into the brilliant sunshine, and, blinking owlishly and shading his eyes with both hands, anxiously searched for Ryder in the crowded poolside area.

Ryder stood and moved into the sunlight, waving an arm to attract Schuyler's attention. Schuyler finally saw him, and threaded his way through the uproar and the tangle of arms and legs around the pool. Ryder could see from across the pool that Schuyler was agitated. Smiling faintly, Ryder thought to himself that Bogart Schuyler would unquestionably prove to be one of the world's worst poker players.

Schuyler arrived, puffing and perspiring, and Ryder, having detained the waiter, said, "Sit down, Boge, and take the load off your feet. You look like you need something tall and cool. What'll it be?"

Schuyler fanned his face with his hands, and looked at Ryder's Planter's Punch. "That does look good. I'll join you." Ryder sent the waiter after another drink, then looked at Bogart Schuyler. "How are you, Boge? I'm sorry I had to leave you holding the bag in Teheran."

Schuyler continued fanning himself. "Oh, I'm fine now. As to Teheran, things weren't as dreadful for me as they looked at first. Except, of course, for poor Mrs. Boubahri. She remained inconsolable, I'm sorry to say."

Ryder shook his head sadly. "I was afraid of that. Ali Boubahri was Anna's whole life."

Schuyler said, "Jeff, I suppose it isn't much consolation, but before I left, Mrs. Boubahri insisted over and over again that I assure you she doesn't blame you in any way for what happened."

Ryder again shook his head. "Well, I hope not. It's bad enough the way it is."

Schuyler went on, "Naturally, she's very confused about the entire affair. But, so is the whole city of Teheran, for that matter!"

Ryder asked in semihumor, "Have they put out 'Wanted' posters on me yet?"

Schuyler shook his head. "Oh, no. Nothing like that. The authorities are simply bewildered. Speaking frankly, I have the distinct feeling that most of those people were actually glad that Hassan Rafat is gone from this world." Schuyler suddenly remembered that he should guard his words, and looked guiltily around.

Ryder noticed Schuyler's look. "No serious problem, Boge. I chose this table for its rotten acoustics. These folks around us can hardly hear themselves think, let alone eavesdrop."

Schuyler lowered his voice anyway. "Well, to go on a little more on that same subject, Jeff, even the higher authorities involved were anxious to hush everything up. They're satisfied that Boubahri's death was not accidental, and they're sure that Hassan Rafat was responsible. They don't seem to care who . . . er . . . eliminated Hassan."

Ryder asked wryly, "What about the rest of the Rafat family? I'll bet *they're* not taking this so quietly!"

Schuyler blanched. "Good Lord, no! I stayed as far away from those terrible people as I could! They are wild with rage, and they have incredible power! Believe it or not, they were given complete access to all the police investigation files! There is nothing official, though, to connect you in any way with the situation."

Ryder squinted, "Well, I'll be watching my rearview mirror in *that* town for quite a while, regardless! But thanks, Boge; it's clear that you did a very good job!"

Schuyler's drink arrived, and Ryder signed the chit. Schuyler leaned back in his chair and gratefully sipped the sweet punch, pleased with Ryder's praise.

Jeff Ryder watched the swimmers for an interval, letting Schuyler sample his drink. Then he asked, "Boge, we seem to have a new subject of conversation to take up. The ambassador said you have something to tell me."

Schuyler lifted the swizzle stick out of his glass, and started drumming it on the table top. He glanced at Ryder through his rimless glasses, then his eyes went back to the dancing swizzle stick in his hand. Sotto voce, he said, "Jeff, I really don't know much about what's been going on. I'm supposed to tell you about something that apparently happened only this morning. Have you heard of a Lebanese village called Ain Safa?"

Ryder thought for a moment, then answered, "I think so. It's up in the hills, just out of town."

Schuyler leaned toward Ryder. "That's right. James Crawford has assigned some people to watch a certain house in Ain Safa. This residence belongs to a wealthy Lebanese named Wahji Ghandhouri, whom I'm sure you've heard of. Everyone has. Well, this morning Ambassador Harte received a message originated by Crawford's lookouts. The report says that a heavy truck came and went from that Ain Safa place during the night. That is what the ambassador wanted me to tell you."

Ryder felt a tingling in the roots of his hair. He heard an echo of Crawford's voice, from their conversation concerning Wahji Ghandhouri by the pool at the Teheran Hilton. He pondered for a moment, then asked, "Is there any more from that message?"

Schuyler answered anxiously, "No, that's all there is to the lookouts' message, Jeff. But Mr. Crawford also asked that you be given this message as soon as you are told about the truck." Schuyler withdrew a sealed, unmarked envelope from an inner jacket pocket, and handed it across to Ryder.

Ryder took the envelope, casually glanced around, then tore it open. Inside was a folded note. It was signed "C. James," and it read: "Jeff: As you can see, I am also contemplating business connections with your new acquaintance here in this vicinity. I suggest you continue forestalling any firm commitments until my negotiations are complete."

Ryder was silent, frowning in thought. Half to himself, he said, "Isn't *this* a pretty pail of eels!"

Schuyler drummed the swizzle stick. "What do you mean? What's wrong?"

Ryder looked at him. "Boge, when you go back to the embassy, tell Ambassador Harte I intend to have a looksee at that Ain Safa layout tomorrow."

Schuyler spoke in a hushed, shocked voice. "Do you think you ought to risk going there?"

Ryder answered, "No big thing, Boge. I've got company business there with Wahji Ghandhouri anyway."

Without comprehending, Schuyler blinked and said, "I see. I see."

Ryder thought for a moment, then he looked at Schuyler. "Boge, thanks again for taking care of Anna Boubahri, and the rest of that snarl in Teheran."

Schuyler again looked pleased. "I'm just glad I could do something to help." He looked at his watch, then asked, "Well, that's all I came to tell you, Jeff. Is there anything else?"

Ryder shrugged his shoulders. "No, Boge. That's it, I guess. If anything else comes up, I'll phone."

Schuyler swallowed the last of his drink, then got up from the chair. With a tentative wave of his hand, he hurried away. Ryder felt his weariness sweep over him. He decided that a short nap would be just right, and headed for his room.

Ryder napped for an hour, and as he'd hoped, awakened feeling refreshed and in a good humor. He splashed some water on his face, toweled himself dry, then went to the telephone, and called Maxton's room. The telephone woke Maxton out of a dead sleep. Ryder heard the groggy basso profundo voice of his friend answer. Ryder said, "Come out of the swamp, King Kong. Sun's over the yardarm."

Maxton groaned, "What day is it?"

Ryder chortled. "If you weren't in a coma, I'd remind you it happens to be Friday the 13th! Wake the hell up! We've got to go fortify ourselves against the evil spirits!"

Maxton, slowly coming out of his fog, said, "Okay, okay. I'll put on my pants, and meet you at the witch doctor's."

Ryder answered, "I'm about to shower and shave. After that I'll meet you down at the lobby bar."

Three-quarters of an hour later, Ryder, perched on a bar stool, watched with amusement the rolling approach of Maxton's powerful, bearlike figure. As Maxton heaved himself onto a stool, Ryder smilingly remarked, "Maxton, you come into a room with the grace of a Sherman tank . . ."

Unperturbed, Maxton finished Ryder's sentence. ". . . which needs refueling!" He signaled for the bartender.

After Maxton had settled himself in front of a double Scotch on the rocks, Ryder told him of their Ain Safa appointment on Saturday with Ghandhouri. He then detailed for Maxton the information Crawford had sent him, and told about Schuyler's report of the nocturnal visit of a truck to Ghandhouri's Ain Safa estate.

Maxton listened to Ryder's account, then said, "What you seem to be telling me is that the next thing you've got in mind is a little breaking and entering. Is that it?"

Ryder grinned. "You're such a blunt son of a bitch, Maxton. But it's just possible that might be in the offing. We'll maybe get to see if Ghandhouri keeps dogs too!"

Maxton grunted, unmoved. "Okay, what's the schedule?"

Ryder spoke seriously. "First we'll finish playing pattyfingers with Ghandhouri on the company's business tomorrow. We can maybe get a feel for the layout of the place while we're there. After that, we'll see."

Maxton, listening, nodded. "Okay. Just one thing. You're *not* cutting me out of *this* donnybrook like you did the last time!"

Ryder smiled and looked at Maxton. "Don't worry, you'll be in on this one up to your Max gluteus!"

Maxton chunked the ice cubes back and forth in his glass. "Well, we might as well milk all the jollies we can out of this trip. If I know you, compadre, this is going to be our swan song out here, because you're going to lose all your cool the next time you cross paths with old P. T. Lane!"

Ryder said, "We don't know all the answers yet."

Maxton opined flatly, "Ghandhouri'll take care of that."

Ryder hunched his shoulders. "I'm afraid you're all too right. That damned fool Lane is heading us into one huge bind. Ghandhouri is bad enough all by himself, not even mentioning this Crawford angle!"

Maxton waved at the bartender, and pointed into his empty glass. "Either way, P. Tuxford Lane is scheduled to spin, crash, and burn. The only thing that's changed is that Crawford's way is probably quicker, I hope."

Ryder nodded sourly. "True. But why? Lane is no fool, even though I call him one."

Maxton then spoke aloud what was really on Ryder's mind. "Come on, Prince Valiant, get your head out of your ass! You know damned well that Ghandhouri's greasing hell out of our P. T.!"

Ryder stared ahead. "And that, by God, makes P. T. Lane rank a slice lower than Ghandhouri."

Maxton quipped in sarcasm, "But look how big they both are."

Ryder added dryly, "For now." He looked at his watch, and saw that it was nearly seven. He said to Maxton, "Let's get some chow. I'm suddenly starved." He made signs to the bartender, asking for the bar tab.

Ain Safa
A Village in Lebanon
MAY 1966

Jefferson Ryder and John Maxton lounged in Ryder's hotel room drinking beer while they waited for arrival of their transport to Wahji Ghandhouri's estate in Ain Safa. Maxton lay stretched out on Ryder's bed, resting on an elbow. Ryder slouched in an upholstered chair, legs stretched out and crossed in front of him. Ryder waved his beer glass at Maxton. "On the way up there, help me keep an eye on the route. We may want to sneak back there sometime, maybe after dark, and we don't want to get lost."

Maxton wiped beer foam from his mouth. "We'll find it. All we have to do is follow the scent of that famous perfumed snot-rag Ghandhouri waves around."

At that moment the telephone rang. Ryder answered. He listened briefly, then said, "Thanks. We'll be right down." He hung up the telephone and glanced at his watch. "Ghandhouri's driver is here, and right on time. It's straight up 11 AM." Maxton rolled off the bed, and got to his feet. The two men headed for the hotel lobby.

The Lebanese driver of the limousine proved to be loquacious and likable. Immensely proud of his English, he regaled the two Americans with a tireless monologue during their ride to Ain Safa. With good-humored and picturesque chatter, amply larded with misused American slang, the driver spared Ryder and Maxton the need for memorizing the route they were following. No landmark of any consequence was passed without a torrential description of its past, present, and predicted future.

The route wended generally south out of Beirut, paralleling the Lebanon Mountains for a few miles, then swung to the east, and started up into the foothills. As the road's elevation climbed, Ryder and Maxton remarked on the decrease in temperature accompanying the ascent. These comments prompted a proud new flood of words on the subject from the talkative driver.

Ultimately they passed through a tiny cluster of buildings that the driver identified as Ain Safa. They continued beyond the village for what Ryder estimated to be another mile. The driver's happy chatter ceased abruptly as he turned the limousine off the main road, into a private and unidentified drive. A short distance along the drive brought them to an iron-gated portal. Huge barred gates stood open to admit the car. Ryder noted the formidable appearance of the gates as they passed through. A high masonry wall extended in solid continuity from either side of the gateway. The wall was capped by an ugly mass of broken glass fragments embedded along its ridge.

Once within the walled confines, they found themselves driving through parklike grounds. The estate was carpeted with vast lawns interspersed with flowering shrubs, and studded with stately shade trees. The paved drive meandered sedately up to a low, rambling residence of modern design. The driver stopped the car under a covered coachway at the entrance to the house. Without comment, he climbed out of the car, and opened the rear doors. Ryder and Maxton left the car and headed for the residence's entry as the driver eased the limousine away from the house.

Before they had reached Ghandhouri's ornate entry door, it swung open. A uniformed butler courteously invited them into the house. He led them through the quiet elegance of the interior, and out to a covered rear patio. Wahji Ghandhouri rose from his seat at a table on which there rested a telephone and a file folder, which Ghandhouri closed. The Lebanese financier strode forward to greet the two Americans. Another man stepped partially into view from the shadows of the house, watching the two arrivals. Ryder recognized him as the obese bodyguard who had been present in Ghandhouri's Beirut office.

Deferring to the informal atmosphere of the residential setting, Wahji wore a white nylon turtleneck shirt under a navy blue blazer. Flashing his grand smile, Ghandhouri extended a limp hand to Jefferson Ryder. "Ah, my dear Mr. Ryder! How nice to see you again!"

Ryder affected a drawl. "Hello there, Mr. Ghandhouri. I'd like you to meet my assistant, Mr. John Maxton."

Ghandhouri sent a vacant smile toward Maxton, but did not extend his hand. He turned his attention immediately back to Ryder, and said, "Our business today will not take long I'm sure, Mr. Ryder. Your vice president, Mr. Lane, and I have settled everything. There is nothing now to do but eliminate a few trivial details." Ghandhouri gestured toward the table at which he had been seated, "Please make yourselves comfortable at the table, gentlemen." He signaled in the direction of the house, and the butler appeared. "Please, gentlemen," Ghandhouri asked. "What would you like to drink before our luncheon is served?"

Ryder looked at the butler and said, "Scotch and water for mine."

Maxton said, "Scotch on the rocks. Double."

The butler nodded silently, and disappeared into the house. Ryder and Maxton were seating themselves across from Ghandhouri when the telephone on the table rang. He picked up the instrument and said, "Ghandhouri." He listened for a moment, then spoke rapidly in Arabic into the telephone. He returned the instrument to its cradle, then waved his hands as though in helpless resignation. He smiled sorrowfully. "Take my advice, gentlemen! Never become wealthy! Life becomes an endless emergency! The telephone has said I must hurry away to Paris this afternoon, and here I have scarcely unpacked from my arrival!"

Ryder smiled blandly, and commented, "That sure is a shame. Mr. Ghandhouri, what with you having such a nice place here and all. I'll bet you hate it every time you have to leave Lebanon!"

Ghandhouri shot a suspicious glance at Ryder, then decided that this rude American couldn't know of the detestable exile terms under which he was obliged to live. He smiled again. "How very true, Mr. Ryder. The peacefulness here allows me at least an occasional moment of rest from my pressures."

As Ghandhouri finished his lament, the butler returned to serve the drinks. He poured a measure of arak into a tumbler for Ghandhouri, following it with ice water. Ghandhouri lifted the milky liquid in a toast. "Gentlemen, to our prosperous future together!" Ryder and Maxton silently tasted their drinks.

Wahji Ghandhouri set his glass down, and leaned back in his chair, smiling at Ryder. "Since we are fortunate enough to have so little to do on this lovely day, I have planned to keep our discussions relaxed and informal." He beckoned to the butler, who waited nearby. "You may bring the *meze* now, Salim." Ghandhouri turned back to Ryder. "If it is agreeable to you, Mr. Ryder, we can chat over luncheon."

Ryder said, "That suits me fine."

Ghandhouri rested a heavily ringed hand on the file folder in front of him. "You will be pleased, I'm sure, to know that your Mr. Lane and I have come to a full understanding. During our meeting in New York on Wednesday, three days ago, Mr. Lane and I signed our agreement. Effective immediately, Mr. Ryder, Wahji Ghandhouri becomes your servant! I am putting the force of my organization and my influence to work for you in twelve countries of this region! And here is a pleasant little surprise for you." Ghandhouri affected a patronizing tone. "In my agreement with Mr. Lane and your company, I have *guaranteed* the sale of eighteen of your big airplanes among those twelve countries!"

Jefferson Ryder looked steadily at Ghandhouri. "Over what period of time, Mr. Ghandhouri?"

Wahji Ghandhouri had not anticipated a counterattack. Momentarily taken aback, he let a flash of annoyance show, then brusquely stated, "My guarantee provides that the eighteen airplanes will be sold within the next twelve-month period."

Ryder smiled easily at Ghandhouri and said, "Let's see now. That's around a quarter of a billion dollars' worth of business in a year. That goes to show you how the big things get done! If the company had left that problem up to me, the best I could have done would be only about a third of that."

Ghandhouri suddenly saw that Ryder was no fool. The Lebanese continued to smile, but a veiled look tightened his eyes. Less than a third was all he expected himself, and that was principally due to past efforts from existing arrangements of the company. He said, "Yes. Your Mr. Lane felt you would be happy to have our help."

The butler approached from the house, pushing a wheeled serving cart laden with more than a dozen of the *meze* dishes. Each of the dishes offered a different food choice. Conversation shifted away from business while the butler arranged linen, silverware, and glassware on a separate nearby table. The remarkable variety of dishes comprising the *meze* was arrayed down the table's center.

In an expansive tone, Wahji Ghandhouri said of the elaborate food display, "A few samples of our poor native fare, gentlemen." Waving his hand in a graceful flaunt toward the lavish spread of foods, he mentioned some of the dishes by their Arabic names. "We have *hummus*, *ful medames*, *mutabbal*, *kibbeh nayeh*, et cetera. Please help yourselves. I only hope that these strange flavors and seasonings are not disagreeable to you. As these are more or less meant as hors d'oeuvres, you may choose to eat sparingly. We shall later be served *shawarma*, which most Americans enjoy, since it resembles their famous barbecue." Ghandhouri laughed lightly. Ryder heard the faint tinge of contempt in the laugh.

At Ghandhouri's invitation, they moved to the luncheon table, and proceeded to eat. Desultory conversation ensued during the meal, exclusively between Ghandhouri and Ryder. John Maxton remained unconcernedly silent. At length, Ryder decided to return to discussion of Ghandhouri's agreement with Lane. He said, "Mr. Ghandhouri, there are details that need settling if we're supposed to work together from now on. I'd like to hear your ideas on how we're going to proceed."

Ghandhouri patted his mouth with a napkin, then replied, "Actually, Mr. Ryder, that will all be very simple. It may come as a pleasant surprise to you, but we shall have to waste very little time in discussion of detailed trivia." The Palestinian-Lebanese financier smiled condescendingly. "Mr. Lane cautioned me that you would be worried about details. Let me reassure you, Mr. Ryder, that from now on, your work will become a holiday out here in my world."

Jefferson Ryder smiled, and looked straight at Ghandhouri. "That would be a mighty fine thing, Mr. Ghandhouri. The only part that bothers me, though, is that I'm trying to figure out how we're going to make this all look kosher, excuse the expression, to the airline folks. They're used to seeing me around a lot of the time, trying to work out a deal with them. All of a sudden now, it looks as though the deals will be coming down on their heads from the top, instead of from the bottom up."

Wahji Ghandhouri smiled patronizingly, and simply nodded his head.

Ryder persisted. "What I'm afraid of mostly, Mr. Ghandhouri, is that I might accidentally screw up these deals you'll be making by saying the wrong thing at the right time."

The smile disappeared from Ghandhouri's face. His gaze sharpened with suspicion as he looked at Ryder. Flicking a glance at Maxton, Ghandhouri said, "Perhaps we do have some details to discuss, Mr. Ryder. But all this must be most boring to your assistant. Possibly he would prefer to relax beside the swimming pool, now that our lunch is finished, while you and I clear up these few little problems."

Maxton stood up. Staring expressionlessly at Wahji Ghandhouri, Maxton emitted a rending belch, then said, "Excuse me. I'd like nothing better than to take a walk. It'll help shake down all that strangely seasoned chow I ate." He turned to Ryder. "If you want me, Chief, just whistle." Maxton then reached out and picked up the opened bottle of arak from the table, and his glass, then sauntered nonchalantly across the patio toward the lawn and the swimming pool.

With a look of vast distaste, Ghandhouri watched Maxton's departure from the table. Forcing himself to smile, he turned back to Ryder. He asked, probingly, "So. You feel that there are things we must discuss in order to avoid inadvertent future damage to our progress in these airplane sales?"

Ryder squinted his eyes and shrugged. "Well, a person never knows, Mr. Ghandhouri. After all, these people do have a tendency to listen to me, what with all these years I've been calling on them."

Ghandhouri studied Ryder's bland face. "Obviously, we must do everything possible to avoid any such damage. There must be some simple way to minimize that likelihood."

Ryder sober faced, said, "Right! There must be some way."

Wahji Ghandhouri smiled, believing he'd correctly analyzed the situation. He leaned back and said, "As an incentive, to stimulate your diligence in avoiding such accidental reverses, Mr. Ryder, I suggest that it will be fair for me to privately offer to you, $1,000 for each airplane sold within the next year. Under the terms of my guarantee to your company, that would mean $18,000 for you. Would such an understanding help diminish the number of unwanted 'accidents'?"

Jefferson Ryder scratched his head and smiled. "I was sure you would see what I was driving at. It makes everything nicer when you're working with somebody you understand."

Ghandhouri smiled in satisfaction. "Then it is settled. You will continue your efforts with the airlines as before, unchanged. I will apply my influence in the meanwhile. You may report to me at suitable intervals regarding your observations, and on any unusual problems you may encounter. Is that acceptable, Mr. Ryder?"

Ryder answered, "Lane told me to listen to your judgment in this arrangement. That's what I intend to do."

Ghandhouri smiled and stood, extending a flaccid hand. Ryder rose, and shook the hand briefly. The financier then adopted a brusque, businesslike manner. "I must now excuse myself from the pleasure of your company. There is much I must do in preparation for my journey to Paris this afternoon."

Ryder nodded, "You go right ahead, Mr. Ghandhouri. I'll collect my assistant, Mr. Maxton, and we'll just hustle on back to the city." As Ryder finished his sentence, both he and Wahji Ghandhouri turned to glance in the direction of the swimming pool. John Maxton was nowhere in sight, although his glass and the arak bottle were visible on one of the poolside tables. Ghandhouri said sharply, "Where is that man?"

Jefferson Ryder said easily, "Finding Max will be no problem. He'll undoubtedly end up alongside your main booze supply."

Ghandhouri displayed no amusement in his reaction to Ryder's flippant remark. He waved an agitated arm signal toward the house, and his butler hurried anxiously into view. Ghandhouri barked a harsh command in Arabic, sending the butler hastening in a half run back the way he'd come. The Palestinian-Lebanese turned a forced smile toward Ryder, and said, "I've ordered your car brought to the house. Shall we find your friend?"

Ryder smiled, and nodded agreeably. He headed across the lawn toward the swimming pool. Ghandhouri strode alongside in uncommunicative silence. The two men came up to the table beside the pool, on which Maxton had left his glass and the arak bottle. From this vantage point, Ryder saw that a low outbuilding was visible, set at some distance from the main house. Ryder said casually, "Maybe Max wandered over there. What's in that building, Mr. Ghandhouri?"

The financier curtly replied, "That is the garage. What possible reason would your friend have for going there?"

Ryder chuckled. "As a matter of fact, I'd bet he's over there swapping stories with that friendly driver you sent to pick us up!"

Ghandhouri stared at Ryder, then started moving at a rapid pace toward the garage. Ryder followed curiously, studying Ghandhouri's uncharacteristically ruffled conduct. As they reached a point halfway to that outbuilding, the car that had brought Ryder and Maxton came backing into view, out of the garage. The car swung around, and headed for the house. John Maxton could be seen seated in front, alongside the driver.

Ryder smiled at Ghandhouri. "There is my wandering boy with your driver, as I thought! I'll tell him to improve on his manners next time!"

Ryder heard Ghandhouri issue an epithet under his breath, and mutter in French that there would never be a "next time." Aloud, Ghandhouri said, "Please overlook my agitation, Mr. Ryder. It is just that I have so many pressing matters that urgently require my attention."

The two men reached the front of the house where the car waited. Ryder turned to Ghandhouri and made his departure amenities, then climbed into the car. The driver solemnly drove away with the two Americans.

The large outdoor clock serving the Phoenicia Hotel's patio read 3 PM by the time Ryder and Maxton had returned from Wahji Ghandhouri's Ain Safa estate. The two men had avoided discussing the Ain Safa luncheon events during their ride back in the chauffeured limousine, and on arrival at the hotel were anxious to compare notes. They stepped out into the crowded activity of the sunlit deck area around the hotel swimming pool.

Surrounded by the inevitable raucous throng of swimmers and sunbathers, the two Americans found the anonymous privacy they sought. They sat down at one of the colorful umbrella tables, had a waiter bring them two bottles of beer, then sat back and relaxed in the canvas deck chairs. Ryder looked at Maxton in amusement. "If I were you, I wouldn't hold my breath waiting for a return invitation to Wahji's house! He thinks your party manners stink!"

Maxton sipped his beer and said dryly, "Fuck him."

Ryder chortled. "It's that kind of narrow-minded thinking that's kept you out of high society, Maxton. If you'd been civil and courteous instead of belching like a bloated boar, Wahji Baby might have offered you one grand for every airplane we sell, like he did me!"

Maxton's eyes widened a fraction. He slanted a look at Ryder. "*Now* will you believe me about Lane? I told you Ghandhouri was shooting grease!" Maxton paused, then looked suspiciously back at Ryder. "I'll bet you baited Ghandhouri all the way into that offer! I heard it start before I shoved off. That gold-hungry bastard would never part with a buck he wasn't forced to!"

Ryder smiled. "I just tried talking in the language he knows best. It worked." Ryder went on, more seriously, "Max, Lane has bought this gold brick of Ghandhouri's lock, stock, and barrel. Our bright boy thinks he's getting a written guarantee! That's unbelievably gullible, and I'm having a hard time swallowing this line. Somebody's getting double- or triple-crossed!"

Maxton swallowed some beer. "Okay, Ryder, it looks to me like you're getting too many balls in the air, but what's the next move?"

Ryder answered slowly. "Like it or not, Lane's got to go. I'm pulling the rug on him when I get back. I'm going over his head this time—way over his head!"

Maxton rumbled, "It's about time."

Ryder studied Maxton's lumpy profile. "All right, now it's your turn at the microphone. What in hell were you doing after you abandoned that arak bottle by the pool?"

Maxton peered at Ryder. "What I did was go pussyfooting around Mr. Superpimp's plantation a little bit. I ended up by bullshitting with that windbag driver of ours out in Ghandhouri's garage."

Ryder said, "Well, let me tell you, amigo, our host got edgier than a Greek on a fag farm when he discovered he'd lost track of your whereabouts! I do believe he's got something to hide up there."

Maxton grunted and looked into his beer bottle. "Yeah. And I figure I know where it's hid!!"

Ryder leaned forward and said sharply, "Let's have it, Max!"

Maxton's eyes swung toward Ryder. "When I escaped from listening to Ghandhouri's horseshit at lunch, I went and parked myself next to the pool with that jug of arak. Sitting there, I got to watching a couple of guys monkeying around down by that garage. I figured our windy driver might be there, so I moseyed over that way to shoot the bull with him, and see what kind of beans he might spill. Anyhow, when I came around the side of the garage, the driver and some other lardbutt were there. The other guy was pulling one of the garage doors shut. When he suddenly spied me, this guy nearly shit! He slammed the damn door closed, and made a wild grab for his armpit! That driver of ours hollered at him in Arabic, telling him to knock off the hysterics. So this lardbutt cooled down. After he gives me a faceful of dirty looks, the lardbutt leaves, and heads for the house. The driver glad-hands me, and hauls out a bottle from the garage. We sat around swapping lies until he gets a telephone call from the house, and then we leave."

Ryder listened carefully to Maxton's account. "Is that all of it, Max?"

Maxton shook his head, and again peered into his beer bottle. "Not quite," he said quietly. "Before that garage door slammed shut, I got a peek inside. There's something in there that's about the right size and shape to be one of your goddamned boxes of goofy dust!"

Ryder's eyebrows lifted. He unconsciously ran a finger over the scar on his cheek. "Somebody's going to have to take a closer look!"

Maxton took a swallow of his beer, and said laconically, "You make it sound so simple."

Brandy and Roses
Beirut, Lebanon
MAY 1966

In spectacular contrast to the unpalatable events of the earlier hours spent with Ghandhouri at Ain Safa, Jefferson Ryder didn't try to suppress the pleasant anticipation he felt that evening as he knocked on the door to Marge Mackenzie's apartment. When the door opened, he filled his eyes with her. She looked the way he thought a woman should—a vision of soft, very feminine loveliness. She stood smiling before him in a long, sleeveless, emerald green dress that clung to her figure, and matched the color of her eyes. The skirt of the dress was slit high on the side, tantalizingly revealing a shapely leg. Marge wore her auburn hair loose and long, rolling softly over her shoulders.

She seized Jeff by the hand and pulled him far enough in to close the door, then threw her arms around his neck, and kissed him eagerly. He reciprocated as well as possible with one arm encumbered by a florist's box of long-stemmed roses and a bottle of Napoleon brandy.

Marge leaned back, hands still clasped behind his neck. She looked happily into his eyes. "Jeff! It's terrible the way the sight of you unravels me inside!"

Ryder crinkled his eyes in a smile. "Same to you, pretty lady. Just look at you! It's the likes of you that causes earthquakes!" He handed the box of roses to Marge, which she accepted with a little pleased sound, and a warm glance into Jeff's eyes. He followed her to her tiny kitchen, noting an appetizing aroma in the apartment from something Marge was cooking. As he tagged along behind, admiring Marge's graceful walk and the gentle movement of her hair, he said, "Marge, you're all kinds of distractions at once! Whatever you're cooking out there smells good enough to make a hungry man hurt!"

In the kitchen, Marge reached into a cupboard and selected a slender vase, then busily began unwrapping the flowers. As she worked, she glanced seductively over her shoulder at Jeff, and said, "I've been plotting ways to distract you ever since you called this afternoon, Jeff Ryder!"

Ryder, having unwrapped the bottle of brandy, left it on the sink, and leaned himself against the jamb of the kitchen doorway. Watching Marge arrange the roses in the vase, he smiled contentedly. "God, you look sexy in that split-up-the-side sorcery you're wearing! I think green has just become my favorite color!"

Marge put down two roses she had in her hand, and swung around to stand very close to Ryder. She raised sultry eyes and gazed wordlessly up at him. Ryder breathed the fresh fragrance of her hair and the scented warmth of her body. Desire for Marge welled up in him. He cupped her upturned face in his hands and kissed her fully. Marge put her arms around his waist and hugged herself tightly against him, leaning her head against his chest. He felt the warmth of her hips pressed against him, and heard her murmur, "And you make me feel sexy, Jeff." She tilted her face up to him, and closed her eyes as she slid her arms around his neck. Jeff pulled her against him, kissing her hungrily and feeling the moist, warm softness of her tongue against his lips. They stood in close embrace as he caressed the warm form of her body, and felt her tremble and curve against him.

He started sliding the zipper down on the back of her dress, and heard her moan softly. In a husky voice, he said, "Maybe we'd better postpone dinner, Marge darling." Mutely, Marge took her arms from around his neck, and drew gently away. She moved to the stove, and extinguished the oven and a pair of burners under low-simmering pots. Ryder watched her turn sensually to him. He saw that Marge was making a private signal when, as she had done once before for him, she made a deliberate thing of slipping out of her shoes. He watched as she looked fully into his eyes, then let the emerald green dress and her loosened brassiere fall to the floor. He saw that she had not worn an underslip, and clad only in panties and nylons, Marge came to him.

Jeff edged drowsily out of his sleep, languishing in a vast sense of well being. He was aware of a cooling touch against his skin, and let his eyes slide lazily open. He found himself lying nude, moist with perspiration, with one leg covered under a rumpled sheet on the disarray of Marge's bed. Marge, legs curled under herself, sat beside him, preoccupied in wiping a cool washcloth gently across his chest.

Marge had brushed her hair into a soft, auburn cloud. She had donned a filmy white peignoir, neglecting to tie it closed over the fullness of her naked breasts. Ryder placidly decided that Marge resembled an earthbound angel, and in a sleep-deepened voice told her so. Marge drew her hands into her lap for a moment, looking fondly into his face. Then she leaned over and kissed him lightly on the lips, letting her breasts rest in two warm centers on the cooled skin of his chest. Straightening up again, Marge smiled softly, and said, "I think you needed that little nap, Jeff."

Jeff eased himself up on an elbow. He looked into Marge's eyes and smiled. "Marge, you're impossibly good for me!" He sat up then, alongside her. Drawing his legs in and crossing them, he put an arm around her middle and hugged her against himself. He made a deep, contented sound.

Marge tilted her head against his cheek. "I want to be, Jeff." She rested, snuggling comfortably against him for a while, then lifted her head, and said, "I think it's time to find out if you're awake enough to eat!"

He exclaimed, "Hey! The dinner! What the devil time did it get to be? Now that you mention it, I'm hungry as a bear!"

Marge laughingly disentangled herself, and scrambled off the bed. She said crisply, "You've only been napping for an hour. While you get yourself all the way awake and decent, I'll go fix things in the kitchen." She quickly slipped her feet into a pair of slippers by the bed, and bustled out of the room. Ryder flopped back against a pillow for a moment, yawning and stretching, then rolled to the edge of the bed, and got up.

Twenty minutes later, showered and dressed, he made his way back to Marge's small kitchen. He found her there, busy at the stove. The kitchen was filled with tempting aromas of good things cooking. Ryder saw that Marge had placed a decanter of Scotch, ice, and glasses out on the sink. He headed for the Scotch. "I'll lend a hand with the drinks. You think of everything, pretty lady!" He fixed a pair of Scotches while Marge, humming little tunes to herself, continued with her cooking. Jeff brought Marge's glass over to her, and, leaning down, kissed the back of her neck. She took her glass from him, and placed it nearby on the stove. She gave him a sultry, sidelong glance, and scolded, "Go on about your business, sir! You're demoralizing the cook! Go put on some nice music for us, and light the candles on the table. We're going to sit down to dinner in about five minutes."

Later, after the tardy, delicious dinner, Marge and Jeff seated themselves comfortably on the couch by the coffee table, sipping from snifters of fine cognac, and quietly listening to soft music from Marge's record collection. In a while, Marge turned to Jeff and said, "There are some things I'd like to tell you, Jeff. Do you mind letting me talk about myself a little?"

Ryder smiled. "That's the most pleasant subject on earth to me right now, Marge."

Marge looked down at her hands, and shook her head slightly. She said quietly, "Maybe it shouldn't be. Let me tell you something." Ryder saw her seriousness and remained silent, studying her face. Marge continued, "This may sound crazy, I guess, but the one thing I'm most frightened of is being happy. Deeply happy, I mean." She hesitated, then went on in a low voice, "And that's what is happening to me now with you, Jeff. I was truly happy one other time earlier in my life, and it ended up hurting me terribly."

Ryder reached out and took her hand. He spoke gently. "Marge, I've found that real happiness can be a very elusive bird. When it comes along, wouldn't it be kind of a mistake to run from it?"

Marge looked away, and said unevenly, "I want to believe that way, Jeff. But I'm thirty-two years old now, and I still haven't rid myself of bitter fear from that other time." She swung around to face him. "When I was twenty-one, I married a man I absolutely worshipped. I stayed married to him for five crushing years, while he put me on display as part of his elegant public image. He cared nothing for me otherwise. He made a frightful fool of me with his two careers: his job, and his endless parade of other women."

Marge leaned back, looking troubled and confused. "Jeff, you're so unlike that man, and our circumstances are so vastly different from that time years ago, that I know there is no basis for comparison." She turned a worried look toward Ryder. "But Ambassador Harte has warned me of the awful hazards of your work. I'm frightened now, not only of the danger, but because I don't want to lose this happiness."

Ryder studied Marge's face fondly. "Look, Marge. Julius Harte is understandably concerned about you. You're important to him, professionally and personally. He's one of the finest men I've ever met, with a heart as big as a house. If that man could, he'd protect the whole cockeyed world from harm. But Marge, nobody can do that. The way I look at it, life is a whole lot of moments, all strung together. You live those moments one by one, and you concentrate on relishing the hell out of the good ones. When the not-so-good ones roll around, you grab hold of your sense of humor, and wade through them. But you have to remember how easy it is to clobber your good moments by spending the time wondering how soon the next bad one is going to crop up."

Marge's eyes had grown wide and misty. Jeff stopped speaking, and reached for both her hands. Holding them clasped in his, he said, quietly, "Listen, Marge. What I said was probably pretty tinny sounding. There's one thing more I'm going to add anyway. You've told me how you were once hurt badly. That's past and done. I want you to be certain of one thing. If it's in my power, I'll never let anyone or anything hurt you again. Above all, and the important thing, I'm not going to hurt you myself, Marge, even if I have to give you up this minute!"

Marge flung her arms around his neck and hugged him fiercely. "Oh, Jeff! Jeff! Please take awfully good care of yourself for me!" She rested her head against his, then murmured, "It's grown awfully late. I don't want to have to start missing you any sooner than I must. Please don't go back to your hotel tonight."

The Equalizers
Ain Safa, Lebanon
MAY 1966

Jeff Ryder was amused to notice in himself a vague feeling of awkwardness accompanying the return to his hotel room at this unaccustomed hour of 9 AM. The undisturbed bed, a lamp left burning, the random disarray of his last occupancy, readying for the previous evening with Marge, a few knowing glances from various hotel employees alert to this departure from Ryder's established routines. He smiled to himself, mentally defying anyone or anything at this moment to intrude on the pleasant state of mind Marge Mackenzie had left him with.

They had shamelessly giggled their way through the considerable upheaval of Marge's usual ordered morning routines brought on by his presence in her bed when the alarm clock had sounded. He had tried at first to help, a quickly abandoned futility, followed instead by a focus on just keeping out of Marge's way. At last, with a flying kiss at the apartment door, she had fled on her way to the embassy.

Ryder leisurely showered and shaved in his own room, dressed himself, then lazed through a late breakfast alone in the hotel's coffee shop. He finished a second cup of coffee, and then, turning his mind somewhat reluctantly to the necessary businesses of the day, picked up a house telephone and arranged to meet John Maxton. Ten minutes later, in acknowledgement of the balmy weather, they settled themselves at a favored table outside on the hotel's patio.

Ryder, acceding to his friend's unavoidable albeit unmentioned curiosity, candidly revealed that he had devoted the previous night to a continuing observance of Maxton's excellent recommendation that he spend more time with Marge Mackenzie. Maxton's face showed a trace of smile to go along with his grunt of approval.

With that small sociable exchange done, Ryder turned the conversation to the Ain Safa episode of the day before with Ghandhouri. He said to Maxton, "We've got to decide what to do about that box you spotted yesterday in Ghandhouri's garage. We probably ought to just go ahead and have a look-see up close ourselves."

Maxton squinted. "You and your stubborn streak. You don't seem to want to admit that this prowling into the bad guys' pit is work for the pros! Why don't you hand over this moldy fig to Crawford's thugs?"

Ryder admitted, "I probably should, I guess. The trouble is, though, by the time we try going through all that, the goddamned goodies might disappear. Don't forget, that lardbutt you bumped into—Ghandhouri's bodyguard, by the way— might figure you saw that box."

Maxton remained silent for a moment, looking at Ryder, then hunched his shoulders. "You're calling the shots, amigo."

Ryder then relented. "Well, I'll tell you what. There's some time available. You go rent us a car and buy a pocket-sized flashlight somewhere, just in case. And while you're doing all that, I'll go see if I can talk to Julius Harte. If he can get this job done without us, fine. If not, you and I will tackle it ourselves."

Maxton nodded. "Now you're making sense. Let's get with it." The two men made their way through the accumulating crowd around the pool and into the hotel lobby. Ryder decided not to telephone ahead, and went directly out of the hotel on his way to the embassy. Maxton set about arranging for a car.

At the embassy, Marge greeted Ryder with a sultry smile. "This is an unexpected pleasure, Mr. Jefferson Ryder!"

Ryder smiled back. "Just trying to keep up my acquaintance, Miss Mackenzie. Also, I wanted a quick word with Ambassador Harte, and took a chance that he might be available."

Marge shook her head regretfully. "I'm sorry, Jeff. The ambassador is away, attending a meeting with the prime minister this afternoon. I'm afraid he won't be back for at least two more hours. Can Bogart Schuyler help you?"

Ryder clucked his tongue and frowned. "I guess I'd better try talking to Boge, Marge. There is a chance he can assist."

Marge pressed a signal button on her intercom. Bogart Schuyler's voice came over the speaker, and Marge told him Ryder was there. Schuyler responded immediately, saying he would come to the ambassador's office. Moments later, Schuyler stepped in. He and Ryder entered the ambassador's empty chambers, and seated themselves on a leather lounge. Ryder gave Schuyler a brief summary of the events at Ghandhouri's Ain Safa estate, and told him that there was a good possibility that one or more of the contraband shipping crates was cached there. Ryder asked Schuyler if James Crawford had provided means by which a clandestine search of Ghandhouri's garage might be arranged.

Schuyler fidgeted with his eyeglasses, and shook his head. "The best I could do for you would be to try to communicate with Crawford in Paris or London, to see what he might offer. To be perfectly frank, I must tell you the outlook for obtaining that sort of help seems very dim. When Crawford advised Ambassador Harte and me that he was having the Ain Safa place watched, he also pointed out that those doing the watching have no idea whatever of the purpose of their assignment. They are, to use Crawford's own words, 'people of limited usefulness.' "

Ryder asked Schuyler, "Are you still receiving reports from those watchers?"

Schuyler nodded his head. "We have a telephone number we may call to receive such reports. Otherwise, they call us hourly."

Ryder said, "Okay, Boge, let's do this. Find out as soon as you can whether those watchers are still on the job. I want them to report to us every movement on or off of that Ain Safa property today, of any kind. If any truck or other vehicle large enough to carry a big shipping crate leaves that place, it is essential that it be followed to its destination. Then, when you've seen to that, try to contact Crawford. Find out for sure if he can have the garage searched, or whether he wants me to do it. I'll hang around my room at the Phoenicia. You can call me there as soon as you have some answers."

Schuyler nodded wordlessly. Ryder stood, and Schuyler followed him to the door. As they left the ambassador's office, Ryder said, "Thanks, Boge. I'll be looking for your call." He sent Marge a fond smile as he passed her desk, and headed out of the embassy on his way to the hotel.

It was nearly five o'clock in the afternoon before Schuyler's call came in for Ryder. Ryder said into the telephone, "Hi, Boge. How's it going?"

Schuyler's careful voice came back. "Not so well, Jeff. I've spoken with the 'watch' people, and they now have your instructions. As of fifteen minutes ago, their report was 100 percent negative. On the other call, though, nothing useful. The principal man has been unavailable this whole time."

Ryder grunted, thought for a moment, then said, "Okay, Boge. So much for that. Thanks for trying. We'll just go ahead on our own."

There was a silence, then Ryder heard Schuyler clear his throat. "I really don't believe you should do that, Jeff. I know that you won't change your mind, though, so good luck."

Ryder smiled at the telephone. "I can't change my mind, Boge, but thanks for the good thoughts. Be seeing you." Ryder hung up the telephone. He made a wry face and muttered, "Into the Valley of Lardbutts rode the six hundred!"

By seven o'clock that evening, both Ryder and Maxton were edgy from the strain of waiting for time to pass and darkness. After a listless dinner that they had tried to prolong, Ryder looked at his watch for the hundredth time. "Max, I can't stand any more of this stalling around. Let's get the hell out of here. If we have to sit on our asses and wait, let's do it up on the goddamn hill."

Maxton let out a sigh of relief. "Anything's better than this! All I can think of is booze! When this is over with, I'm planning to get drunk as a pigeon-toed Paiute!"

The two men headed out of the hotel. On their way to the parked automobile that Maxton had rented, Ryder remarked, "I tossed a blanket into the car earlier. We might need some padding if we have to climb over that broken glass on top of Ghandhouri's outside wall."

Maxton grunted, "Not bad. Did you pack your shootin' iron?"

Ryder patted the bulge under his left arm. "Yep. And I brought a couple of small tools too. I wish you had an equalizer of some kind."

Maxton held up two thick-fingered hands. "These'll do just fine."

Their drive to Ain Safa proved uneventful. Ryder drove leisurely. Thanks to the verbose travelogue from Ghandhouri's driver, they found no difficulty navigating themselves back over the route to the tiny village, despite the darkness. As they eased through Ain Safa's brief limits, Ryder said, "One of the weird aspects of this expedition is that Crawford's watchers will be watching us. I hope those clowns don't do anything to crab the act, if they do happen to see us."

Maxton peered around at the deserted-looking village as their headlights reflected from darkened windows on the few buildings. There was no pedestrian traffic, and apart from a dim glow in one or two windows, and excepting a few parked automobiles, no signs of life. Maxton commented, "There could be an army looking us over, and we'd never know it in this black hole!"

Beyond Ain Safa, Ryder drove slowly onward through the darkness, watching the side of the road. Occasional cars sped past them, honking angrily. A level thicket of shrubbery appeared in the headlights on the right. Ryder picked what looked like a small break in the wall of black leaves, and deliberately nosed the car into it. Amid the shriek of much scraping and scratching on the car's exterior, he forced the lurching vehicle deep into the thicket, and turned off the lights and engine.

Out of the black silence that followed, Maxton's voice said, "When P. T. Lane fires you from the company, you'll be able to make an easy living in LA as a parking lot attendant!"

Ryder couldn't help laughing. "Maxton, you'll be cracking wise at your own wake!"

Maxton said, "And you just ruined the joke with that remark!"

Ryder laughed again, then said, "Let's see if we can get out of this sardine can." He and Maxton pushed their way through the tangle of branches in the darkness, and met at the rear of the automobile. Ryder carried the blanket he had brought from the hotel. He said, "Let's hoof it up the road, and try to keep out of sight the best we can." The two men started walking toward the Ghandhouri estate.

Half an hour and a few minor rips and bruises later, having made good use of the hotel's blanket in surmounting Ghandhouri's eight-foot high perimeter wall, the two men crouched on the well-tended lawn of the estate, and took stock of their position. They had eased their way through a tedious detour, wide of the few lighted windows marking the main residence, and now could make out the vague outline of Ghandhouri's garage ahead through the darkness. The garage building loomed as a rectangle of solid blackness in front of them, outlined by faint light reflections from the few windows glowing hospitably in the main house. Ryder looked at the luminous dial of his wristwatch. Nearly nine o'clock. In a low voice he said, "Max, I think we'd be smart to park here for a while. Maybe whoever's in the house will go to bed, or else leave."

Maxton's hushed voice answered, "Suits me." With the aid of a few grunts, Maxton stretched his powerful torso out on the cool grass. Ryder eased himself into a sitting position, legs crossed under him, and settled down to watch the house and wait.

Time passed slowly. Ryder remained alert, shifting his position occasionally, now and then standing to flex his legs and enliven his blood circulation. A silent hour went by with no apparent change at the house. Ryder decided to continue the vigil. He let another half hour inch slowly by.

As the hands on his watch slipped past ten thirty, Ryder concluded that further delay was pointless. He was on the verge of alerting Maxton when he saw some of the lighted windows darken at the main house. He nudged Maxton. As Maxton sat up and stared at the house, all remaining lights were extinguished. The premises of Ghandhouri's estate suddenly stood in total darkness.

Ryder whispered, "It's finally our turn." The two men stood. Ryder waited, then said, "I'm going down to the back of that garage to look for a way in. Stay behind me a ways, Max, and keep your eyes peeled for trouble." Ryder moved off toward the garage, with Maxton lagging silently behind.

Ryder, groping his way carefully through the darkness, came up to the back wall of the garage. He covered the end of his flashlight with the fingers of one hand, then switched on the light, allowing a tiny beam to escape between his fingers. He swung its faint illumination through a low arc across the wall, and saw that there were three equally spaced, barred windows. The end stall on Ryder's left, the one in which Maxton had seen a shipping crate, had the only rear door.

Ryder turned away from the building and moved back across the grass to find Maxton. With an exchange of quick blips from their lights, the two men met again. Maxton growled, "I saw that door."

Ryder whispered, "Okay. Post yourself off to the left, then, where you can see both this back door and the approaches from the house. I'm going in through that door somehow. When I come out, I'll signal with the light and wait until you show up, then we'll cut out of here."

Maxton rumbled, "I hope you don't take all night. All I want between me and this creep joint is a whole lot of gone!"

Ryder said, "ASAP," then moved away through the night. He groped his way back to the garage and then along the rear wall until his hands found the lone door. Shielding the flashlight, Ryder studied the door's fastenings. He found a conventional latch and doorknob, and above that a hasp and padlock. Looking closely, Ryder saw that the hasp had been poorly installed. He took a screwdriver from his pocket, and with it was able to loosen by several turns each of the hasp screws behind the padlock. He then took out some pliers. Using the handle as a pry, Ryder ripped the loosened screws out from the soft wood of the doorjamb.

Despite the care taken as he worked, Ryder unavoidably disturbed the silence. Perspiration beaded his forehead as he stood tautly, waiting and listening for any sounds of alarm. The enveloping darkness remained utterly silent, however. Ryder turned back to the door. Gingerly, he grasped the dangling padlock in one hand to keep it from rattling, and gripped the doorknob in the other. He turned the knob, then gently pushed to open the door. Ryder was appalled to hear a nerve-shattering complaint shrill from the door's unoiled hinges. He left the door ajar, and hurriedly slipped into the total blackness within the garage, then stopped. He stood tensely, straining his ears and senses against the black stillness. Nothing stirred. Then, just as he started to move, Ryder heard a furtive rustling sound. He felt his stomach contract and a chill run along his spine. He drew the automatic pistol from his shoulder holster, and held the gun ready in the darkness. Perspiration ran across the scar on his cheek. Then the furtive sound repeated, stopped, and repeated again. In relief, Ryder muttered half aloud, "Rats!"

Still holding the gun, but feeling his tension ease, Ryder flicked on the pencil-beamed flashlight in his left hand. He squatted down and swung the focused shaft of light low around the room. He saw the ugly gray shapes of several large rats dart frantically into concealment. He watched as one of them raced through an interconnecting doorway into the solid blackness of the adjoining garage stall. In the brief swing of his light, Ryder also saw the large wooden shipping crate that stood in the middle of the floor. Rising to his feet, Ryder moved to the box. He played the thin beam of light over the wooden surface facing him, and carefully studied the stenciled Arabic markings that the light revealed. They looked familiar. Familiar enough to cause the hairs to rise on the back of Ryder's neck.

Bending toward the box, Ryder engrossed himself in scanning the wooden surface thoroughly, searching for the telltale brass screwhead with the S-shaped slot. Then the flashlight's beam found it for him, when its yellow rays gleamed back from the burnished brass surface, like the stare of a tiny, golden eye.

Then with blinding, shattering suddenness, simultaneous with a quick succession of sounds from somewhere behind Ryder, the black darkness changed to dazzling bright light! The overhead lights within the garage had abruptly been switched on. The instantaneous change of light virtually deprived Ryder of his vision. Instinctively, he flung his right arm up to shield his squinted eyes as he spun to face the sounds behind him. A gun roared in the confined room, and Ryder felt himself slammed upright against the crate behind him by a sledge hammer blow on his right shoulder. His pistol fell from the nerveless fingers of his right hand as he saw Ghandhouri's burly, fat bodyguard grinning gloatingly at him from the connecting doorway. The guard was taking deliberate aim at Ryder's head across the sights of a smoking revolver. Ryder saw the muzzle flash as the revolver roared again, and as suddenly as they had appeared in Jefferson Ryder's eyes moments before, the bright lights exploded and vanished into blackness.

The fat Lebanese gunman let the muzzle of his pistol sag. He took a step into the lighted garage and watched carefully for any sign of life from the still form of Jefferson Ryder, laying sprawled on the floor in a growing pool of blood in front of the packing crate.

The obese Lebanese, with his attention fixed in murderous elation on his victim, was too slow with his gun hand. With a terrible roar of rage, John Maxton burst slamming through the opened back door into the garage left ajar by Ryder. Head down, Maxton rammed like a charging wild bull into the big Lebanese. As Maxton struck, his powerful arm came slicing through the air in a great, unerring, chopping arc, bringing the edge of his hand down with lethal accuracy across the wrist of the fat bodyguard's gun hand. Between the violent force of the blow and the weight of the gun, the man's wrist bones broke cleanly. The pistol clattered to the floor as the Lebanese guard was hurled against the wall by the impact of Maxton's rampaging charge.

John Maxton, crouched and weaving like a wrestler, then eased back a pace from the dazed Lebanese. With a savage smile on his face, Maxton beckoned gently to the fat, sweating gunman, inviting him to combat. The bodyguard's eyes searched wildly for the fallen gun. Maxton, wearing a malevolent, rictal grin, pointed out the pistol's location, then pointed to the gunman's uselessly dangling right hand. Again, Maxton beckoned for the fat bodyguard to come and fight.

Suddenly, the Lebanese screamed and rushed at Maxton, flailing wildly with his left arm. Maxton met the man's rush coolly. Ducking under the violent blow from the bodyguard's left arm, Maxton dropped a shoulder and absorbed the heavy charge without budging. As the man crashed grunting against him, Maxton straightened and brought a knee up with all his strength into the man's groin. The Lebanese howled, and doubled up from the sudden agony in his crotch. John Maxton seized the fat man by the back of the collar and by the back of his belt. He ran the man, bent over, headfirst across the width of the garage. Maxton smashed the top of the bodyguard's head with terrible force against the garage's concrete wall. Maxton released his hold on the man and watched the fat Lebanese drop limply to the floor with blood running from the nose, mouth, and both ears. Ghandhouri's bodyguard was abruptly quite dead.

Cadaqués
Costa Brava, Spain
<u>MAY 1966</u>

In the tiny village of Cadaqués on Spain's Costa Brava, Wahji Ghandhouri sat at a sunny table in front of a small sidewalk café and stared vaguely at the Mediterranean. He sat in tense silence, ignoring glances from occasional tourists and villagers passing by. Ghandhouri remained unaware of the comfortable warmth of the Spanish sunlight, and of the light spring breeze that rippled the red and white tablecloth gently against his knees. He failed to appreciate the simple splendor in the colorful cluster of timeworn buildings around him, or this village's claim as one of the Costa Brava's loveliest. He had only listlessly sampled the heaped serving of paella that grew cold in front of him.

Wahji Ghandhouri's life had conditioned him to expect infallible, flamboyant success. Nothing less was imaginable. Yet, Wahji Ghandhouri now found himself forced to endure the humiliation of a calamitous error. He shivered, his soul naked and cornered, unable to conceive of himself in defeat. The idea alone made him physically ill. Here, seated among these alien and humble surroundings, anonymously clothed in nondescript, repellent garments, the Lebanese-Palestinian financier struggled to reinstate his own crushed confidence. A bitter retrospection invaded his thoughts, however, and Ghandhouri stared gloomily at this peasant hamlet that to him simply stank of fish—a village all too reminiscent of harsh scenes from his childhood. Fate seemed, incredibly, to have closed back on itself.

Ghandhouri labored to hearten himself. In his mind he reviewed the ruinous events of the preceding week, carefully clinging to the commendable aspects of his own performance in the face of threatening disaster. He thought back to that shocking, dead-of-the-night telephone call from Ain Safa. At three o'clock in the morning, disturbed from deep sleep, how he had suddenly been obliged to face life-or-death decisions. He remembered the immediate clarity of his thinking, and how superbly he had reacted!

Ghandhouri recalled how a scheme for escape had formed almost instantly in his mind. He had been able to respond with the customary Ghandhouri decisiveness. His commands had been crisp when he ordered his Ain Safa people to rush that shipping crate and the bodyguard's corpse away in the night, to Beirut's waterfront and on to that cargo ship fortuitously awaiting his orders.

Ghandhouri's thoughts swerved around to a second tangent. He dwelled on his own shrewd foresight in having begun, months before, the secret provisions accommodated to just such an emergency as this. He lauded himself for having set aside, carefully packed into two ordinary suitcases, more than a million dollars in American currency. He comforted himself in the thought that those two suitcases now rested safely, a few hours' drive away, in the custody of the baggage check room at Barcelona's international airport. Ghandhouri admired his own cleverness for having provided himself with the forged French and Brazilian passports now resting in the inner pocket of his jacket.

All that remained was to wait out the fortnight, posing here in Cadaqués as a visiting artist, while the cargo ship reached Barcelona from Beirut. The rest would be quite simple, Ghandhouri mused. Arrangements for disposition of the morphine had all been carefully completed prior to the Ain Safa intrusion, and in fact largely paid for in advance. Once certain that the box containing the morphine had safely reached the right people in Barcelona, he would make a sudden, unexpected appearance there in person, and simply negotiate a revision of the previously agreed timetable toward a much earlier date.

Ghandhouri conceded to himself that the negotiation might require sacrifice of some of his emergency reserves of cash from the suitcases. Surely not much more, though, he thought with gloating satisfaction, than the $50,000 cash for which he had sold the location of the Palestinian Asad Tabet's current secret hiding place!

But after all, Ghandhouri told himself, the sacrifice of some of that cash would be handsomely repaid. How better to invest the money, in light of the astronomic profits that lay ahead?

Somewhat easier of mind, Wahji Ghandhouri roused himself from his solitary reflections. He left the sunlit table and the uneaten food, and strolled slowly down to watch the gently swaying fishing boats moored along the Cadaqués quay.

The Briefing
Beirut, Lebanon
MAY 1966

Consciousness returned to Jefferson Ryder in infinitesimal bits. Annoyingly faint fragments of irregular sound began to penetrate the comfortable silence of his mind. The threshold sounds did not arouse his interest or even curiosity. He vaguely wished they would fade away and leave him alone. Instead, however, the muted, occasional dissonances became more audible, seemingly nearer. At odd intervals, they repeated. Finally, he began waiting for them, puzzling over their identity. Listening seemed to require great effort. Stubbornly, he concentrated on hearing those sounds. Gradually the sounds became murmuring voices, vaguely distinct.

Ryder decided to open his eyes. Doing so, he discovered that his vision was as blurred and vague as the sounds had been. Then, disappointingly, as he struggled to bring his eyes to a focus, the sounds retreated. Ryder thought, *Okay, then, one thing at a time.* He let his eyes droop closed, concentrated his thoughts on seeing better, then slowly opened them again. His vision still swam, but it had improved. In the hazy wash of gray tones, he thought he could pick out indistinct forms. One of them seemed to move gently. Ryder let his eyelids fall again, contented that with a little more effort, everything would clear up fine. For now, though, he felt an overpowering need for sleep, and gave in to it.

Doctor Allan Rostow straightened up from his scrutiny of the bandage-swathed figure on the hospital bed, and made a professionally satisfied sound. He picked up the patient's clipboard chart from the bedside table, adjusted his eyeglasses, and looked at his watch. He fished a pen from his pocket, and scribbled a number of entries onto the chart. Dr. Rostow swung around, and handed the clipboard to a nurse standing attentively by. "We're not going to lose him. He's over the hump. He doesn't know it, but he just fell asleep. Keep him on the plasma IV through tonight. No visitors of any kind until I check him again in the morning, even if he wakes up." The doctor glanced down at the still figure on the bed, then peered over the tops of his glasses at the nurse. "And he probably will. He seems to have a constitution like a water buffalo, and a skull like a bowling ball." The doctor strode out of the room.

By noon of the following day, Jefferson Ryder was fully aware of the world he found around him, and entirely dissatisfied with it. After prolonged badgering of the nurses attending him, he learned that he was confined in a private hospital near Beirut; that his right arm was immobilized by a cast while a bullet hole and two broken bones in his shoulder healed; that his head was swathed in bandages because he had been hit there by a bullet that should have killed him; and that he had been unconscious for three days. He had also been informed that under no circumstances could he leave the bed, and that until Doctor Rostow said differently, he was permitted no visitors.

In another part of the hospital, two men were shown into Dr. Rostow's office. The first man introduced himself. "Dr. Rostow? I'm James Crawford." Indicating his companion, Crawford added, "This is Mr. John Maxton." The doctor shook hands with the two visitors and invited them to be seated. Crawford opened the conversation. "What can you tell us now about Jeff Ryder's condition? On the telephone this morning I believe you said we might be able to see him this afternoon."

Dr. Rostow smiled. He looked at John Maxton. "Yes, and it will be a relief to everyone around here when you do, especially you, Mr. Maxton. Your Mr. Ryder is fully in control of his senses now, and quite out of danger. Despite being weak, he is already behaving like a caged animal. He is giving me—and more particularly the nurses—fits! Since awakening this morning, he has continually demanded that we produce you, Mr. Maxton. For some reason he doubts that we can!"

Maxton said, "Well, hell, let's oblige him!" Without further comment, the doctor pressed a signal button on his desk, and a nurse promptly entered. Dr. Rostow directed that the two visitors be escorted to Jefferson Ryder's room.

Crawford and Maxton were led through the hospital's corridors to a counter that barred the hallway. Facing them from behind the counter, in addition to an attendant nurse, stood a US Marine. Beyond him, posted outside of Ryder's door, another marine stood on guard. Both of the sentries were armed.

After a brief delay for the inspection of their authorizing credentials, Crawford and Maxton were permitted to proceed to Ryder's room. The escorting nurse entered the room first, but stayed by the door, and as Maxton and Crawford entered, the nurse slipped back out behind them. Ryder, hearing the sounds of their entry, turned his eyes to the visitors, and saw Maxton. His face creased into a smile. In a tone of relief, Ryder said, "You beautiful, ape-faced son of a bitch! I thought you were dead too!" Ryder reached up with his left hand.

John Maxton stuck his own left hand out and gripped Ryder's. He stood there mutely, his homely, lumpy face working around a great grin as he looked down at the inert form of his friend. Tears suddenly started from Maxton's crinkled eyes. He wiped the corners of his eyes, and said, "Goddamn your ass, Ryder! The last time I bawled was when my dog died!"

Ryder laughed. Still smiling, he swung his eyes to James Crawford. "Hi, Jim. Sorry I clobbered my big scene."

Crawford smiled enigmatically. "There are a few things you need to hear before you make any apologies, Jeff. The main thing now, though, is that you're okay. The doctor says you might gripe some about your shoulder when the weather's cold, but otherwise you'll come out of this like new."

Maxton added, "He also says you should rent your head out as an anvil!"

The three men laughed, then Ryder said, "They tell me I've been in a blackout for three days here. How about filling in some of the holes for me? The last thing I can remember is watching Ghandhouri's fat bodyguard shooting at my face!"

James Crawford spoke up. "After you were shot, Max made quite a mess out of that fat bodyguard. He won't be shooting people any more."

Ryder asked, "And what about that damned shipping box we were after?"

Crawford looked over toward Maxton. "Maxton broke all the Lebanese speed laws getting you down from Ain Safa. He headed directly to our embassy, and he and the embassy guard got Ambassador Harte out of bed to take charge of things. Harte made a couple of judicious telephone calls, and Ghandhouri's Ain Safa place was immediately invaded by the Lebanese police. They found no one there. Both the box and bodyguard's corpse were gone from the garage. A feeble attempt had been made to make the garage look normal, but they couldn't hide the bloodstains, nor a serving of the bodyguard's brains from one wall. On that basis, the police conducted a search of the entire property. Ambassador Harte, I might add, saw to it that one of *our* people was on that police investigating team. Although no one found the box, they did find this in Ghandhouri's wall safe."

Crawford drew a folded document from the inner pocket of his jacket, and waved it. He said, "This is a copy of Ghandhouri's private agreement with your vice president, P. T. Lane. I'm afraid this will be very damaging to Mr. Lane's reputation in your company."

Ryder's eyes shifted interestedly to Maxton's face. "Kickback? "

Maxton said laconically, "A whopper. P. T. stood to collect a hundred grand for every bird we sold out here."

Ryder whistled, then smiled sardonically. Crawford returned the incriminating document to his pocket. He said, "When the Lebanese authorities searched Ghandhouri's place, they also discovered a number of items that *they* consider very interesting. They've obviously wanted for a considerable while just such an opportunity as this. It would be most unwise of Mr. Ghandhouri to let himself be seen anywhere in Lebanon, as things now stand."

Ryder, still curious about the shipping crate that had so nearly caused his end, asked, "Jim, what about those guys you had watching the Ain Safa layout? Didn't they see anything that night?"

Crawford smiled. "I see you're still spotting all the angles! Yes, they listened to the shooting, and then, evidently about an hour and a half later, saw a truck pull into the front gate. After a short while the truck came out again, and one of my watching agents followed it, per your relayed instructions. The truck took that box and the dead guard down to the docks. The box and the body were loaded aboard a freighter that night."

Ryder speculated, "I wonder what that all means."

Crawford said, "You might as well stop wondering. We'll find all the answers very soon, thanks to the help you've already put in. For the present, your job is done, except to get back on your feet again. Maxton and I have already overstayed our visit, and right now we're leaving. We'll be looking in on you regularly, Jeff."

Ryder protested, but both Crawford and Maxton were firm with him. After again assuring Ryder that he would be receiving frequent visits, the two men departed.

After Crawford and Maxton had gone, Jeff Ryder let himself relax. As he did so, he grimaced in pain, and admitted to himself that his head was spinning, and that he seemed to ache from head to foot. He guessed it would be a day or two yet before he felt "as good as new" again.

Five days later, Jefferson Ryder walked across the hospital room, and stood in front of the full-length mirror on the bathroom door. He stared curiously at his own reflection, expecting to find that he looked as peculiar as he felt, now that he was dressed in street clothes again for the first time in the eight days since arriving at the hospital.

He was mildly surprised to find that he didn't look much different at all. Of course there was the unwieldy cast on his right shoulder and arm, and then the crown of gauze and adhesive tape on his head. Otherwise, he decided, he looked pretty much the same as always. Color wasn't bad, weight about the same. No serious differences. Ryder grunted his satisfaction, and glanced down at his watch. Nearly eleven o'clock. Crawford and Maxton were due to arrive to rescue him from the hospital's clutches.

The hospital was situated several miles north of Beirut on a rising, orcharded foothill overlooking the sea, and half an hour later Ryder found himself genuinely enjoying his restored freedom as he gazed out over the panoramic view while Crawford drove the car at an easy pace down the road to the south.

Ryder contentedly watched the scenery for a while, then addressed himself to Crawford. "Jim, you two guys have been damn closemouthed about this CIA deal for the past week. What's been happening?"

Crawford smiled and nodded his head as he drove. He admitted, "Security was partly the problem. The other part was doctor's orders. Dr. Rostow instructed us to avoid getting you excited. He said you were getting enough excitement for a man in your condition all day long, trying to bluster your way out of that hospital! Now that you're out, though, there are a few details you'll be interested to learn."

Crawford drove on in silence for a moment. He then said, "Let's take it from the top. The most important thing, Jeff, is that we've succeeded in cutting the flow of contraband arms into Jordan to a trickle. That was a major goal, and it's been met for now."

Ryder asked, "What about the morphine/heroin mess?"

Crawford replied with emphatic satisfaction, "That's been busted wide open."

Ryder leaned back. "Well, what about some of the bad guys? What's happened to them? Like the Rafats, for instance?"

Crawford's answer was succinct. "We've come down on all the guilty parties involved, by recruiting the help of the several governments concerned. The Syrians and the Iraqis weren't very enthusiastic, but we've had fine cooperation from the governments of Jordan, Israel, Lebanon, Turkey, Iran, Afghanistan, and France. In the case of the Rafats, as it happened not a great deal needed to be done. The Rafat family's underworld activities have always been directed almost solely by old Mohammed, the father. He has suffered a fatal stroke, attributed in the large part to the violent death of his eldest son, Hassan. The old man Mohammed Rafat died of a brain hemorrhage two weeks ago. He died before the Iranian officials ever confronted him over his smuggling activities."

Ryder then asked, "Okay, then what about Lane's pal, Ghandhouri?"

Crawford hesitated, then answered carefully, "I've told you that the box you saw in Ghandhouri's garage was loaded aboard a freighter that same night. That freighter has since headed westward through the Mediterranean, and is being tracked. In the meanwhile an unexpected development has arisen. Wahji Ghandhouri has vanished. He disappeared from Paris a week ago, shortly after your episode in Ain Safa, and hasn't been seen since. I'm sorry to have to admit that we don't know where he is. The people in his various enterprises are alarmed. Rumors are already spreading like wildfire in Beirut that the Lebanese government will be obliged to step in as underwriters, due to pressure from people who have invested fortunes with Ghandhouri."

Ryder pondered Crawford's words. He remarked, "It'll be too bad if that son of a bitch gets away."

Crawford glanced sideways with a grim smile. "There's more. This weapons and narcotics scheme was mutually sponsored by the Palestinians and by an international crime syndicate, part offshoot of the Mafia, headquartered in New York. Ghandhouri tried to double-cross them, and failed. As you might guess, now *they* are also after him! Mr. Wahji Ghandhouri will remain a lot healthier if *we* catch up with him first, but in either case the man is finished." Crawford again shot a quick look at Ryder. "Now, at the risk of inviting total disillusionment on your part, there's another thing I'd better tell you before you find out somewhere else. About that shipping container at Ain Safa. It did not contain morphine."

Ryder's eyebrows climbed. "Oh?" He paused, then demanded, "Well, then, what in hell were we chasing it for?"

Crawford answered evenly, "Don't forget, it was Ghandhouri we were after. What happened was this. When one of the contraband shipments moved out of Teheran westward, it went through Aleppo in Syria, en route to Marseille. At Aleppo, one of the boxes containing morphine was cleverly stolen from that shipment by Ghandhouri's people. They replaced the box with one identically marked, but containing hides. In other words, Ghandhouri stole a fortune in morphine from the master smuggling organization of which he was a member!" Crawford interrupted the account. "And by the way, at that time we didn't know who the traitor was. We only knew that whoever engineered that theft was operating from Beirut. You see, my people observed that entire action."

Crawford returned to his discourse. "Ghandhouri's crew set out with the stolen box, on their way to Beirut from Aleppo. They were followed by the CIA. During that trip, certain of my people managed to get at the box and to substitute for the morphine that they removed an equal weight of worthless material. That was the condition of the box when you two saw it in Ain Safa." Crawford smiled to himself. "I would dearly love to watch the faces on the ones who unpack Ghandhouri's stolen 'morphine'!"

Ryder and Maxton listened with avid attention to Crawford's disclosures. As Crawford finished the story, Ryder spoke in a somewhat cynical tone. "That wasn't exactly cricket, was it? It sounds like Max and I risked getting our ashes hauled trying to salvage a box full of nothing! It would've been a little nicer if you'd leveled with us, my friend!"

Crawford nodded without smiling. "It may seem so, but in this business no one has much time to wonder if he's being nice. Under similar circumstances, next time I probably will level with you. You've got to appreciate that every move made in this business has to have a set of odds assigned to it. The odds are always uncertain, and practically always against. Whenever there's even a slight chance of improving the odds, you have no choice but to grab it. That's all I was doing, Jeff. Improving the odds of the moment by not mentioning the stolen morphine to you."

Ryder sat silently for a moment. He shrugged. "I suppose I can get used to that. Put your way, it figures." Ryder studied the CIA man's face. He abruptly changed the subject. "Crawford, how come the Mafia has made it onto the CIA hit parade, along with your regular list of overseas ugly cousins?"

James Crawford's reply was evasive and cryptic. "We just take it as it comes."

The three men rode along without conversation. Then Crawford broke the silence. "There is another subject I want to broach with you, Jeff. Now that you've seen and heard the worst, this is probably as good a time as any." He looked at Ryder. "I'd like to see you accept a more permanent arrangement of some kind with the CIA. You could do a lot for us." Before Ryder could comment, Crawford added, "Don't try to answer now, Jeff. But please begin to give the idea some thought." The CIA man looked around at Maxton. "If your friend here comes along, Max, you are invited too."

Ryder said slowly, "Okay. I'll think it over."

Ten minutes later, Crawford slowed the car and stopped in front of the seldom-used side entrance to the Phoenicia Hotel. He left the car's engine running, and turned to face Ryder. "You can reach me through Bogart Schuyler if there's anything you want me for until I leave Beirut tomorrow. Otherwise I probably won't see you two for a while. In the meantime, Ambassador Harte asked me to tell you he would like to see both you and Max at two this afternoon."

Crawford reached out and shook left hands with Ryder, then shook hands with Maxton, and thanked them both. He told Ryder, "I can't say exactly when, but I will see you one of these days, probably in California."

Ryder smiled and nodded as he managed to open the car door. He and Maxton climbed out of the car, and headed up the stairway to the hotel entrance as Crawford drove away.

As the big glass entry doors to the lobby had just eased closed behind them, Ryder stopped. With a light touch on the arm, he halted Maxton too. He said, with a hint of surprise threading through his voice, "Max, it has just hit me! This is the first moment I've been free to do what I please, ever since the lights went out up in Ghandhouri's garage! Look around us! No doctors! No nurses! No marines! Not even a Crawford!"

Maxton smiled indulgently at his bandage-swathed friend. "Yes, and its high time you gave up all that coddling! There's a whole lot of housekeeping you've got to catch up on!" The two men resumed a slow stroll into the lobby. Maxton abruptly added, "And I think you might just as well get started right now." He stepped across in front of Ryder and blocked his way, while gesturing to one side.

Ryder swung his eyes around, barely in time to see Marge Mackenzie rushing toward him before she happily called out his name, unabashedly wrapped her arms around his neck, and kissed him soundly on the mouth. Marge leaned her head back, smiling gaily up into his face, "Jeff! At last! Do you know that they wouldn't let me see you? They've been guarding you like Fort Knox!"

Ryder did the best he could to participate in the welcoming embrace, hindered discouragingly by the plaster-and-gauze barrier immobilizing his right shoulder and arm. He smilingly shook his head. "Well, all that guard stuff is over now, and *I'm* giving the orders! From now on, Miss Marge Mackenzie, you have a permanent free pass!"

The two continued to stand there, smiling into each other's faces, until Maxton graveled, "Come on, you two, break it up! I made lunch reservations for the three of us, and I'm hungry. You two can neck while I'm eating my clam chowder!" He stepped between them and seized each by an elbow, then steered the trio to an elevator, en route to the hotel's elegant penthouse restaurant.

Maxton, a clam chowder fanatic, had ordered their lunch ahead. The three ended up seated around a huge, covered tureen of hot chowder, reinforced on the side by heaped dishes of thin-sliced smoked salmon and deep-fried jumbo prawns. As they lunched, Maxton divided his time between contentedly demolishing repeated bowlfuls of the steaming chowder, and in briefing Ryder on the accumulated backlog of company communications. He also advised Ryder that their airline reservations were confirmed from Beirut to Los Angeles for departure on the following afternoon. This brought Ryder's glance around to Marge's face, but he saw by her small, forlorn nod that this was not news to her. She interjected, in a transparent effort to brighten her own mood, "But before you may leave Beirut, Mr. Jefferson Ryder, there is one more thing you must do! Tonight! Tonight, you must take me back to Dimitri's, to help me finish that bottle of brandy with our names on it!"

Ryder noticed that, as a matter of fact, his own spirits had sagged at the sudden mention of leaving, and he fought off the sensation. He announced, "And *that*, pretty lady, is a date!" Ryder glanced down at his watch, then back at Marge. "Our friend Crawford said that your boss wants to see me and Max at two, which is pretty soon. If you're ready and willing, we'd like to escort you back to the embassy."

Promptly at two o'clock, Ryder and Maxton entered the ambassador's office in the embassy. Julius Harte's smiling face beamed as he came around his desk to greet them. He exclaimed to Ryder, "Well, Jeff! It's a treat to see you on your feet again! Sit down now, and make yourselves comfortable."

The ambassador waited while Ryder, maneuvering the awkward cast, seated himself alongside Maxton. Harte then returned to his place behind the desk. He asked, "Now tell me truthfully, how do you really feel, Jeff? James Crawford assures me you're all right, but I'd like to hear it from you. If you're not up to par, please tell me. We can easily postpone this talk."

Ryder smiled and wagged a hand. "I'm fine, Ambassador Harte. Just fine! It's good medicine, getting back into the swing of things a little."

Harte continued to smile. He picked up a folded paper from his desk, "In that case, I believe this message will suffice as a starting place for our conversation today. Why don't you read it aloud?" The ambassador reached across the desk, handing the folded page to Ryder. Ryder opened it and read:

PERSONAL TO JEFFERSON RYDER C/O US AMBASSADOR JULIUS HARTE BEIRUT LEBANON EMBASSY STOP HAVE BEEN ADVISED IN DETAIL OF YOUR RECENT MERITORIOUS ENDEAVORS AND OF YOUR ASSOCIATED INJURIES STOP YOU ARE HEREWITH COLON PAREN ONE END PAREN GRANTED THIRTY DAYS SABBATICAL LEAVE WITH FULL PAY AND EXPENSES EFFECTIVE THIS DATE STOP PAREN TWO END PAREN OFFERED POSITION AS VICE PRESIDENT COMMA INTERNATIONAL MARKETING COMMA REPORTING DIRECTLY TO JOHN MORREL COMMA EFFECTIVE AS OF DATE OF RECEIPT HERE YOUR WRITTEN ACCEPTANCE STOP PAREN THREE END PAREN ADVISED OF FULL AND FINAL SEPARATION FROM THIS COMPANY OF PALMER TUXFORD LANE STOP NEW SUBJECT STOP OUR BEST PERSONAL REGARDS AND GRATITUDE

The message was signed by the chairman of the board for the company.

When Ryder had finished reading, he looked up and found the ambassador studying his face. Julius Harte said quietly, "I sincerely hope that offer represents something you wanted, Jeff. It is surely well deserved."

Ryder smiled a little and glanced at Maxton, then back at the message in his hand. "Thanks for saying so, sir." He chuckled. "Today seems to be my day for job offers!"

The ambassador sat without speaking for a moment, then slowly got to his feet, and turned to stare through the great window behind his desk.

Observing the ambassador's apparent change of mood, Ryder and Maxton remained silent. At length Julius Harte swung back and said, "All right," in a tone indicating an unspoken decision. He looked straight at the two men across the desk from him. "I'm going to intrude somewhat into matters that are not, strictly speaking, my affair."

Harte turned, and started slowly pacing. "I am aware that James Crawford wants you to continue in this CIA kind of work. He is understandably impressed with you."

The ambassador halted momentarily and looked at Ryder. "What it comes down to is that you in particular, Jeff, are confronted with a rather drastic choice." Harte's voice was intense. "You have a choice between two almost diametrically opposite extremes. I'm referring to the offers from your company"—he pointed to the message form in Ryder's hand—"and from Crawford."

Harte returned to his pacing. "It is not my intention to meddle in your decision. However, in view of the profound effect this choice will assuredly have on your future, it is only reasonable that you be made aware of as much as possible about the alternatives. There are some things I want you to know about the events you've just been through."

Harte paced in silence for a moment, head bowed, apparently pondering his next words. "Let me begin with this. You, personally, have had a very narrow escape. Obviously you know all about that." The ambassador swung around. "What you do not know is that at the same time, the United States has had an equally narrow escape out of this! What I'm saying is that in both cases, the results verged on catastrophe!"

Ryder frowned, trying to comprehend. He watched the stern expression on Julius Harte's face. The ambassador looked back at him. "Intermixed with this conspiracy you've been up against is a program of steps being taken by certain manipulators of organized crime. They have become emboldened enough to send tentacles deeply into the government of the United States!"

Harte went back to his pacing. "To return to cases, it was by no coincidence that a particular man named Jefferson Ryder was selected for approach by the CIA. You were painstakingly searched out by them *after* they had observed Wahji Ghandhouri and your Mr. Lane begin their unsavory negotiations late last year, and after they'd watched the Rafats commence undertaking their massive smuggling project. That is, the CIA has been on the trail of this incredible, Mafia-inspired international intrigue for quite some time."

Ryder's face showed puzzlement. "That part all sounds for the good."

Harte responded, "Yes, it does sound that way. But it should make you wonder why a vast and sophisticated organization like the CIA would look to an unschooled person such as you for help. It certainly made *me* wonder! Well, Jeff, it was discovered in the midst of the CIA's pursuit of this giant conspiracy, that the Mafia had managed to invade the *CIA's own ranks*!"

Ryder's eyes widened. Harte saw the look, and nodded in emphasis. "Through information provided from within the CIA, this conspiracy learned the structure of our Middle East intelligence system! Furthermore, they were informed of every foreign espionage agent on whom the CIA kept dossiers pertaining to this region!"

Harte continued, "That is why James Crawford himself was thrown into the breach, and why people such as you were sought out. Crawford holds a high position within the CIA, and is no longer expected to participate in field operations. But he is a man of unquestioned trust, and they were forced to employ his experience. Jeff, this has had the proportions of a national crisis! This bold scheme very nearly succeeded! We have had no more than a handful of men standing in the way of an unprecedented attempt to subvert a basic governmental function, and to destroy our efforts to prevent a Middle East war!"

The ambassador stopped speaking. Ryder leaned forward in his chair. "I follow you through all that, Ambassador Harte. But tell me—if those kinds of people are able to make their way into such key government areas, what else is in sight? Is it really that bad?"

Harte answered flatly, "It is every bit as bad as that. There will be more from these people." The ambassador pondered for a moment, then resumed. "There is a terrible magnitude to the consequences when highly placed men succumb to avarice and extraordinary greed. There is far too much of that in our midst these days. You've just seen it at your own back twice. In one instance, at the top of a highly respected, blue ribbon corporation. In the second instance, among the very people we employ to rid us of such debilitating influences. We may be forced to admit that corruption is a fact of life, but we cannot accept it at epidemic levels! Every incident of this kind exacts a terrible price. When too many of those kinds of people succeed, the entire world becomes the loser."

Ryder stirred. "A damned bleak picture, especially coming from you, Ambassador Harte." He settled back in his chair and smiled bleakly. "Well, sir, I see what you mean about my choice between extremes! I get to choose between super luxury and my turn at the Big Trough, or sticking my nose into a meat grinder! Some choice!"

Julius Harte laughed a little at Ryder's words. He got up from his chair, then came around the desk and extended his hand. "I doubt that the things I've said will frighten you very much, Jefferson Ryder. I'll be watching to see what you do, and either way, I wish you well." The ambassador shook Maxton's hand, then watched as the two men departed.

Barcelona
Spain
JUNE 1966

Wahji Ghandhouri's spirits soared. This first day of June had dawned fittingly in a glorious example of Spanish Mediterranean weather. At last, back amid the clamor and rush of a big city's lively commerce, Ghandhouri felt a full return of confidence. In their old familiar pattern, his business affairs were now going beautifully according to plan. Ghandhouri relaxed grandly in the back seat of the luxurious rented limousine, behind a hired, uniformed chauffeur. He basked in the flood of admiring and envious stares from the audience provided by Barcelona's ordinary street traffic.

The limousine cruised sedately through the city's thronged commercial center, then headed into a section of Barcelona's industrial suburbs. Ghandhouri noted on his golden wristwatch that it was just ten minutes before four o'clock in the afternoon when his limousine pulled up in front of the drab entrance to a sprawling brick factory building, buried within the tawdry maze of Barcelona's industrial complex.

Ghandhouri remained within the sanctuary of the limousine for an interval before entering the building, reviewing the significant elements of the discussions he planned to sponsor. He had ascertained that these Spanish producers of heroin had, indeed, taken delivery of his box of morphine. Earlier, he had made a personal check on the undisturbed security of his two suitcases of currency. He had carefully checked news releases covering the past two weeks, and had found nothing incriminating about himself. Lastly, he reached up to feel the reassuring bulk of the envelope in his pocket that contained fifty $1,000 bills. This amount, he planned, would be the maximum penalty he might agree to pay as a fee for accommodation of his new timing demands by the Spaniards.

Ghandhouri brusquely ordered the chauffeur to wait, then climbed out of the car, and headed confidently into the stolid building's entry. Within the building, he found the way barred by a reception counter. Two men stood behind the counter. One, an elderly, menial-looking Spaniard in a guard's uniform, watched dully as Ghandhouri approached. The other, an athletic-looking, impeccably dressed young man, greeted Ghandhouri flatly, although courteously, in English. He asked, "You are Mr. Ghandhouri, from Paris?"

Ghandhouri replied officiously, "I am Wahji Ghandhouri. Please direct me to the offices of the leading executive."

The young man nodded expressionlessly and opened a gate at one side of the counter. Ghandhouri stepped through, and at the young Spaniard's gestured invitation, followed him down a silent, echoing corridor. Ghandhouri was led deep into the hushed, chill building, to a waiting elevator. In silence, the two men entered the lift. Ghandhouri watched as the young man pressed the topmost button on the elevator's control panel. The elevator lurched into motion, and trundled unevenly upward at a very slow pace. It finally came to a swaying stop. The young man slid aside its heavy door, and held it open for the Lebanese financier. Ghandhouri exited from the elevator, relieved to escape its uncertain behavior. He found himself in a carpeted hallway that impressed him as somber but well appointed. The hallway was deserted and silent.

Dark-paneled, heavily varnished doors faced the hall at intervals along both walls. Each door carried a gilt-lettered title. Ghandhouri followed the young man down the length of the hallway to a great double door that faced the hall at its end. This door was not labeled. The young man paused at the door, and pressed a button at its side. After a moment's delay the door swung inward, and a portly, black-haired man in a dark business suit soberly greeted Ghandhouri by name, and politely invited him to enter.

Wahji Ghandhouri stepped through the doorway, followed by the young escort. Ponderously, the door closed and latched itself behind them. The portly, middle-aged man introduced himself. "We have looked forward to your arrival, Mr. Ghandhouri. I am Hilario Ortiz, the secretary to our chairman, Don Fernando Miguel. Don Fernando will be pleased to speak with you in the inner chamber."

Ortiz bowed slightly, then stepped to an ornately carved door nearby. Opening the door, he stood aside, and with another small bow, silently invited Ghandhouri to enter.

Wahji Ghandhouri had grown impatient to be done with the business at hand. Rudely he brushed past Ortiz, and strode on into the office beyond. Then, abruptly, he halted to a frozen standstill. He stood rigidly in the center of the room he had entered, the color draining from his face. He stared into the eyes of the men confronting him. Seated behind a massive table, Luigi Carini and Alfonzo Bonifacio coolly looked back into the terrified confusion in Ghandhouri's eyes. A third man, unrecognized by Ghandhouri, stood to one side, impassively looking on.

Quietly, the young man who had escorted Ghandhouri through the building positioned a chair behind the stiff figure of of the visibly trembling financier.

Luigi Carini allowed the stunned Lebanese to stand in terrified silence for an interval, then he leaned comfortably back in his chair, and said, "Why don't you sit down, Wahji? You look as though you should."

With spasmodic head movements, Ghandhouri peered wildly around the room. He saw that the door he had come through was the sole exit. Ortiz and the athletic young escort stood silently in front of it, watching him. Ghandhouri shakily seated himself, and turned back to face Carini and Bonifacio.

Carini was busy lighting a cigar. As he puffed the cigar alight, he glanced up at Ghandhouri across the flame of his lighter. He extinguished the lighter and returned it to his pocket, then said, "Well, Wahji, old friend, where the hell are your elegant manners? You haven't even said hello to Alfonzo and me!" The Mafia chief turned to the tall, phlegmatic Spaniard standing beside the table. He said, "Don Fernando, I must apologize for the rude conduct of this miserable acquaintance of ours. He appears, though, to be upset about something, so maybe you'll forgive him. Possibly you could offer him a belt of booze. Maybe that will relax his guts."

The impassive Spaniard flicked his eyes to his secretary, Ortiz. Ortiz moved to a concealed panel door on one of the walls, and slid it aside. The opened panel revealed a well-stocked liquor bar. Ortiz poured a glass of excellent brandy, and offered it to the seated figure in the center of the room. Wordlessly, Wahji Ghandhouri accepted the glass, then swallowed some of the brandy.

Luigi Carini, cigar in mouth, tilted forward in his chair again, and rested his elbows on the table. Speaking around the cigar, he said, "Okay, Wahji, you're all rested and refreshed now. It's time to get down to business. I want you to understand that we intend to be fair about this. Alfonzo and I are going to listen while you tell us what the hell you're doing here in Barcelona."

Wahji Ghandhouri took another drink from the brandy glass. Fear filled his body with an icy tension. His mind raced, seeking an avenue of escape. He looked at Carini, and in a strained voice, said, "As you must already know, I am here to conduct business with these Spanish people."

Carini smiled around the cigar, and leaned back in his chair. He said, "You're doing fine, Wahji! You haven't lied to us once since you walked in!" The Mafia chief chuckled, then said, "You're so right! We *do* know you're here on business. And now, we're going to let you in on a trade secret, Wahji! Our friend Bonifacio is going to tell you *how* we know!"

The Corsican, Alfonzo Bonifacio, had not taken his eyes from Ghandhouri's face. Unlike Carini, he made no effort to be jocular. He said acidly, "You are the worst kind of fool, Ghandhouri! You, who swallows pitiful sardines so grandly, have let your filthy appetite lead you into swallowing a shark." Bonifacio stared silently at Ghandhouri for a moment, then resumed. "I have made a mistake about you. I have considered you both shrewd and dangerous. You are neither. You have insulted me with your gross stupidity. Ghandhouri, only a fool would believe that I, in my position, would have no knowledge of what my competing neighbors are doing! What is the matter with your geography, you with your vast 'empire'? Cannot you see how near to Marseille is Barcelona? Don Fernando and I have enjoyed nothing but mutual respect and friendly liaison for years."

Ghandhouri heard neither mercy nor leniency whatsoever in Bonifacio's harsh condemnation of him. Shuddering inwardly, he looked at Carini. The Mafia chief was smiling sardonically. Wahji Ghandhouri asked, "Then, what do you want from me? I'm sure there is a way that this may all be rectified?"

Carini's eyes narrowed over a fatuous smile. He said, "Wahji, there is just one thing in this wide world that might save you. I will be frank with you about your situation." Carini paused and puffed on his cigar, letting the Lebanese sweat. He resumed, "In Bonifacio's eyes, there is *nothing* that can save you! So, it is up to me to persuade him not to feed you to his friends, the sharks! But first, Wahji, as you can see, it is up to *you* to persuade *me*!" Luigi Carini let a lethal grin cross his face as he eased the cigar's ash into an ashtray.

Ghandhouri's eyes watched Carini's blunt fingers manipulate the cigar. In a low, fearful voice, he asked, "And what is this one thing you speak of?"

Carini answered, "Look behind me, Ghandhouri."

Wahji Ghandhouri stared in bewilderment at Carini. He saw only that a blank wall stood close to the Mafia chief's back. Then he realized that the wall was actually an accordioned curtain that could be moved aside.

Carini signaled to the men standing behind Ghandhouri. Ghandhouri heard the click of a switch, then the faint whirring of an unseen electric motor. The curtain wall began to fold itself aside, opening quietly from left to right. As the opening grew, Ghandhouri saw that he and the others were occupying only half of an immense office. The curtain slid further aside, and Ghandhouri felt his throat constrict. There, in the center of the now vast room, standing intact behind the seated figures of Carini and Bonifacio, was Ghandhouri's stolen box of morphine. Resting on top of that travel-worn shipping crate were the two suitcases that contained Ghandhouri's money. Wahji Ghandhouri stared speechlessly at the sight.

Big Lou Carini rose leisurely from his chair, and moved back to stand beside the box. He flicked ashes from his cigar onto the crate, then looked at Ghandhouri. He said, "Wahji, from the look on your face, I would guess that these three articles seem familiar to you. It might even be that you think they are yours. But looks can be deceiving, though, Wahji, *n'est ce pas*, as you would say? There is only one way to be sure whether or not these are what they seem to be."

Carini reached out and grabbed one of the suitcases by its handle. He pulled the suitcase over onto its side. He unfastened the latches, and lifted the bag open. Carini looked across the room at the pale Lebanese. He asked, "Is this yours, Wahji?" With that, Carini tipped the opened suitcase forward, and let the neat bundles of currency fall in a huge cascade to the floor. With deliberate movements, he then repeated the performance with the second suitcase.

Lou Carini stood beside the heaped fortune on the floor, and stared malevolently at Ghandhouri. At length, he demanded, "That *was* yours, wasn't it, Wahji?"

Ghandhouri nodded weakly, but made no sound.

Carini thrust his head forward, and patted the palm of his hand smartly against the top of the shipping crate. He said, "That solves the mystery of two of our puzzles, then. That leaves one more, this great big box. Now, we will see if its contents are also yours!"

Carini flung the two emptied suitcases roughly to the floor. He gestured to the men behind Ghandhouri, and Ortiz came forward. Together, Lou Carini and Ortiz lifted the top from the shipping crate, and leaned it against the back of the great box. It was obvious that the box had been opened before. Then, Carini and Ortiz reached down into the outer crate, and lifted out the lid from a second, inner box. This too they propped against the rear of the crate. Ortiz stepped away. A disgusting stench escaped into the room. In a sudden rage, Lou Carini scooped into the box with both hands, then rushed at the seated Lebanese, and shoved the contents of his cupped hands into Ghandhouri's terrified face. Carini roared, *"That box is filled with sand, dog shit, and dirty rags, Ghandhouri! All that must be yours too!"*

Carini stood, shaking with fury, staring down at the pallid, dung-smeared face of Wahji Ghandhouri.

Bonifacio, holding his nose, gestured to Ortiz, and together, he and the Spaniard returned the lids to the two nested boxes. Ortiz opened some windows, then returned to his position by the door. Carini reached down roughly and yanked the silk handkerchief from Wahji Ghandhouri's breast pocket. Using the perfumed handkerchief, he methodically wiped the foul-smelling filth from his hands. He then wafted the handkerchief across Ghandhouri's face several times. He said, "That dog-shit perfume suits you better, Mr. Pimp!" Carini flung the stinking handkerchief into Ghandhouri's face, then strode to the sink at the liquor bar, and washed and dried his hands. He then returned to his seat behind the table. Don Fernando had moved a chair over, and seated himself next to one of the opened windows.

Wahji Ghandhouri was a pathetic sight. His efforts to clean his face had only produced worse smears. Clotted chunks of evil-smelling ordure clung in his hair and to the front of his clothes. Ghandhouri sat slumped in the chair, his head hanging forward. Suddenly, he vomited into his own lap.

Carini watched in silent disgust. He turned to Don Fernando and said, "I'm sorry we've fouled up your office this way, Don Fernando. The cleaning bill will be on my puking friend over there. I don't think this will take much longer, and he can't do much more damage unless he shits in his pants."

Carini then stared furiously back at Ghandhouri's slumped figure. He said, loudly, "You're onstage now, pretty boy! All you have to do is answer one simple question! If you answer it right, you can go take a bath and keep your health. If your answer doesn't satisfy me, you never walk out of this room!" Carini drew a finger across his throat. At this signal, the young Spaniard stepped quickly up behind Ghandhouri, and slipped a thin loop of wire over Ghandhouri's slumped head. Crossing the ends of wire behind Ghandhouri's neck, the young man jerked the Lebanese into an upright position by pulling back on the wire. Ghandhouri sobbed with fright.

Carini stared at Ghandhouri, then said, "I presume you get the picture, Wahji. All I have to do is move my hand, and that wire noose is going to close your windpipe. Forever. You can be useful to me in one of two ways. Dead, you will serve as an example to a few other people I know who are capable of getting ideas such as the mistaken one that brought you here. Alive, you can remain that way by telling us *where the goddamned hell those hundred kilos of morphine are* that belong in that box! Now, speak up!"

Wahji Ghandhouri's mouth opened and closed repeatedly, but he made no sound. His eyes shot back and forth wildly between Carini and Bonifacio. He finally managed to stammer, "Tell him to take this thing off my neck! I'll tell you anything you want to know!"

Carini solemnly shook his head. He looked grimly into Ghandhouri's face, and said, "Time is flying by for you, Wahji. The noose stays. Where is the morphine?"

Ghandhouri groaned, and wagged his head. His eyes continued to roll frantically. He muttered, "Someone discovered I had the box. They murdered my guard. I thought it was you." Ghandhouri's voice faded into a whisper. "I have no idea where the morphine is. I thought the box was filled with it."

Big Lou Carini jerked himself into a standing position. He leaned forward, his weight against his hands on the tabletop. His face flushed red with his rage as he shouted, "*Ghandhouri, this is it! Where the hell is that morphine?*"

Wahji Ghandhouri turned helpless eyes to Bonifacio, then to the silent face of Don Fernando, then back at Carini's savage look. In a pleading voice, he began, "I can help you find it. I will tell you how they murdered my guard. I will . . ." Carini cut him off with a roar of fury, and chopped the air viciously with his hand. Carini, Bonifacio, Don Fernando, and the secretary, Ortiz, watched as the wire noose suddenly disappeared into the flesh of Wahji Ghandhouri's neck. Ghandhouri's eyes bulged. He struggled violently, flailing his legs and clawing with his fingers at his own throat. The young man knew his business. He drew the wire loop steadily tighter, letting Ghandhouri's desperate convulsions work against his victim. Slowly, Ghandhouri's frenzied struggling subsided. Tongue and eyes protruded hideously from the gruesomely contorted blue face. Finally, the spasmodic jerking of Wahji Ghandhouri's body ceased entirely. The Lebanese financier's execution and his career were finished.

Lisbon
Portugal
JUNE 1966

The echoing message boomed through the cavernous passenger terminal of Lisbon's International Airport. "Announcing departure of Swissair Flight 801, nonstop from Lisbon to New York. First-class passengers joining Flight 801 at Lisbon will kindly proceed to Gate 4 for immediate boarding. Tourist-class passengers will board through Gate 5. Transit passengers continuing from Geneva on Flight 801 will kindly show their boarding passes at Gate 7."

Jefferson Ryder and John Maxton mingled with the last of the line of transit passengers trailing through Gate 7. They joined the straggle of people meandering across the paved ramp toward Swissair's sleek DC-8. Ryder carried a folded copy of the Herald Tribune's foreign edition. Strolling beside Maxton, he studied an article on the newspaper's front page. "Look at this, Max," he remarked, holding the folded paper toward his friend. "Today is Friday, isn't it? June third? It says here they're launching Gemini 4 from Cape Kennedy today. When they get into orbit, one of those two guys is going to get out and walk in space! How'd you like to be in on *that* action?"

Maxton glanced at the newspaper in Ryder's left hand. He grunted and shook his head, "Uh-uh. Not this kid. I'll stick with these tin birds that carry booze and babes." He waved in the direction of the airliner.

The two friends continued their idle conversation while they approached the boarding stairway leading to the airliner's first-class compartment. Neither Ryder nor Maxton took any particular notice of the tall, fleshy, silver-haired man with the scowl who climbed the boarding stairs ahead of them, nor of his slender, hard-eyed, more youthful companion.

Neither did Luigi Carini nor his alert bodyguard pay more than casual heed to the smiling, dark-haired American with the bandaged head and cast on his arm, nor to his burly, taciturn friend.

On this sunny day in June, the mind of each of these four men was occupied with private thoughts of his own.

END

Joseph C. "José" Pimentel (1920-2004) was an overseas commercial aircraft sales manager in the 1950s and 1960s, like his alter ego Jefferson Ryder. While working for Douglas Aircraft in the Middle East, Pimentel was recruited by the CIA to assist in breaking up an international smuggling ring. Previously, the author had been a Disney Studios cartoonist, then an AAF fighter pilot in WWII (one of the last to fly *under* the Eiffel Tower) who wound up his military career as a lieutenant colonel in the Air Force Reserves. (Some of Pimentel's wartime exploits were recounted in Jim Doyle's book *Flying Through Time*.) A UCLA aeronautical engineering graduate, the Fresno native retired from aircraft-related work in 1970 to buy and work a cattle ranch in far northern California's Scott Valley. In addition to running his ranch, driving cattle in the Marble Mountains, and continuing to fly, Pimentel returned to cartooning in his later years, publishing a book-length collection, *Saddleburrs*, in 1982 and serving as a longtime editorial cartoonist for the *Pioneer Press*.